'Mr Vidal interweaves with ingenuity and wit the well-established patterns of human credulity and revolution. The result is a satirical fantasy of real brilliance: horribly relevant to our follies and dreadfully funny' *Sunday Times*

'Mr Vidal has written a book which can be bracketed with Huxley and Orwell in its realistic handling of fantasy' *Guardian*

'There is no question of Gore Vidal's talent, his promise, or the possibility, still, of his development. The prelude to *Messiah* is an attractive essay on modern times, witty and discerning'
New York Times Book Review

Also by Gore Vidal in Panther Books

Williwaw
The City and the Pillar
Julian
Washington, DC
Myra Breckinridge

Gore Vidal

Messiah

Panther

Granada Publishing Limited
Published in 1973 by Panther Books Ltd
York Road, St. Albans, Hertfordshire.

First published in Great Britain by
William Heinemann Ltd 1955
Made and printed in Great Britain by
Hunt Barnard Printing Ltd
Aylesbury, Bucks
Set in Monotype Times

For Tennessee Williams

I sometimes think the day will come when all the modern nations will adore a sort of American god, a god who will have been a man that lived on earth and about whom much will have been written in the popular press; and images of this god will be set up in the churches, not as the imagination of each painter may fancy him, not floating on a Veronica kerchief, but established, fixed once and for all by photography. Yes, I foresee a photographed god, wearing spectacles.

On that day civilization will have reached its peak and there will be steam-propelled gondolas in Venice.

November, 1861: *The Goncourt Journals*

ONE

ONE

I envy those chroniclers who assert with reckless but sincere abandon: "I was there. I saw it happen. It happened thus." Now I too, in every sense, was there, yet I cannot trust myself to identify with any accuracy the various events of my own life, no matter how vividly they may seem to survive in recollection . . . if only because we are all, I think, betrayed by those eyes of memory which are as mutable and particular as the ones with which we regard the material world, the vision altering, as it so often does, from near in youth to far in age. And that I am by a devious and unexpected route arrived at a great old age is to me a source of some complacency, even on those bleak occasions when I find myself attending inadvertently the body's dissolution, a process as imperceptible yet sure as one of those faint, persistent winds which shift the dunes of sand in that desert of dry Libya which burns, white and desolate, beyond the mountains I see from the window of my room, a window facing, aptly enough, the west where all the kings lie buried in their pride.

I am also conscious that I lack the passion for the business of familiar life which is the central preoccupation of our race while, worse still, I have never acquired the habit of judging the usual deeds of men . . . two inconvenient characteristics which render me uncertain whenever I attempt to recall the past, confounding me sadly with the knowledge that my recollections are, after all, tentative and private and only true in part.

Then, finally, I have never found it easy to tell the truth, a temperamental infirmity due not so much to any wish or compulsion to distort reality that I might be reckoned virtuous but, rather, to a conception of the inconsequence of human activity which is ever in conflict with a profound love of those essential powers that result in human action, a paradox certainly, a dual vision which restrains me from easy judgments.

I am tempted to affirm that historic truth is quite impossible, although I am willing to accept the philosophic notion that it may exist abstractly, perfect and remote in the imagination. A windy attic filled with lovely objects has always been my personal image of those absolutes Aristotle conceived with such mellifluous optimism . . . and I have always liked the conceits of philosophy, the more extravagant the better. I am especially devoted to Parmenides, who was so strenuously obsessed with the idea of totality that he was capable, finally, of declaring that nothing ever changed, that what has been must still exist if it it is yet remembered and named, a metaphysical conception which will, I suspect, be of some use to me as I journey in memory back to that original crisis from which I have for so long traveled and to which, despite the peril, I must return.

I do not say, then, that what I remember is all true but I can declare that what I shall recall is a relative truth as opposed to that monstrous testament the one-half world believes, entrenching deep thereby a mission at whose birth I officiated and one whose polished legend has since become the substantial illusion of a desperate race. That both mission and illusion were false, I alone can say with certainty, with sorrow, such being the unsuspected and terrible resolution of brave days. Only the crisis, which I shall record, was real.

I have said I am not given to making judgments. That is not precise. It is true that in most "wicked" acts I have been able, with a little effort, to perceive the possibilities for good either in actual intention or (and to me more important) in uncalculated result; yet, ultimately, problems in ethics have never much concerned me: possibly because they have been the vital interest of so many others who, through custom, rule society, more agreeably than not. On that useful moral level I have been seldom, if ever, seriously engaged. But once on another, more arduous plane I was forced to make a choice, to judge, to act; and act I did in such a way that I am still startled by the implications of my choice, of my life's one judgment.

I chose the light in preference to the dreamless dark, destroying my own place in the world, and then, more painful still, I chose the light in preference to the twilight region of indeterminate visions and ambiguities, that realm where decision was impossible and where the potentialities of choice were endless and exquisite to contemplate. To desert these beloved ghosts and incalculable powers was the greater pain, but I have lived on, observing with ever-increasing intensity that blazing disc of fire which is the symbol as well as material source of the reality I have accepted entirely, despite the sure dominion in eternity of the dark other.

But now, as my private day begins to fade, as the wind in the desert gathers in intensity, smoothing out the patterns in the sand, I shall attempt to evoke the true image of one who assumed with plausibility in an age of science the long-discarded robes of prophecy, prevailing at last through ritual death and becoming, to those who see the universe in man, that solemn idea which is yet called by its resonant and antique name, god.

TWO

Stars fell to earth in a blaze of light, and where they fell, monsters were born, hideous and blind.

The first dozen years after the second of the modern wars were indeed "a time of divination," as one religious writer unctuously described them. Not a day passed but that some omen or portent was remarked by an anxious race, suspecting war. At first, the newspapers delightedly reported these marvels, getting the details all wrong but communicating a sense of awfulness that was to increase as the years of peace uneasily lengthened until a frightened people demanded government action, the ultimate recourse in those innocent times.

Yet these omens, obsessive and ubiquitous as they were, would not yield their secret order to any known system. For instance, much of the luminous crockery which was seen in the sky was never entirely explained. And explanation, in the end, was all that the people required. It made no difference how extraordinary the explanation was, if only they could know *what* was happening: that the shining globes which raced in formation over Sioux Falls, South Dakota, were mere residents of the Andromeda Galaxy, at home in space, omnipotent and eternal in design, on a cultural visit to our planet . . . if only this much could definitely be stated, the readers of newspapers would have felt secure, able in a few weeks' time to turn their attention to other problems, the visitors from farther space forgotten. It made little difference whether these mysterious blobs of light were hallucinations, intergalactic visitors or military weapons; the important thing was to explain them.

To behold the inexplicable was perhaps the most unpleasant experience a human being of that age could know, and during that gaudy decade many wild phenomena were sighted and recorded.

In daylight, glittering objects of bright silver maneuvered at unearthly speed over Washington, D.C., observed by hundreds, some few reliable. The government, with an air of spurious calm, mentioned weather balloons, atmospheric reflections, tricks-of-eye, hinting, too, as broadly as it dared, that a sizable minority of its citizens were probably subject to delusions and mass hysteria. This cynical view was prevalent inside the administration, though it could not of course propound such a theory publicly since its own tenure was based, more or less solidly, on the franchise of those same hysterics and irresponsibles.

Shortly after the mid-point of the century, the wonders increased, becoming daily more bizarre. The recent advance in atomic research and in jet propulsion had made the Western world disagreeably aware of other planets and galaxies, and the thought that we would soon be making expeditions into space was disquieting, if splendid, giving rise to the not illogical thought that life might be developing on other worlds somewhat more brilliantly than here at home and, further, that it was quite conceivable that we ourselves might receive visitors long before our own adventuring had begun in the starry blackness which contains our life, like a speck of phosphorus in a quiet sea. And since our people were (and no doubt still are) barbarous and drenched in superstition, like the dripping "Saved" at an old-time Texas baptism, it was generally felt that these odd creatures whose shining cars flashed through our poor heavens at such speed must, of necessity, be hostile and cruel and bent on world dominion, just like ourselves or at least our geographic neighbors.

The evidence was horrific and plentiful:

In Berlin a flying object of unfamiliar design was seen to land by an old farmer who was so close to it that he could make out several little men twinkling behind an arc of windows. He fled, however, before they could eat him. Shortly after his breathless announcement to the newspapers, he was absorbed by an Asiatic government whose mission it was at that time to regularize the part of humanity fortunate enough to live within its curiously elastic boundaries, both temporal and spiritual.

In West Virginia, a creature ten feet tall, green with a red face and exuding a ghastly odor, was seen to stagger out of a luminous globe, temporarily grounded. He was observed by a woman and four boys, all of unquestionable probity; they fled before he could eat them. Later in the company of sheriff and well-armed posse, they returned to the scene of horror only to find both monster and conveyance gone. But even the skeptical sheriff and his men could detect, quite plainly, an unfamiliar odor, sharp and sickening among the clean pines.

This particular story was unique because it was the first to describe a visitor as being larger instead of smaller than a man, a significant proof of the growing anxiety: we could handle even the cleverest little creature, but something huge and green, with an awful odor . . . it was too much.

I myself, late one night in July of the mid-century, saw quite plainly from the eastern bank of the Hudson River, where I lived, two red globes flickering in a cloudless sky. As I watched, one moved to a higher point at a forty-five-degree angle above the original plane which had contained them both. For several nights I watched these eccentric twins but then, carried away by enthusiasm, I began to confuse Mars and Saturn with my magic lights until at last I thought it wise to remain indoors, except for those brief days at summer's end when I watched, as I always used to do, the lovely sudden silver arcs meteors plunging make.

In later years, I learned that, concurrently with the celestial marvels, farm communities were reporting an unusual number of calves born two-headed, chickens hatched three-legged, and lambs born with human faces; but since the somewhat vague laws of mutation were more or less well understood by the farmers these curiosities did not alarm them. An earlier generation would have known instinctively that so many irregularities forecast an ill future, full of spite.

Eventually all was satisfactorily explained or, quite as good, forgotten. Yet the real significance of these portents was not so much their mysterious reality as the profound effect they had upon a people who, despite their emphatic materialism, were as easily shattered by the unexpected as their ancestors who had beheld eagles circling the Capitoline Hill, observed the sky grow leaden on Golgotha, shivered in loud storms when the rain was red as blood and the wind full of toads, while in our own century, attended by a statesman-Pope, the sun did a dance over Portugal.

Considering the unmistakable nature of these signs, it is curious how few suspected the truth: that a new mission had been conceived out of the race's need, the hour of its birth already determined by a conjunction of terrible new stars.

It is true of course that the established churches duly noted these spectacular happenings and, rather slyly, used them to enhance that abstract power from which their own mystical but vigorous authority was descended. The more secular, if no less mystical, dogmas . . . descended variously from an ill-tempered social philosopher of the nineteenth century and an energetic, unreasonably confident mental therapist, a product of that century's decline . . . maintained, in the one case, that fireworks had been set off by vindictive employers to bedazzle the poor workers for undefined but patently wicked ends, and, in the other case, that the fiery objects represented a kind of atavistic recession to the childish world of marvels; a theory which was developed even further in a widely quoted paper by an ingenious disciple of the dead therapist. According to this worthy, the universe was the womb in symbol and the blazing lights which many people thought they saw were only a form of hallucination, harking back to some prenatal memory of ovaries bursting with a hostile potential life which would, in time, become sibling rivals. The writer demanded that the government place all who had seen flying objects under three years' close observation to determine to what extent sibling rivalry, or the absence of it (the proposition worked equally well either way), had affected them in life. Although this bold synthesis was universally admired and subsequently read into the Congressional Record by a lady Representative who had herself undergone nine years' analysis with striking results, the government refused to act.

THREE

But although nearly every human institution took cognizance of these signs and auguries, none guessed the truth, and those few individuals who had begun to suspect what might be happening preferred not to speak out, if only because, despite much private analysis and self-questioning, it was not a time in which to circulate ideas which might prove disagreeable to any minority, no matter how lunatic. The body politic was more than usually upset by signs of nonconformity. The atmosphere was not unlike that of Britain during the mad hour of Titus Oates.

Precisely why my countrymen behaved so frantically is a problem for those historians used to the grand, eternal view of human events. Yet I have often thought that much of our national irritability was closely related to the unexpected and reluctant custody of the world the second war had pressed upon the confused grandchildren of a proud, isolated people, both indifferent and strange to the ways of other cultures.

More to the point, however, was the attitude of our intellectuals, who constituted at this time a small, militantly undistinguished minority, directly descended in spirit if not in fact from that rhetorical eighteenth-century Swiss whose romantic and mystical love for humanity was magically achieved through a somewhat obsessive preoccupation with himself. His passion for self-analysis flourished in our mid-century, at least among the articulate few who were capable of analyzing and who, in time, like their great ancestor, chose the ear of the world for their confessional.

Men of letters lugubriously described their own deviations (usually political or sexual, seldom aesthetic), while painters worked devotedly at depicting unique inner worlds which were not accessible to others except in a state of purest empathy hardly to be achieved without a little fakery in a selfish world. It was finally, the accepted criterion that art's single function was the fullest expression of a private vision . . . which was true enough, though the visions of men lacking genius are not without a certain gloom. Genius, in this time, was quite as rare as in any other and, to its credit, it was not a self-admiring age. Critics found merit only in criticism, a singular approach which was to amuse the serious for several decades.

Led by artists, the intellectuals voiced their guilt at innumerable cocktail parties where it was accepted as an article of faith that each had a burden of guilt which could, once recognized, be exorcised. The means of recognition were expensive but rewarding: a trained and sympathetic listener would give the malaise a name and reveal its genesis; then, through confession (and occasionally "reliving"), the guilt would vanish along with asthma, impotence and eczema. The process, of course, was not easy. To facilitate therapy, it became the custom among the cleverer people to set aside all the traditional artifices of society so that both friends and strangers could confess to one another their worst deeds, their most squalid fantasies, in a series of competitive monologues conducted with arduous sincerity and surprisingly successful on every level but that of communication.

I am sure that this sort of catharsis was not entirely valueless: many of the self-obsessed undoubtedly experienced relief when dispensing secrets. It was certainly an instructive shock for them to find that even their most repellent aberrations were accepted quite perfunctorily by strangers too intent on their own problems to be outraged, or even greatly interested. This discovery was not always cheering. There is a certain dignity and excitement in possessing a dangerous secret life. To lose it in maturity is hard. Once promiscuously shared, vice becomes ordinary, no more troublesome than obvious dentures.

Many cherished private hells were forever lost in those garrulous years, and the vacuum each left was invariably filled with a boredom which, in its turn, could be dispelled only by faith. As a result, the pursuit of the absolute, in one guise or another, became the main preoccupation of these romanticists who professed with some pride a mistrust of reason, derived quite legitimately from their own incapacity to assimilate the social changes created by machinery, their particular Lucifer. They rejected the idea of the reflective mind, arguing that since both logic and science had failed to establish the first cause of the universe or (more important) humanity's significance, only the emotions could reveal to us the nature of reality, the key to meaning. That it was no real concern of this race why or when or how the universe came into being was an attitude never, so far as I can recall, expressed by the serious-minded of the day. Their searching, however, was not simply the result of curiosity; it was more than that: it was an emotional, senseless plunging into the void, into the unknowable and the irrelevant. It became, finally, the burden of life, the blight among the flowers: the mystery which must be revealed, even at the expense of life. It was a terrible crisis, made doubly hard since the eschewal of logic left only one path clear to the heart of the dilemma: the way of the mystic, and even to the least sensible it was sadly apparent that, lacking a superior and dedicated organization, one man's revelation is not apt to be of much use to another.

Quantities of venerable attitudes were abandoned and much of the preceding century's "eternal truths and verities" which had cast, rocklike, so formidable and dense a shadow were found, upon examination, to be so much sand, suitable for the construction of fantastic edifices but not durable, nor safe from the sea's tide.

But the issue was joined: dubious art was fashioned, authorities were invoked, dreams given countenance and systems constructed on the evidence of private illumination.

For a time, political and social action seemed to offer a way out, or in. Foreign civil wars, foreign social experiments were served with a ferocity difficult to comprehend; but later, when the wars and experiments went wrong, revealing, after such high hopes, the perennial human inability to order society, a disillusion resulted, bitterly resolved in numerous cases by the assumption of some mystical dogma, preferably one so quaintly rich with history, so sweeping and unreasonable in its claims, as to be thoroughly acceptable to the saddened romanticist who wanted, above all else, to *feel*, to know without reasoning.

So in these portentous times, only the scientists were content as they constructed ever more fabulous machines with which to split the invisible kernels of life while the anti-scientifics leaped nervously from one absolute to another . . . now rushing to the old for grace, now to the new for salvation, no two of them really agreeing on anything except the need for agreement, for the last knowledge. And that, finally, was the prevailing note of the age, since reason had been declared insufficient, only a mystic could provide the answer, only he could mark the boundaries of life with a final authority, inscrutably revealed. It was perfectly clear. All that was lacking was the man.

TWO

ONE

The garden was at its best that first week in the month of June. The peonies were more opulent than usual and I walked slowly through the green light on the terrace above the white river, enjoying the heavy odor of peonies and of new roses rambling in hedges.

The Hudson was calm, no ripple revealed that slow tide which even here, miles to the north of the sea, rises brackishly at the moon's disposition. Across the river the Catskills, water-blue, emerged sharply from the summer's green as though the earth in one vivid thrust had attempted sky, fusing the two elements into yet another, richer blue . . . but the sky was only framed, not really touched, and the blue of hills was darker than the pale sky with its protean clouds all shaped by wind, like the stuff of auguries and human dreaming.

The sky that day was like an idiot's mind, wild with odd clouds, but lovely too, guileless, natural, elusive.

I did not want to go in to lunch, although there was no choice in the matter. I had arrived at one o'clock; I was expected at one-thirty. Meanwhile, avoiding the house until the last possible moment, I had taken a neighbour's privilege of strolling alone about the garden; the house behind me was gray and austere, granitic, more English than Hudson Valley. The grounds swept softly down toward the river nearly a mile away. A vista had been cleaned from the central terrace, a little like the one at Versailles but more rustic, less royal. Dark green trees covered the hills to left and right of the sweep of the lawn and meadow. No other house could be seen. Even the railroad between the terrace and the water was invisible, hidden by a bluff.

I breathed the air of early summer gladly, voluptuously. I lived my life in seasonal concert with this river and, after grim March and confusing sharp April, the knowledge that at last the trees were in leaf and the days warm was quite enough to create in me a mood of euphoria, of marvelous serenity. I contemplated love affairs. I prepared to meet strangers. The summer and I would celebrate our triumph soon; but, until the proper moment, I was a spectator: the summer love as yet unknown to me, the last dark blooming of peonies amid the wreckage of white lilacs still some weeks away, held in the future with my love. I could only anticipate; I savored my disengagement in this garden.

But then it was time to go in and I turned my back resolutely on the river and ascended the wide stone steps to the brick terrace which fronted the house on the river side, pausing only to break the stem of a white and pink peony, regretting immediately what I had done: brutally, I had wished to possess the summer, to fix the instant, to bear with me into the house a fragment of the day. It was wrong; and I stood for a moment at the French door holding the great peony in my hand, its odor like a dozen roses, like all the summers I had ever known. But it was impractical. I could not stuff it into my buttonhole for it was as large as a baby's head, while I was fairly certain that my hostess would be less than pleased to receive at my hands one of her best peonies, cut too short even to place in water. Obscurely displeased with myself and the day, I plunged the flower deep into a hedge of boxwood until not even a glimmer of white showed through the dense dark green to betray me. Then, like a murderer, the assaulted day part-spoiling, I went inside.

TWO

"You have been malingering in the garden," Clarissa said, offering me her face like a painted plate to kiss. "I saw you from the window."

"Saw me ravage the flowers?"

"They all do," she said obscurely, and led me after her into the drawing room, an oblong full of light from French windows opening upon the terrace. I was surprised to see that she was alone.

"She'll be along presently. She's upstairs changing."

"Who?"

"Iris Mortimer . . . didn't I tell you? It's the whole reason."

Clarissa nodded slyly from the chair opposite me. A warm wind crossed the room and the white curtains billowed like spinnakers in a regatta. I breathed the warm odor of flowers, of burned ash remnants from the fireplace: the room shone with silver and porcelain. Clarissa was rich despite the wars and crises that had marked our days, leaving the usual scars upon us, like trees whose cross-sections bear a familiar resemblance of concentric rings, recalling in detail the weather of past years . . . at least those few rings we shared in common, for Clarissa, by her own admission, was twenty-two hundred years old with an uncommonly good memory. None of us had ever questioned her too closely about her past. There is no reason to suspect, however, that she was insincere. Since she felt she had lived that great length of time and since her recollections were remarkably interesting and plausible, she was much in demand as a conversationalist and adviser, especially useful in plots which required great shrewdness and daring. It was perfectly apparent that she was involved in some such plot at the moment.

I looked at her thoughtfully before I casually rose to take the bait of mystery she had trailed so perfunctorily before me. She knew her man. She knew I would not be difficult in the early stages of any adventure.

"Whole reason?" I repeated.

"I can say no more!" said Clarissa with a melodramatic emphasis which my deliberately casual tone did not entirely justify. "You'll love Iris, though."

I wondered whether loving Iris, or pretending to love Iris, was to be the summer's game. But before I could inquire further, Clarissa, secure in her mystery, asked me idly about my work and, as idly, I answered her, the exchange perfunctory yet easy, for we were used to one another.

"I am tracking him down," I said. "There is so little to go on, but what there is is quite fascinating, especially Ammianus."

"Fairly reliable as military men go," said Clarissa, suddenly emerging from her polite indifference. Any reference to the past she had known always interested her. Only the present seemed to bore her, at least that ordinary unusable present which did not contain promising material for one of her elaborate human games.

"Did you know him?" I never accepted, literally, Clarissa's unique age. Two thousand years is an unlikely span of life even for a woman of her sturdy unimaginativeness; yet there was no ignoring the fact that she *seemed* to have lived that long, and that her references to obscure episodes, where ascertainable, were nearly always right and, more convincing still, where they differed from history's records, differed on the side of plausibility, the work of a memory or a mind completely unsuperstitious and unenthusiastic. She *was* literal and, excepting always her central fantasy, matter-of-fact. To her the death of Caesar was the logical outcome of a system of taxation which has not been preserved for us, while the virtue of the Roman republic and the ambitions of celebrated politicians she set aside as being less than important. Currency and taxation were her forte and she managed to reduce all the martial splendor of ancient days to an economic level.

She had one other obsession, however, and my reference to Ammianus reminded her of it.

"The Christians!" she exclaimed significantly; then she paused. I waited. Her conversation at times resembled chapter headings chosen haphazardly from an assortment of Victorian novels. "*They* hated him."

"Ammianus?"

"No, your man Julian. It *is* the Emperor Julian you are writing about."

"Reading about."

"Ah, you *will* write about him," she said with an abstracted Pythoness stare which suggested that I was indefatigable in my eccentric purpose, the study of history in a minor key.

"Of course they hated him. As well they should have . . . that's the whole point to my work."

"Unreliable, the lot of them. There is no decent history from the time they came to Rome up until that fat little Englishman . . . you know, the one who lived in Switzerland . . . with the *staring* eyes."

"Gibbon."

"Yes, that one. Of course he got all the facts wrong, poor man, but at least he tried. The facts of course were all gone by then. They saw to that . . . burning things, rewriting things . . . not that I really ever *read* them . . . you know how I am about reading. I prefer a mystery novel any day. But at least Gibbon got the tone right."

"Yet . . ."

"Of course Julian was something of a prig, you know. He *posed* continually and he wasn't . . . what do they call him now? an apostate. He *never* renounced Christianity."

"He what? . . ."

Clarissa in her queer way took pleasure in rearranging all accepted information. I shall never know whether she did it deliberately to mystify or whether her versions were the forgotten reality.

"He was a perfectly good Christian *au fond* despite his peculiar diet. He was a vegetarian for some years but wouldn't eat beans, as I recall, because he thought they contained the souls of the dead, an old orphic notion."

"Which is hardly Christian."

"Isn't that part of it? No? Well, in any case the first Edict of Paris was intended . . ." But I was never to hear Julian's intent, for Iris was in the doorway, slender, dressed in white, her hair dark and drawn back in a classical line from her calm face. She was handsome and not at all what I had expected, but then Clarissa had, as usual, not given me much lead. Iris Mortimer was my own age, I guessed, about thirty, and although hardly a beauty she moved with such ease, spoke with such softness and created such an air of serenity that one gave her perhaps more credit for the possession of beauty than an American devoted to regular features ought, in all accuracy, to have done. The impression was one of lightness, of this month of June in fact . . . I linger over her description a little worriedly, conscious that I am not really getting her right (at least as she appeared to me that afternoon) for the simple reason that our lives were to become so desperately involved in the next few years and my memories of her are now encrusted with so much emotion that any attempt to evoke her as she actually was when I first saw her in that drawing room some fifty years ago is not unlike the work of a restorer of paintings removing layers of glaze and grime in an attempt to reveal an original pattern in all its freshness somewhere beneath. Except that a restorer of course is a workman who has presumably no prejudice and, too, he did not create the original image only to attend its subsequent distortion, as the passionate do in life; for the Iris of that day was, I suppose, no less and no more than what she was to become; it was merely that I could not suspect the bizarre course our future was to take. I had no premonition of our mythic roles, though the temptation is almost overpowering to assert, darkly, that even on the occasion of our first meeting I *knew*. The truth is that we met; we became friends; we lunched amiably and the future cast not one shadow across the mahogany table around which we sat, listening to Clarissa and eating fresh shad caught in the river that morning.

"Eugene here is interested in Julian," said our hostess, lifting a spring asparagus to her mouth with her fingers.

"Julian who?"

"The Emperor of Rome. I forget his family name but he was a cousin, I think, of Constantius, who was dreary, too, though not such a bore as Julian. Iris, try the asparagus. We get them from the garden."

Iris tried an asparagus and Clarissa recalled that the Emperor Augustus's favorite saying was: "Quick as boiled asparagus." It developed that *he* had been something of a bore, too. "Hopelessly involved in office work. Of course it's all terribly important, no doubt of that . . . after all the entire Empire was based on a first-rate filing system; yet, all in all, it's hardly *glamorous*."

"Whom *did* you prefer?" asked Iris, smiling at me. She too was aware of our hostess's obsession; whether or not she believed is a different matter. I assumed not; yet the assumption of truth is perhaps, for human purposes, the same as truth itself, at least to the obsessed.

"None of the obvious ones," said Clarissa, squinting near-sightedly at the window through which a pair of yellow-spangled birds were mating on the wing like eccentric comets against the green of box. "But of course, I didn't know everyone, darling. Only a few. Not all of them were accessible. Some never dined out and some that did go out were impossible. And then of course I travelled a good deal. I loved Alexandria and wintered there for over two hundred years, missing a great deal of the unpleasantness at Rome, the *unstability* of those tiresome generals . . . although Vitellius was great fun, at least as a young man. I never saw him when he was Emperor that time, for five minutes, wasn't it? Died of greed. Such an appetite! Once as a young man he ate an entire side of beef at my place in Baiae. Ah, Baiae, I do miss it. Much nicer than Bath or Biarritz and certainly more interesting than Newport. I had several houses there over the years. Once when Senator Tullius Cicero was travelling with that poisonous daughter of his, they stopped . . ."

We listened attentively as one always did to Clarissa . . . does? I wonder if she is still alive. If she is, then perhaps the miracle has indeed taken place and one human being has finally avoided the usual fate. It is an amiable miracle to contemplate.

Lunch ended without any signs of the revelation Clarissa had led me to expect. Nothing was said that seemed to possess even a secret significance. Wondering idly whether or not Clarissa might, after all, be entirely mad, I followed the two women back into the drawing room, where we had our coffee in a warm mood of satiety made only faintly disagreeable for me by the mild nausea I always used to experience when I drank too much wine at lunch. Now of course I never drink wine, only the Arabs' mint tea and their sandy bitter coffee which I have come to like.

Clarissa reminisced idly. She possessed a passion for minor detail which was often a good deal more interesting than her usual talks on currency devaluation.

Neither Iris nor I spoke much; it was as if we were both awaiting some word from Clarissa which would throw into immediate relief this lunch, this day, this meeting of strangers. But Clarissa continued to gossip; at last, when I was beginning to go over in my mind the various formulae which make departure easy, our hostess, as though aware that she had drawn out the overture too long, said abruptly, "Eugene, show Iris the garden. She has never seen it before." And then, heartily firing fragments of sentences at us as though in explanation of this move of hers, she left the room, indicating that the rest was up to us.

Puzzled, we both went onto the terrace and into the yellow afternoon. We walked slowly down the steps toward the rose arbors, a long series of trellis arches forming a tunnel of green, bright with new flowers and ending in a cement fountain of ugly tile with a bench beside it, shaded by elms.

We got to facts. By the time we had burrowed through the roses to the bench, we had exchanged those basic bits of information which usually make the rest fall (often incorrectly) into some pattern, a foundation for those various architectures people together are pleased to build to celebrate friendship or enmity or love or, on very special occasions, in the case of a grand affair, a palace with rooms for all three, and much else besides.

Iris was from the Middle West, from a rich suburb of Detroit. This interested me in many ways, for there still existed in those days a real disaffection between East and Midwest and Far West which is hard to conceive nowadays in that gray homogeneity which currently passes for a civilized nation. I was an Eastener, a New Yorker from the Valley with Southern roots, and I felt instinctively that the outlanders were perhaps not entirely civilized. Needless to say, at the time, I would indignantly have denied this prejudice had someone attributed it to me, for those were the days of tolerance in which all prejudice had been banished, from conversation at least . . . though of course to banish prejudice is a contradiction in terms since, by definition, prejudice means prejudgment, and though time and experience usually explode for us all the prejudgments of our first years, they exist, nevertheless, as part of our subconscious, a sabotaging irrational force, causing us to commit strange crimes indeed, made so much worse because they are often secret even to ourselves, I was, then, prejudiced against the Midwesterner, and against the Californian too. I felt that the former especially was curiously hostile to freedom, to the interplay of that rational Western culture which I had so lovingly embraced in my boyhood and grown up with, always conscious of my citizenship in the world, of my role as a humble but appreciative voice in the long conversation. I resented the automobile manufacturers who thought only of manufacturing objects, who distrusted ideas, who feared the fine with the primitive intensity of implacable ignorance. Could this cool girl be from Detroit? From that same rich suburb which had provided me with a number of handsome vital classmates at school? Boys who had combined physical vigor with a resistance to all ideas but those of their suburb, which could only be described as heroic considering the power of New England schools to crack even the toughest prejudices, at least on the rational level. That these boys did not possess a rational level had often occurred to me, though I did, grudgingly, admire, even in my scorn, their grace and strength as well as their confidence in that assembly line which had done so well by them.

Iris Mortimer was one of them. Having learned this there was nothing to do but find sufficient names between us to establish the beginnings of the rapport of class which, even in that late year of the mid-century, still existed: the dowdy aristocracy to which we belonged by virtue of financial security, at least in childhood, of education, of self-esteem and of houses where servants had been in some quantity before the second of the wars; all this we shared and of course those names in common of schoolmates, some from her region, others from mine, names which established us as being of an age. We avoided for some time any comment upon the names, withholding our true selves during the period of identification. I discovered too that she, like me, had remained unmarried, an exceptional state of affairs, for all the names we had mentioned represented two people now instead of one. Ours had been a reactionary generation. We had attempted to combat the time of wars and disasters by a scrupulous observance of our grandparents' customs, a direct reaction to the linking generation whose lives had been so entertainingly ornamented with untidy alliances and fortified by suspect gin. The result was no doubt classic but, at the same time, it was a little shocking. The children were decorous, subdued; they married early, conceived glumly, surrendered to the will of their own children in the interests of enlightened psychology; their lives enriched by the best gin in the better suburbs, safe among their own kind. Yet, miraculously, I had escaped and so apparently had Iris.

"You live here alone?" She indicated the wrong direction though taking in, correctly, the river on whose east bank I did live, a few miles to the north of Clarissa.

I nodded. "Entirely alone . . . in an old house."

"No family?"

"None here. Not much anywhere else. A few in New Orleans, my family's original base." I waited for her to ask if I ever got lonely living in a house on the river, remote from others; but she saw nothing extraordinary in this.

"It must be fine," she said slowly. She broke a leaf off a flowering bush whose branch, heavy with blooming, quivered above our heads as we sat on the garden bench and watched the dim flash of goldfish in the muddy waters of the pond.

"I like it," I said, a little disappointed that there was now no opportunity for me to construct one of my familiar defenses of a life alone. I had, in the five years since my days of travel had temporarily ended, many occasions on which to defend and glorify the solitary life I had chosen for myself beside this river. I had an ever-changing repertoire of feints and thrusts: for instance, with the hearty, I invariably questioned, gently of course, the virtue of a life in the city, confined to a small apartment with uninhibited babies and breathing daily large quantities of soot; at other times I assumed a prince of darkness pose, alone with his crimes in an ancient house, a figure which could, if necessary, be quickly altered to the more engaging one of remote observer of the ways of men, a Stoic among his books, sustained by the recorded fragments of forgotten bloody days, evoking solemnly the pure essences of nobler times, a chaste intelligence beyond the combat, a priest celebrating the cool memory of his race. My theater was extensive and I almost regretted that with Iris there was no need for even a brief curtain raiser, much less one of my exuberant galas.

Not accustomed to the neutral response, I stammered something about the pleasures of gardens. Iris's calm indifference saved me from what might have been a truly mawkish outburst calculated to interest her at any cost (mawkish because, I am confident, none of our deepest wishes or deeds is, finally, when honestly declared, very wonderful or mysterious: simplicity, not complexity, is at the center of our being; fortunately the trembling "I" is seldom revealed, even to paid listeners, for, conscious of the appalling directness of our needs, we wisely disguise their nature with a legerdemain of peculiar cunning). Much of Iris's attraction for me . . . and at the beginning that attraction did exist . . . was that one did not need to discuss so many things. Of course the better charades were not called into being, which, creatively speaking, was a pity. But then it was a relief *not* to pretend and, better still, a relief not to begin the business of plumbing shallows under the illusion that a treasure chest of truth might be found on the mind's sea floor . . . a grim ritual which was popular in those years, especially in the suburbs and housing projects where the mental therapists were ubiquitous and busy.

With Iris, one did not suspend, even at a cocktail party, the usual artifices of society. All was understood, or seemed to be, which is exactly the same thing. We talked about ourselves as though of absent strangers. Then: "Have you known Clarissa long?" I asked.

She shook her head. "I met her only recently."

"Then this is your first visit here? to the Valley?"

"The first," she smiled, "but it's a little like home, you know. I don't mean Detroit, but a memory of home, got from books."

I thought so too. Then she added that she did not read any longer and I was a little relieved. With Iris one wanted not to talk about books or the past. So much of her charm was that she was entirely in the present. It was her gift, perhaps her finest quality, to invest the moment with a significance which in recollection did not exist except as a blurred impression of excitement. She created this merely by existing. I was never to learn the trick, for her conversation was not, in itself, interesting and her actions were usually predictable, making all the more unusual her peculiar effect. She asked me politely about my work, giving me then the useful knowledge that, though she was interested in what *I* was doing, she was not much interested in the life of the Emperor Julian.

I made it short. "I want to do a biography of him. I've always liked history and so, when I settled down in the house, I chose Julian as my work."

"A life's work?"

"Hardly. But another few years. It's the reading which I most enjoy, and that's treacherous. There is so much of interest to read that it seems a waste of time and energy to write anything . . . especially if it's to be only a reflection of reflections."

"Then why do it?"

"Something to say, I suppose. Ot at least the desire to define and illuminate, from one's own point of view, of course."

"Then why . . . Julian?"

Something in the way she said the name convinced me she had forgotten who he was if she had ever known.

"The apostasy; the last stand of paganism against Christianity."

She looked truly interested, for the first time. "They killed him, didn't they?"

"No, he died in battle. Had he lived longer he might at least have kept the Empire divided between the old gods and the new messiah. Unfortunately his early death was their death, the end of the gods."

"Except they returned as saints."

"Yes, a few found a place in Christianity, assuming new names."

"Mother of god," she murmured thoughtfully.

"An unChristian concept, one would have thought," I added, though the beautiful illogic had been explained to me again and again by Catholics: how god could and could not at the same time possess a mother, that gleaming queen of heaven, entirely regnant in those days.

"I have often thought about these things," she said, diffidently. "I'm afraid I'm not much of a student but it fascinates me. I've been out in California for the past few years, working. I was on a fashion magazine." The note was exactly right. She knew precisely what that world meant and she was neither apologetic nor pleased. We both resisted the impulse to begin the names again, threading our way through the maze of fashion, through that frantic world of the peripheral arts.

"You kept away from Vedanta?" A group of transplanted English writers at this time had taken to Oriental mysticism, under the illusion that Asia began at Las Vegas. Swamis and temples abounded among the billboards and orange trees; but but since it was *the* way for some, it was, for those few at least, honorable.

"I came close," She laughed. "But there was too much to read and even then I always felt that it didn't work for us, for Americans, I mean. It's probably quite logical and familiar to Asiatics, but we come from a different line, with a different history. Their responses aren't ours. But I did feel it was possible for others, which is a great deal."

"Because so much is *not* possible?"

"Exactly. But then I know very little about these things." She was direct. No implication that what she did not know either did not exist or was not worth the knowing, the traditional response in the fashionable world.

"Are you working now?"

She shook her head. "No, I gave it up. The magazine sent

somebody to take my place out there (I didn't have the 'personality' they wanted) and so I came on to New York, where I've never really been, except for weekends from school. The magazine had some idea that I might work into the New York office, but I was through. I have worked."

"And had enough?"

"Of that sort of thing, yes. So I've gone out a lot in New York, met many people; thought a little . . ." She twisted the leaf that she still held in her fingers, her eyes vague as though focused on the leaf's faint shadow which fell in depth upon her dress, part upon her dress and more on a tree's branch ending finally in a tiny fragment of shadow on the ground, like the bottom step of a frail staircase of air.

"And here you are, at Clarissa's."

"What an extraordinary woman she is!" The eyes were turned upon me, hazel, clear, luminous with youth.

"She collects people, but not according to any of the usual criteria. She makes them all fit, somehow, but what it is they fit, what design, no one knows. *I* don't know, that is."

"I suppose I was collected. Though it might have been the other way around, since I am sure she interests me more than I do her."

"There is no way of telling."

"Anyway, I'm pleased she asked me here."

We talked of Clarissa with some interest, getting nowhere. Clarissa was truly enigmatic. She had lived for twenty years on the Hudson. She was not married but it was thought she had been. She entertained with great skill. She was in demand in New York and also in Europe, where she often travelled. But no one knew anything of her origin or of the source of her wealth and, oddly enough, although everyone observed her remarkable *idêe fixe*, no one ever discussed it, as though in tactful obedience to some obscure sense of form. In the half-dozen years that I had known her, not once had I discussed with anyone her eccentricity. We accepted in her presence the reality of her mania, and there it ended. Some were more interested by it than others. I was fascinated, and having suspended both belief and doubt found her richly knowing in matters which interested me. Her accounts of various meetings with Libanius in Antioch were brilliant, all told most literally, as though she had no faculty for invention, which perhaps, terrifying thought, she truly lacked, in which case . . . but we chose not to speculate. Iris spoke of plans.

"I'm going back to California."

"Tired of New York?"

"No, hardly. But I met someone quite extraordinary out there, someone I think I should like to see again." Her candor made it perfectly clear that her interest was not romantic. "It's rather in line with what we were talking about. I mean your Julian and all that. He's a kind of preacher."

"That doesn't sound promising," A goldfish made a popping sound as it captured a dragonfly on the pond's surface.

"But he isn't the usual sort at all. He's completely different but I'm not sure just how."

"An evangelist?" In those days loud men and women were still able to collect enormous crowds by ranging up and down the country roaring about that salvation which might be found in the bosom of the Lamb.

"No, his own sort of thing entirely. A little like the Vedanta teachers, only he's American, and young."

"What does he teach?"

"I . . . I'm not sure. No, don't laugh. I met him only once. At a friend's house in Santa Monica. He talked very little but one had the feeling that, well, that it was something unusual."

"It must have been if you can't recall what he said." I revised my first estimate. It was romantic after all. A man who was young, fascinating . . . I was almost jealous as a matter of principle.

"I'm afraid I don't make much sense." She gestured and the leaf fell into its own shadow on the grass. "Perhaps it was the effect he had on the others that impressed me. They were clever people, worldly people, yet they listened to him like children."

"What does he do? does he live by preaching?"

"I don't know that either. I met him the night before I left California."

"And now you think you want to go back to find out?"

"Yes. I've thought about him a great deal these last few weeks. You'd think one would forget such a thing, but I haven't."

"What was his name?"

"Cave. John Cave."

"A pair of initials calculated to amaze the innocent." Yet even while I invoked irony, I felt with a certain chill in the heat that *this* was to be Clarissa's plot, and for many days afterward that name echoed in my memory, long after I had temporarily forgotten Iris's own name, had forgotten, as one does, the whole day, the peony in the boxwood, the leaf's fall and the catch of the goldfish; instants which now live again in the act of re-creation, details which were to fade into a yellow-green blur of June and of the girl beside me in a garden and of that name spoken in my hearing for the first time, becoming in my imagination like some bare monolith awaiting the sculptor's chisel.

THREE

ONE

I did not see Iris again for some months. Nor, for that matter, did I see Clarissa, who the day after our lunch disappeared on one of her mysterious trips. Clarissa's coming and goings doubtless followed some pattern though I could never make much sense of them. I was very disappointed not to see her before she left because I had wanted to ask her about Iris and also . . .

* * *

It has been a difficult day. Shortly after I wrote the lines above, this morning, I heard the sound of an American voice on the street side of the hotel; the first American voice I've heard in some years. Except for me, none has been allowed in Upper Egypt for twenty years. The division of the world has been quite thorough, religiously and politically, and had not some official long ago guessed my identity, it is doubtful that I should have been granted asylum even in this remote region.

I tried to continue with my writing but it was impossible: I could recall nothing. My attention would not focus on the past, on those wraiths which have lately begun to assume again such startling reality as I go about the work of memory . . . but the past was lost to me this morning. The doors shut and I was marooned in the meager present.

Who was this American who had come to Luxor? and why?

For a moment the serenity which I have so long practiced failed me and I feared for my life. Had the long-awaited assassins finally come? But then that animal within who undoes us all with his fierce will to live grew quiet, accepting again the discipline I have so long maintained over him, his obedience due less perhaps to my strong will than to his fatigue, for he is no longer given to the rages and terrors and exultations that once dominated me as the moon does the tide; his defeat is my old age's single victory, and a bitter one.

I took the pages that I had written and hid them in a wide crack in the marble-topped Victorian washstand. I then put on a tie and linen jacket and, cane in hand, my most bemused and guileless expression upon my face, I left the room and walked down the tall dim corridor to the lobby, limping perhaps a little more than was necessary, exaggerating my genuine debility to suggest, if possible, an even greater helplessness. If they had come at last to kill me, I thought it best to go to them while I still held in check the creature terror. As I approached the lobby, I recalled Cicero's death and took courage from his example. He too had been old and tired, too exasperated at the last even to flee.

My assassin (if such he is and I still do not know) looks perfectly harmless: a red-faced American in a white suit crumpled from heat and travel. In atrocious Arabic he was addressing the manager, who, though he speaks no English, is competent in French and accustomed to speaking it to Occidentals. My compatriot, however, was obstinate and smothered with a loud voice the polite European cadences of the manager.

I moved slowly to the desk, tapping emphatically with my cane on the tile floor. Both turned. It was the moment which I have so long dreaded. The eyes of an American were turned upon me once again. Would he know? *Does* he know? I felt all the blood leave my head. With a great effort, I remained on my feet. Steadying my voice, which has nowadays a tendency to quaver even when I am at ease, I said to the American, in our own language, the language I had not once spoken in nearly twenty years, "Can I be of assistance, sir?" The words sounded strange on my lips and I was aware that I had given them an ornateness which was quite unlike my usual speech. His look of surprise was, I think, perfectly genuine. I felt a cowardly relief: not yet, not yet.

"Oh!" The American stared at me stupidly for a moment (his face is able to suggest a marvelous range of incomprehension, as I have since discovered).

"My name is Richard Hudson," I said, pronouncing carefully the name by which I am known in Egypt, the name with which I have lived so long that it sometimes seems as if all my life before was only a dream, a fantasy of a time which never was except in reveries, in those curious waking dreams which I often have these days when I am tired, at sundown usually, and the mind loses all control over itself and the memory grows confused with imaginings, and I behold worlds and splendors which I have never known, yet they are vivid enough to haunt me even in the lucid mornings. I am dying, of course, and my brain is only letting up, releasing its images with a royal abandon, confusing everything like those surrealist works of art which had some vogue in my youth.

"Oh," said the American again and then, having accepted my reality, he pushed a fat red hand toward me. "The name is Butler, Bill Butler. Glad to meet you. Didn't expect to find another white . . . didn't expect to meet up with an American in these parts," I shook the hand.

"Let me help you," I said, releasing the hand quickly. "The manager speaks no English."

"I been studying Arabic," said Butler with a certain sullenness. "Just finished a year's course at Ottawa Center for this job. They don't speak it here like *we* studied it."

"It takes time," I said soothingly. "You'll catch the tone."

"Oh, I'm sure of that. Tell them I got a reservation." Butler mopped his full glistening cheeks with a handkerchief.

"You have a reservation for William Butler?" I asked the manager in French.

He shook his head, looking at the register in front of him. "Is he an American?" He looked surprised when I said that he was. "But it didn't sound like English."

"He was trying to speak Arabic."

The manager sighed. "Would you ask him to show me his passport and authorizations?"

I did as directed. Butler pulled a bulky envelope from his pocket and handed it to the manager. As well as I could, without appearing inquisitive, I looked at the papers. I could tell nothing. The passport was evidently in order. The numerous authorizations from the Egyptian Government in the Pan-Arabic League, however, seemed to interest the manager intensely.

"Perhaps . . ." I began, but he was already telephoning the police. Though I speak Arabic with difficulty, I can understand it easily. The manager was inquiring at length about Mr. Butler and about his status in Egypt. The police chief evidently knew all about him and the conversation was short.

"Would you ask him to sign the register?" The manager's expression was puzzled. I wondered what on earth it was all about.

"Don't know why there's all this confusion," said Butler, carving his name into the register with the ancient pen. "I wired for a room last week from Cairo."

"Communications have not been perfected in the Arab countries," I said (fortunately for me, I thought to myself).

When he had done registering, a boy came and took his bags and the key to his room.

"Much obliged to you, Mr. Hudson."

"Not at all."

"Like to see something of you, if you don't mind. Wonder if you could give me an idea of the lay of the land."

I said I should be delighted and we made a date to meet for tea in the cool of the late afternoon, on the terrace.

When he had gone, I asked the manager about him but though my old friend has been manager for twelve years and looks up to me as an elder statesman, since I have lived in the hotel longer than anyone, he would tell me nothing. "It's too much for me, sir." And I could get no more out of him.

TWO

The terrace was nearly cool when we met at six o'clock, the hour when the Egyptian sun, having just lost its unbearable gold, falls, a scarlet disc, into the white stone hills across the river which, at this season, winds narrowly among the mud flats, a third of its usual size, diminished by heat.

"Don't suppose we could order a drink . . . not that I'm much of a drinking man. But you get quite a thirst on a day like this."

I told him that since foreigners had ceased to come here, the bar had been closed down. Moslems for religious reasons did not use alcohol.

"I know, I know," he said. "Studied all about them, even read the Koran. Frightful stuff, too."

"No worse than most documents revealed by heaven," I said

gently, not wanting to get on to that subject. "But tell me what brings you to these parts."

"I was going to ask *you* the same thing," said Butler genially, taking the cup of mint tea which the servant had brought him. On the river a felucca with a red sail tacked slowly in the hot breeze. "The manager tells me you've been here for twenty years."

"You must have found a language in common."

Butler chuckled. "These devils understand you well enough if they want to. But you . . ."

"I was an archaeologist at one time," I said, and I told him the familiar story which I have repeated so many times now that I have almost come to believe it. "I was from Boston originally. Do you know Boston? I often think of those cold winters with a certain longing. Too much light can be as trying as too little. Some twenty years ago, I decided to retire, to write a book of memoirs." This was a new, plausible touch, "Egypt was always my single passion and so I came to Luxor, to this hotel where I've been quite content, though hardly industrious."

"How come they let you in? I mean there was all that trouble back when the Pan-Arabic League shut itself off from civilization."

"I was very lucky, I suppose. I had many friends in the academic world of Cairo and they were able to grant me a special dispensation."

"Old hand, then, with the natives?"

"But a little out of practice. All my Egyptian friends have seen fit to die and I live now as if I were already dead myself."

This had the desired effect of chilling him. Though he was hardly fifty, the immediacy of death, even when manifested in the person of a chance acquaintance, does inspire a certain gravity.

He mumbled something which I did not catch. I think my hearing has begun to go. Not that I am deaf but I have, at times, a monotonous buzzing in my ears which makes conversation difficult. According to the local doctor my arteries have hardened and at any moment one is apt to burst among the convolutions of the brain, drowning my life. But I do not dwell on this, at least not in conversation.

"There's been a big shake-up in the Atlantic Community.

Don't suppose you'd hear much about it around here since from the newspapers I've seen in Egypt they have a pretty tight censorship."

I said I knew nothing about recent activities in the Atlantic Community or anywhere else, other than Egypt.

"Well they've worked out an alliance with Pan-Arabia that will open the whole area to us. Of course no oil exploitation is allowed but there'll still be a lot of legitimate business between our sphere and these people."

I listened to him patiently while he explained the state of the world to me. It seemed unchanged. The only difference was that there were now new and unfamiliar names in high places. He finished with a patriotic harangue about the necessity of the civilized to work in harmony together for the good of mankind. "And this opening up of Egypt has given us the chance we've been waiting for for years, and we mean to take it."

"You mean to extend trade?"

"No, I mean the Word."

"The Word?" I repeated numbly, the old fear returning.

"Why sure. I'm a Cavite Communicator." He rapped perfunctorily on the table twice. I tapped feebly with my cane on the tile: in the days of the Spanish persecution such signals were a means of secret communication (not that the persecution had really been so great, but it had been our decision to dramatize it in order that our people might become more conscious of their splendid if temporary isolation and high destiny); it had not occurred to me that, triumphant, the Cavites should still cling to those bits of fraternal ritual which I had conceived with a certain levity in the early days. But of course the love of ritual, of symbol, is peculiar to our race, and I reflected bleakly on this as I returned the signal which identified us as brother Cavites.

"The world must have changed indeed," I said at last. "It was a Moslem law that no foreign missionaries be allowed in the Arab League."

"Pressure!" Butler looked very pleased. "Nothing obvious, of course; had to be done, though."

"For economic reasons?"

"No, for Cavesword. That's what we're selling because that's the one thing we've got." And he blinked seriously at the remnant of scarlet sun; his voice husky, like that of a man selling some commodity on television in the old days. Yet the note of sincerity, whether simulated or genuine, was unmistakably resolute.

"You may have a difficult time," I said, not wanting to go on with this conversation but unable to direct it short of walking away. "The Moslems are very stubborn in their faith."

Butler laughed confidently. "We'll change all that. It may not be easy at first because we've got to go slow, feel our way, but once we know the lay of the land, you might say, we'll be able to produce some big backing, some real big backing."

His meaning was unmistakable. Already I could imagine those Squads of the Word in action throughout this last terrestrial refuge. Long ago they had begun as eager instruction teams. After the first victories, however, they had become adept at demoralization, at brainwashing and auto-hypnosis, using all the psychological weapons that our race in its ingenuity had fashioned in the mid-century, becoming so subtle with the passage of time that imprisonment or execution for unorthodoxy was no longer necessary. Even the most recalcitrant, virtuous man could be reduced to a sincere and useful orthodoxy, no different in quality from his former antagonists, his moment of rebellion forgotten, his reason anchored securely at last in the general truth. I was also quite confident that their methods had improved even since my enlightened time.

"I hope you'll be able to save these poor people," I said, detesting myself for this hypocrisy.

"Not a doubt in the world," he clapped his hands. "They don't know what happiness we'll bring them." Difficult as it was to accept such hyperbole, I believed in his sincerity. Butler is one of those zealots without whose offices no large work in the world can be successfully propagated. I did not feel more than a passing pity for the Moslems. They were doomed but their fate would not unduly distress them, for my companion was perfectly right when he spoke of the happiness which would be theirs: a blithe mindlessness that would in no way affect their usefulness as citizens. We had long since determined that this was the only humane way of ridding the mass of superstition in the interest of Cavesword and the better life.

"Yet it *is* strange that they should let you in," I said, quite aware that he might be my assassin after all, permitted by the

Egyptian government to destroy me and, with me, the last true memory of the mission. It was not impossible that Butler was an accomplished actor, sounding me out before the final victory of the Cavites, the necessary death and total obliteration of the person of Eugene Luther, now grown old with a false name in a burning land.

If Butler is an actor, he is a master. He thumped on interminably about America, John Cave and the necessity of spreading his word throughout the world. I listened patiently as the sun went abruptly behind the hills and all the stars appeared against the moonless waste of sky. Fires appeared in the hovels on the far shore of the Nile, yellow points of light like fireflies hovering by that other river which I shall never see again.

"Must be nearly suppertime."

"Not quite," I said, relieved that Butler's face was now invisible. I was not used to great red faces after my years in Luxor among the lean, the delicate and the dark. Now only his voice was a dissonance in the evening.

"Hope the food's edible."

"It isn't bad, though it may take some getting used to."

"Well, I've got a strong stomach. Guess that's why they chose me for this job."

This job? could it mean . . .? But I refused to let myself be panicked. I have lived too long with terror to be much moved now; especially since my life by its very continuation has brought me to nothing's edge. "Are there many of you?" I asked politely. The day was ending and I was growing weary, all senses blunted and some confused. "Many Communicators?"

"Quite a few. They've been training us for the last year in Canada for the big job of opening up Pan-Arabia. Of course we've known for years that it was just a matter of time before the government got us in here."

"Then you've been thoroughly grounded in the Arab culture? and disposition?"

"Oh sure. Of course I may have to come to you every now and then, if you don't mind." He chuckled to show that his patronage would be genial.

"I should be honoured to assist."

"We anticipate trouble at first. We have to go slow. Pretend we're just available for instruction while we get to know the local big shots. Then, when the time comes . . ." He left the ominous sentence unfinished. I could imagine the rest. Fortunately, nature by then, with or without Mr. Butler's assistance, would have removed me as a witness.

Inside the hotel the noise of plates being moved provided a familiar reference. I was conscious of being hungry. As the body's mechanism jolts to a halt, it wants more fuel than it ever did at its optimum. I wanted to go in, but before I could gracefully extricate myself Butler asked me a question. "You the only American in these parts?"

I said that I was.

"Funny, nothing was said about there being *any* American up here. I guess they didn't know you were here."

"Perhaps they were counting me among the American colony at Cairo," I said smoothly. "I suppose, officially, I am a resident of that city. I was on the Advisory Board of the Museum." This was not remotely true but since, to my knowledge, there is no Advisory Board it would be difficult for anyone to establish my absence from it.

"That must be it." Butler seemed easily satisfied, perhaps too easily. "Certainly makes things a lot easier for us, having somebody like you up here, another Cavite, who knows the lingo."

"I'll help in any way I can. Although I'm afraid I have passed the age of usefulness. Like the British king, I can only advise."

"Well, that's enough. I'm the active one anyway. My partner takes care of the other things."

"Partner? I thought you were alone."

"No. I'm to dig my heels in first; then my colleague comes on in a few weeks. That's standard procedure. He's a psychologist and an authority on Cavesword. We all are, of course—authorities, that is—but he's gone into the early history and so on a little more thoroughly than us field men usually do."

So there was to be another one, a clever one. I found myself both dreading and looking forward to the arrival of this dangerous person. It would be interesting to deal with a good mind again, or at least an instructed one, though Butler has not given me much confidence in the new Cavite Communicators. Nevertheless, I am intensely curious about the Western world since my flight from it. I have been effectively cut off from any real knowledge of the West for two decades. Rumors, stray bits of information, sometimes penetrate as far as Luxor but I can make little sense of them, for the Cavites are, as I well know, not given to candor, while the Egyptian newspapers exist in a fantasy world of Pan-Arabic dominion. There was so much I wished to know that I hesitated to ask Butler, not for fear of giving myself away but because I felt that any serious conversation with him would be pointless. I rather doubted if he knew what he was supposed to know, much less all the details that I wished to know and that even a moderately intelligent man, if not hopelessly zealous, might be able to supply me with.

I had a sudden idea. "You don't happen to have a recent edition of the Testament, do you? Mine's quite old and out of date."

"What date?" This was unexpected.

"The year? I don't recall. About thirty years old, I should say."

There was a silence. "Of course yours is a special case, being marooned like this. There's a ruling about it which I think will protect you fully since you've had no contact with the outside. Anyway, as a Communicator, I must ask you for your old copy."

"Why, certainly, but . . ."

"I'll give you a new one, of course. You see it is against the law to have any Testament which predates the second Cavite Council."

I was beginning to understand. After the schism a second Council had been inevitable even though no reference to it has ever appeared in the Egyptian press. "The censorship here is thorough, " I said. "I had no idea there had been a new Council."

"What a bunch of savages!" Butler groaned with disgust. "That's going to be one of our main jobs, you know, education, freeing the press. There has been almost no communication between the two spheres of influence . . ."

"Spheres of influence." How easily the phrase came to his lips! All the jargon of the journalists of fifty years ago has, I gather, gone into the language, providing the inarticulate with a number of made-up phrases calculated to blur their none too clear meanings. I assume of course that Butler is as inarticulate as he seems, that he is typical of the first post-Cavite generation.

"You must give me a clear picture of what has been happening in America since my retirement." But I rose to prevent him from giving me, at that moment at least, any further observations on "spheres of influence."

I stood for a moment, resting on my cane. I had stood up too quickly and as usual suffered a spell of dizziness. I was also ravenously hungry. Butler stamped out a cigarette on the tile.

"Be glad to tell you anything you want to know. That's my business." He laughed shortly. "Well, time for chow. I've got some anti-bacteria tablets they gave us before we came out, supposed to keep the food from poisoning us."

"I'm sure you won't need them here."

He kept pace with my slow shuffle. "Well, it increases eating pleasure, too." Inadvertently, I shuddered as I recognized yet another glib phrase from the past; it had seemed such a good idea to exploit the vulgar language of the advertisers. I suffered a brief spasm of guilt.

THREE

We dined together in the airy salon, deserted at this season except for a handful of government officials and businessmen who eyed us without much interest, even though Americans are not a common sight in Egypt. They were of course used to me although, as a rule, I keep out of sight, taking my meals in my room and frequenting those walks along the river bank which avoid altogether the town of Luxor.

I found, after I had dined, that physically I was somewhat restored, better able to cope with Butler. In fact, inadvertently, I actually found myself, in the madness of my great age, enjoying his company, a sure proof of loneliness if not of senility. He too, after taking pills calculated to fill him "chock full of vim and vigor" (that is indeed the phrase he used), relaxed considerably and spoke of his life in the United States. He had no talent for evoking what he would doubtless call "the big picture" but in a casual, disordered way he was able to give me a number of details about his own life and work which did suggest the proportions of the world from which he had so recently come and which I had, in my folly, helped create.

On religious matters he was unimaginative and doctrinaire, concerned with the letter of the commands and revelations rather than with the spirit, such as it was or is. I could not resist the dangerous maneuver of asking him, at the correct moment of course (we were speaking of the time of the schisms), what had become of Eugene Luther.

"Who?"

The coffee cup trembled in my hand. I set it carefully on the table. I wondered if *his* hearing was sound. I repeated my own name, long lost to me, but mine still in the secret dimness of memory.

"I don't place the name. Was he a friend of the Liberator?"

"Why, yes. I even used to know him slightly but that was many years ago, before your time. I'm curious to know what might have become of him. I suppose he's dead."

"I'm sorry but I don't place the name." He looked at me with some interest. "I guess you must be almost old enough to have seen *him*."

I nodded, lowering my lids with a studied reverence, as though dazzled at the recollection of great light. "I saw him several times."

"Boy, I envy you! There aren't many left who have seen *him* with their own eyes. What was he like?"

"Just like his photographs," I said, shifting the line of inquiry: there is always the danger that a trap is being prepared for me. I was noncommittal, preferring to hear Butler talk of himself. Fortunately, he preferred this too, and for nearly an hour I learned as much as I shall ever need to know about the life of at least one Communicator of Cavesword. While he talked, I watched him furtively for some sign of intention but there was none that I could detect. Yet I am suspicious. He had not known my name and I could not understand what obscure motive might cause him to pretend ignorance, unless of course he *does* know who I am and wishes to confuse me, preparatory to some trap.

I excused myself soon afterward and went to my room, after first accepting a copy of the newest Testament handsomely bound in Plasticon (it looks like plastic) and promising to give him my old proscribed copy the next day.

The first thing that I did, after locking the door to my room, was to take the book over to my desk and open it to the index.

My eye traveled down that column of familiar names until it came to the L's.

At first I thought that my eyes were playing a trick upon me. I held the page close to the light, wondering if I might not have begun to suffer delusions, the not unfamiliar concomitant of solitude and old age. But my eyes were adequate and the hallucination, if real, was vastly convincing. My name was no longer there. Eugene Luther no longer existed in that Testament which was largely his own composition.

I let the book shut of itself, as new books will. I sat down at the desk, understanding at last the extraordinary ignorance of Butler. I had been obliterated from history. My place in time was erased. It was as if I had never lived.

FOUR

ONE

I have had in the last few days some difficulty in avoiding the company of Mr. Butler. Fortunately, he is now very much involved with the local functionaries and I am again able to return to my narrative. I don't think Butler has been sent here to assassinate me but, on the other hand, from certain things he has said and not said, I am by no means secure in his ignorance; however, one must go on. At best, it will be a race between him and those hardened arteries which span the lobes of my brain. My only curiosity concerns the arrival next week of his colleague, who is, I gather, of the second generation and of a somewhat bookish turn according to Butler—who would not, I fear, be much of a judge. Certain things that I have learned during the last few days about Iris Mortimer make me more than ever wish to recall our common years as precisely as possible, for what I feared might happen has indeed, if Butler is to be believed, come to pass, and it is now with a full burden of hindsight that I revisit the scenes of a half century ago.

TWO

I had got almost nowhere with my life of Julian. I had become discouraged with his personality though his actual writings continued to delight me. As so often happens in history I had found it difficult really to get at him. The human attractive part of Julian was undone for me by those bleak errors in deed and in judgment which depressed me even though they derived most logically from the man and his time: that fatal wedding which finally walls off figures of earlier ages from the present, keeping them strange despite the most intense and imaginative re-creation. They are not we. We are not they. And I refused to resort to the low trick of fashioning Julian in my own image. I respected his integrity in time and deplored the division of centuries. My work at last came to a halt and, somewhat relieved, I closed my house in the autumn of the year and traveled west to California.

I had a small income which made modest living and careful travel easy for me . . . a happy state of affairs since, in my youth, I was of an intense disposition, capable of the passions and violence of a Rimbaud without, fortunately, the will to translate them into reality. Had I had more money, or none, I might have died young, leaving behind the brief memory of a minor romanticist. As it was, I had a different role to play in the comedy; one for which I was, after some years of reading beside my natal river, peculiarly fitted to play.

I journeyed to southern California, where I had not been since my service in one of the wars. I had never really explored that exotic land and I was curious about it, more curious than I have ever been before or since about any single part of the world. Egypt one knows without visiting it, and China the same; but Los Angeles is unique in its bright horror.

Naturally, one was excited by the movies, even though at that time they had lost much of their hold over the public imagination, unlike earlier decades when the process of film before light could project, larger than life, not only on vast screens but also upon the impressionable minds of an enormous audience made homogeneous by a common passion, shadowy figures which, like the filmy envelopes of Stoic deities, floated to earth in public dreams, suggesting a brave and perfect world where love reigned and only the wicked died. But then time passed and the new deities lost their worshipers. There were too many gods and the devotees got too used to them, realizing finally that they were only mortals, involved not in magical rites but in a sordid business. Television (the home altar) succeeded the movies and their once populous and ornate temples, modeled tastefully on baroque and Byzantine themes, fell empty, as the old gods moved to join the new hierarchies, becoming the domesticated godlings of television which, although it held the attention of the majority of the population, did not enrapture, nor possess dreams or shape days with longing and with secret imaginings the way the classic figures of an earlier time had. Though I was of an age to recall the gallant days of the movies, the nearly mythical power which they had held for millions of people, not all simple, I was more intrigued by the manners, by the cults, by the works of this coastal people so unlike the older world of the East and so antipathetic to our race's first home in Europe. Needless to say, I found them much like everyone else, except for minor differences of no real consequence.

I stayed at a large hotel not too happily balanced in design between the marble-and-potted-palm décor of the Continental Hotel in Paris and the chrome and glass of an observation car on a train.

I unpacked and telephoned friends, most of whom were not home. The one whom I found in was the one I knew the least, a minor film writer who had recently married money and given up the composition of films, for which the remaining moviegoers were no doubt thankful. He devoted his time to assisting his wife in becoming the first hostess of Beverly Hills. She had, I recalled from one earlier meeting, the mind of a child of twelve, but an extremely active child and a good one.

Hastings, such was the writer's name (her name was either Ethel or Valerie, two names which I always confuse because of a particularly revolutionary course I once took in mnemonics), invited me to a party. I went.

It seemed like spring though it was autumn, and it seemed like an assortment of guests brought together in a ship's dining room to celebrate New Year's Eve, though in fact the gathering was largely made up of close acquaintances. Since I knew almost no one, I had a splendid time.

After a brilliant greeting my hostess, a gold figure all in green with gold dust in her hair, left me alone. Hastings was more solicitous, a nervous gray man with a speech impediment which took the form of a rather charming sigh before any word which began with an aspirate.

"We, ah, have a better place coming up. Farther up the hills with a marvelous view of the, ah, whole city. You will love it, Gene. Ah, haven't signed the lease yet, but soon." While we talked he steered me through the crowds of handsome and bizarre people (none of them was from California, I discovered). I was introduced to magnificent girls exactly resembling their movie selves. I told a striking blonde that she would indeed be excellent in a musical version of Bhagavad-Gita. She thought so too and my host and I moved on to the patio.

Beside a jade-green pool illuminated from beneath (and a little dirty, I noticed, with leaves floating upon the water: the décor was becoming tarnished, the sets had been used too long and needed striking. Hollywood was becoming old without distinction), a few of the quieter guests sat in white iron chairs while paper lanterns glowed prettily on the palms and everywhere, untidily, grew roses, jasmine and lilac, all out of season and out of place. The guests beside the pool were much the same; except for one: Clarissa.

"You know each other?" Hastings's voice, faintly pleased, was drowned by our greetings and I was pulled into a chair by Clarissa, who had elected to dress herself like an odalisque which made her look more indigenous than any of the other guests. This was perhaps her genius: her adaptiveness.

"We'll be quite happy here," said Clarissa, waving our host away. "Go and abuse your other guests."

Hastings trotted off. Those who had been talking to Clarissa talked to themselves and beneath a flickering lantern the lights of Los Angeles, revealed in a wedge between two hills, added the proper note of lunacy, for at the angle from which I viewed those lights they seemed to form a monster Christmas tree, poised crazily in the darkness.

Clarissa and I exchanged notes on the months that had intervened since our luncheon.

"And you gave up Julian, too?"

"Yes . . . but why 'too'?" I was irritated by the implication.

"I feel you don't finish things, Eugene. Not that you should; but I *do* worry about you."

"It's good of you," I said, discovering that at a certain angle the Christmas tree could be made to resemble a rocket's flare arrested in space.

"Now don't take that tone with me. I have your interest at heart." She expressed herself with every sign of sincerity in that curious flat language which she spoke so fluently yet which struck upon the ear untruly, as though it were, in its homeliness, the highest artifice.

"But I've taken care of everything, you know. Wait and see.

If you hadn't come out here on your own I should have sent for you . . ."

"And I would have come?"

"Naturally." She smiled.

"But for what?"

"For . . . *she's* here. In Los Angeles."

"You mean that girl who came to lunch?" I disguised my interest, but Clarissa, ignoring me, went on talking as energetically and as obliquely as ever.

"She's asked for you several times, which is a good sign. I told her I suspected you'd be along but that one never could tell, especially if you were still tied up with Julian, unlikely as that prospect was."

"But I do finish some things."

"I'm sure you do. In any case, the girl has been here over a month and you must see her as soon as possible."

"I'd like to."

"Of course you would. I still have my plot, you know. Oh, you may think I forget things but I don't. My mind is a perfect filing system."

"Could you tell me just *what* you are talking about?"

She chuckled and wagged a finger at me. "Soon you'll know. I know I meddle a good deal, more than I should, but after all this time it would be simply impossible for me *not* to interfere. I see it coming, one of those really exciting moments, and I want just to give it a tickle here, a push there to set it rolling. Oh, what fun it will be!"

Hastings crept back among us, diffidently pushing a star and a producer in our direction. "I think you all ought to know each other, Clarissa . . . and, ah, Gene too. This is Miss . . . and Mr. . . .and here in Hollywood . . . when you get to New York. . . house on the river, wonderful, old . . . new film to cost five million . . . runner-up for the Academy Award." He did it all very well, I thought. Smiles gleamed in the patio's half-light. The star's paste jewels, borrowed from her studio, glimmered like an airliner's lighted windows. I moved toward the house, but Clarissa's high voice restrained me at the door: "You'll call Iris tomorrow, won't you?" and she shouted an exchange and a number. I waved to show that I'd heard her; then, vowing I would never telephone Iris, I rejoined the party and watched with fascination as the various performers performed in the living room to the accompaniment of a grand piano just barely out of tune.

THREE

I waited several days before I telephoned Iris. Days of considerable activity, of visiting friends and acquaintances, of attending parties where the guests were precisely the same as the ones I had met at Hastings's house.

I met Iris at the house where she was staying near the main beach of Santa Monica, in a decorous Spanish house, quiet among palms and close to the sea. The day was vivid; the sea made noise; the wind was gentle, smelling of salt.

I parked my rented car and walked around to the sea side of the house. Iris came forward to meet me, smiling, hand outstretched. Her face, which I had remembered as being remarkably pale, was flushed with sunlight.

"I hoped you'd come," she said, and she slipped her arm in mine as though we had been old friends and led me to a deck chair adjoining the one where she'd been seated reading. We sat down. "Friends let me have this place. They went to Mexico for two months."

"Useful friends."

"Aren't they? I've already put down roots here in the sand and I'll hate to give it back."

"Don't."

"Ah, wouldn't it be wonderful." She smiled vaguely and looked beyond me at the flash of sea in the flat distance. An automobile horn sounded through the palms; a mother called her child; we were a part of the world, even here.

"Clarissa told me you've been here several months."

Iris nodded. "I came back. I think I told you I was going to."

"To see the man?"

"Would you like something to drink?" She changed the subject with a disconcerting shift of gaze from ocean to me, her eyes still dazzled with the brilliance of light on water. I looked away and shook my head.

"Too early in the day. But I want to take you to dinner tonight if I may. Somewhere along the coast."

"I'd like it very much."

"Do you know of a place?"

She suggested several. Then we went inside and she showed me a room where I might change into my bathing suit.

We walked through the trees to the main road, on the other side of which the beach glowed in the sun. It was deserted at this point although, in the distance, other bathers could be seen, tiny figures, moving about like insects on a white cloth.

For a time we swam contentedly, not speaking, not thinking, our various urgencies (or their lack) no longer imposed upon the moment. At such times, in those days, I was able through the body's strenuous use to reduce the miserable demands of the yearning self to a complacent harmony, with all things in proper proportion: a part of the whole and not the whole itself, though, metaphorically speaking, perhaps whatever conceives reality is reality itself. But such nice divisions and distinctions were of no concern to me that afternoon in the sun, swimming with Iris, the mechanism which spoils time with questioning switched off by the body's euphoria.

And yet, for all this, no closer to one another, no wiser about one another in any precise sense, we drove that evening in silence to a restaurant on the beach to the north: a ramshackle, candle-lit place, smelling of tar and hung with old nets. After wine and fish and coffee, we talked.

"Clarissa is bringing us together."

I nodded, accepting the plain statement as a fact. "The match-making instinct is, I suppose . . ."

"Not that at all." Her face was in a half-light and looked as it had when we first met: pale, withdrawn, all the day's color drained out of it. Into the sea, the evening star all silver set. We were early and had the place to ourselves.

"Then what? Clarissa never does anything that doesn't contribute to some private design . . . though what she's up to half the time I don't dare guess."

Iris smiled. "Nor I. But she is at least up to something which concerns us both and I'm not sure that she may not be right, about the two of us, I mean . . . though of course it's too soon to say."

I was conventional enough at first to assume that Iris was speaking of ourselves, most boldly, in terms of some emotional attachment and I wondered nervously how I might indicate without embarrassment to her that I was effectively withdrawn from all sexuality and that, while my emotions were in no way impaired, I had been forced to accept a physical limitation to any act of affection which I might direct at another; consequently, I avoided as well as I could those situations which might betray me, and distress another. Though I have never been unduly grieved by this incompletion, I had come to realize only too well from several disquieting episodes in my youth that this flaw in me possessed the unanticipated power of shattering others who, unwarily, had moved to join with me in the traditional duet only to find an implacable surface where they had anticipated a creature of flesh like themselves, as eager as they, as governed by the blood's solemn tide. I had caused pain against my will and I did not want Iris hurt.

Fortunately, Iris had begun to move into a different, an unexpected, conjunction with me, one which had in it nothing of the familiar or even of the human. It was in that hour beneath Orion's glitter that we were, without warning, together volatilized onto that archetypal plane where we were to play with such ferocity at being gods, a flawed Mercury and a dark queen of heaven, met at the sea's edge, disguised as human beings but conscious of one another's true identity, for though our speeches, our arias, were all prose, beneath the usual talk recognition had occurred, sounding with the deep resonance of a major chord struck among dissonances.

We crossed the first division easily. She was, in her way, as removed as I from the flesh's wild need to repeat itself in pleasure. There was no need for us ever to discuss my first apprehension. We were able to forget ourselves, to ignore the mortal carriage. The ritual began simply enough.

"Clarissa knows what is happening here. That's why she has come West, though she can't bear California. She wants to be in on it the way she's in on everything else, or thinks she is."

"You mean John Cave, your *magus*?" It was the first time

I had ever said that name. The sword was between us now, both edges sharp.

"You guessed? or did she tell you that was why I came back?"

"I assumed it. I remembered what you said to me last spring."

"He is more than . . . *magus*, Eugene." And this was the first time she had said *my* name: closer, closer. I waited. "You will see him." I could not tell if this was intended as a question or a prophecy. I nodded. She continued to talk, her eyes on mine, intense and shining. Over her shoulder the night was black and all the stars flared twice, once in the sky and once upon the whispering smooth ocean at our feet, one real and one illusion, both light.

"It is really happening," she said and then, deliberately, she lightened her voice. "You'll see when you meet him. I know of course that there have been thousands of these prophets, these saviors in every country and in every time. I also know that this part of America is particularly known for religious maniacs. I started with every prejudice, just like you."

"Not prejudice . . . skepticism; perhaps indifference. Even if he should be one of the chosen wonder-workers, should I care? I must warn you, Iris, that I'm not a believer. And though I'm sure that the revelations of other men must be a source of infinite satisfaction to them individually, I shouldn't for one second be so presumptuous as to make a choice among the many thousands of recorded revelations of truth, accepting one at the expense of all the others. I might so easily choose wrong and get into eternal trouble. And you must admit that the selection is wide, and dangerous to the amateur."

"You're making fun of me," said Iris, but she seemed to realize that I was approaching the object in my own way. "He's not like that at all."

"But obviously if he is to be useful he must be accepted and he can't be accepted without extending his revelation or whatever he calls it, and I fail to see how he can communicate, short of hypnotism or drugs, the sense of his vision to someone like myself who, in a sloppy but devoted way, has wandered through history and religion, acquiring with a collector's delight the more colorful and obscure manifestations of divine guidance, revealed to us through the inspired systems of philosophers and divines, not to mention such certified prophets as the custodians of the Sibylline books. '*Illo die hostem Romanorum esse periturum*' was the instruction given poor Maxentius when he marched against Constantine. Needless to say he perished and consequently fulfilled the prophecy by *himself* becoming the enemy of Rome, to his surprise I suspect. My point, though, in honoring you with the only complete Latin sentence which I can ever recall is that at no time can we escape the relativity of our judgments. Truth for us, whether inspired by messianic frenzy or merely illuminated by reason, is, after all, inconstant and subject to change with the hour. You believe now whatever it is this man says. Splendid. But will the belief be true to you at another hour of your life? I wonder. For even if you wish to remain consistent and choose to ignore inconvenient evidence in the style of the truly devoted, the truly pious, will not your prophet *himself* have changed with time's passage? No human being can remain the same, despite the repetition of . . ."

"Enough, enough!" she laughed aloud and put her hand between us as though to stop the words in air. "You're talking such nonsense."

"Perhaps. It's not at all easy to say what one thinks when it comes to these problems or, for that matter, to any problem which demands statement. Sometimes one is undone by the flow of words assuming its own direction, carrying one, protesting, away from the anticipated shore to *terra incognita*. Other times, at the climax of a particularly telling analogy, one is aware that in the success of words the meaning has got lost. Put it this way, finally, *accurately*: I accept no man's authority in that realm where we are all equally ignorant. The beginning and the end of creation are not our concern. The eventual disposition of the human personality which we treasure in our conceit as being the finest ornament of an envious universe is unknown to us and shall so remain until we learn the trick of raising the dead. God, or what have you, will not be found at the far end of a syllogism, no matter how brilliantly phrased and conceived. We are prisoners in our flesh, dullards in divinity as the Greeks would say. No man can alter this, though of course human beings can be made to *believe* anything. You can teach that fire is cold and ice is hot but nothing changes except the words. So what can your *magus* do? What can he celebrate except what is visible and apparent to all eyes? What can he offer me that I should accept his authority, and its source?"

She sighed. "I'm not sure he wants anything for himself; acceptance, authority . . . one doesn't think of such things, at least not now. As for his speaking with the voice of some new or old deity, he denies the reality of any power other than the human . . ."

"A strange sort of messiah."

"I've been trying to tell you this." She smiled. "He sounds at times not unlike you just now . . . not so glib perhaps."

"Now *you* mock *me*."

"No more than you deserve for assuming facts without evidence."

"If he throws over all the mystical baggage, what is left? an ethical system?"

"In time, I suppose, that will come. So far there is no system. You'll see for yourself soon enough."

"You've yet to answer any direct question I have put to you."

She laughed. "Perhaps there is a significance in that; perhaps you ask the wrong questions."

"And perhaps you have no answers."

"Wait."

"For how long?"

She looked at her watch by the candles' uncertain light. "For an hour."

"You mean we're to see him tonight?"

"Unless you'd rather not."

"Oh, I want to see him, very much."

"He'll want to see you too, I think." She looked at me thoughtfully but I could not guess her intention; it was enough that two lines had crossed, both moving inexorably toward a third, toward a terminus at the progression's heart.

FOUR

It is difficult now to recall just what I expected. Iris deliberately chose not to give me any clear idea of either the man or of his teachings or even of the meeting which we were to attend. We talked of other things as we drove by starlight north along the ocean road, the sound of waves striking sand loud in our ears.

It was nearly an hour's drive from the restaurant to the place where the meeting was to be held. Iris directed me accurately and we soon turned from the main highway into a neon-lighted street; then off into a suburban area of comfortable-looking middle-class houses with gardens. Trees lined the streets; dogs barked; yellow light gleamed at downstairs windows. Silent families were gathered in after-dinner solemnity before television sets, absorbed by the spectacle of blurred gray figures telling jokes.

As we drove down the empty streets, I imagined ruins and dust where houses were and, among the powdery debris of stucco all in mounds, the rusted antennae of television sets like the bones of awful beasts whose vague but terrible proportions will alone survive to attract the unborn stranger's eye. But the loathing of one's own time is a sign of innocence, of faith. I have come since to realize the wholeness of man in time. That year, perhaps that ride down a deserted evening street of a California suburb, was my last conscious moment of specified disgust: television, the Blues and the Greens, the perfidy of Carthage, the efficacy of rites to the moon . . . all are at last the same.

"That house over there, with the light in front, with the clock."

The house, to my surprise, was a large neo-Georgian funeral parlor with a lighted clock in front crowned by a legend discreetly fashioned in Gothic gold on black: *Whitaker and Dormer, Funeral Directors.* Since a dozen cars had been parked in front of the house, I was forced to park nearly a block away.

We walked along the sidewalk; street lamps behind trees cast shadows thick and intricate upon the pavement. "Is there any particular significance?" I asked. "I mean in the choice of meeting place?"

She shook her head. "Not really, no. We meet wherever it's convenient. Mr. Dormer is one of us and has kindly offered his chapel for the meetings."

"Is there any sort of ritual I should observe?"

She laughed. "Of course not. This isn't at all what you think."

"I think nothing."

"Then you are prepared. But I should tell you that until this year when a number of patrons made it possible for him" (already I could identify the "him" whenever it fell from her lips, round with reverence and implication) "to devote all his time to teaching, he was for ten years an undertaker's assistant in Washington."

I said nothing. It was just as well to get past this first obstacle all at once. There was no reason of course to scorn that necessary if overwrought profession; yet somehow the thought of a savior emerging from those unctuous ranks seemed ludicrous. I reminded myself that a most successful messiah had been a carpenter and that another had been a politician . . . but an embalmer! My anticipation of great news was chilled. I prepared myself for grim comedy.

Iris would tell me nothing more about the meeting or about *him* as we crossed the lawn. She opened the door to the house and we stepped into a softly lighted anteroom. A policeman and a civilian, the one gloomy and the other cheerful, greeted us.

"Ah, Miss Mortimer!" said the civilian, a gray, plump pigeon of a man. "And a friend, how good to see you both." No, this was not *he*. I was introduced to Mr. Dormer, who chirped on until he was interrupted by the policeman.

"Come on, you two, in here. Got to get the prints and the oath."

Iris motioned me to follow the policeman into a sideroom. I'd heard of this national precaution but until now I had had no direct experience of it. Since the attempt of the communists to control our society had, with the collapse of Russian foreign policy, failed, our government in its collective wisdom decided that never again would any sect or party, other than the traditional ones, be allowed to interrupt the rich flow of the nation's life. As a result, all deviationist societies were carefully watched by the police, who fingerprinted and photographed those who attended meetings, simultaneously exacting an oath of allegiance to the Constitution and the Flag which ended with that powerful invocation which a recent President's speechwriter had, in a moment of inspiration, struck off to the delight of his employer and nation: "In a true democracy there is no place for a serious difference of opinion on great issues." It is a comment on those years, now happily become history, that only a few ever considered the meaning of this resolution, proving of course that words are never a familiar province to the great mass which prefers recognizable pictures to even the most apposite prose.

Iris and I repeated dutifully in the presence of the policeman and an American flag the various national sentiments. We were then allowed to go back to the anteroom and to Mr. Dormer, who himself led us into the chapel where several dozen people—perfectly ordinary men and women—were gathered.

The chapel, nonsectarian, managed to combine a number of decorative influences with a blandness quite remarkable in its success at not really representing anything while suggesting, at the same time, everything. The presence of a dead body, a man carefully painted and wearing a blue serge suit, gently smiling in an ebony casket behind a bank of flowers at the chapel's end, did not detract as much as one might have supposed from the occasion's importance. After the first uneasiness, it was quite possible to accept the anonymous dead man as part of the décor. There was even, in later years, an attempt made by a group of Cavite enthusiasts to insist upon the presence of an embalmed corpse at every service, but fortunately other elements prevailed, though not without an ugly quarrel and harsh words.

John Cave's entrance followed our own by a few minutes, and it is with difficulty that I recall what it was that I felt on seeing him for the first time. Though my recollections are well known to all (at least they *were* well known, although now I am less certain, having seen Butler's Testament so strangely altered), I must record here that I cannot, after so many years, recall in any emotional detail my first reaction to this man who was to be the world's peculiar nemesis as well as my own.

But, concentrating fiercely, emptying my mind of later knowledge, I can still see him as he walked down the aisle of the chapel, a small man who moved with some grace. He was younger than I had expected or, rather, younger-looking, with short straight hair, light brown in color, a lean regular face which would not have been noticed in a crowd unless one got close enough to see the expression of the eyes: large silver eyes with black lashes like a thick line drawn on the pale skin, focusing attention to them, to the congenitally small pupils which glittered like the points of black needles, betraying the will and the ambition which the impassive, gentle face belied . . . but I am speaking with future knowledge now. I did not that evening think of ambition or will in terms of John Cave. I was merely curious, intrigued by the situation, by the intensity of Iris, by the serene corpse behind the bank of hothouse flowers, by the thirty or forty men and women who sat close to the front of the chapel, listening intently to Cave as he talked.

At first I paid little attention to what was being said, more interested in observing the audience, the room and the appearance of the speaker. Immediately after Cave's undramatic entrance, he moved to the front of the chapel and sat down on a gilt chair to the right of the coffin. There was a faint whisper of interest at his appearance. Newcomers like myself were being given last-minute instruction by the habitués who had brought them there. Cave sat easily on the gilt chair, his eyes upon the floor, his small hands, bony and white, folded in his lap, a smile on his narrow lips. He could not have looked more ineffectual and ordinary. His opening words by no means altered this first impression.

The voice was good, though Cave tended to mumble at the beginning, his eyes still on the floor, his hands in his lap, motionless. So quietly did he begin that he had spoken for several seconds before many of the audience were aware that he had begun. His accent was the national one, learned doubtless from the radio and the movies: a neutral pronunciation without any strong regional overtone. The popular if short-lived legend of the next decade that he had begun his mission as a backwoods revivalist was certainly untrue.

Not until Cave had talked for several minutes did I begin to listen to the sense rather than to the tone of his voice. I cannot render precisely what he said but the message that night was not much different from the subsequent ones which are known to all. It was, finally, the manner which created the response, not the words themselves, though the words were interesting enough, especially when heard for the first time. His voice, as I have said, faltered at the beginning and he left sentences unfinished, a trick which I later discovered was deliberate, for he had been born a remarkable actor, an instinctive rhetorician. What struck me that first evening was the purest artifice of his performance. The voice, especially when he came to his climax, was sharp and clear while his hands stirred like separate living creatures and the eyes, those splendid unique eyes, were abruptly revealed to us in the faint light, displayed at that crucial moment which had been as carefully constructed as any work of architecture or of music: the instant of communication.

Against my will and judgment and inclination, I found myself absorbed by the man, not able to move or to react. The magic that was always to affect me, even when later I knew him only too well, held me fixed to my chair as the words, supported by the clear voice, came in a resonant line from him to me alone, to each of us alone, separate from the others . . . and both restless general and fast-breathing particular were together his.

The moment itself lasted only a second in actual time; it came suddenly, without warning: one was riven; then it was over and he left the chapel, left us chilled and weak, staring foolishly at the gilt chair where he had been.

It was some minutes before we were able to take up our usual selves again.

Iris looked at me. I smiled weakly and cleared my throat. I was conscious that I ached all over. I glanced at my watch and saw that he had spoken to us for an hour and a half, during which time I had not moved. I stretched painfully and stood up. Others did the same. We had shared an experience and it was the first time in my life that I knew what it was like to be the same as others, my heart's beat no longer individual, erratic, but held for at least this one interval of time in concert with those of strangers. It was a new, disquieting experience: to be no longer an observer, a remote intelligence. For ninety minutes to have been a part of the whole.

Iris walked with me to the anteroom, where we stood for a moment watching the others who had also gathered here to talk in low voices, their expressions bewildered.

She did not have to ask me what I thought. I told her immediately, in my own way, impressed but less than reverent. "I see what you mean. I see what it is that holds you, fascinates you, but I still wonder what it is really all about."

"You saw. You heard."

"I saw an ordinary man. I heard a sermon which was interesting, although I might be less impressed if I read it to myself . . ." Deliberately I tried to throw it all away, that instant of belief, that paralysis of will, that sense of mysteries revealed in a dazzle of light. But as I talked, I realized that I was not really dismissing it, that I could not alter the experience even though I might dismiss the man and mock the text: something *had* happened and I told her what I thought it was,

"It is not truth, Iris, but hypnosis."

She nodded. "I've often thought that. Especially at first when I was conscious of his mannerisms, when I could see, as only a woman can perhaps, that this was just a man. Yet something *does* happen when you listen to him, when you get to know him. You must find that out for yourself; and you will. It may not prove to be anything which has to do with him. There's something in oneself which stirs and comes alive at his touch, through his agency." She spoke quickly, excitedly.

I felt the passion with which she was charged. But suddenly it was too much for me. I was bewildered and annoyed. I wanted to get away.

"Don't you want to meet him?"

I shook my head. "Another time maybe, but not now. Shall I take you back?"

"No. I'll get a ride in to Santa Monica. I may even stay over for the night. He'll be here a week."

I wondered again if she might have a personal interest in Cave. I doubted it, but anything was possible.

She walked me to the car, past the lighted chapel, over the summery lawn, down the dark street whose solid prosaicness helped to dispel somewhat the madness of the hour before.

We made a date to meet later on in the week. She would tell Cave about me and I would meet him. I interrupted her then. "What *did* he say, Iris? What did he say tonight?"

Her answer was as direct and as plain as my question. "That it is good to die."

FIVE

ONE

This morning I reread the last section, trying to see it objectively, to match what I have put down with the memory I still bear of that first encounter with John Cave. I have not, I fear, got it. But this is as close as I can come to recalling long-vanished emotions and events.

I was impressed by the man and I was shaken by his purpose. My first impression was, I think, correct. Cave was a natural hypnotist and the text of that extraordinary message was, in the early days at least, thin, illogical and depressing if one had not heard it spoken. Later of course I, among others, composed the words which bear his name and we gave them, I fancy, a polish and an authority which, with his limited education and disregard for the works of the past, he could not have accomplished on his own, even had he wanted to.

I spent the intervening days between my first and second encounters with this strange man in a state of extreme tension and irritability. Clarissa called me several times but I refused to see her, excusing myself from proposed entertainments and hinted tête-à-têtes with an abruptness which anyone but the iron-cast Clarissa would have found appallingly rude. But she merely said that she understood and let me off without explaining what it was she understood, or thought she did. I avoided all acquaintances, keeping to my hotel room, where I contemplated a quick return to the Hudson and to the coming autumn. Finally Iris telephoned to fix a day for me to meet John Cave. I accepted her invitation, with some excitement.

We met in the late afternoon at her house. Only the three of us were present. In the set of dialogues which I composed and published in later years I took considerable liberties with our actual conversations, especially this first one. In fact, as hostile critics were quick to suggest, the dialogues were created by me with very little of Cave in them and a good deal of Plato, rearranged to fit the occasion. But in time, my version was accepted implicitly, if only because there were no longer any hostile critics.

Cave rose promptly when I came out onto the patio, shook my hand vigorously but briefly and sat down again, indicating that I sit next to him while Iris went for tea. He was smaller and more compact than I had thought, measuring him against myself as one does unconsciously, with an interesting stranger. He wore a plain brown suit and a white shirt open at the neck. The eyes, which at first I did not dare look at, were, I soon noticed, sheathed . . . an odd word which was always to occur to me when I saw him at his ease, eyes half-shut, ordinary, not in the least unusual. Except for a restless folding and unfolding of the hands (suggesting a recently reformed cigarette smoker) he was without physical idiosyncrasy.

"It's a pleasure to meet you" were the first words, I fear, that John Cave ever spoke to me; so unlike the dialogue on the spirit which I later composed to celebrate the initial encounter between master and disciple-to-be. "Iris has told me a lot about you." His voice was light, without resonance now. He sat far back in a deck chair. Inside the house I could hear Iris moving plates. The late afternoon sun had just that moment gone behind trees and the remaining light was warmly gold.

"And I have followed your . . . career with interest too." I said, knowing that "career" was precisely the word he would not care to hear used but, since neither of us had yet got the range of the other, we fired at random.

"Iris tells me you write history."

I shook my head. "No, I only read it. I think it's all been written anyway." I was allowed to develop this novel conceit for some moments, attended by a respectful silence from my companion, who finally dispatched my faintly hysterical proposition with a vague "Maybe so"; and then we got to him.

"I haven't been East, you know." He frowned at the palm trees. "I was born up in Washington state and I've spent all my life in the Northwest, until last year." He paused as though he expected me to ask him about *that* year. I did not. I waited for him to do it in his own way. He suddenly turned about and faced me; those disconcerting eyes suddenly trained upon my own. "You were there the other night, weren't you?"

"Why yes."

"Did you feel it too? Am I right?"

The quick passion with which he said this, exploding all at once the afternoon's serenity, took me off guard. I stammered, "I don't think I know what you mean. I . . ."

"You know exactly what I mean, what I meant." Cave leaned closer to me and I wondered insanely if the deck chair might not collapse under him. It teetered dangerously. My mind went blank, absorbed by the image of deck chair and prophet together collapsing at my feet. Then, as suddenly, satisfied perhaps with my confusion, he settled back, resumed his earlier ease, exactly as if I had answered him, as though we had come to a crisis and together fashioned an agreement. He was most alarming.

"I want to see New York especially. I've always thought it must look like a cemetery with all those tall gray buildings you see in photographs." He sighed conventionally. "So many interesting places in the world. Do you like the West?"

Nervously, I said that I did. I still feared a possible repetition of that brief outburst.

"I like the openness," said Cave, as though he had thought long about this problem. "I don't think I'd like confinement. I couldn't live in Seattle because of those fogs they used to have. San Francisco's the same. I don't like too many walls, too much fog." If he'd intended to speak allegorically he could not have found a better audience; even at this early stage, I was completely receptive to the most obscure histrionics. But in conversation, Cave was perfectly literal. Except when he spoke before a large group, he was quite simple and prosaic and, though conscious always of his dignity and singular destiny, not in the least portentous.

I probably did not put him at his ease, for I stammered a good deal and made no sense, but he was gracious, supporting me with his own poise and equanimity.

He talked mostly of places until Iris came back with tea. Then, as the sky became florid with evening and the teacups gradually grew cold, he spoke of his work and I listened intently.

"I can talk to you straight," he said. "This just happened to me. I didn't start out to do this. No sir, I never would have believed ten years ago that I'd be traveling about, talking to people like one of those crackpot fanatics you've got so many of in California." I took a sip of the black, fast-cooling tea, hoping he was not sufficiently intuitive to guess that I had originally put him down, provisionally of course, as precisely that.

"I don't know how much Iris may have told you or how much you might have heard, but it's pretty easy to pass the whole thing off as another joke. A guy coming out of the backwoods with a message." He cracked his knuckles hard and I winced at the sound. "Well, I didn't quite come out of the woods. I had a year back at State University and I had a pretty good job in my field with the best firm of funeral directors in Washington state. Then I started on this. I just *knew* one day, and so I began to talk to people and they knew too and I quit my job and started talking to bigger and bigger crowds all along the Coast. There wasn't any of this revelation stuff. I just knew one day, that was all. And when I told other people *what* I knew, they seemed to get it. And that's the strange part. Everybody gets ideas about things which he thinks are wonderful but usually nothing happens to the people he tries to tell them to. With me, it's been different from the beginning. People have listened, and agreed. What I know *they* know. Isn't that a funny thing? Though most of them probably would never have thought it out until they heard me and it was all clear." His eyes dropped to his hands and he added softly: "So since it's been like this, I've gone on. I've made this my life. This is it. I will come to the people."

There was silence. The sentence had been spoken which I was later to construct the first dialogue upon: "I will come to the people." The six words which were to change our lives were spoken softly over tea.

Iris looked at me challengingly over Cave's bowed head.

I remember little else about that evening. We dined, I think, in the house and Cave was most agreeable, most undemanding. There was no more talk of the mission. He asked me many questions about New York, about Harvard, where I had gone to school, about Roman history. He appeared to be interested in paganism and my own somewhat tentative approach to Julian. I was to learn later that though he seldom read he had a startling memory for any fact he thought relevant. I am neither immodest nor inaccurate when I say that he listened to me attentively for some years and many of his later views were a result of our conversations.

I should mention, though, one significant omission in his

conversation during those crucial years. He never discussed ethical questions. That was to come much later. At the beginning he had but one vision: Death is nothing; literally nothing; and since, demonstrably, absence of things is a good; death which is no thing is good. On this the Cavite system was constructed, and what came after in the moral and ethical spheres was largely the work of others in his name. Much of this I anticipated in that first conversation with him, so unlike, actually, the dialogue which I composed and which ended with the essential lines—or so I still think complacently, despite the irony with which time has tarnished all those bright toys for me: "Death is neither hard nor bad. Only the dying hurts." With that firmly postulated, the rest was inevitable.

Cave talked that evening about California and Oregon and Washington (geography and places were always to fascinate and engage him while people, especially after the early years, ceased to be remarkable to him; he tended to confuse those myriad faces which passed before him like successive ripples in a huge sea). He talked of the cities he had visited on the Coast, new cities to him. He compared their climates and various attractions like a truly devoted tourist, eager to get the best of each place, to encounter the *genius loci* and possess it.

"But I don't like staying in any place long." Cave looked at me then and again I felt that sense of a power being focused on me . . . it was not unlike what one experiences during an X-ray treatment when the humming noise indicates that potent rays are penetrating one's tissue and though there is actually no sensation, *something* is experienced, power is felt. And so it invariably was that, right until the end, Cave could turn those wide bleak eyes upon me whenever he chose, and I would experience his force anew.

"I want to keep moving, new places, that's what I like. You get a kind of charge traveling. At least I do. I always thought I'd travel but I never figured it would be like this; but then of course I never thought of all this until just a while ago."

"Can you remember when it was? how it was exactly you got . . . started?" I wanted a sign. Constantine's *labarum* occurred to me: *in hoc signo vinces*. Already ambition was stirring, and the little beast fed ravenously on every scrap that came its way, for in that patio I was experiencing my own revelation, the compass needle no longer spinning wildly but coming to settle at last with many hesitancies and demurs, upon a direction, drawn to a far pole's attraction.

John Cave smiled for the first time. I suppose, if I wanted, I could recall each occasion over the years when, in my presence at least, he smiled. His usual expression was one of calm resolve, of that authority which feels secure in itself, a fortunate expression which lent dignity to even his casual conversation. I suspected the fact that this serene mask hid a nearly total intellectual vacuity as early in my dealings with him as this first meeting; yet I did not mind, for I had experienced his unique magic and already I saw the possibilities of channeling that power, of using that force, of turning it like a flame here, there, creating and destroying, shaping and shattering . . . so much for the spontaneous nature of my ambition at its least responsible, and at its most exquisite! I could have set the one-half world aflame for the sheer splendor and glory of the deed. For this fault my expiation has been long and my once exuberant pride is now only an ashen phoenix consumed by flames but not quite tumbled into dust, nor re-created in the millennial egg, only a gray shadow in the heart which the touch of a finger of windy fear will turn to dust and air.

Yet the creature was aborning that day: one seed had touched another and a monster began to live.

"The first day? The first time?" The smile faded. "Sure, I remember it. I'd just finished cosmeticizing the face of this big dead fellow killed in an automobile accident. I didn't usually do make-up but I like to help out and I used to do odd jobs when somebody had too much to do and asked me to help; the painting isn't hard either and I always like it, though the faces are cold like . . . like . . ." He thought of no simile and went on: "Anyway I looked at this guy's face and I remembered I'd seen him play basketball in high school. He was in a class or two behind me. Big athlete. Ringer, we called them . . . full of life . . . and here he was, with me powdering his face and combing his eyebrows. Usually you don't think much about the stiff (that's our professional word) one way or the other. It's just a job. But I thought about this one suddenly. I started to feel sorry for him, dead like that, so sudden, so young, so good-looking with all sorts of prospects. Then I felt it." The voice grew low and precise. Iris and I listened intently, even the sun froze in the wild sky above the sea; and the young night stumbled in the darkening east.

With eyes on the sun, Cave described his sudden knowledge that it was the dead man who was right, who was a part of the whole, that the living were the sufferers from whom, temporarily, the beautiful darkness and non-being had been withdrawn. In his crude way, Cave struck chord after chord of meaning and, though the notes were not in themselves new, the effect was all its own . . . and not entirely because of the voice, of the cogency of this magician.

"And I knew it was the dying which was the better part," he finished. The sun, released, drowned in the Pacific.

In the darkness I asked, "But you, you still live?"

"Not because I want to," came the voice, soft as the night. "I must tell the others first. There'll be time for me."

I shuddered in the warmth of the patio. My companions were only dim presences in the failing light. "Who told you to tell this to everyone?"

The answer came back, strong and unexpected: "I told myself. The responsibility is mine."

That was the sign for me. He had broken with his predecessors. He was on his own. He knew. And so did we.

TWO

I have lingered over that first meeting, for in it was finally all that was to come. Later details were the work of others, irrelevant periphery to a simple but powerful center. Not until late that night did I leave the house near the beach. When I left, Cave stayed on and I wondered again if perhaps he was living with Iris.

We parted casually and Iris walked me to the door while Cave remained inside, gazing in his intent way at nothing at all; day-dreaming, doubtless, of what was to come.

"You'll help?" Iris stood by the car's open door, her features indistinct in the moonless night.

"I think so. But I'm not sure about the scale."

"What do you mean?"

"Must *everyone* know? Can't it just be kept to ourselves? for the few who do know him?"

"No. We must let them all hear him. Everyone." And her voice assumed that zealous tone which I was to hear so often again and again from her lips and those of others.

I made my first and last objection. "I don't see that quantity has much to do with it. If this thing spreads it will become organized. If it becomes organized, secondary considerations will obscure the point. The truth is no truer because only a few have experienced it."

"You're wrong. Even for purely selfish reasons, ruling out all altruistic considerations, there's an excellent reason for allowing this to spread. A society which knows what we know, which believes in Cave and what he says, will be a pleasanter place in which to live, less anxious, more tolerant." She spoke of a new Jerusalem in our sallow and anxious land, nearly convincing me.

The next day I went to Hastings's house for lunch. He was alone; his wife apparently had a life of her own which required his company only occasionally. Clarissa, sensible in tweed and dark glasses, was the only other guest. We lunched on a wrought-iron table beside the gloomy pool in which, among the occasional leaves, I saw, quite clearly, a cigarette butt delicately unfolding like an ocean flower.

"Good to, ah, have you, Eugene. Just a bit of pot luck. Clarissa's going back to civilization today and wanted to see you. I did too, of course. The bride's gone out. Told me to convey her . . ."

Clarissa turned her bright eyes on me and, without acknowledging the presence of our host, said right off, "You've met him at last."

I nodded. The plot was finally clear to me; the main design at least. "We had dinner together last night."

"I know. Iris told me. You're going to help out of course."

"I'd like to but I don't know what there is I might do. I don't think I'd be much use with a tambourine on street corners, preaching the word."

"Don't be silly!" Clarissa chuckled. "We're going to handle this quite, *quite* differently."

"We?"

"Oh, I've been involved for over a year now. It's going to be the greatest fun . . . you wait and see."

"But . . ."

"*I* was the one who got Iris involved. I thought she looked a little peaked, a little bored. I had no idea of course she'd get in so deep, but it will probably turn out all right. I think she's in love with him."

"Don't be such a gossip," said Hastings sharply. "You always reduce everything to . . . to biology. Cave isn't that sort of man."

"You know him too?" How fast it was growing, I thought.

"Certainly. Biggest thing I've done since . . ."

"Since you married that brassy blonde," said Clarissa with her irrepressible rudeness. "Anyway, my dear, Iris took to the whole thing like a born proselyte, if that's the word I mean . . . the other's a little boy, isn't it? and it seems, from what she's told me, that you have too."

"I wouldn't say that." I was a little put out at both Iris and Clarissa taking me so much for granted.

"Say anything you like. It's still the best thing that's ever happened to you . Oh God, *not* avocado again!" The offending salad was waved away while Hastings muttered apologies. "Nasty, pointless things, all texture and no taste." She made a face. "But I suppose that we must live off the fruits of the country and this is the only thing that will grow in California." She moved without pause from Western flora to the problem of John Cave. "As for your own contribution, Eugene, it will depend largely upon what you choose to do. As I said, I never suspected that Iris would get in so deep and you may prove to be quite as surprising. This is the ground floor of course . . . wonderful expression, isn't it? the spirit of America, the slogan that broke the plains . . . in any case, the way is clear. Cave liked you. You can write things for them, rather solid articles based on your inimitable misreadings of history. You can educate Cave, though this might be unwise since so much of his force derives from his eloquent ignorance. Or you might become a part of the organization which is getting under way. I suppose Iris will explain that to you. It's rather her department at the moment. All those years in the Junior League gave her a touching faith in the power of committees, which is just as well when handling Americans. As for the tambourines and cries of 'Come and Be

Saved' you are some twenty years behind the times. We have more up-to-date plans."

"Committees? What committees?"

Clarissa unfolded her mushroom omelet with a secret smile. "You'll meet our number-one committee member after lunch. He's coming, isn't he?" She looked at Hastings as though suspecting him of a treacherous ineptitude.

"Certainly, certainly, at least he *said* he was." Hastings motioned for the servingwoman to clean away the lunch, and we moved to other chairs beside the pool for coffee.

Clarissa was in fine form, aggressive, positive, serenely indifferent to the effect she was having on Hastings and me. "Of course I'm just meddling," she said in answer to an inquiry of mine. "I don't really give two cents for Mr. Cave and his message."

"Clarissa!" Hastings was genuinely shocked.

"I mean it. Not that I don't find him fascinating and of course the whole situation is delicious . . . what we shall do! or *you* shall do!" she looked at me maliciously. "I can foresee no limits to this."

"It no doubt reminds you of the period shortly after Mohammed married Khadija." But my own malice could hardly pierce Clarissa's mad equanimity.

"Vile man, sweet woman. But no, this is all going to be different, although the intellectual climate (I think *intellectual* is perhaps optimistic but you know what I mean) is quite similar. I can't wait for the first public response."

"There's already been some," said Hastings, crossing his legs, which were encased in pale multicolor slacks with rawhide sandals on his feet. "There was a piece yesterday in the *News* about the meeting they had down near Laguna."

"What did they say?" Clarissa scattered tiny saccharine tablets into her coffee like a grain goddess preparing harvest.

"Oh, just one of those short suburban notes about how a Mr. Joseph Cave, they got the name wrong, was giving a series of lectures at a funeral parlor which have been surprisingly well attended."

"They didn't mention what the lectures were about?"

"No, just a comment; the only one so far in Los Angeles."

"There'll be others soon, but I shouldn't think it's such a good idea to have too many items like that before things are really under way."

"And the gentleman who is coming here will be responsible for getting them under way?" I asked.

"Pretty much, yes. It's been decided that the practical details are to be left to him. Cave will continue to speak in and around Los Angeles until the way has been prepared. Then, when the publicity begins, he will be booked all over the country, all over the world!" Clarissa rocked silently for a moment in her chair, creating a disagreeable effect of noiseless laughter which disconcerted both Hastings and me.

"I don't like your attitude," said Hastings, looking at her gloomily. "You aren't *serious.*"

"Oh I am, my darling, I am. You'll never know how serious." And on that high note of Clarissa's, Paul Himmell stepped out onto the patio, blinking in the light of noon.

Himmell was a slender man in his fortieth and most successful year, hair only just begun to gray, a lined but firmly modeled face, all bright with ambition. The initial impression was one of neatly contained energy, of a passionate temperament skillfully channeled. Even the twist to his bow tie was the work of a master craftsman.

Handshake agreeable; smile quick and engaging; yet the effect on me was alarming. I had detested this sort of man all my life and here at last, wearing a repellently distinguished sports coat, was the archetype of all such creatures, loading with a steady hand that cigarette holder without which he might at least have seemed to me still human. He was identified by Hastings, who with a few excited snorts and gasps told me beneath the conversation that this was the most successful young publicist in Hollywood, which meant the world.

"I'm happy to meet you, Gene," Himmel said as soon as we were introduced. He was perfectly aware that he had been identified while the first greetings with Clarissa had been exchanged. He had the common gift of the busy worldling of being able to attend two conversations simultaneously, profiting from both. I hate being called by my first name by strangers, but in his world there were no strangers: the freemasonry of self-interest made all men equal in their desperation. He treated me like a buddy. He knew (he was, after all, clever) that I detested him on sight and on principle, and that presented him with a challenge to which he rose with confidence . . . and continued to rise through the years, despite the enduring nature of my disaffection. But then to be liked was his business, and I suspect that his attentions had less to do with me, or any sense of failure in himself for not having won me, than with a kind of automatic charm, a response to a situation which was produced quite inhumanly, mechanically: the smile, the warm voice, the delicate flattery . . . or not so delicate, depending on the case.

"Iris and Cave both told me about you and I'm particularly glad to get a chance to meet you . . . and to see you too, Clarissa . . . will you be long in the East?" Conscious perhaps that I would need more work than a perfunctory prelude, he shifted his attention to Clarissa, saving me for later.

"I never have plans, Paul, but I've one or two chores I've got to do. Anyway I've decided that Eugene is just the one to give the enterprise its tone . . . a quality concerning which you, dear Paul, so often have so much to say."

"Why, yes," said the publicist genially, obviously not understanding. "Always use more tone. You're quite right."

Clarissa's eyes met mine for a brief amused instant. She was on to everything; doubtless on to me too in the way one can never be about oneself; I always felt at a disadvantage with her.

"What we're going to need for the big New York opening is a firm historical and intellectual base. Cave hasn't got it and of course doesn't need it. We are going to need commentary and explanation and though you happen to be a genius in publicity you must admit that that group which has been characterized as intellectual, the literate few who in their weakness often exert enormous influence, are not apt to be much moved by your publicity; in fact, they will be put off by it."

"Well, now I'm not sure my methods are *that* crude. Of course I never . . ."

"They are superbly, triumphantly, providentially crude and you know it. Eugene must lend dignity to the enterprise. He has a solemn and highly unimaginative approach to philosophy which will appeal to his fellow intellectuals. He and they are quite alike: liberal and ineffectual, irresolute and lonely. When he addresses them they will get immediately his range, you might say, pick up his frequency, realizing he is one of them, a man to be trusted. Once they are reached the game is over, or begun." Clarissa paused and looked at me expectantly.

I did not answer immediately. Hastings, as a former writer, felt that he too had been addressed and he worried the subject of "tone" while Paul gravely added a comment or two. Clarissa watched me, however, conscious perhaps of the wound she had dealt.

Was it all really so simple? was *I* so simple? so typical? Vanity said not, but self-doubt, the shadow which darkens even those triumphs held at noon, prevailed for a sick moment or two. I was no different from the others, from the little pedagogues and analysts, the self-obsessed and spiritless company who endured shame and a sense of alienation without even that conviction of virtue which can dispel guilt and apathy for the simple, for all those who have accepted without question one of the systems of absolutes which it has amused both mystics and tyrants to construct for man's guidance.

I had less baggage to rid myself of than the others; I was confident of that. Neither Christianity nor Marxism nor the ugly certainties of the mental therapists had ever engaged my loyalty or suspended my judgment. I had looked at them all, deploring their admirers and servants, yet interested by their separate views of society and of the potentialities of a heaven on earth (the medieval conception of a world beyond life was always interesting to contemplate, even if the evidence in its favor was whimsical at best, conceived either as a system of rewards and punishments to control living man or else as lovely visions of what might be were man indeed consubstantial with a creation which so often resembled the personal aspirations of gifted divines rather than that universe the rest of us must observe with mortal eyes). No, I had had to dispose of relatively little baggage and, I like to think, less than my more thoughtful contemporaries who were forever analyzing themselves, offering their psyches to doctors for analysis or, worse, giving their immortal souls into the hands of priests who would then assume much of their *Weltschmerz*, providing them with a set of grown-up games every bit as appealing as the ones of childhood which had involved make-believe or, finally, worst of all, the soft acceptance of the idea of man the mass, of man the citizen, of society the organic whole for whose greater good all individuality must be surrendered.

My sense then of all that I had *not* been, negative as it was, saved my self-esteem. In this I was unlike my contemporaries. I had, in youth, lost all respect for the authority of men; and since there is no other discernible (the "laws" of nature are only relative and one cannot say for certain that there is a beautiful logic to everything in the universe as long as first principles remain unrevealed, except of course to the religious, who *know* everything, having faith), I was unencumbered by belief, by reverence for any man or groups of men, living or dead; yet human wit and genius often made my days bearable since my capacity for admiration, for aesthetic response, was highly developed even though, with Terence, I did not know, did not *need* to know through what wild centuries roves back the rose.

Nevertheless, Clarissa's including me among the little Hamlets was irritating, and when I joined in the discussion again I was careful to give her no satisfaction; it would have been a partial victory for her if I had denied a generic similarity to my contemporaries.

Paul spoke of practical matters, explaining to us the way he intended to operate in the coming months; and I was given a glimpse of the organization which had spontaneously come into being only a few weeks before.

"Hope we can have lunch tomorrow, Gene. I'll give you a better picture then, the overall picture and your part in it. Briefly, for now, the organization has been set up as a company under California law with Cave as president and myself, Iris and Clarissa as directors. I'm also secretary-treasurer but only for now. We're going to need a first-rate financial man to head our campaign fund and I'm working on several possibilities right now."

"What's the . . . company called?" I asked.

"Cavite, Inc. We didn't want to call it anything, but that's the law here and since we intended to raise money we had to have a legal setup."

"Got a nice sound, ah, Cavite," said Hastings, nodding.

"What on earth should we have done if he'd had *your* name, Paul?" exclaimed Clarissa, to the indignation of both Hastings and Paul. They shut her up.

Paul continued smoothly, "I've had a lot of experience, of

course, but this is something completely new for me, a real challenge and one which I'm glad to meet head-on."

"How did you get into it?" I asked.

Paul pointed dramatically to Hastings. "Him! He took me to a meeting in Burbank last year. I was sold the first time. *I got the message.*"

There was a hush as we were allowed to contemplate this awesome information. Then, smiling in a fashion which he doubtless would have called "wry," the publicist continued, "I knew this was it. I contacted Cave immediately and found we talked the same language. He was all for the idea and so we incorporated. He said he wasn't interested in the organizational end and left that to us, with Iris sort of representing him, though of course we all do since we're all Cavites. This thing is big and we're part of it." He almost smacked his lips. I listened, fascinated. "Anyway he's going to do the preaching part and we're going to handle the sales end, if you get what I mean. We're selling something which nobody else ever sold before, and you know what that is?" He paused dramatically and we stared at him a little stupidly. "Truth!" His voice was triumphant. "We're selling the truth about life and that's something that nobody, but nobody, has ever done before!"

Clarissa broke the silence which had absorbed his last words. "You're simply out of this world, Paul! If I hadn't heard you, I'd never have believed it. But you don't have to sell *us*, dear. We're in on it too. Besides, I have to catch a plane." She looked at her watch. She stood up and we did too. She thanked Hastings for lunch and then, before she left the patio on his arm, she said: "Now you boys get on together and remember what I've told you. Gene must be used, and right away. Get him to write something dignified, for a magazine." We murmured assent. Clarissa said goodby and left the patio with Hastings. Her voice, shrill and hard, could be heard even after she left. "The truth about life! Oh, it's going to be priceless!"

I looked quickly at Paul to see if he had heard. But if he had he ignored it. He was looking at me intently, speculatively. "I think we're going to get along fine, Gene, just fine," leaving me only a fumbled word or two of polite corroboration with which to express my sincere antipathy; then we went our separate ways.

THREE

I met Paul the next day at his office for a drink and not for lunch, since at the last minute his secretary had called me to say he was tied up and could I possibly come at five. I said that I could. I did.

Paul's offices occupied an entire floor of a small skyscraper on the edge of Beverly Hills. I was shown through a series of rooms done in natural wood and beige with indirect lighting and the soft sound of Strauss waltzes piped in from all directions: the employees responded best to three-quarter time, according to the current efficiency reports.

Beneath an expensive but standard mobile, Paul stood, waiting for me. His desk, a tiny affair of white marble on slender iron legs, had been rolled off to one side, and the office gave, as had been intended, the impression of being a small drawing room rather than a place of business. I was greeted warmly. Hand was shaken firmly. Eyes were met squarely for the regulation length of time. Then we sat down on a couch which was like the open furry mouth of some great soft beast and his secretary rolled a portable bar toward us.

"Name your poison," said the publicist genially. We agreed on a cocktail, which he mixed with the usual comments one expects from a regular fellow.

Lulled by the alcohol and the room, disarmed by the familiar patter in which one made all the correct responses, our conversation as ritualistic as that of a French dinner party, I was not prepared for the abrupt, "You don't like me, do you, Gene?"

Only once or twice before had anyone ever said this to me and each time that it happened I had vowed grimly that the *next* time, no matter where or with whom, I should answer with perfect candor, with merciless accuracy, "No, I don't." But since I am neither quick nor courageous, I murmured a pale denial.

"It's all right, Gene. I know how you probably feel." And the monster was magnanimous; he treated me with pity. "We've got two different points of view. That's all. I have to make my way in this rat race and you don't. You don't have to do anything, so you can afford to patronize us poor hustlers."

"Patronize isn't quite the word." I was beginning to recover from the first shock. A crushing phrase or two occurred to me, but Paul knew his business and he changed course before I could begin my work of demolition.

"Well, I just wanted you to know that there are no hard feelings. In my business you get used to this sort of thing: occupational hazard, you might say. I've had to fight my way every inch and I know that a lot of people are going to be jostled in the process, which is just too bad for them." He smiled suddenly, drawing the sting. "But I've got a hunch we're going to be seeing a lot of each other, so we ought to start on a perfectly plain basis of understanding. You're on to me and I'm on to you." The man was diabolic in the way he could enrage yet not allow his adversary sufficient grounds for even a perfunctory defense. He moved rapidly, with a show of spurious reason which quite dazzled me. His was what he presently called "the common-sense view."

I told him I had no objection to working with him; that everything I had heard about him impressed me; that he was wrong to suspect me of disdaining methods whose efficacy was so well known. I perjured myself for several impassioned minutes, and on a rising note of coziness we took up the problem at hand, congenial enemies for all time. The first round was clearly his.

"Clarissa got you into this?" He looked at me over his glass.

"More or less. Clarissa to Iris to Cave was the precise play."

"She got me to Cave last summer, or rather to Hastings first. I was sold right off. I think I told you that yesterday. This guy's got everything. Even aside from the message, he's the most remarkable salesman I've ever seen, and please believe me when I tell you there isn't *anything* I don't know about salesmen."

I agreed that he was doubtless expert in these matters.

"I went to about a dozen of those early meetings and I could see he was having the same effect on everyone, even on Catholics, people like that. Of course, I don't know what happens when they get home, but while they're there they're sold, and that's all that matters, because in the next year we're going to have him *there*, everywhere, and all the time."

I told him I didn't exactly follow this metaphysical flight.

"I mean we're going to have him on television, on movie screens, in the papers, so that everybody can feel the effect of his personality, just like he was there in person. This prayer-meeting stuff he's been doing is just a warming up, that's all. It's outmoded; can't reach enough people even if you spoke at Madison Square every night for a year. But it's good practice, to get him started. Now the next move is a half-hour TV show once a week, and when that gets started we're in."

"Who's going to pay for all this?"

"We've got more money than you can shake a stick at." He smiled briefly and refilled our glasses with a flourish. "I haven't been resting on my laurels and neither has Clarissa. We've got three of the richest men in L.A. drooling at the mouth for an opportunity to come in with us. They're sold. They've talked to him, they've heard him. That's been enough."

"Will you sell soap on television at the same time?"

"Come off it, Gene. *Cave* is the product."

"Then in what way will you or his sponsors profit from selling him?"

"In the first place, what he says is the truth and that's meant a lot to them, to the tycoons. They'll do anything to put him across."

"I should think that the possession of the truth and its attendant sense of virtue is in itself enough, easily spoiled by popularization," I said with chilling pomp.

"Now that's a mighty selfish attitude to take. Sure it makes me happy to know at last nothing matters a hell of a lot since I'm apt to die any time and that's the end of yours truly. A nice quiet nothing, like sleeping pills after a busy day. All that's swell, but it means a lot more to me to see the truth belong to everybody. Also, let's face it, I'm ambitious. I like my work. I want to see this thing get big, and with me part of it. Life doesn't mean a thing and death is the only reality, like he says, but while we're living we've got to keep busy and the best thing for me, I figured about six months ago, was to put Cave over with the public, which is just what I'm going to do. Anything wrong with that?"

Since right and wrong had not yet been reformulated and codified, I gave him the comfort he hardly needed. "I see what you mean. I suppose you're right. Perhaps the motive is the same in every case, mine as well as yours. Yet we've all experienced Cave and that should be enough."

"No, we should all get behind it and push, bring it to the world."

"That, of course, is where we're different. Not that I don't intend to propagate the truth, but I shall do it for something to do, knowing that nothing matters, not even *this* knowledge matters." In my unction, I had stumbled upon the first of a series of paradoxes which were to amuse and obsess our philosophers for a generation. However, Paul gave me no opportunity to elaborate; his was the practical way and I followed. We spoke of means not ends.

"Cave likes the idea of the half-hour show and as soon as we get all the wrinkles ironed out, buying good time, not just dead air, we'll make the first big announcement, along around January. Until then we're trying to keep this out of the papers. Slow but sure; then fast and hard."

"What sort of man is Cave?" I wanted very much to hear the reaction of a practical man.

Paul was candid; he did not know. "How can you figure a guy like that out? At times he seems a little feeble-minded, this is between us by the way, and other times when he's talking to people, giving with the message, there's nothing like him."

"What about his early life?"

"Nobody knows very much. I've had a detective agency prepare a dossier on him. Does that surprise you? Well, I'm going far out on a limb for him and so are our rich friends. We had to be sure we weren't buying an ax murderer or a commie or something."

"Would that have made any difference to the message?"

"No, *I* don't think so but it sure would have made it impossible for us to sell him on a big scale."

"And what did they find?"

"Not much. I'll let you read it. Take it home with you. Confidential, of course, and, as an officer of the company, I must ask you not to use any of it without first clearing with me."

I agreed and his secretary was sent for. The dossier was a thin bound manuscript.

"It's a carbon but I want it back. You won't find anything very striking but you ought to read it for the background. Never been married, no girl friends that anybody remembers . . . no boy friends either (what a headache *that* problem is for a firm like ours). No police record. No tickets for double parking, even. A beautiful, beautiful record on which to build."

"Perhaps a little negative."

"That's what we like. As for the guy's character, his I.Q., your guess is as good as mine, probably better. When I'm with him alone, we talk about the campaign and he's very relaxed, very sensible, businesslike. Doesn't preach or carry on. He seems to understand all the problems of our end. He's cooperative."

"Can you look him straight in the eye?"

Paul laughed. "Gives you the creeps, doesn't it? No, I guess I don't look at him very much. I'm glad you mentioned that because I've a hunch he's a hypnotist of some kind, though there's no record of his ever having studied it. I think I'll get a psychologist to take a look at him."

"Do you think he'll like that?"

"Oh, he'll never know unless he's a mindreader. Somebody to sort of observe him at work. I've already had him checked physically."

"You're very thorough."

"Have to be. He's got a duodenal ulcer and there's a danger of high blood pressure when he's older; otherwise he's in fine shape."

"What do you want me to do first?"

He became serious. "A pamphlet. You might make a highbrow magazine article out of it for the *Reader's Digest* or something first. We'll want a clear, simple statement of the Cavite philosophy."

"Why don't you get him to write it?"

"I've tried. He says he can't write anything. In fact he even hates to have his sermons taken down by a recorder. God knows why. But in a way it's all to the good, because it means we can get all the talent we like to do the writing for us, and that way, sooner or later, we can appeal to just about everybody."

"Whom am I supposed to appeal to in this first pamphlet?"

"The ordinary person, but make it as foolproof as you can. Leave plenty of doors open so you can get out fast in case we switch the party line along the way."

I laughed. "You're extraordinarily cynical."

"Just practical. I had to learn everything the hard way. I've been kicked around by some mighty expert kickers in my time."

I checked his flow of reminiscence. "Tell me about Cave and Iris." This was the secondary mystery which had occupied my mind for several days. But Paul did not know or, if he did, would not say. "I think they're just good friends, like we say in these parts. Except that I doubt if anything is going on . . . they don't seem the type and she's so completely gone on what he has to say . . ."

A long-legged girl secretary in discreet black entered the room unbidden and whispered something to the publicist. Paul started as though she had given him an electric shock from the thick carpeting. He spoke quickly. "Get Furlow. Tell him to stand bail. I'll be right down."

She hurried from the room. Paul pushed the bar away from him and it rolled aimlessly across the floor, bottles and glasses chattering. Paul looked at me distractedly. "He's in jail. Cave's in jail."

SIX

ONE

Last night the noise of my heart's beating kept me awake until nearly dawn. Then, as the gray warm light of the morning patterned the floor, I fell asleep and dreamed uneasily of disaster, my dreams disturbed by the noise of jackals, by that jackal-headed god who hovers over me as these last days unfold confusedly before my eyes: it will end in heat and terror, alone beside a muddy river, all time as one and that soon gone. I awakened, breathless and cold, with a terror of the dying still ahead.

After coffee and pills, those assorted pellets which seem to restore me for moments at a time to a false serenity, I put aside the nightmare world of the previous restless hours and idly examined the pages which I had written with an eye to rereading them straight through, to relive for a time the old drama which is already, as I write, separating itself from my memory and becoming real only in the prose. I think now of these events as I have told them and not as they occur to me in memory. For the memory now is of pages and not of scenes or of actual human beings still existing in that baleful, tenebrous region of the imagination where fancy and fact together confuse even the most confident of narrators. I have, thus far at least, exorcised demons, and to have lost certain memories to my narrative relieves my system, as would the excision of a cancer from a failing organism.

The boy brought me my morning coffee and the local newspaper, whose Arabic text pleases my eye though the sense, when I do translate it, is less than strange. I asked the boy if Mr. Butler was awake and he said that he had gone out already. These last few days I have kept to my room even for the evening meal, delaying the inevitable revelation as long as possible.

After the boy left and while I drank coffee and looked out upon the river and the western hills, I was conscious of a sense of well-being which I have not often experienced in recent years.

Perhaps the work of evoking the past has, in a sense, enhanced the present for me. I thought of the work done as life preserved, as part of me which will remain.

Then, idly, I riffled the pages of John Cave's Testament for the first time since I had discovered that my name had been expunged.

The opening was the familiar one which I had composed so many years before in Cave's name. The time of divination: a straightforward account of the apparent wonders which had preceded the mission. No credence was given the supernatural but a good case was made (borrowed a little from the mental therapists) for the race's need of phenomena as a symptom of unease and boredom and anticipation. I flicked through the pages. An entire new part had been added which I did not recognize: it was still written as though by Cave but obviously it could not have been composed until at least a decade after his death.

I read the new section carefully. Whoever had written it had been strongly under the influence of the pragmatic philosophers, though the style was somewhat inspirational, a guide to popularity crossed with the Koran. A whole system of ideal behaviour was sketched broadly for the devout, so broadly as to be fairly useless, though the commentary and the interpretive analysis of such lines as "Property really belongs to the world though individuals may have temporary liens on certain sections" must be already prodigious.

I was well into the metaphysics of the Cavites when there was a knock on my door. It was Butler, looking red and uncomfortable from the heat, a spotted red bandana tied, for some inscrutable reason, about his head in place of a hat.

"Hope you don't mind my barging in like this, but I finished a visit with the mayor earlier than I thought." He crumpled, on invitation, into a chair opposite me. He sighed gloomily. "This is going to be tough, tougher than I ever imagined back home."

"I told you it would be. The Moslems are very obstinate."

"I'll say! and the old devil of a mayor practically told me point-blank that if he caught me proselytizing he'd send me back to Cairo. Imagine the nerve!"

"Well, it *is* their country," I said, reasonably, experiencing my first real hope. Might the Cavites not get themselves expelled from Islam? I knew the mayor of Luxor, a genial merchant who still enjoyed the obsolete title of Pasha. The possibilities of a daring plot occurred to me. All I needed was another year or two, by which time nature would have done its work in any case and the conquest of humanity by the Cavites could then continue its progress without my bitter presence.

I looked at Butler speculatively. He is such a fool. I could, I am sure, undo him, for a time at least. Unless of course he is, as I first expected, an agent come to finish me in fact as absolutely as I have been finished in effect by those revisionists who have taken my place among the Cavites, arranging history . . . I had experienced, briefly, while studying Butler's copy of the Testament, the unnerving sense of having never lived, of having dreamed the past entire.

"Maybe it is their country but we got the truth, and like Paul Himmell said: 'A truth known to only half the world is but half a truth."

"Did he say that?"

"Of course he did. Don't you . . ." he paused, aware of the book in my hand. His expression softened, like a parent in anger noticing suddenly an endearing resemblance to himself in the offending child. "But I forget how isolated you've been up here. If I've interrupted your studies, I'll go away."

"Oh no. I was finished when you came. I've been studying for several hours, which is too long for an old man."

"If a contemplation of Cavesword can ever be too long." said Butler reverently. "Yes, Himmell wrote that even before Cavesword, in the month of March, I believe, though we'll have to ask my colleague when he comes. He knows all the dates, all the facts. Remarkable guy. He is the brains of the team." And Butler laughed to show that he was not entirely serious.

"I think they might respond to pressure," I said, treacherously. "One thing the Arabs respect is force."

"You may be right. But our instructions are to go slow. Still, I didn't think it would be as slow as this. Why, we haven't been able to get a building yet. They've all been told by the Pasha fellow not to rent to us."

"Perhaps I could talk to him."

"Do you know him well?"

"We used to play backgammon quite regularly. I haven't seen

much of him in the past few years, but if you'd like I'll pay him a call."

"He's known all along you're a Cavite, hasn't he?"

"We have kept off the subject of religion entirely. As you've probably discovered, since the division of the world there's been little communication between East and West. I don't think he knows much about the Cavites except that they're undesirable."

"Poor creature," said Butler, compassionately.

"Outer darkness," I agreed.

"But mark my words: before ten years have passed they will have the truth."

"I have no doubt of that, Communicator, none at all. If the others who come out have even a tenth of your devotion the work will go fast."The easy words of praise came back to me mechanically from those decades when a large part of my work was organizational, spurring the mediocre on to great deeds . . . and the truth of the matter has been, traditionally, that the unimaginative are the stuff from which heroes and martyrs are made.

"Thanks for those kind words," said Butler, flushed now with pleasure as well as heat. "Which reminds me, I was going to ask you if you'd like to help us with our work once we get going."

"I'd like nothing better but I'm afraid my years of useful service are over. Any advice, however, or perhaps influence that I may have in Luxor . . ." There was a warm moment of mutual esteem and amiability, broken only by a reference to the Squad of Belief.

"We'll have one here eventually. Fortunately, the need for them in the Atlantic Community is nearly over. Of course there are always a few malcontents, but we have worked out a statistical ratio of nonconformists in the population which is surprisingly accurate. Knowing their incidence, we are able to check them early. But in general, truth is ascendant everywhere in the civilized world."

"What are their methods now?"

"The Squad of Belief's? Psychological indoctrination. We now have methods of converting even the most obstinate lutherist. Of course where usual methods fail (and once in every fifteen hundred they do), the Squad is authorized to remove a section of brain which effectively does the trick of making the lutherist conform, though his usefulness in a number of other spheres is somewhat impaired. I'm told he has to learn all over again how to talk and to move around."

"Lutherist? I don't recognize the word."

"You certainly have been cut off from the world." Butler looked at me curiously, almost suspiciously. "I thought even in your day that was a common expression. It means anybody who refuses willfully to know the truth."

"What does it come from?"

"Come from?" Semantics was either no longer taught or else Butler had never been interested in it. "Why, it just means, well, a lutherist."

"I wonder, though, what the derivation of it was," I was excited. This was the first sign that I had ever existed, a word of obscure origin connoting nonconformist.

"I'm afraid we'll have to ask my sidekick when he comes. I don't suppose it came from one of those Christian sects . . . you know, the German one that broke with Rome."

"That must be it," I said. "I don't suppose in recent years there have been as many lutherists as there once were."

"Very, very few. As I say, we've got it down to a calculable minority and our psychologists are trying to work out some method whereby we can spot potential lutherists in childhood and indoctrinate them before it's too late . . . but of course the problem is a negligible one in the Atlantic Community. We've had no serious trouble for forty years."

"Forty years . . . that was the time of all the trouble," I said.

"Not so *much* trouble," said Butler, undoing the bandana and mopping his face with it. "The last flare-up, I gather, of the old Christians. History makes very little of it but at the time it must have seemed important. Now that we have more perspective we can view things in their proper light. I was only a kid in those days and, frankly, I don't think I paid any attention to the papers. Of course *you* remember it." He looked at me suddenly, his great vacuous eyes focussed. My heart missed one of its precarious beats: was this the beginning? had the inquisition begun?

"Not well," I said. "I was seldom in the United States. I'd been digging in Central America, in and around the Petén. I missed most of the trouble."

"You seem to have missed a good deal." His voice was equable, without a trace of secondary meaning.

"I've had a quiet life. I'm grateful though for your coming here. Otherwise, I should have died without any contact with America, without ever knowing what was happening outside the Arab League."

"Well, we'll shake things up around here."

"Shake well before using," I quoted absently.

"What did you say?"

"I said I hoped all would be well."

"I'm sure it will. By the way, I brought you the new edition of Cave's prison dialogues." He pulled a small booklet from his back pocket and handed it to me.

"Thank you." I took the booklet: dialogues between Cave and Iris Mortimer. I had not heard of this particular work. "Is this a recent discovery?" I asked.

"Recent? Why no. It's the newest edition but of course the text goes right back to the early days when Cave was in prison."

"Oh, yes, in California."

"Sure; it was the beginning of the persecutions. Well, I've got to be on my way." He arranged the bandana about his head. "Somebody stole my hat. Persecuting *me*, I'll bet my bottom dollar . . . little ways. Well, I'm prepared for them. They can't stop us. Sooner or later the whole world will be Cavite."

"Amen," I said.

"What?" He looked at me with shock.

"I'm an old man," I said hastily. "You must recall I was brought up among Christians. Such expressions still linger on, you know."

"It's a good thing there's no Squad of Belief in Luxor," said Butler cheerily. "They'd have you up for indoctrination in a second."

"I doubt if it would be worth their trouble. Soon I shall be withdrawing from the world altogether."

"I suppose so. You haven't thought of taking Cavesway, have you?"

"Of course, many times, but since my health has been good I've been in no great hurry to leave my contemplation of those hills." I pointed to the western window. "And now I should hesitate to die until the very last moment, out of curiosity. I'm eager to learn, to help as much as possible in your work here."

"Well, of course that is good news, but should you ever want to take His Way let me know. We have some marvelous methods now, extremely pleasant to take and, as he said, 'It's not death which is hard but dying.' We've finally made dying simply swell."

"Will wonders never cease?"

"In that department, never! It is the firm basis of our truth. Now I must be off."

"Is your colleague due here soon?"

"Haven't heard recently. But I don't suppose the plans have been changed. You'll like him."

"I'm sure I shall."

TWO

And so John Cave's period in jail was now known as the time of persecution, with a pious prison dialogue attributed to Iris. Before I returned to my work of recollection I glanced at the dialogue, whose style was enough like Iris's to have been her work. But of course her style was not one which could ever have been called inimitable since it was based on the most insistent of twentieth-century advertising techniques. I assumed the book was the work of one of those anonymous counterfeiters who have created, according to a list of publications on the back of the booklet, a wealth of Cavite doctrine.

The conversation with Cave in prison was lofty in tone and seemed to deal with moral problems. It was apparent that since the task of governing is largely one of keeping order, with the passage of time it had become necessary for the Cavite rulers to compose in Cave's name different works of ethical instruction to be used for the guidance and control of the population. I assume that since they now control all records and original sources, it is an easy matter for them to "discover" some relevant text that gives clear answer to any moral or political problem not anticipated in previous commentaries. The work of falsifying records and expunging names is, I should think, somewhat more tricky but they seem to have accomplished it in Cave's Testament, brazenly assuming that those who recall the earlier versions will die off in time, leaving a generation which knows only what they wish it to know, excepting of course the "calculable minority" of nonconformists, of base lutherists.

Cave's term in prison was far less dramatic than official legend, though more serious. He was jailed for hit-and-run driving on the highway from Santa Monica into Los Angeles.

I went to see him that evening with Paul. When we arrived at the jail, we were not allowed near him though Paul's lawyers had been permitted to go inside a few minutes before our arrival.

Iris was sitting in the outer office, pale and shaken. A bored policeman in uniform sat at a desk, ignoring us.

"They're the best lawyers in L.A.," said Paul quickly. "They'll get him out in no time."

Iris looked at him bleakly.

"What happened?" I asked, sitting down beside her on the bench. "How did it happen?"

"I wasn't with him." She shook her head several times as though to dispel a profound daydream. "He called me and I called you. They *are* the best, Paul?"

"I can vouch for that . . ."

"Did he kill anybody?"

"We . . . we don't know yet. He hit an old man and went on driving. I don't know why. I mean why he didn't stop. He just went on and the police car caught him. The man's in the hospital now. They say it's bad. He's unconscious, an old man . . ."

"Any reporters here?" asked Paul. "Anybody else we know besides us?"

"Nobody. You're the only person I called."

"This could wreck everything." Paul was frightened.

But Cave was rescued, at considerable expense to the company. The old man chose not to die immediately, while the police and the courts of Los Angeles, at that time well known for their accessibility to free-spending reason, proved more than obliging. After a day and a night in prison, Cave was released on bail, and when the case came to court it was handled discreetly by the magistrate.

The newspapers, however, had discovered John Cave at last and there were photographs of "Present-Day Messiah in Court." As ill luck would have it, the undertakers of Laguna had come to the aid of their prophet with banners which proclaimed his message. This picketing of the court was photographed and exhibited in the tabloids. Paul was in a frenzy. Publicist though he was, in his first rage he expressed to me the novel sentiment that not all publicity was good.

"But we'll get back at those bastards," he said grimly, not identifying which ones he meant but waving toward the city hidden by the Venetian blinds of his office window.

I asked for instructions. The day before, Cave had gone back to Washington state to lie low until the time was right for a triumphant reappearance. Iris had gone with him; on a separate plane, to avoid scandal. Clarissa had sent various heartening if confused messages from New York while Paul and I were left to gather up the pieces and begin again. Our close association during those difficult days impressed me with his talents and though, fundamentally, I still found him appalling, I couldn't help but admire his superb operativeness.

"I'm going ahead with the original plan . . . just like none of this happened. The stockholders are willing and we've got enough money, though not as much as I'd like, for the publicity build-up. I expect Cave'll pick up some more cash in Seattle. He always does, wherever he goes."

"Millionaires just flock to him?"

"Strange to tell, yes. But then, nearly everybody does."

"It's funny, since the truth he offers is all there is to it. Once it is experienced, there's no longer much need for Cave or for an organization." This of course was the paradox which time and the unscrupulous were bloodily to resolve.

Paul's answer was reasonable."That's true, but there's the problem of sharing it. If millions felt the same way about death the whole world would be happier and, if it's happier why, it'll be a better place to live in."

"Do you really believe this?"

"Still think of me as a hundred per cent phony?" Paul chuckled good-naturedly. "Well, it so happens, I *do* believe that. It also so happens that if this thing clicks we'll have a world organization and if we have, there'll be a big place for number one in it. It's all mixed up, Gene. I'd like to hear *your* motives, straight from the shoulder."

I was not prepared to answer him, or myself. In fact, to this day, my own motives are a puzzle to which there is no single key, no easy answer. One is not, after all, like those classic or neo-classic figures who wore with such splendid monomaniacal consistency the scarlet of lust or the purple of dominion or the bright yellow of madness, existing not at all beneath their identifying robes. Power appealed to me in my youth but only as a minor pleasure and not as an end in itself or even as a means to any private or public end. I enjoyed the idea of guiding and dominating others, preferably in the mass; yet, at the same time, I did not like the boredom of power achieved, or the silly publicness of a great life. But there was something which, often against my will and judgment, precipitated me into deeds and attitudes where the logic of the moment controlled me to such an extent that I could not lessen, if I chose, the momentum of my own wild passage, or chart its course.

I would not have confided this to Paul even had I in those days thought any of it out, which I had not. Though I was conscious of some fundamental ambivalence in myself, I always felt that should I pause for a few moments and question myself, I could easily find answers to these problems. But I did not pause. I never asked myself a single question concerning motive. I acted like a man sleeping who was only barely made conscious by certain odd incongruities that he dreams. The secret which later I was to discover was still unrevealed to me as I faced the efficient vulgarity of Paul Himmell across the portable bar which reflected his competence so brightly in its crystal.

"My motives are perfectly simple," I said, half believing what I said. In those days the more sweeping the statement, the more apt I was to give it my fickle allegiance. Motives are simple, splendid! Simple they are. "I want something to do. I'm fascinated by Cave and I believe what he says . . . not that it is so supremely earth-shaking. It's been advanced as a theory off and on for two thousand years. Kant wrote that he anticipated with delight the luxurious sleep of the grave, and the Gnostics came close to saying the same thing when they promised a glad liberation from life. The Eastern religions, about which I know very little, maintain . . ."

"That's it!" Paul interrupted me eagerly. "That's what we want. You just keep on like that. We'll call it 'An Introduction to John Cave.' Make a small book out of it. Get it published in New York. Then the company will buy up copies and we'll pass it out free."

"I'm not so sure that I know enough formal philosophy to . . ."

"To hell with that stuff. You just root around and show how the old writers were really Cavites at heart and then you come to him and put down what he says. Why we'll be half there even before he's on TV!" Paul lapsed for a moment into a reverie of promotion. I had another drink and felt quite good myself, although I had serious doubts about my competence to compose philosophy in the popular key. But Paul's faith was infectious and I felt that, all in all, with a bit of judicious hedging and recourse to various explicit summaries and definitions, I might put together a respectable ancestry for Cave, whose message, essentially, ignored *all* philosophy, empiric and orphic, moving with hypnotic effectiveness to the main proposition: death and man's acceptance of it. The problems of life were always quite secondary to Cave, if not to the rest of us.

"When will you want this piece done?"

"The sooner the better. Here," he scribbled an address on a pad of paper. "This is Cave's address. He's on a farm outside Spokane. It belongs to one of his undertaker friends."

"Iris is with him?"

"Yes. Now you . . ."

"I wonder if that's wise, Iris seeing so much of him. You know he's going to have a good many enemies before very long and they'll dig around for any scandal they can find."

"Oh, it's perfectly innocent, I'm sure. Even if it isn't, I can't see how it can do much harm."

"For a public relations man you don't seem to grasp the possibilities for bad publicity in this situation."

"All pub . . ."

"Is good. But Cave, it appears, is a genuine ascetic." And the word "genuine" as I spoke it was like a knife blade in my heart. "And, since he is, you have a tremendous advantage in building him up. There's no use in allowing him, quite innocently, to appear to philander."

Paul looked at me curiously. "You wouldn't by any chance be interested in Iris yourself?"

And of course that was it. I had become attached to Iris in precisely the same sort of way a complete man might have been but of course for me there was no hope, nothing. The enormity of that nothing shook me, despite the alcohol I had drunk. Fortunately, I was sufficiently collected not to make the mistake of vehemence. "I like her very much but I'm more attached to the idea of Cave than I am to her. I don't want to see the business get out of hand. That's all. I'm surprised that you, of all people, aren't more concerned."

"You may have a point. I suppose I've got to adjust my views to this thing . . . it's different from my usual work building up show business types. In that line the romance angle is swell, just as long as there're no bigamies or abortions involved. I see your point, though. With Cave we have to think in sort of Legion of Decency terms. No rough stuff. No nightclub pictures or posing with blondes. You're absolutely right. Put that in your piece: doesn't drink, doesn't go out with dames . . ."

I laughed. "Maybe we won't have to go that far. The negative virtues usually shine through all on their own. The minute you draw attention to them you create suspicion. People are generally pleased to suspect the opposite of every avowal."

"You talk just like my analyst." And I felt that I had won, briefly, Paul's admiration. "Anyway, you go to Spokane; talk to Iris; tell her to lay off . . . in a tactful way of course. But don't mention it to him. You never can tell how he'll react. She'll be reasonable even though I suspect she is stuck on the man. Try and get your piece done by the first of December. I'd like to have it in print for the first of the New Year, Cave's year."

"I'll try."

"By the way, we're getting an office, same building as this."

"Cavites, Inc.?"

"We could hardly call it the Church of the Golden Rule," said Paul with one of the few shows of irritability I was ever to observe in his equable disposition. "Now, on behalf of the directors, I'm authorized to advance you whatever money you might feel you need for this project. That is, within . . ."

"I won't need anything except, perhaps, a directorship in the company." My own boldness startled me. Paul laughed.

"That's a good boy. Eye on the main chance. Well, we'll see what we can do about that. There aren't any more shares available right now but that doesn't mean . . . I'll let you know when you get back from Spokane."

Our meeting was ended by the appearance of his secretary, who called him away to other business. As we parted in the outer office, he said, quite seriously, "I don't think Iris likes him the way you think but if she does be careful. We can't upset Cave now. This is a tricky time for everyone. Don't show that you suspect anything. Later, when we're under way and there's less pressure, I'll handle it. Agreed?"

I agreed, secretly pleased at being thought in love . . . "in love" —to this moment the phrase has a strangely foreign sound to me, like a classical allusion not entirely understood in a scholarly text. "In love," I whispered to myself in the elevator as I left Paul that evening: in love with Iris.

THREE

We met at the Spokane railroad station and Iris drove me through the wide, clear, characterless streets to a country road which wound east into the hills, in the direction of a town with the lovely name of Coeur d'Alene.

She was relaxed. Her ordinarily pale face was fairly burned from the sun, while her hair, which I recalled as darkly waving, was now streaked with light and loosely bound at the nape of the neck. She wore no cosmetics and her dress was simple cotton beneath the sweater she wore against the autumn's chill. She looked younger than either of us actually was.

At first we talked of Spokane. She identified mountains and indicated hidden villages with an emphasis on place which sharply recalled Cave. Not until we had turned off the main highway into a country road, dark with fir and spruce, did she ask me about Paul. I told her. "He's very busy preparing our New Year's debut. He's also got a set of offices for the company in Los Angeles and he's engaged me to write an introduction to Cave . . . but I suppose you knew that when he wired you I was coming."

"It was my idea."

"My coming? or the introduction?"

"Both."

"And I thought he picked it out of the air while listening to me majestically place Cave among the philosophers."

Iris smiled. "Paul's not obvious. He enjoys laying traps and as long as they're for one's own good, he's very useful."

"Implying he could be destructive?"

"Immensely. So be on your guard even though I don't think he'll harm any of us."

"How is Cave?"

"I'm worried, Gene. He hasn't got over that accident. He talks about it continually."

"But the man didn't die."

"It would be better if he did . . . as it is, there's a chance of a lawsuit against Cave for damages."

"But he has no money."

"That doesn't prevent them from suing. But worst of all, there's the publicity. The whole thing has depressed Cave terribly. It was all I could do to keep him from announcing to the press that he had almost done the old man a favor."

"You mean by killing him?"

Iris nodded, quite seriously. "That's actually what he believes and the reason why he drove on."

"I'm glad he said nothing like that to the papers."

"But it's true; his point of view *is* exactly right."

"Except that the old man might regard the situation in a different light and, in any case, he was badly hurt and did not receive Cave's gift of death."

"Now you're making fun of us." She frowned and drove fast on the empty road.

"I'm doing no such thing. I'm absolutely serious. There's a moral problem involved which is extremely important and if a precedent is set too early, a bad one like this, there's no predicting how things will turn out."

"You mean the . . . the gift, as you call it, should only be given voluntarily?"

"Exactly . . . *if* then, and only in extreme cases. Think what might happen if those who listened to Cave decided to make all their friends and enemies content by killing them."

"Well, I wish you'd talk to him." She smiled sadly. "I'm afraid I don't always see things clearly when I'm with him. You know how he is . . . how he convinces."

"I'll talk to him tactfully. I must also get a statement of belief from him."

"But you have it already. We all have it."

"Then I'll want some moral application of it. We still have so much ground to cover."

"There's the farm, up there on the hill." A white frame building stood shining among spruce on a low hill at the foot of blue sharp mountains. She turned up a dirt road and, in silence, we arrived at the house.

An old woman, the cook, greeted us familiarly and told Iris that *he* could be found in the study.

In a small warm room, sitting beside a stone fireplace empty of fire, Cave sat, a scrapbook on his knees, his expression vague, unfocused. Our arrival recalled him from some dense reverie. He got to his feet quickly and shook hands. "I'm glad you came," he said.

It was Cave's particular gift to strike a note of penetrating sincerity at all times, even in his greetings, which became, as a result, disconcertingly like benedictions. Iris excused herself and we sat beside the fireplace.

"Have you seen these?" Cave pushed the scrapbook toward me.

I took the book and saw the various newspaper stories concerning the accident. It had got a surprisingly large amount of space as though, instinctively, the editors had anticipated a coming celebrity for "Hit-and-Run Prophet."

"Look what they say about me."

"I've read them," I said, handing the scrapbook back to him, a little surprised that, considering his unworldliness, he had bothered to keep such careful track of his appearance in the press. It showed a new, rather touching side to him; he was like an actor hoarding notices, good and bad. "I don't think it's serious. After all you were let off by the court, and the man didn't die."

"It was an accident, of course. Yet that old man nearly received the greatest gift a man can have, a quick death. I wanted to tell the court that. I could have convinced them, I'm sure, but Paul said no. It was the first time I've ever gone against my own instinct and I don't like it." Emphatically, he shut the book.

The cook came into the room and lit the fire. When the first crackling filled the room and the pine had caught, she left, observing that we were to eat in an hour.

"You want to wash up?" asked Cave mechanically, his eyes on the fire, his hands clasped in his lap like those dingy marble replicas of hands which decorate medieval tombs. That night there was an unhuman look to Cave: pale, withdrawn, inert . . . his lips barely moving when he spoke, as though another's voice spoke through senseless flesh.

"No thanks," I said, a little chilled by his remoteness. Then I got him off the subject of the accident as quickly as possible and we talked until dinner of the introduction I was to write. It was most enlightening. As I suspected, Cave had read only the Bible and that superficially, just enough to be able, at crucial moments to affect the seventeenth-century prose of the translators and to confound thereby simple listeners with the familiar authority of his manner. His knowledge of philosophy did not even encompass the names of the principals. Plato and Aristotle rang faint, unrelated bells and with them the meager carillon ended.

"I don't know why you want to drag in those people," he said, after I had suggested Zoroaster as a possible point of beginning. "Most people have never heard of them either. And what I have to say is all my own. It doesn't tie in with any of them or, if it does, it's a coincidence, because I never picked it up anywhere."

"But I think that it *would* help matters if we provided a sort of family tree for you, to show . . ."

"I don't." He gestured with his effigy-hands. "Let them argue about it later. For now, act like this is a new beginning, which it is. I have only one thing to give people and that is the way to die without fear, gladly, to accept nothing for what it is, a long and dreamless sleep."

I had to fight against that voice, those eyes which as always, when he chose, could dominate any listener. Despite my close association with him, despite the thousands of times I heard him speak, I was never, even in moments of lucid disenchantment, quite able to resist his power. He was a magician in the great line of Simon Magus. That much, even now, I will acknowledge. His divinity, however, was and is the work of others, shaped and directed by the race's recurrent need.

I surrendered in the name of philosophy with a certain relief, and he spoke in specific terms of what he believed that I should write in his name.

It was not until after dinner that we got around, all three of us, to a problem which was soon to absorb us all, with near-disastrous results.

We had been talking amiably of neutral things and Cave had emerged somewhat from his earlier despondency. He got on to the subject of the farm where we were, of its attractiveness and remoteness, of its owner who lived in Spokane.

"I always liked old Smathers. You'd like him too. He's got one of the biggest funeral parlors in the state. I used to work for him and then, when I started on all this, he backed me to the hilt. Loaned me money to get as far as San Francisco. After that of course it was easy. I paid him back every cent."

"Does he come here often?"

Cave shook his head. "No, he lets me use the farm but he keeps away. He says he doesn't approve of what I'm doing. You see, he's Catholic."

"But he still likes John," said Iris, who had been stroking a particularly ugly yellow cat beside the fire. So it was John now, I thought. Iris was the only person ever to call him by his first name.

"Yes. He's a good friend."

"There'll be a lot of trouble, you know," I said.

"From Smathers?"

"No, from the Catholics, from the Christians."

"You really think so?" Cave looked at me curiously. I believe that until that moment he had never realized the inevitable collision of his point of view with that of the established religions.

"Of course I do. They've constructed an entire ethical system upon a supernatural foundation whose main strength is the promise of a continuation of human personality after death. You are rejecting grace, heaven, hell, the Trinity . . ."

"I've never said anything about the Trinity or about Christianity."

"But you'll *have* to say something about it sooner or later. If —or rather when—the people begin to accept you, the churches will fight back, and the greater the impression you make, the more fierce their attack."

"I suspect John *is* the Antichrist," said Iris, and I saw from her expression that she was perfectly serious. "He's come to undo all the wickedness of the Christians."

"Though not, I hope, of Christ," I said. "There's some virtue in his legend, even as corrupted at Nicea three centuries after the fact."

"I'll have to think about it," said Cave. "I don't know that I've ever given it much thought before. I've spoken always what I knew was true and there's never been any opposition, at least that I've been aware of, to my face. It never occurred to me that people who like to think of themselves as Christians couldn't accept both me and Christ at the same time. I know I don't promise the kingdom of heaven but I *do* promise oblivion and the loss of self, of pain . . ."

"Gene is right," said Iris. "They'll fight you hard. You must get ready now while you still have time to think it out, before Paul puts you to work and you'll never have a moment's peace again."

"As bad as that, you think?" Cave sighed wistfully. "But how to get ready? What should I do? I never think things out, you know. Everything occurs to me on the spot. I can never tell what may occur to me next. It happens only when I speak to people. When I'm alone, I seldom think of the . . . the main things. But when I'm in a group talking to them I hear . . . no, not hear, I *feel* voices telling me what I should say. That's why I never prepare a talk, why I don't really like to have them taken down. There are some things which are meant only for the instant they are conceived . . . a child, if you like, made for just a moment's life by the people listening and myself speaking. I don't mean to sound touched," he added, with a sudden smile. "I'm not really *hearing* things but I do get something from those people, something besides the thing I tell them. I seem to become a part of them, as though what goes on in their minds also goes on in me at the same time, two lobes to a single brain."

"We know that, John," said Iris softly. "We've felt it."

"I suppose, then, that's the key," said Cave. "Though it isn't much to write about. I don't suppose you can put it across without me to say it."

"You may be wrong there," I said. "Of course in the beginning you will say the word but I think in time, properly managed, everyone will accept it on the strength of evidence and statement, responding to the chain of forces you have set in motion." Yet for all the glibness with which I spoke, I did not really believe that Cave would prove to be more than an interesting momentary phenomenon whose "truth" about death might, at best, contribute in a small way to the final abolition of those old warring superstitions which had mystified and troubled men through all the dark centuries. A doubt which displayed my basic misunderstanding of our race's will to death and, worse, to a death in life made radiant by false dreams, by desperate adjurations.

But that evening we spoke only of a bright future: "To begin again is the important thing," I said. "Christianity, though strong as an organization in this country, is weak as a force because, finally, the essential doctrine is not accepted by most of the people: the idea of a manlike God dispensing merits and demerits at time's end."

"We are small," said Cave. "In space, on this tiny planet, we are nothing. Death brings us back to the whole. We lose this instant of awareness, of suffering, like spray in the ocean. There it forms, there it goes back to the sea."

"I think people will listen to you because they realize now that order, if there is any, has never been revealed, that death *is* the end of personality even for those passionate, self-important 'I's' who insist upon a universal diety like themselves, presented eponymously in order not to give the game away."

"How dark, how fine the grave must be! Only sleep and an end of days, an end of fear. The end of fear in the grave as the 'I' goes back to nothing . . ."

"Yes, Cave, life will be wonderful when men no longer fear dying. When the last superstitions are thrown out and we meet death with the same equanimity that we have met life. No longer will children's minds be twisted by evil gods whose fantastic origin is in those babaric tribes who feared death and lightning, who feared life. That's it: life is the villian to those who preach reward in death, through grace and eternal bliss, or through dark revenge . . ."

"Neither revenge nor reward, only the not-knowing in the grave which is the same for all."

"And without those inhuman laws, what societies we might build! Take the morality of Christ. Begin there, or even earlier with Plato or earlier yet with Zoroaster. Take the best ideas of the best men and should there be any disagreement as to what is best, use life as the definition, life as the measure. What contributes most to the living is the best."

"But the living is soon done and the sooner done the better. I envy those who have already gone."

"If they listen to you, Cave, it will be like the unlocking of a prison. At first they may go wild but then, on their own, they will find ways to life. Fear of punishment in death has seldom stopped the murderer's hand. The only two things which hold him from his purpose are, at the worst, fear of reprisal from society and, at the best, a feeling for life, a love for all that lives. And not the wide-smiling idiot's love but a sense of the community of the living, of life's marvelous regency. Even the most ignorant has felt this. Life is all while death is only the irrelevant shadow at the end, the counterpart to that instant before the seed lives."

Yes, I believed all that, all that and more too, and I felt Cave was the same as I. By removing fear with that magic of his, he would fulfill certain hopes of my own and (I flatter myself perhaps) of the long line of others, nobler than I, who had been equally engaged in attempting to use life more fully. And so that evening the one true conviction of a desultory life broke through the chill hard surface of disappointment and disgust that had formed a brittle carapace about my heart. I had, after all, my truth too, and Cave had got to it, broken the shell, and for that I shall remain grateful to him, until we are at last the same, both taken by dust.

Excitedly, we talked. I talked mostly. Cave was the theme and I the counterpoint, or so I thought. He had stated it and I built upon what I conceived to be the luminosity of his vision. Our dialogue was one of communion. Only Iris guessed that it was not. From the beginning she saw the difference; she was conscious of the division which that moment had, unknown to either of us, separated me from Cave. *Each time I said "life," he said "death."* In true amity but false concord, the fatal rift began.

Iris, more practical than we, deflated our visions by pulling the dialogue gently back to reality, to ways and dull means.

It was agreed that we had agreed on fundamentals: the end of fear was desirable; superstition should be exorcised from human affairs; the ethical systems constructed by the major religious figures from Zoroaster to Mohammed all contained useful and applicable ideas of societal behavior which need not be discarded.

At Iris's suggestion, we left the problem of Christianity itself completely alone. Cave's truth was sufficient cause for battle. There was no reason, she felt, for antagonizing the ultimate enemy at the very beginning.

"Let them attack *you*, John. You must be above quarreling."

"I reckon I *am* above it," said Cave and he sounded almost cheerful for the first time since my arrival. "I want no trouble, but if trouble comes I don't intend to back down. I'll just go on saying what I know."

At midnight, Cave excused himself and went to bed.

Iris and I sat silent before the last red embers on the hearth. I sensed that something had gone wrong but I could not tell what it was.

When Iris spoke, her manner was abrupt. "Do you really want to go on with this?"

"What an odd time to ask me that. Of course I do. Tonight's the first time I really saw what it was Cave meant, what it was I'd always felt but never before known; consciously, that is. I couldn't be more enthusiastic."

"I hope you don't change."

"Why so glum? What are you trying to say? After all, you got me into this."

"I know I did and I think I was right. It's only that this evening I felt . . . well, I don't know. Perhaps I'm getting a bit on edge," She smiled and, through all the youth and health, I saw that she was anxious and ill at ease.

"That business about the accident?"

"Mainly, yes. The lawyers say that now that the old man's all right he'll try to collect damages. He'll sue Cave."

"Nasty publicity."

"The worst. It's upset John terribly . . . he almost feels it's an omen."

"I thought we were dispensing with all that, with miracles and omens." I smiled but she did not.

"Speak for yourself." She got up and pushed at the coals with a fire shovel. "Paul says he'll handle everything but I don't see how. There's no way he can stop a lawsuit."

But I was tired of the one problem which was out of our hands anyway. I asked her about herself and Cave.

"Is it wise my being up here with John, alone? No, I'm afraid not but that's the way it is." Her voice was hard and her back, now turned to me, grew stiff, her movements with the fire shovel angry and abrupt.

"People will use it against both of you. It may hurt him, and all of us."

She turned suddenly, her face flushed. "I can't help it, Gene. I swear I can't. I've tried to keep away. I almost flew East with Clarissa but when he asked me to join him here, I did. I couldn't leave him."

"Will marriage be a part of the new order?"

"Don't joke." She sat down angrily in a noise of skirts crumpling. "Cave must never marry. Besides it's . . . it isn't like that."

"Really? I must confess I . . ."

"Thought we were having an affair? Well, it's not true." The rigidity left her as suddenly as it had possessed her. She grew visibly passive, even helpless, in the worn upholstered chair, her eyes on me, the anger gone and only weakness left. "What can I do?" It was a cry from the heart. All the more touching because, obviously, she had not intended to tell me so much. She had turned to me because there was no one else to whom she could talk.

"You . . . love him?" that word which whenever I spoke it in those days always stuck in my throat like a diminutive sob.

"More, more," she said distractedly. "But I can't *do* anything or *be* anything. He's complete. He doesn't need anyone. He doesn't want me except as . . . a companion, and adviser like you or Paul. It's all the same to him."

"I don't see that it's hopeless."

"Hopeless!" The word shot from her like a desperate deed. She buried her face in her hands but she did not weep. I sat watching her. The noise of a clock's dry ticking kept the silence from falling in about our heads.

Finally, she dropped her hands and turned toward me with her usual grace. "You mustn't take me too seriously," she said. "Or I mustn't take myself too seriously, which is more to the point. Cave doesn't really need me or anyone and we . . . I, perhaps you, certainly others, need him. It's best no one try to claim him all as a woman would do, as I might, given the chance." She rose. "It's late and you must be tired. Don't ever mention to anyone what I've told you tonight, especially to John. If he knew the way I felt . . ." She left it at that. I gave my promise and we went to our rooms.

I stayed two days at the farm, listening to Cave, who continually referred to the accident. He was almost petulant, as though the whole business were an irrelevant, gratuitous trick played on him by a malicious old man.

Cave's days were spent reading his mail (there was quite a bit of it even then), composing answers which Iris typed out for him, and walking in the wooded hills that surrounded the farm.

The weather was sharp and bright and the wind, when it blew, tasted of ice from the glaciers in the vivid mountains. Winter was nearly upon us and red leaves decorated the wind. Only the firs remained unchanged, warm and dark in the bright chill days.

Cave and I would walk together while Iris remained indoors, working. He was a good walker, calm, unhurried, surefooted, and he knew all the trails beneath the fallen yellow and red leaves. He agreed with most of my ideas for the introduction. I promised to send him a first draft as soon as I had got it done. He was genuinely indifferent to the philosophic aspect of what he preached. He acted almost as if he did not want to hear of those others who had approached the great matter in a similar way. When I talked to him of the fourth-century Donatists who detested life and loved heaven so much that they would request strangers to kill them, and magistrates to execute them for no crime, he stopped me. "I don't want to hear all that. That's finished. All that's over. We want new things now."

Iris, too, seemed uninterested in any formalizing of Cave's thought though she saw its necessity and wished me well, suggesting that I not ever intimate derivation since, in fact, there had been none. What he was he had become on his own, uninstructed.

During our walks, I got to know Cave as well as I was ever to know him. He was indifferent, I think, to everyone. He gave one his attention in precise ratio to one's belief in him and the importance of his work. With groups he was another creature:

warm, intoxicating, human, yet transcendent, a part of each man who beheld him, the long desired and pursued whole achieved.

And though I found him without much warmth or mind, I nevertheless identified him with the release I had known in his presence, and for this new certainty of life's value and of death's irrelevance, I loved him.

On the third day I made up my mind to go back East and do the necessary writing in New York, away from Paul's distracting influence and Cave's advice. I was asked to stay the rest of the week but I could see that Iris regarded me now as a potential danger, a keeper of secrets who might, despite promises, prove to be disloyal; and so, to set her mind at ease as well as to suit my own new plans, I told her privately after lunch on the third day that I was ready to leave that evening if she would drive me to Spokane.

"You're a good friend," she said. "I made a fool of myself the other night. I wish you'd forget it . . . forget everything I said."

"I'll never mention it. Now, the problem is how can I leave here gracefully. Cave just asked me this morning to stay on and . . ."

But I was given a perfect means of escape. Cave came running into the room, his eyes shining. "Iris! I've just talked to Paul in L.A. It's all over! No heirs, nothing, no lawsuit. No damages to pay."

"What's happened?" Iris stopped him in his excitement.

"The old man's dead!"

"O Lord!" Iris went gray. "That means a manslaughter charge!"

"No, no . . . not because of the accident. He was in *another* accident. A truck hit him the day after he left the hospital. Yesterday. He was killed instantly . . . lucky devil. And of course we're in luck too."

"Did they find who hit him?" I asked, suddenly suspicious. Iris looked at me fiercely. She had got it too.

"No. Paul said it was a hit-and-run. He said this time the police didn't find who did it. Paul said his analyst calls it 'a will to disaster' . . . the old man *wanted* to be run over. Of course that's hardly a disaster but the analyst thinks the old way."

I left that afternoon for New York, leaving Cave jubilantly making plans for the New Year. Everything was again possible. Neither Iris nor I mentioned what we both suspected. Each in his different way accommodated the first of many crimes.

SEVEN

ONE

"The tone, dear Gene, has all the unction, all the earnest turgidity of a trained theologian. You are perfect." Clarissa beamed at me wickedly over lunch in the Plaza Hotel. We sat at a table beside a great plate-glass window through which was visible the frosted bleak expanse of Central Park, ringed by buildings, monotonous in their sharp symmetry. The sky was sullen, dingy with snow ready to fall. The year was nearly over.

"I thought it quite to the point," I said loftily but with an anxious glance at the thin black volume which was that day to be published, the hasty work of one hectic month, printed in record time by a connection of Paul Himmell's.

"It's pure nonsense, the historical part. *I* know, though I confess I was never one for philosophers, dreary *egotistical* men, worse than actors and not half so lovely. Waiter, I will have a melon. Out of season I hope. I suggest you have it too. It's light."

I ordered *pot-de-crême*, the heaviest dessert on the menu.

"I've made you angry." Clarissa pretended contrition. "I was only trying to compliment you. What I meant was that I think the sort of thing you're doing is nonsense only because action is what counts, action on any level, not theorizing."

"There's a certain action to *thinking*, you know, even to writing about the thoughts of others."

"Oh, darling, don't sound so stuffy. Your dessert, by the way, poisons the liver. Oh, isn't that Bishop Winston over there by the door, in tweed? In mufti, eh, Bishop?"

The Bishop, who was passing our table in the company of a handsomely pale youth whose contemplation of orders shone in his face like some cherished sin, stopped and with a smile shook Clarissa's hand.

"Ah, how are you? I missed you the other night at Agnes's. She told me you've been engaged in social work."

"A euphemism, Bishop." Clarissa introduced me and the prelate moved on to his table.

"Catholic?"

"Hardly. Episcopal. I like them the best, I think. They adore society and good works . . . spiritual Whigs you might call them, a civilizing influence. Best of all, so few of them believe in God, unlike the Catholics or those terrible Calvinist peasants who are forever damning others."

"I think you're much too hard on the Episcopalians. I'm sure some of them must believe what they preach."

"Well, we shall probably never know. Social work! I knew Agnes would come up with something altogether wrong. Still, I'm just as glad it's not out yet. Not until the big debut tomorrow afternoon. I hope you've made arrangements to be near a television set. No? Then come to my place and we'll see it together. Cave's asked us both to the station, by the way, but I think it better if we not distract him."

"Iris came East with him?"

"Indeed she did. They both arrived last night. I thought you'd talked to her."

"No. Paul's the only one I ever see."

"He keeps the whole thing going, I must say. One of those born organizers. Now! what about you and Iris?"

This came so suddenly, without preparation, that it took me a suspiciously long time to answer, weakly, "I don't know what you mean. What about Iris and me?"

"Darling, I know *everything*." She looked at me in her eager, predatory way. I was secretly pleased that, in this particular case at least, she knew nothing.

"Then tell *me*."

"You're in love with her and she's classically involved with Cave."

"Classical seems to be the wrong word. Nothing has happened and nothing *will* happen."

"I suppose she told you this herself."

I was trapped for a moment. Clarissa, even in error, was shrewd and if one was not on guard she would quickly cease to be in error, at one's expense.

"No, not exactly. But Paul who I think does know everything

about our affairs, assures me that nothing has happened, that Cave is not interested in women."

"In men?"

"I thought you were all-knowing. No, not in men nor in wild animals, nor, does it seem, from the evidence Paul's collected, in anything except John Cave. Sex does not happen for him."

"Oh," said Clarissa, exhaling slowly, significantly, inscrutably. She abandoned her first line of attack to ask, "But *you* are crazy about Iris, aren't you? That's what I'd intended, you know, when I brought you two together."

"I thought it was to bring me into Cave's orbit."

"That too, but somehow I saw you and Iris . . . well, you're obviously going to give me no satisfaction so I shall be forced to investigate on my own."

"Not to sound too auctorial, too worried, do you think it will get Cave across? my Introduction?"

"I see no reason why not. Look at the enormous success of those books with titles like 'Eternal Bliss Can Be Yours for the Asking' or 'Happiness at Your Beck and Call.' "

"I'm a little more ambitious."

"Not in the least. But the end served is the same. You put down the main line of Cave's thinking, if it can be called thinking. And your book, along with his presence, should have an extraordinary effect."

"Do you really think so? I've begun to doubt."

"Indeed I do. They are waiting, all those sad millions who want to believe will find him exactly right for their purposes. He exists only to be believed in. He's a natural idol. Did you know that when Constantine moved his court to the East, his heirs were trained by Eastern courtiers to behave like idols and when his son came in triumph back to Rome (what a day that was! hot, but exciting) he rode for hours through the crowded streets without once moving a finger or changing expression, a perfectly trained god. We were all so impressed."

I cut this short. "Has it occurred to you that they might not want to believe anything, just like you and me?"

"Nonsense . . . and it's rude to interrupt, dear, even a garrulous relic like myself . . . yet after all, in a way, we *do* believe what Cave says. Death is there and he makes it seem perfectly all right, oblivion and the rest of it. And dying does rather upset a lot of people. Have you noticed one thing that the devoutly superstitious can never understand—that though we do not accept the fairy tale of reward or punishment beyond the grave we still are reluctant to 'pass on,' as the nuts say? As though the prospect of nothing isn't really, in its way, without friend Cave to push one into acceptance, perfectly ghastly, *much* worse than toasting on a grid like poor Saint Lawrence. But now I must fly. Come to the apartment at seven and I'll give you dinner. He's on at eight. Afterward they'll all join us." Clarissa flew.

I spent the afternoon gloomily walking up and down Fifth Avenue filled with doubt and foreboding, wishing now that I had never lent myself to the conspiracy, confident of its failure and of the rude laughter or, worse, the tactful silence of friends who would be astonished to find that after so many years of promise and reflection my first book should prove to be an apologia for an obscure evangelist whose only eminence was that of having mesmerized myself and an energetic publicist, as well as a handful of others more susceptible perhaps than we.

The day did nothing to improve my mood, and it was in a most depressed state that I went finally to Clarissa's Empire apartment on one of the good streets to dine with her and infect her, I was darkly pleased to note, with my own grim mood. By the time Cave was announced on the television screen, I had reduced Clarissa, for one of the few times in our acquaintance, to silence.

Yet as the lights in the room mechanically dimmed and an announcer came into focus, I was conscious of a quickening of my pulse, of a certain excitement. Here it was at last, the result of nearly a year's careful planning. Soon, in a matter of minutes, we would know.

To my surprise Paul Himmell was introduced by the announcer, who identified him perfunctorily, saying that the following half hour had been bought by Cavite, Inc.

Paul spoke briefly, earnestly. He was nervous, I could see, and his eyes moved from left to right disconcertingly as he read his introduction from cards out of view of the camera. He described Cave briefly as a teacher, as a highly regarded figure in the West. He implied it was as a public service, the rarest of philanthropies, that a group of industralists and businessmen were sponsoring Cave this evening.

Then Paul walked out of range of the camera, leaving briefly, a view of a chair and a table behind which a handsome velvet curtain fell in rich graceful folds from the invisible ceiling to an imitation marble floor. An instant later, Cave walked into view.

Both Clarissa and I leaned forward in our chairs tensely, eagerly, anxiously. We were there as well as he. This was our moment too. My hands grew cold and my throat dry.

Cave was equal to the moment. He looked tall. The scale of the table and chair was exactly right. He wore a dark suit and a dark unfigured tie with a light shirt that gave him an austereness which, in person, he lacked. I saw Paul's stage-managing in this.

Cave moved easily into range, his eyes cast down. Not until he had placed himself in front of the table and the camera had squarely centered him did he look directly into the lens. Clarissa gasped and I felt suddenly pierced: the camera and lights had magnified rather than diminished his power. It made no difference now what he said. The magic was working.

Clarissa and I sat in the twilight of her drawing room, entirely concentrated on the small screen, on the dark figure, the pale eyes, the hands which seldom moved. It was like some fascinating scene in a skillful play which, quite against one's wish and aesthetic judgment, becomes for that short time beyond real time, a part of one's own private drama of existence, sharpened by artifice, and a calculated magic.

Not until Cave was nearly finished did those first words of his, spoken so easily, so quietly, begin to come back to me as he repeated them in his coda, the voice increasing a little in volume, yet still not hurrying, not forcing, not breaking the mood that the first glance had created. The burden of his words was, as always, the same. Yet this time it seemed more awesome, more final, undeniable . . . in short, the truth. Though I had always accepted his first premise, I had never been much impressed by the ways he found of stating it. This night, before the camera and in the sight of millions, he perfected his singular art of communication and the world was his.

When he finished, Clarissa and I sat for a moment in complete silence, the chirping of a commercial the only sound in the room. At last she said, "The brandy is over there on the console. Get me some." Then she switched off the screen and turned on the lights.

"I feel dragged through a wringer," she said after her first mouthful of brandy.

"I had no idea it would work so well on television." I felt strangely empty, let down. There was hardly any doubt now of Cave's effectiveness, yet I felt joyless and depleted, as though part of my life had gone, leaving an ache.

"What a time we're going to have." Clarissa was beginning to recover. "I'll bet there are a million letters by morning and Paul will be doing a jig."

"I hope this is the right thing, Clarissa. It would be terrible if it weren't."

"Of course it's right. Whatever *that* means. If it works it's right. Perfectly simple. Such conceptions are all a matter of fashion anyway. One year women expose only their ankle; the next year their *derrière*. What's right one year is wrong the next. If Cave captures the popular imagination, he'll be right until someone better comes along."

"A little cynical." But Clarissa was only repeating my own usual line. I was, or had been until that night on the Washington farm, a contented relativist. Cave, however, had jolted me into new ways and I was bewildered by the change, by the prospect.

TWO

That evening was a time of triumph, at least for Cave's companions. They arrived noisily. Paul seemed drunk, maniacally exhilarated, while Iris glowed in a formal gown of green shot with gold. Two men accompanied them, one a doctor whose name I did not catch at first and the other a man from the television network who looked wonderfully sleek and pleased and kept patting Cave on the arm every now and then, as if to assure himself he was not about to vanish in smoke and fire.

Cave was silent. He sat in a high brocaded chair beside the fire and drank tea that Clarissa, knowing his habits, had ordered in advance for him. He responded to compliments with grave nods.

After the first burst of greetings at the door, I did not speak to Cave again and soon the others left him alone and talked around him, about him yet through him, as though he had become invisible, which seemed the case when he was not speaking, when those extraordinary eyes were veiled or cast down, as they were now, moodily studying the teacup, the pattern in the Aubusson rug at his feet.

I crossed the room to where Iris sat beside the doctor, who said, "Your little book, sir, is written in a complete ignorance of Jung."

This was sudden but I answered, as graciously as possible, that I had not intended writing a treatise on psychoanalysis.

"Not the point, sir, if you'll excuse me. I am a psychiatrist, a friend of Mr. Himmell's" (so this was the analyst to whom Paul so often referred) "and I think it impossible for anyone today to write about the big things without a complete understanding of Jung."

Iris interrupted as politely as possible. "Dr. Stokharin is a zealot, Gene. You must listen to him but, first, did you see John tonight?"

"He was remarkable, even more so than in person."

"It is the isolation," said Stokharin, nodding. Dandruff fell like a dry snow from thick brows to dark blue lapels. "The camera separates him from everyone else. He is projected like a dream into . . ."

"He was so afraid at first," said Iris, glancing across the room at the silent Cave, who sat, very small and still in the brocaded chair, the teacup still balanced on one knee. "I've never seen him disturbed by anything before. They tried to get him to do a rehearsal but he refused. He can't rehearse, only the actual thing."

"Fear is natural when . . . " but Stokharin was in the presence of a master drawing-room tactician. Iris was a born hostess. For all her ease and simplicity she was ruthlessly concerned with keeping order, establishing a rightness of tone.

"At first we hardly knew what to do." Iris's voice rose serenely over the East European rumblings of the doctor. "He'd always made such a point of the audience. He needed actual people to excite him. Paul wanted to fill the studio with a friendly audience but John said no, he'd try it without. When the talk began there were only a half dozen of us there; Paul, myself, the technicians. No one else."

"How did he manage?"

"It was the camera. He said when he walked out there he had no idea if anything would happen or not, if he could speak. Paul was nearly out of his mind with terror. We all were. Then John saw the lens of the camera. He said looking into it gave him a sudden shock, like a current of electricity passing through him, for there, in front of him, was the eye of the world and the microphone above his head was the ear into which at last he could speak. When he finished, he was transfigured. I've never seen him so excited. He couldn't recall what he had said but the elation remained until . . ."

"Until he got here."

"Well, nearly." Iris smiled. "He's been under a terrible strain these last two weeks."

"It'll be nothing like the traumatizing shocks in store for him during the next few days," said Stokharin, rubbing the bole of a rich dark pipe against his nose to bring out its luster (the pipe's luster, for the nose, straight, thick, proud, already shone like a baroque pearl). "Mark my words, everyone will be eager to see this phenomenon. When Paul first told me about him, I said, ah, my friend, you have found that father for which you've searched since your own father was run over by a bus in your ninth (the crucial) year. Poor Paul, I said, you will be doomed to disappointment. The wish for the father is the sign of your immaturity. For a time you find him here, there . . . in analysis you transfer to me. Now you meet a spellbinder and you turn to him, but it will not last. Exactly like that I talked to him. Believe me, I hold back nothing. Then I met this Cave. I watched him. Ah, what an analyst he would have made! What a manner, what power of communication! A natural healer. If only we could train him. Miss Mortimer, to you I appeal. Get him to study. The best people, the true Jungians are all here in New York. They will train him. He would become only a lay analyst but, even so, what miracles he could perform, what therapy! We must not waste this native genius."

"I'm afraid, Doctor, that he's going to be too busy wasting himself to study your . . . procedures." Iris smiled engagingly but with dislike apparent in her radiant eyes. Stokharin, however, was not sensitive to hostility, no doubt attributing such emotions to some sad deficiency in the other's adjustment.

Iris turned to me. "Will you be in the city the whole time?"

"The whole time Cave's here? Yes. I wouldn't miss it for anything."

"I'm glad. I've so much I want to talk to you about. So many things are beginning to happen. Call me tomorrow. I'll be staying at my old place. It's in the book."

"Cave?"

"Is staying with Paul, out on Long Island at someone's house. We want to keep him away from pests as much as possible."

"Manic depressions, I should say," said Stokharin thoughtfully, his pipe now clenched between his teeth and his attention on Cave's still figure. "With latent schizoid tendencies which . . . Miss Mortimer, you must have an affair with him. You must marry him if necessary. Have children. Let him see what it is to give live to others, to live in a balanced . . ."

"Doctor, you are quite mad," said Iris. She rose and crossed the room, cool in her anger. I too got away from the doctor as quickly as I could. "False modesty, inhibited behaviour, too-early bowel training," and similar phrases ringing in my ears.

Paul caught me at the door. I had intended to slip away without saying good night, confident that Clarissa would understand, that the others would not notice. "Not going so soon, are you?" He was a little drunk, his face dark with excitement. "But you ought to stay and celebrate." I murmured something about having an early appointment the next day.

"Well, see me tomorrow. We've taken temporary offices in the Empire State Building. The money has begun to roll in. If this thing tonight turns out the way I think it will, I'm going to be able to quit my other racket for good and devote full time to Cave." Already the name Cave had begun to sound more like that of an institution than of a man.

"By the way, I want to tell you what I think of the Introduction. Superior piece of work. Tried it out on several highbrow friends of mine and they liked it."

"I'm afraid . . ."

"That, together with the talks on television, should put this thing over with the biggest bang in years. We'll probably need some more stuff from you, historical background, rules and regulations, that kind of thing, but Cave will tell you what he wants. We've hired a dozen people already to take care of the mail and inquiries. There's also a lecture tour being prepared, all the main cities, while . . ."

"Paul, you're not trying to make a religion of this, are you?" I could hold it back no longer even though both time and occasion were all wrong for such an outburst.

"Religion? Hell, no . . . but we've got to organize. We've got to get this to as many people as we can. People have started looking to us (to him, that is) for guidance. We can't let them down."

Clarissa's maid ushered in a Western Union messenger, laden with telegrams. "Over three hundred," said the boy. "The station said to send them here."

Paul paid him jubilantly, and in the excitement, I slipped away.

THREE

The results of the broadcast were formidable. My Introduction was taken up by excited journalists who used it as a basis for hurried but exuberant accounts of the new marvel.

One night a week for the rest of that winter Cave appeared before the shining glass eye of the world, and on each occasion new millions in all parts of the country listened and saw and pondered this unexpected phenomenon, the creation of their own secret anxieties and doubts, a central man.

The reactions were too numerous for me to recollect in any order or with any precise detail; but I do recall the first few months vividly.

A few days after the first broadcast, I went to see Paul at the offices he had taken in the Empire State Building, as high up as possible, I noted with amusement: always the maximum, the optimum.

Halfway down a corridor, between lawyers and exporters, Cavite, Inc., was discreetly identified in black upon a frosted-glass door. I went inside.

It appeared to me the way I had always thought a newspaper office during a crisis might look. Four rooms opening off one another, all with doors open, all crowded with harassed secretaries and clean-looking young men in blue serge suits carrying papers, talking in loud voices; the room sounded like a hive at swarming time.

Though none of them knew me, no one made any attempt to ask my business or to stop me as I moved from room to room in search of Paul. Everywhere there were placards with Cave's picture on them, calm and gloomy-looking, dressed in what was to be his official costume, dark suit, unfigured tie, white shirt. I tried to overhear conversations as I passed the busy desks and groups of excited debaters, but the noise was too loud. Only one word was identifiable, sounding regularly, richly emphatic like a cello note: Cave, Cave, Cave.

In each room I saw piles of my Introduction, which pleased me even though I had come already to dislike it.

The last room contained Paul, seated behind a desk with a Dictaphone in one hand, three telephones on his desk (none fortunately ringing at this moment) and four male and female attendants with notebooks and pencils eagerly poised. Paul sprang from his chair when he saw me. The attendants fell back. "Here he is!" He grabbed my hand and clung to it vise-like. I could almost feel the energy pulsing in his fingertips, vibrating through his body; his heartbeat was obviously two to my every one.

"Team, this is Eugene Luther."

The team was properly impressed and one of the girls, slovenly but intelligent-looking, said, "It was you who brought me here. First you I mean . . . and then of course Cave."

I murmured vaguely and the others told me how "clear" I had made all philosophy in the light of Cavesword. (I believe it was that day, certainly that week, Cavesword was coined by Paul to denote the entire message of John Cave to the world.)

Paul then shooed the team out with instructions that he was not to be bothered. The door, however, was left open.

"Well, what do you think of them?" He leaned back, beaming at me from his chair.

"They seem very . . . earnest," I said, wondering not only what I was supposed to think but, more to the point, what I *did* think of the whole business.

"I'll say they are! I tell you, Gene, I've never seen anything like it. The thing's bigger even than that damned crooner I handled . . . you know the one. Everyone has been calling up and, look!"

He pointed to several bushel baskets containing telegrams and letters. "This is only a fraction of the response since the telecast. From all over the world. I tell you, Gene, we're in."

"What about Cave? Where is he?"

"He's out on Long Island. The press is on my tail trying to interview him but I say no, no go, fellows, not yet. And does that excite them! We've had to hire guards at the place on Long Island just to keep them away."

"How is Cave taking it all?"

"In his stride, absolute model of coolness, which is more than I am. He agrees that it's better to keep him under wraps while the telecasts are going on. It means that curiosity about him will increase like nobody's business. Look at this." He showed me a proof sheet of a tabloid story: "Mystery Prophet Wows TV Audience," with a photograph of Cave taken from the telecast and another one showing Cave ducking into a taxi, his face turned away from the camera. The story seemed most provocative and, for that complacent tabloid, a little bewildered.

"Coming out Sunday," said Paul with satisfaction. "There's also going to be coverage from the big circulation media. They're going to monitor the next broadcast even though we said nobody'd be allowed on the set while Cave was speaking." He handed me a bundle of manuscript pages bearing the title "Who Is Cave?" "That's the story I planted in one of the slick magazines. Hired a name writer, as you can see, to do it." The name writer's name was not known to me, but presumably it would be familiar to the mass audience.

"And, biggest of all, we got a sponsor. We had eleven offers already and we've taken Dumaine Chemicals. They're paying us enough money to underwrite this whole setup here, and pay for Cave and me as well. It's terrific but dignified. Just a simple 'through the courtesy of' at the beginning and another at the end of each telecast. What do you think of that?"

"Unprecedented!" I had chosen my word some minutes before.

"I'll say. By the way, we're getting a lot of letters on that book of yours." He reached in a drawer and pulled out a manila folder which he pushed toward me. "Take them home if you like. Go over them carefully, might give you some ideas for the next one, you know—ground which needs covering."

"Is there to be a next one?"

"Man, a flock of next ones! We've got a lot to do, to explain. People want to know all kinds of things. I'm having the kids out in the front office do a breakdown on all the letters we've received, to get the general reaction, to find what it is people most want to hear; and, believe me, we've been getting more damned questions, and stuff like, 'Please, Mr. Cave, I'm married to two men and feel maybe it's a mistake since I have to work nights anyway,' Lord, some of them are crazier than that."

"Are you answering all of them?"

"Oh, yes, but in my name. All except a few of the most interesting which go to Cave for personal attention. I've been toying with the idea of setting up a counselor service for people with problems."

"But what can *you* tell them?" I was more and more appalled.

"Everything in the light of Cavesword. You have no idea how many questions that answers. Think about it and you'll see what I mean. Of course we follow standard psychiatric procedure, only it's speeded up so that after a couple of visits there can be a practical and inspirational answer to their problems. Stokharin said he'd be happy to give it a try, but we haven't yet worked out all the details."

I changed the subject. "What did you have in mind for me to do?"

"Cavesword applied to everyday life."He spoke without hesitation; he had thought of everything. "We'll know more what people want to hear after a few more telecasts, after more letters and so on. Then supply Cavesword where you can and, where you can't, just use common sense and standard psychiatric procedure."

"Even when they don't always coincide?"

Paul roared with laughter. "Always the big knocker, Gene. That's what I like about you, the disapproving air. It's wonderful. I'm quite serious. People like myself . . . visionaries, you might say, continually get their feet off the ground and it's people like you who pull us back, make us think. Anyway, I hope you'll be able to get to it soon. We'll have our end taken care of by the time the telecasts are over."

"Will you show Cave to the world then? I mean in person?"

"I don't know. By the way, we're having a directors' meeting Friday morning. You'll get a notice in the mail. One of the things we're going to take up is just that problem, so you be thinking about it in the meantime. I have a hunch it may be smart to keep him away from interviewers for good."

"That's impossible."

"I'm not so sure. He's pretty retiring except when he speaks. I I don't think he'd mind the isolation one bit. You know how dull he gets in company when he's not performing."

"Would he consent?"

"I think we could persuade him. Anyway, for now he's a mystery man. Millions see him once a week but no one knows him except ourselves. A perfect state of affairs, if you ask me."

"You mean there's always a chance he might make a fool of himself if a tough interviewer got hold of him?"

"Exactly, and believe me there's going to be a lot of them after his scalp."

"Have they begun already?"

"Not yet. We have you to thank for that, too, making it so clear that though what we say certainly conflicts with all the churches we're really not competing with them, that people listening to Cavesword can go right on being Baptists and so on."

"I don't see how, if they accept Cave."

"Neither do I, but for the time being that's our line."

"Then there's to be a fight with the churches?"

Paul nodded grimly. "And it's going to be a honey. People don't take all the supernatural junk seriously these days but they do go for the social idea of the church, the uplift kind of thing. That's where we'll have to meet them, where we'll have to lick them at their own game."

I looked at him for one long moment. I had of course anticipated something like this from the moment that Cave had become an organization and not merely one man talking. I had realized that expansion was inevitable. The rule of life is more life and of organization more organization, increased dominion. Yet I had not suspected Paul of having grasped this so promptly, using it so firmly to his and our advantage. The thought that not only was he cleverer than I had realized but that he might, indeed, despite his unfortunate approach, be even cleverer than myself, disagreeably occurred to me. I had until then regarded myself as the unique intellectual of the Cavites, the one sane man among maniacs and opportunists. It seemed now that there were two of us with open eyes and, of the two, he alone possessed ambition and energy.

"You mean this to be a religion, Paul?"

He smiled, "Maybe, yes . . . something on that order perhaps. Something workable, though, for now. I've thought about what you said the other night."

"Does Cave want this?"

Paul shrugged. "Who can tell? I should think so but this is not really a problem for him to decide. He has happened. Now *we* respond. Stokharin feels that a practical faith, a belief in ways of behavior which is the best modern analysts are agreed on as being closest to ideal, might perform absolute miracles. No more guilt feeling about sex if Cave were to teach that all is proper when it does no harm to others . . . and the desire to do harm to others might even be partly removed if there were no false mysteries, no terrible warnings in childhood and so on. Just in that one area of behavior we could work wonders! Of course there would still be problems, but the main ones could be solved if people take to Cave and to us. Cavesword is already known and it's a revelation to millions . . . we know that. Now they are looking to him for guidance in other fields. They know about death at last. Now we must tell them about living and we are lucky to have available so much first-rate scientific research in the human psyche. I suspect we can even strike on an ideal behavior pattern by which people can measure themselves."

"And to which they will be made to conform?" Direction was becoming clear already.

"How can we force anyone to do anything? Our whole power is that people come to us, to Cave, voluntarily because they feel here, at last, is the answer." Paul might very well have been sincere. There is no way of determining, even now.

"Well, remember, Paul, that you will do more harm than good by attempting to supplant old dogmas and customs with new dogmas. It will be the same in the end except that the old is less militant, less dangerous than a new order imposed by enthusiasts."

"Don't say 'you.' Say 'we.' You're as much a part of this as I am. After all, you're a director. You've got a say-so in these matters. Just speak up Friday." Paul was suddenly genial and placating. "I don't pretend I've got all the answers. I'm just talking off the top of my head, like they say."

A member of the team burst into the office with the news that Bishop Winston was outside.

"Now it starts," said Paul with a grimace.

The Bishop did not recognize me as we passed one another in the office. He looked grim and he was wearing clerical garb.

"He's too late," said a lean youth, nodding at the churchman's back.

"Professional con men," said his companion with disgust. "They've had their day."

And with that in my ears, I walked out into the snow-swirling street; thus did Cave's first year begin.

I was more alarmed than ever by what Paul had told me and by what I heard on every side. In drugstores and bars and restaurants, people talked of Cave. I could even tell when I did not hear the name that it was of him they spoke: a certain intentness, a great curiosity, a wonder. In the bookstores, copies of my Introduction were displayed together with large blown-up photographs of Cave.

Alone in a bar on Madison Avenue where I'd taken refuge from the cold, I glanced at the clippings Paul had given me. There were two sets. The first were the original perfunctory ones which had appeared. The reviewers, knowing even less philosophy than I, tended to question my proposition that Cavesword was anything more than a single speculation in a rather large field. I had obviously not communicated his magic, only its record which, like the testament of miracles, depends entirely on faith: to inspire faith one needed Cave himself.

"What do you think about the guy?" The waiter, a fragile Latin with parchment-lidded eyes, mopped the spilled gin off my table (he'd seen a picture of Cave among my clippings).

"It's hard to say," I said. "How does he strike you?"

"Boy, like lightning!" The waiter beamed. "Of course I'm Catholic but this is something new. Some people been telling me you can't be a good Catholic and go for this guy. But why not? I say. You still got Virginmerry and now you got him, too, for right now. You ought to see the crowd we get here to see the TV when he's on. It's wild."

It was wild, I thought, putting the clippings back into the

folder. Yet it might be kept within bounds. Paul had emphasized my directorship, my place in the structure. Well, I would show them what should be done or, rather, *not* done.

Then I went out into the snow-dimmed street and hailed a cab. All the way to Iris's apartment I was rehearsing what I would say to Paul when next we met. "Leave them alone," I said aloud. "It is enough to open the windows."

"Open the windows!" The driver snorted. "It's damn near forty in the street."

FOUR

Iris occupied several rooms on the second floor of a brownstone in a street with, pleasantest of New York anachronisms, trees. When I entered, she was doing yoga exercises on the floor, sitting crosslegged on a mat, her slender legs in a leotard and her face flushed with strain. "It just doesn't work for me!" she said and stood up without embarrassment.

Since I'd found the main door unlocked, I had opened this one too, without knocking.

"I'm sorry, Iris, the downstairs door was . . ."

"Don't be silly." She rolled up the mat efficiently. "I was expecting you but I lost track of time . . . which means it must be working a little. I'll be right back." She went into the bedroom and I sat down, amused by this unexpected side to Iris. I wondered if perhaps she was a devotee of wheat germ and mint tea as well. She claimed not. "It's the only real exercise I get," she said, changed now to a heavy robe that completely swathed her figure as she sat curled up in a great armchair, drinking Scotch, as did I, the winter outside hid by drawn curtains, by warmth and light.

"Have you done it long?"

"Oh, off and on for years. I never get anywhere but it's very restful and I've felt so jittery lately that anything which relaxes me . . ." her voice trailed off idly. She seemed relaxed now.

"I've been to see Paul," I began importantly.

"Ah."

But I could not, suddenly, generate sufficient anger to speak out with eloquence. I went around my anger stealthily, a murderer stalking his victim. "We disagreed."

"In what?"

"In everything, I should say."

"That's so easy with Paul." Iris stretched lazily; ice chattered in her glass; a car's horn melodious and foreign sounded in the street below. "We need him. If it weren't Paul, it might be someone a great deal worse. At least he's intelligent and devoted. That makes up for a lot."

"I don't think so. Iris, he's establishing a sort of supermarket, short-order church for the masses."

She laughed delightedly. "I like that! And, in a way, you're right. That's what he *would* do left to himself."

"He seems in complete control."

"Only of the office. John makes all the decisions."

"I wish I could be sure of that."

"You'll see on Friday. You'll be at the meeting, won't you?"

I nodded. "I have a feeling that between Paul and Stokharin this thing is going to turn into a world-wide clinic for mental health."

"I expect worse things *could* happen, but Paul must still contend with me and you and of course the final word is with John."

"How is Cave, by the way?"

"Quite relaxed, unlike the rest of us. Come out to Long Island and see. I go nearly every day for a few hours. He's kept completely removed from everyone except the servants and Paul and me."

"Does he like that?"

"He doesn't seem to mind. He walks a good deal . . . It's a big place and he's used to the cold. He reads a little, mostly detective stories . . . and then of course there's the mail that Paul sends on. He works at that off and on all day. I help him and when we're stuck (you should see the questions!) we consult Stokharin, who's very good on some things, on problems . . ."

"And a bore the rest of the time."

"That's right," Iris giggled. "I couldn't have been more furious the other night, but, since then, I've seen a good deal of him and he's not half bad. We've got him over the idea that John should become a lay analyst. The response to the telecast finally convinced Stokharin that here was a 'racial folk father figure' . . . his very own words. Now he's out to educate the father so that he will fulfill his children's needs on the best Jungian lines."

"Does Cave take him seriously?"

"He's bored to death with him. Stokharin's the only man who's ever had the bad sense to lecture John . . . who absolutely hates it. But he realizes that Stokharin's answers to some of the problems we're confronted with are ingenious. All that . . . hints to the love-lorn is too much for John, so we need Stokharin to take care of details."

"I hope Cave is careful not to get too involved."

"John's incorruptible. Not because he is so noble or constant but because he can only think a certain way and other opinions, other evidence, don't touch him."

I paused, wondering if this was true. Then: "I'm going to make a scene on Friday. I'm going to suggest that Paul is moving in a dangerous direction, towards organization and dogma, and that if something is not done soon we'll all be ruined by what we most detest, a militant absolutist doctrine."

Iris looked at me curiously. "Tell me, Gene, what *do* you want? Why are you still with Cave, with all of us, when you so apparently dislike the way we are going? You've always been perfectly clear about what you did *not* want (I can recall, I think, every word you said at the farm that night), but to be specific, what would you like all this to become? How would you direct things if you could?"

I had been preparing myself for such a question for several months, I still had no single answer to make which would sharply express my own doubts and wishes. But I made an attempt. "I would not organize, for one thing. I'd have Cave speak regularly, all he likes, but there would be no Cavite, Inc., no Paul planting articles and propagandizing. I'd keep just Cave, nothing more. Let him do his work. Then, gradually, there will be effects, a gradual end to superstition . . ."

Iris looked at me intently. "*If* it were possible, I would say we should do what you suggest, but it would be ruinous not only for us but for everyone . . ."

"Why ruinous? A freedom to come to a decision on one's own without . . ."

"That's it. No one can be allowed that freedom. One doesn't

need much scholarship or even experience to see that. Everywhere people are held in check by stifling but familiar powers. People are used to tyranny. They expect governments to demand their souls, and they have given up decisions on many levels for love of security. What you suggest is impossible with this race at this time."

"You're talking nonsense. After all, obeisance to established religions is the order of the day, yet look at the response to Cave, who is undermining the whole Christian structure."

"And wait until you see the fight they're going to put up!" said Iris grimly. "Fortunately, Cavesword is the mortal blow though Cave himself would be their certain victim if he were not protected, if there were no organization to guard him and the Word."

"So Paul and his—his team, his proselytizers are to become merely an equivalent power, combating the old superstitions with their own weapons."

"More or less, yes. That's what it has come to."

"Even though Cave's talking to the people would be enough? Let them use him, not he them."

"A good slogan," Iris smiled. "But I think I'm right. No one would have a chance to see or hear him if it weren't for Paul. You should read the threatening letters we've been getting."

"I thought all the mail was most admiring?"

"All that came from people who've actually *heard* him, but there's a lot coming in now from religious fanatics. They are very extreme. And of course the churches, one by one, are starting to take notice.

"I saw Bishop Winston in Paul's office today."

"He's been trying to see John all week. He finally settled for Paul, I gather. In any case, after the next telecast there will really be a storm."

"The next? What's going to happen then?"

"John will tell them that there's no need for the churches, that their power derives from superstition and bloody deeds."

I was startled. "When did this occur to him? I thought he intended to go on as he was, without ever coming out openly against them."

"I was surprised too. He told me yesterday: he'd been brooding all day and, suddenly, he started to attack them. It's going to be murderous."

"I hope not for him."

"Oh, he'll convince, I'm sure of that. But their revenge . . ." She gave a troubled sigh. "Anyway, Gene, you do see why we can't, for our own safety, dispense with Paul and his financiers and press agents and all the squalid but necessary crew."

"It may be too late," I agreed. "But I fear the end."

"No one can tell. Besides, as long as you and I are there with John it will be all right."

I felt her confidence was not entirely justified, but I determined to defer my attack on Paul's methods until a safer time.

We argued about the wisdom of the coming telecast. Was it really necessary to confront the enemy explicitly? and in his own country, so to speak? Iris was not sure, but she felt Cave's instinct was right even though he had, perhaps, been goaded into action sooner than anticipated by the harsh letters of Christian zealots.

And then by slow degrees, by careful circling, the conversation grew personal.

"I've never told anyone else," said Iris, looking at me speculatively.

"Don't worry: I haven't repeated any of it." And, as always at such times, I feel a warm flood of guilt. Any direct statement of personal innocence has always made me feel completely criminal.

"But since I've told you, I . . . it's a relief to have someone I can talk to about John. I don't dare mention his name to my family, to my old friends. I don't think they even know that I know him."

"I thought it has all been in the papers."

"I haven't been mentioned but, after Friday, everyone will know. Paul says there's no way for us to duck inquiries. After the directors' meeting he'll issue a statement naming directors, stockholders and so on."

"But even then, why should anyone suspect you were interested in Cave or he in you? It's possible merely to be a director, isn't it?"

Iris shrugged. "You know how people are. Clarissa keeps wanting to have what she calls a comfy chat about *everything* and I keep putting her off. Stokharin now takes it for granted that John and I sleep together, that he is the father image to me and I the mother to him."

It had an odd ring to it and I laughed. "Do you think that's a sound Jungian analysis?"

Iris smiled faintly. "Whatever it is, the feeling, such as it is, is all on my side."

"He shows no sign of returning your affection?"

"None at all. He's devoted to me, I think. He relies on my judgment. He trusts me, which is more than he does anyone else I know of . . ."

"Even me?" Always the "I" coming between me and what I wished to know: that insatiable, distressing "I".

"Yes, even you, dear, and Paul too. He's on guard against everyone, but not in a nasty or suspicious way. He . . . what is the phrase? he keeps his own counsel."

"And you are the counsel?"

"In a sense, and nothing more."

"Perhaps you should give up. It would seem that . . . love was not possible for him. If so, it's unwise for you to put yourself in such a position . . . harmful, too."

"But there's still the other Cave. I love him as well and the two are, finally, the same."

"A *metaphysique*?"

"No, or at least I don't see a paradox. It's something else; it's like coming out of an illness with no past at all, only a memory of pain and dullness which soon goes in the wonderful present."

"It?"

"My love is *it*." Her voice grew strong. "I've learned that in loving him I love life, which I never did before. Why I can even value others now, value all those faceless creatures whom I knew without ever bothering to see, to bring in focus the dim blurs of all *that* world alive. I lived asleep. Now I am awake."

"He does not love you."

"Why should he? It's gone beyond that. I'm no longer the scales most lovers are, weighing the deeds and gifts and treasures proffered against those received or stolen from the other, trying always to bring into fatal balance two separate things. I give myself and what I take is life, the knowledge that there is another creature in the world whose wonder, to me at least, is all satisfying by merely being."

"Is it so terrible to be alive?"

"Beyond all expectation, my poor friend." And then I left her to return to winter, to the snow-filled streets and my old pain.

FIVE

The second telecast had the anticipated effect. The day after, Friday, nearly a hundred thousand letters and telegrams had been received, and Cave's life had been threatened four times over the telephone.

I was awakened at five o'clock on Friday morning by a newspaperman begging an interview. Half asleep, irritably, I told him to go to hell and hung up though not before I'd heard the jeer: "Thought you fellows did away with hell." This woke me up and I made coffee, still keeping my eyes half shut in the dim winter light, hoping sleep might return to its accustomed perch; but more telephone calls demoralized my fragile ally and I was left wide awake, unshaven, with fast-beating heart beside the telephone, drinking coffee.

Every few minutes there was a call from some newspaperman or editor requesting information. They had all been shocked by the telecast. When I told them to get in touch with Cave himself, or at least with Paul's office, they only laughed. Thousands were trying to speak to Paul, tens of thousands to Cave; the result was chaos. Shakily, I took the phone off its hook and got dressed. When I opened my door to get the morning paper, a thin young man leaped past me into my living room and anchored himself to a heavy chair.

"What . . ." I began; he was only too eager to explain the what and the why.

"And so," he ended, breathlessly, "the *Star* has authorized me to advance you not only *that* money but expenses, too, for an exclusive feature on Cave and the Cavites."

"I wish," I said, very gentle in the presence of such enthusiasm, "that you would go away. It's five in the morning . . ."

"You're our only hope," the boy wailed. "Every paper and news service has been trying to get past the gate out on Long Island for three weeks and failed. They couldn't even shoot him at long range."

"Shoot him?"

"Get a picture. Now please . . ."

"Paul Himmell is your man. He's authorized to speak for Cave. He has an office in the Empire State Building and he keeps respectable hours; so why don't you . . ."

"We haven't been able to get even a release out of him for three days now. It's censorship, that's what it is."

I had to smile. "We're not the government. Cave is a private citizen and this is a private organization. If we choose not to give interviews you have no right to pester us."

"Oh, come off it." The young man was at an age where the needs of ambition were often less strong than the desire for true expression; for a moment he forgot that he needed my forebearance and I liked him better. "This is the biggest news that's hit town since V-E Day. You guys have got the whole country asking questions and the big one is: who is Cave?"

"There'll be an announcement today, I think, about the company. As for Cave, I suggest you read a little book called 'An Introduction to . . .' "

"Of course I've read it. That's why I'm here. Now, please, Mr. Luther, give me an exclusive even if you won't take the *Star's* generous offer. At least tell me something I can use."

I sat down heavily; a bit of coffee splattered from cup to saucer to the back of my hand and dried stickily. I felt worn out already, the day only just begun. "What do you want me to tell you? What would you most like to hear? What do you expect me to say since, being a proper journalist, that is what you'll write no matter what I tell you?"

"Oh, that's not true. I want to know what Cave's all about as a person, as a teacher."

"Well, what do *you* think he's up to?"

"Me? Why . . . I don't know. I never heard him on the air until last night. It was strong stuff."

"Were you convinced?"

"In a way, yes. He said a lot of things I agreed with but I was a little surprised at his going after the churches. Not that I like anything about *them*, but still it's some stunt to get up and talk like that in front of millions of people. I mean you just don't say those things any more, even if you do think them . . . can't offend minorities. That's what you learn first in journalism school."

"There's part of your answer then. Cave is a man who, unlike others, says what he thinks is true even if it makes him unpopular. There's some virtue in that."

"I guess he can afford to in his position," said the boy vaguely. "You know we got Bishop Winston to answer him for the *Star*. Signed him last night after Cave went off the air. I'm sure he'll do a good job. Now . . ."

We wrestled across the room. Since I was the stronger, I won my privacy though muffled threats of exposure were hurled at me from behind the now-bolted door.

Acting on an impulse, I left the apartment as soon as I was sure my visitor had gone. I was afraid that others would try to find me if I stayed home; fears which were justified. According to the elevator man, he had turned away several men already. The one who did get through had come up the fire escape.

I walked quickly out into the quiet street, the snow now gone to slush as gray as the morning sky. Fortunately, the day was neither windy nor cold and I walked to a Times Square Automat for an early breakfast.

I was reassured by anonymity. All around me sleepy men and women clutching newspapers, briefcases and lunch boxes sat sullenly chewing their breakfast, sleep not yet departed.

I bought a roll, more coffee, hominy grits, which I detested in the North but occasionally tried in the hope that, by accident, I might stumble upon the real thing. These were not the real thing and I left them untouched while I read my paper.

Cave was on the front page. Not prominent but still he was there. The now-standard photograph looked darkly from the page. The headline announced that: "Prophet Flays Churches as Millions Listen." There followed a paraphrase of the telecast which began with those fateful and soon to be famous words: "Our quarrel is not with Christ but with his keepers." I wondered, as I read, if anyone had ever taken one of the telecasts down in shorthand and made a transcript of it. I, for one should have been curious to see in cold print one of those sermons. Cave himself knew that without his presence they would not stand up, and he allowed none of them to be transcribed. As a result, whenever there was a report of one of his talks it was, necessarily, paraphrased, which gave a curious protean flavor to his doctrine, since the recorded style was never consistent, changing always with each paraphraser just as the original meaning was invariably altered by each separate listener as he adapted the incantation to his private needs.

A fat yellow-faced woman sat down with a groan beside me and began to ravish a plate of assorted cakes. Her jaws grinding, the only visible sign of life, for her eyes were glazed from sleep and her body, incorrectly buttoned into a cigarette-ash-dusted dress, was as still as a mountain; even the work of lungs was obscured by the torpid flesh.

I watched her above the newspaper, fascinated by the regularity with which jaws ground bits of cake. Her eyes looked past me into some invisible world of pastry.

Then, having finished the report on Cave's telecast, I put the newspaper down and ate with deliberate finesse my own biscuit. The rustling of the newspaper as it was folded and placed on the table disturbed my companion and, beneath the fat, her will slowly sent out instructions to the extremities. She cleared her throat. The chewing stopped. A bit of cake was temporarily lodged in one cheek, held in place by a sturdy plate. She squinted at the newspaper. "Something about that preacher fellow last night?"

"Yes. Would you like to see it?" I pushed the paper toward her.

She looked at the picture, carefully spelling out the words of the headlines with heavy lips and deep irregular breaths. "Did you see him last night?" she asked when her eye finally got to the small print where it stopped, as though halted by a dense jungle.

"Yes. As a matter of fact, I did."

"He sure gave it to them bastards, didn't he?" Her face lit up joyously. I thought of *ça ira*.

"You mean the clergy?"

"That's just what I mean. They had it too good, too long. People afraid to say anything. Takes somebody like him to tell us what we know and tell *them* where to head in."

"Do you like what he said about dying?"

"About there being nothing? Why, hell, mister, I knew it all along."

"But it's good to hear someone else say it?"

"Don't do no harm." She belched softly. "I expect they're going to be on his tail," she added with gloomy pleasure, spearing a fragment of éclair which she had missed on her first circuit of the crowded dish.

I spent that morning in the street buying newspapers and eavesdropping. I heard several arguments about Cave. The religiously orthodox were outraged but clearly interested. The others were triumphant though all seemed to feel that *they*, as the Automat woman had said, would soon be on his tail. Ours was no longer a country where the nonconformist could escape disaster if he unwisely showed a strange face to the multitude.

I tried to telephone Iris and then Clarissa but both telephones were busy. I rang the office but was told by a mechanical voice that if I left my name and address and business Mr. Himmell would get back to me as soon as possible. The siege had begun.

I arrived at the Empire State Building half an hour before the meeting was to begin, hoping to find out in advance from Paul what was happening and what we were supposed to do about it.

A line of pickets marched up and down before the entrance, waving banners, denouncing Cave and all his works in the names of various religious groups. A crowd was beginning to gather and the police, at least a score, moved frantically about, not certain how to keep the mob out of the building. When I stepped off the elevator at Cave's floor, I found myself a part of a loud and confused mass of men and women all shoving toward the door which was marked Cavite, Inc. Policemen barred their way.

Long before I had got to the door, a woman's shoe went hurtling through the air, smashing a hole in the frosted glass. One policeman cocked his revolver menacingly. Another shouted, "Get the riot squad!" But still the crowd raved and shouted and quarreled. Some wanted to lynch Cave in the name of the Lamb, while others begged to be allowed to touch him, just once. I got to the door at last, thanks to a sudden shove which landed me with a crash into a policeman. He gasped and then, snarling, raised his club. "Business!" I shouted with what breath was left me. "Got business here. Director."

I was not believed but, after some talk with a pale secretary through the shattered glass door, I was admitted. The crowd roared when they saw this and moved in closer. The door slammed shut behind me.

"It's been like this since nine o'clock," said the secretary, looking at me with frightened eyes.

"You mean after two hours the police still can't do anything?"

"We didn't call them right away. When we did it was too late. We're barricaded in here."

But Paul was not in the least disturbed. He was standing by the window in his office looking out. Clarissa, her hat and her hair together awry, a confusion of straw and veil and bolts of reddish hair apparently not all her own, was making up in a pocket mirror.

"Ravenous wild beasts!" she hailed me. "I've seen *their* likes before."

"Gene, good fellow! Got through the mob all right? Here, have a bit of brandy. No? Perhaps some Scotch?"

I said it was too early for me to drink. Shakily, I sat down. Paul laughed at the sight of us. "You both look like the end of the world has come."

"I'd always pictured the end as being quite orderly . . ." I began stuffily, but Doctor Stokharin's loud entrance interrupted me. His spectacles were dangling from one ear and his tie had been pulled around from front to back quite neatly. "No authority!" he bellowed, ignoring all of us. "The absence of a traditional patriarch, the center of the tribe, has made them insecure. Only together do they feel warmth in great *swarming* hives!" His voice rose sharply and broke on the word "hives" into a squeak. He took the proffered brandy and sat down, his clothes still dis-arranged.

"My hair," said Clarissa grimly, "will never come out right again today." She put the mirror back into her purse, which she closed with a loud snap. "I don't see, Paul, why you didn't have the foresight to call the police in advance and demand protection."

"I had no idea it would be like this. Believe me, it's not deliberate." But from Paul's excited chuckling, I could see that he was delighted with the confusion, a triumph of the publicist's dark art. I wondered if he might not have had a hand in it. It was a little reminiscent of the crowds of screaming women which in earlier decades, goaded by publicists, had howled and, as Stokharin would say, swarmed about singers and other theatrical idols.

Paul anticipated my suspicions. "Didn't have a thing to do with it, I swear. Doctor, your tie is hanging down your back."

"I don't mind," said Stokharin disagreeably, but he did adjust his glasses.

"I had a feeling we'd have a few people in to see us but no idea it would be like this." He turned to me as the quietest, the least dangerous of the three. "You wouldn't believe the response to last night's telecast if I told you."

"Why don't you tell me?" The comic aspects were becoming apparent: Stokharin's assaulted dignity and the ruin of Clarissa's ingenious hair both seemed to me suddenly funny. I tried not to smile. Paul named some stupendous figures with an air of triumph. "And there are more coming all the time. Think of that!"

"Are they favorable?"

"Favorable? Who cares?" Paul was pacing the floor quickly, keyed to the breaking point had he possessed the metabolism of a normal man. "We'll have a breakdown over the weekend. Hired more people already. Whole bunch working all the time. By the way, we're moving."

"Not a moment too soon," said Clarissa. "I suggest, in fact, we move now while there are even these few police to protect us. When they go home for lunch (they all eat enormous lunches, one can tell), that crowd is going to come in here and throw us out the window."

"Or suffocate us with love," said Paul.

Stokharin looked at Clarissa thoughtfully; with his turned-around necktie he had a sacerdotal look. "Do you often think of falling from high places? of being pushed from windows or perhaps high trees?"

"Only when I'm on a top floor of the world's highest building surrounded by raving maniacs do such forebodings occur to me, Doctor. If you had any sense of reality you might be experiencing the same fear."

Stokharin clapped his hands happily. "Classic, classic. To believe she alone knows reality. Madam, I suggest that you . . ."

There was a roar of sound from the hallway; a noise of glass shattering; a revolver went off with a sharp report and, frozen with alarm, I waited for its echo. There was none; only shouts of Cave! Cave! Cave!

Surrounded by police, Cave and Iris were escorted into the office. More police held the door, aided by the office crew who, suddenly inspired, were throwing paper cups full of water into the crowd. Flashbulbs like an electric storm flared in all directions as the newspapermen invaded the office, let in by the police who could not hold them back.

Iris looked frightened and even Cave seemed alarmed by the rioting.

Once the police lieutenant had got Cave and Iris into the office, he sent his men back to hold the corridor. Before he joined them he said sternly, breathing hard from the struggle, "We're going to clear the hall in the next hour. When we do we'll come and get you people out of here. You got to leave whether you want to or not. This is an emergency."

"An hour is all we need, officer." Paul was smooth. "And may I say that my old friend the Commissioner is going to hear some extremely nice things about the efficiency and good sense of his men." Before the lieutenant had got around to framing a suitably warm answer, Paul had maneuvered him out of the inner office; and locked the door behind him.

"There," he said, turning to us, very business like. "It was a mistake meeting here after last night. I'm sorry, Cave."

"It's not your fault." Cave, having found himself an uncomfortable straight chair in a corner of the room, sat very erect, like a child in serious attendance upon adults. "I had a hunch we should hold the meeting out on Long Island."

Paul scowled. "I hate the idea of the press getting a look at you. Spoils the mystery effect. But it was bound to happen. Anyway you won't have to talk to them."

"Oh, but I will," said Cave easily, showing who was master here, this day.

"But . . . well, after what we decided, the initial strategy being . . ."

"No. It's all changed now. I'll have to face them, at least this once. I'll talk to them the way I always talk. They'll listen," His voice grew dreamy. He was indifferent to Paul's opposition.

"Did you find a new place?" asked Iris, suddenly, to divert the conversation.

"What? Oh yes. A whole house, five stories on East Sixty-first Street. Should be big enough. At least for now." The interoffice communicator sounded. Paul spoke quickly into it: "Tell the newspaper people to wait out there. We'll have a statement in exactly an hour and they'll be able . . ." he paused and looked at Cave for some reprieve; seeing none, he finished: "They'll be able to interview Cave." He flipped the machine off. Through the locked door, we heard a noise of triumph from the gathered journalists and photographers.

"Well, come along," said Clarissa. "I thought this was to be a board of directors' meeting. Cave, dear, you've got to preside."

But, though he said he'd rather not, Clarissa, in a sudden storm of legality, insisted that he must. She also maliciously demanded a complete reading of the last meeting's minutes by Paul, the secretary. We were able to save him by a move to waive the reading, which was proposed, recorded and passed by a show of hands, only Clarissa dissenting. Cave conducted the meeting solemnly. Then Clarissa demanded a report from the treasurer and this time Paul was not let off.

For the first time I had a clear picture of the company of which I was a director. Shares had been sold. Control was in the hands of Clarissa, while Paul and several West Coast industralists whose names were not familiar to me also owned shares. The main revenue of the company now came from the sponsor of Cave's television show. There was also a trickle of contributions which, in the last few weeks, had increased considerably.

Then Paul read from a list of expenses, his voice hurrying a little over his own salary, which was, I thought, too large. Cave's expenses were recorded and, with Clarissa goading from time to time, Paul gave an accounting of all that had been spent since the arrival in New York. John Cave was a big business.

"The books are audited at standard intervals," said Paul, looking at Clarissa as he finished, some of his good humor returning. "We will not declare dividends unless Mrs. Lessing insists the company become a profit-making enterprise."

"It might not be a bad idea," said Clarissa evenly. "Why not get a little return . . ."

But Paul had launched into policy. We listened attentively. From time to time, Cave made a suggestion. Iris and I made no comment. Stokharin occasionally chose to illuminate certain human problems as they arose and Paul, at least, heard him out respectfully. Clarissa wanted to know all about costs and her interruptions were always brief and shrewd.

Several decisions were made at that meeting. It was decided

that a Center be established where Dr. Stokharin could minister to those Cavites whose problems might be helped by therapy. "We just apply classical concepts to their little troubles," he said.

"But it shouldn't *seem* like a clinic," said Iris suddenly. "It's all part of John, of what John says."

"We'll make that perfectly clear," said Paul quickly.

Stokharin nodded agreeably. "After all, it is in his name they come to us. We take it from there. No more problems . . . all is contentment." He smacked his lips.

It was then decided that Cave would spend the summer quietly and, in the autumn, begin a tour of the country to be followed by more telecasts in the following winter. "The summer is to think a little in," were Cave's words.

Next, I was assigned the task of writing a defense of Cave for certain vast syndicates. I was also requested to compose a set of dialogues which would record Cave's views on such problems as marriage, the family, world government, problems all in urgent need of solution. I suggested diffidently that it would be very useful if Cave were to tell me what he thought about such things before I wrote my dialogues. Cave said, quite seriously, that we would have the summer in which to handle all these subjects.

Paul then told us the bad news; there was a good deal of it. "The Cardinal, in the name of all the Diocesan Bishops, has declared that any Catholic who observes the telecasts of John Cave or attends in person his blasphemous lectures commits a mortal sin. Bishop Winston came to tell me that not only is he attacking Cave in the press but that he is quite sure, if we continue, the government will intervene. It was a hint, and not too subtle."

"On what grounds intervene?" asked Cave. "What have I done that breaks one of their laws?"

"They'll trump up something," said Clarissa.

"I'm afraid you're right. They can always find something to get us on."

"But can they?" I asked. "Free speech is still on the books."

Paul chuckled. "That's just where it stays, too." And he quoted the national credo: In a true democracy there is no place for a serious difference of opinion on great issues. "Sooner or later they'll try to stop Cave."

"But they can't!" said Iris. "The people won't stand for it."

"He's the father of too many now," said Stokharin sagely. "No son will rise to dispute him, yet."

"Let's cross that bridge when we come to it." Paul was reasonable. "Now let's get a statement ready for the press."

While Paul and Cave worked over the statement, the rest of us chatted quietly about other problems. Stokharin was just about to explain the origin of alcoholism in terms of the new Cavite pragmatism when Iris said, "Look!" and pointed to the window where, bobbing against the glass, was a bright red child's balloon on which had been crudely painted, "Jesus Saves."

Stokharin chuckled when he saw it. "Very ingenious. Someone gets on the floor beneath and tries to shake us with his miracle. Now we produce the counter-miracle." He slid the window open. The cold air chilled us all. He took his pipe and touched its glowing bowl to the balloon, which exploded loudly; then he shut the window beaming. "It will be that easy," he said. "I promise you. a little fire, and pop! these superstitions disappear like bad dreams."

EIGHT

ONE

The six months after the directors' meeting were full of activity and danger. Paul was forced to hire bodyguards to protect Cave from disciples as well as from enemies, while those of us who were now known publicly to be Cave's associates were obliged to protect our privacy with unlisted telephone numbers and numerous other precautions, none of which did much good, for we were continually harassed by madmen and interviewers.

The effect Cave had made on the world was larger than even Paul, our one optimist, had anticipated. I believe even Cave himself was startled by the vastness and the variety of the response.

As I recall, seldom did a day pass without some new exposé or interpretation of this phenomenon. Bishop Winston attacked after nearly every telecast. The Catholic Church invoked its entire repertory of anathemas and soon it was whispered in devout Christian circles that the Antichrist had come at last, sent to test the faith. Yet, despite the barrage of attacks, the majority of those who heard Cave became his partisans and Paul, to my regret but to the delight of everyone else, established a number of Cavite Centers in the major cities of the United States, each provided with a trained staff of analysts who had also undergone an intensive indoctrination in Cavesword. Stokharin headed these clinics. Also at Cave's suggestion, one evening a week, the same evening, Cavites would gather to discuss Cavesword, to meditate on the beauty of death, led in their discussions and meditations by a disciple of Cave who was, in the opinion of the directors, equal to the task of representing Cave and his Word.

Iris was placed in charge of recruiting and training the proselytizers, while Paul handled the business end, obtaining property in different cities and managing the large sums which poured in from all over the world. Except for Cave's one encounter with the press that day in the Empire State Building (an occasion which, despite its ominous beginning, became a rare triumph: Cave's magic had worked even with the hostile), he was seen by no one except his intimates and the technicians at the television studio. Ways were found to disguise him so that he would not be noticed in the lobbies or elevators of the television network building. Later he spoke only from his Long Island retreat, his speeches recorded on film in advance.

By summer there were more than three million registered Cavites in the United States and numerous believers abroad. Paul was everywhere at once; flying from city to city (accompanied by two guards and a secretary); he personally broke ground in Dallas for what was to be the largest Cavite Centre in the United States; and although the inaugural ceremonies were nearly stopped by a group of Baptist ladies carrying banners and shouting "Onward Christian Soldiers," no one was hurt and the two oil millionaires who had financed the Centre gave a great barbecue on the foundation site.

Iris was entirely changed by her responsibilities. She had become, in the space of a few months, brisk and energetic, as deeply involved in details as a housewife with a new home. I saw very little of her that spring. Her days were mostly spent in a rented loft in the Chelsea district, where she lectured the candidates for field work and organized a makeshift system of indoctrination for potential Residents, as the heads of the various centers were known.

Iris was extraordinarily well fitted for this work, to my surprise, and before the year ended she had what was in fact a kind of university where as many as three hundred men and women at a time were transformed into Residents and Deputy Residents and so on down through an ever proliferating hierarchy. For the most part, the first men and women we sent out to the country were highly educated, thoughtful people, entirely devoted to Cavesword. They were, I think, the best of all, for later, when it became lucrative to be a Resident, the work was largely taken over by energetic careerists whose very activity and competence diminished their moral effectiveness.

Iris used me unmercifully those first months. I lectured her students. I taught philosophy until in exasperation at the absurdity of *that*, I told her to hire a professional teacher of philosophy, which she did.

Yet I enjoyed these men and women. Their sincerity and excitement communicated itself to me and I became aware of something I had known before only from reading, from hearsay: the religious sense which I so clearly lacked, as did both Paul and Stokharin. I don't think Cave really possessed it either because although he believed entirely in himself and in the miraculous truth of his Word, he did not possess that curious power to identify himself with creation, to transcend the self in contemplation of an abstraction, to sacrifice the personality to a mystical authority; none of us, save Iris in love, possessed this power which, as nearly as I can get at it, is the religious sense in man. I learned about it only from those who came to learn from us in that Chelsea loft. In a sense I pitied them, for I knew that much of what they evidently believed with such passion was wrong. But at the same time, I was invigorated by their enthusiasm, by the hunger with which they devoured Cavesword, by the dignity their passion lent to an enterprise that in Paul's busy hands resembled, more often than not, a cynical commercial venture. And I recognised in them (oh, very early, perhaps in the first weeks of talking to them) that in their goodness and their love they would, with Cavesword, smudge each bright new page of life as it turned; yet, suspecting this, I did not object nor did I withdraw. Instead, fascinated, I was borne by the tide to the shore whose every rock I could imagine, sharp with disaster.

Once a week the directors met on Long Island in the walled estate where Cave now lived with his guards. The meetings soon demonstrated a division in our ranks; between Paul and Stokharin on the one side and Iris, Clarissa and Cave on the other with myself as partisan, more often than not, to Cave. The division was amiable but significant. Paul and Stokharin wanted to place the Centers directly under the supervision of the analysts, while the rest of us, led by Iris (Cave seldom intervened, but we had already accepted the fact that Iris spoke for him), preferred that the Centers be governed by the Residents. "It is certainly true that the therapists are an important part of each Center," said Iris briskly, at the end of a long wrangle with Stokharin. "But these are *Cavite* Centers and not clinics for the advancement of Jungian analysis. It is Cavesword which draws people to the Centers, not mental illness. Those who have problems are of course helped by Stokharin's people but, finally, it is Cave who has made it possible for them to face death. Something no one has done before." And thus the point was won in our council, though Stokharin and Paul were still able at times, slyly, to insinuate their own creatures into important Residencies.

My own work went on fitfully. I composed an answer to Bishop Winston which brought down on my head a series of ecclesiastical thunderbolts, each louder than the one before. I wrote a short life of Cave in simple declarative sentences which enjoyed a considerable success for many years and, finally, seriously, in my first attempt at a true counter attack, I began the several dialogues in which Cave and I purportedly traversed the entire field of moral action.

I felt that in these dialogues I could quietly combat those absolutist tendencies which I detected in the disciples. Cave himself made no pretense of being final on any subject other than death, where, even without his particular persuasiveness, he stood on firm, even traditional ground. The attacks he received he no longer noticed. It was as simple as that. He had never enjoyed reading, and to watch others make telecasts bored him, even when they spoke of him. After the fateful Empire State Building conference he ceased to attend the world; except for a few letters which Paul forwarded to him and his relations with us, he was completely cut off from ordinary life, and perfectly happy. For though human contacts had been reduced to a minimum, he still possessed the polished glass eye of the world before whose level gaze he appeared once a week and experienced what he called "Everyone. All of them, listening and watching everywhere."

In a single year Cave had come a long way from the ex-embalmer who had studied a book of newspaper clippings on a Washington farm and brooded about an old man in a hospital. Though Paul was never to refer again to the victim of Cave's driving, I was quite sure that he expected, sooner or later, that mysterious death would return to haunt us all.

By midsummer, Cave had grown restless and bored, and since the telecasts had been discontinued until the following November, he was eager to travel. He was never to lose his passion for places. It was finally decided that he spend the summer on one of the Florida Keys, a tiny island owned by a Cavite who offered to place everything at the master's disposal. And, though warned that the heat might be uncomfortable, Cave and his retinue left secretly one night by chartered seaplane from Long Island Sound and for at least a month the press did not know what had happened to him.

I declined to accompany Cave and Iris. Paul remained in New York, while Iris's work was temporarily turned over to various young enthusiasts trained by her. I went back to the Hudson Valley, to my house and . . .

TWO

I have not been able to write for several days. According to the doctor it is a touch of heat, but I suspect that this is only his kind euphemism.

I had broken off in my narrative to take a walk in the garden last Friday afternoon when I was joined by Butler, whose attentions lately had been more numerous than I should like.

"He'll be here Sunday, Hudson. Why don't we all three have dinner together that night and celebrate."

I said that nothing could give me more pleasure, as I inched along the garden path, moving toward the hot shaded center where, beneath fruit trees, a fine statue of Osiris stood, looted in earlier days by the hotel management from one of the temples. I thought, however, with more longing of the bench beside the statue than of the figure itself, whose every serene detail I had long since memorized. Butler adjusted his loose long stride to my own uneven pace. I walked as I always do now, with my eyes upon the ground, nervously avoiding anything which might make me stumble, for I have fallen down a number of times in the last few years and I have a terror of broken bones, the particular scourge of old bodies.

I was as glad as not that I didn't have to watch my companion while we chatted, for his red honest face, forever dripping sweat, annoyed me more than was reasonable.

"And he'll be pleased to know I've got us a Center. Not much of one but good enough for a start."

I paused before a formidable rock that lay directly in my path. It would take some doing to step over it, I thought, as I remarked, "I'm sure the Pasha doesn't know about this."

"Not really." Butler laughed happily. "He thinks we're just taking a house for ourselves to study the local culture. Later, after we get going, he can find out."

"I'd be very careful," I said and, very careful myself, I stepped over the rock; my legs detested the extra exertion; one nearly buckled as it touched the ground. I threw my weight on my cane and was saved a fall. Butler had not noticed.

"Jessup is going to bring in the literature. We'll say it's our library. All printed in Arabic, too. The Dallas Center thinks of everything."

"Are they . . . equipped for such things?"

"Oh yes. That's where the main university is now. Biggest one in the world. I didn't go there myself. Marks weren't good enough, but Jessup did. He'll tell you all about it. Quite a crew they turn out: best in the business, but then they get the cream of the crop to begin with."

"Tell me, are the Residents still in charge of the Centers or do they share the administration with the therapists?"

"Therapists?" Butler seemed bewildered.

"In the old days there used to be the Resident and his staff and then a clinic attached where . . ."

"You really are behind the times." Butler looked at me as though I'd betrayed a firsthand knowledge of earth's creation. "All Residents and their staffs, including the Communicators like myself, get the same training; part of it is in mental therapy. Those who show particular aptitude for therapy are assigned clinical work just as I do communication work in foreign countries. People who get to be Residents are usually teachers and administrators. Sometimes a Communicator will even get a Residency in his old age as a reward for the highest services." He then explained to me the official, somewhat Byzantine, structure of the Cavites. There were many new titles, indicating a swollen organization under the direction of a Counsel of Residents which, in turn, was responsible for the election from among their number of a unique Chief Resident whose reign lasted for the remainder of his lifetime.

With relief, I sat down on the bench beside Osiris. Butler joined me. "Dallas of course is the main Residency," he said.

"It used to be in New York, years ago," I said, thinking of the brownstone house, of the loft on Twenty-third Street.

"Around twenty years ago it was moved to Dallas by the Chief Resident. Not only did they have the best-equipped Center there but the Texans make just about the best Cavites in the country. What they won't do for Cavesword isn't worth mentioning. They burned the old churches, you know . . . every one in the state."

"And one or two Baptist ministers as well?"

"You can't break eggs without making an omelet," said Butler sententiously.

"I see what you mean. Still, Cave was against persecution. He always felt it was enough for people to hear Cavesword . . ."

"You got a lot of reading to do," said Butler sharply. "Looks like you've forgotten your text: 'And, if they persist in superstition, strike them, for one idolator is like a spoiled apple in the barrel, contaminating the others,' " Butler's voice, as he quoted, was round and booming, rich in vowel sounds, while his protruding eyes gazed without blinking into the invisible radiance of truth which hovered, apparently, above a diseased hibiscus bush.

"I've forgotten that particular quotation," I said.

"Seems funny you should, since it's just about the most famous of the texts." But, though my ignorance continued to startle Butler, I could see that he was beginning to attribute it to senility rather than to laxity or potential idolatry.

"I was a close follower in the first few years," I said, currying favor. "But I've been out of touch since and I suppose that after Cave's death there was a whole mass of new doctrine with which I am unfamiliar, to my regret."

"Doctrine!" Butler was shocked. "We have no doctrine. We are not one of those heathen churches with claims to 'divine' guidance. We're simply listeners to Cavesword. That's all. He was the first to tell the plain truth and naturally we honor him, but there is no doctrine even though he guides us the way a good father does his children."

"I am very old," I said in my best dying-fall voice. "You must remember that when you are with me you are in the company of a man who was brought up in the old ways, who uses Christian terms from time to time. I was thirty when Cave began his mission. I am, as a matter of fact, nearly the same age as Cave himself if he were still alive."

That had its calculated effect. Butler looked at me with some awe. "Golly!" he said. "It doesn't really seem possible, does it?

Of course there're still people around who were alive in those days, but I don't know of anybody who actually *saw* Cave. You did tell me you saw him?"

"Once only."

"Was he like the telecasts?"

"Oh yes. Even more effective, I think."

"He was big of course, six feet one inch tall."

"No, he was only about five feet eight inches, a little shorter than I . . ."

"You must be mistaken because, according to all the texts, he was six feet one."

"I saw him at a distance, of course. I was only guessing." I was amused that they should have seen fit to change even Cave's stature.

"You can tell he was a tall man from the telecasts."

"Do they still show them?"

"Still show them! They're the main part of our weekly Get-togethers. Each Residency has a complete library of Cave's telecasts, one hundred and eight including the last. Each week, a different one is shown by the Resident's staff, and the Resident himself or someone assigned by him discusses the message."

"And they still hold up after fifty years?"

"Hold up? We learn more from them each year. You should see all the books and lectures on Cavesword . . . several hundred important ones which we have to read as part of our communication duties, though they're not for the laymen. We discourage nonprofessionals from going into such problems, much too complicated for the untrained mind."

"I should think so. Tell me, is there any more trouble with the idolators?"

Butler shook his head. "Just about none. They were licked when the parochial schools were shut down. That took care of Catholicism. Of course there were some bad times. I guess you know all about them."

I nodded. Even in Egypt I had heard of massacres and persecutions. I could still recall the morning when I opened the Cairo paper and saw a large photograph of St. Peter's smoldering in its ruins, a fitting tomb for the last Pope and martyr who had perished there when a mob of Cavites had fired the Vatican. The Cairo paper took an obvious delight in these barbarities and I had not the heart to read of the wanton destruction of works of

Michelangelo and Bernini, the looting of the art galleries, the bonfire which was made in the Papal gardens of the entire Vatican library. Later, word came of a certain assistant Resident of Topeka who, with a group of demolition experts and Cavite enthusiasts, ranged across France and Italy destroying the cathedrals with the approval of the local governments, as well as the Cavite crowds who gathered in great numbers to watch, delightedly, the crumbling of these last monuments to superstition. Fortunately, the tourist bureaus were able to save a few of the lesser churches.

"The Edict of Washington which outlawed idolatrous schools did the trick. The Atlantic Community has always believed in toleration. Even to this day it is possible for a man to be a Christian, though unlikely since the truth is so well known."

"But the Christian has no churches left and no clergy."

"True, and if that discourages him he's not likely to remain too long in error. As I've told you, though, we have our ways of making people see the truth."

"The calculable percentage."

"Exactly."

I looked at Osiris in the green shade. His diorite face smiled secretly back at me. "Did you have much trouble in the Latin countries?"

"Less than you might think. The ignorant were the big problem because, since they didn't know English, we weren't able to use the telecasts. Fortunately, we had some able Residents and after a little showmanship, a few miracles (or what they took to be miracles), they came around, especially when many of their ex-priests told them about Cavesword. Nearly all of the older Residents in the Mediterranean countries were once Catholic priests."

"Renegades?"

"They saw the truth. Not without some indoctrination, I suspect. We've had to adapt a good many of our procedural methods to fit local customs. The old Christmas has become Cavesday and what was Easter is now Irisday."

"Iris Mortimer?"

"Who else? And then certain festivals which . . ."

"I suppose she's dead now."

"Why, yes. She died six years ago. She was the last of the Original Five."

"Ah, yes, the five: Paul Himmell, Iris Mortimer, Ivan Stokharin, Clarissa Lessing and . . ."

"And Edward Hastings. We still use his Introduction even though it's been largely obsoleted by later texts. His dialogues will of course be the basis for that final book of Cave, which our best scholars have been at work on for over twenty years."

Hastings, of all people! I nearly laughed aloud. Poor feckless Hastings was now the author of *my* dialogues with Cave. I marveled at the ease with which the innumerable references to myself had been deleted. I began to doubt my own existence. I asked if Hastings was still alive and was told that he too was long dead.

I then asked again about Iris.

"Some very exciting things have come to light," said Butler. "Certain historians at the Dallas Center feel that there is some evidence that she was Cave's sister."

I was startled by this. "How could that be? Wasn't she from Detroit? and wasn't he from Seattle? and didn't they meet for the first time in southern California at the beginning of his mission?"

"I see you know more Cavite history than you pretend," said Butler amiably. "That of course has been the traditional point of view. Yet as her influence increased in the world (in Italy, you know, one sees her picture nearly as often as Cave's) our historians became suspicious. It was all perfectly simple, really. If she could exert nearly the same power as Cave himself then she must, in some way, be related to him. I suppose you know about the Miami business. No? Well, their Resident, some years ago, openly promulgated the theory that Cave and Iris Mortimer were man and wife. A great many people believed him and though the Chief Resident at Dallas issued a statement denying the truth of all this, Miami continued in error and it took our indoctrination team several years to get the situation back to normal. But the whole business *did* get everyone to thinking and, with the concurrence of Dallas, investigations have been made. I don't know many of the details but my colleague probably will. He keeps track of that kind of thing."

"If she is proven to be Cave's sister will she have equal rank with him?"

"Certainly not. Cavesword is everything. But she will be equal to him on the human level though his inferior in truth. At least that appears to be the Dallas interpretation."

"She was very active, I suppose?"

"Right until the end. She traveled all over the world with Cavesword and, when she grew too old to travel, she took over the Residency of New York City, which she held until she died. As a matter of fact, I have a picture of her which I always carry. It was taken in the last years." He pulled out a steel-mesh wallet in which, protected by cellophane, was a photograph of Iris, the first I had seen in many many years. My hand shook as I held the picture up to the light.

For a split second I felt her presence, saw in the saddened face, framed by white hair, my summer love which had never been except in my own dreaming where I was whole and loved this creature whose luminous eyes had not altered with age, their expression the same as that night beside the western sea. But then my fingers froze. The wallet fell to the ground. I fainted into what I supposed with my last vestige of consciousness to be death, to be nothing.

THREE

I awakened in my own bed with my old friend Dr. Riad beside me. He looked much concerned while, at the foot of the bed, stood Butler, very solemn and still. I resolved not to die with him in the room.

"My apologies, Mr. Butler," I said, surprised that I could speak at all. "I'm afraid I dropped your picture." I had no difficulty in remembering what had happened. It was as if I had suddenly shut my eyes and opened them again, several hours having passed instead of as many seconds. Time, I decided, was all nonsense.

"Think nothing of it. I'm only . . ."

"You must not strain yourself, Mr. Hudson," said the doctor. A few days in bed, plenty of liquids, a pill or two, and then I was left alone with a buzzer beside my bed which would summon the houseboy if I should have a coherent moment before taking a last turn for the worse. The next time, I think, will be the final one and though I detest the thought, these little rehearsals over the last few years—the brief strokes, the sudden flooding of parts of the brain with the blood of capillaries in preparation for that last arterial deluge—have got me used to the idea. My only complaint is that odd things are done to my memory by these strokes which, light as they have been, tend to alter those parts of the brain which hold the secrets of the past. I have found this week, while convalescing from Tuesday's collapse, that most of my childhood has been washed clean out of my memory. I knew of course that I was born on the banks of the Hudson but I cannot for the life of me recall what schools I attended; yet memories from college days on seem unimpaired, though I have had to reread this memoir attentively to resume my train of thought, to refresh a dying memory. It is strange indeed to have lost some twenty years as though they had never been and, worse still, to be unable to find out about oneself in any case, since the will of others has effectively abolished one. I do not exist in the world and very soon (how soon I wonder?), I shall not exist even to myself, only this record a fragile proof that I once lived.

Now I am able to work again. Butler pays me a daily visit, as does the doctor. Both are very kind but both tend to treat me as a thing which no longer matters. I have been written off in their minds. I'm no longer really human since soon, perhaps in a few days, I shall not be one of them but one of the dead whose dust motes the air they breathe. Well, let it come. The fraternity of the dead, though nothing, is the larger kingdom.

I am able to sit up in bed (actually I can get around as well or as badly as before but it tires me too much to walk so I remain abed). Sunday is here at last, and from the excited bustle in the air, which I feel rather than hear, Butler's colleague must have arrived. I am not ready for him yet and I have hung a "Do Not Disturb" sign on the door, composed emphatically in four languages. It should keep them out for a few days.

I have a premonition of disaster which, though it is no doubt perfectly natural at my age with the last catastrophe almost upon me, seems to be of a penultimate nature, a final *human* crisis. All that I have heard from Butler about this young man, this colleague of his, disposes me to fear him. For although my existence has been kept a secret from the newer generations, the others, the older ones, the chief counselors are well aware of me. Though I have so far evaded their agents and though they undoubtedly assume that I am long since dead, it is still possible that a shrewd young man with a career in the making might grow suspicious, and one word to the older members of the hierarchy would be enough to start an inquisition which could end in assassination (ironic that I should fear *that* at this point!) or, more terrible, in a course of indoctrination where my apostasy would be reduced by drugs to conformity. It would be the most splendid triumph for Cave, if, in my last days, I should recant. The best victory of all, the surrender of the original lutherist upon his deathbed.

Yet I have a trick or two up my sleeve and the game's not yet over. Should the new arrival prove to be the one I have so long awaited, I shall know how to act. I have planned for this day. My adversary will find me armed.

But now old days draw me back: the crisis approaches in my narrative.

FOUR

The first summer was my last on the Hudson, at peace. Iris wrote me regularly from the Florida Keys. Short, brisk letters completely impersonal and devoted largely to what "he" was doing and saying. It seems that "he" was enchanted by the strangeness of the Keys, yet was anxious to begin traveling again. With some difficulty, I gathered between the lines, Iris had restrained him from starting out on a world tour. "He says he wants to see Saigon and Samarkand and so forth soon because he likes the names. I don't see how he can get away yet, though maybe in the fall after his tour. They say now he can make his talks on film all at once, which will mean of course he won't have to go through anything like last winter again." There followed more news, an inquiry into my health (in those days I was confident I should die early of a liver ailment; my liver now seems the one firm organ in my body; in any case, I enjoyed my hypochondria) and a reference to the various things I was writing for the instruction of converts and detractors both. I pushed the letter away and looked out across the river.

I was alone, awaiting Clarissa for tea. I had actually prepared tea since she never drank alcohol and I myself was a non-drinker that summer when my liver rested (so powerful is imagination) like a brazen cannonball against the cage of bones.

I sat on my porch, which overlooked the lawn and the water; unlike most other houses on that river, mine had the railroad behind it instead of in front of it, an agreeable state of affairs; I don't mind the sound of trains but the sight of their tracks depresses me.

Beside me, among the tray of tea things, the manuscript of my dialogue lay neglected. I had not yet made up my mind whether or not to read it to Clarissa. Such things tended to bore her; yet, if she could be enticed into attention, her opinion would be useful. Such a long memory of old customs would be invaluable to me as I composed, with diligence rather than inspiration, an ethical system whose single virtue was that it tended to satisfy the needs of human beings as much as was possible without inviting chaos. I had, that morning over coffee, abolished marriage. During lunch, served me by my genteel but impoverished housekeeper (although servants still existed in those days in a few great houses, people like myself were obliged to engage the casual services of the haughty poor), I decided to leave marriage the way it was but make divorce much simpler. After lunch, suffering from a liver-inspired headache, I not only abolished marriage again but resolutely handed the children over to the impersonal mercies of the state.

Now, bemused, relaxed, my eyes upon the pale blue Catskills and the summer green, ears alert to the noise of motorboats like great waterbugs, I brooded upon the implications of what I was doing and, though I was secretly amused at my own confidence, I realized, too, that what I felt and did and wrote, though doubtless unorthodox to many, was, finally, not really the work of my own inspiration but a logical result of all that was in the world. A statement of the dreams of others which I could formulate only because I shared them. Cave regarded his own words as revelation when, actually, they only echoed the collective mind, a plausible articulation of what most men felt even though their conscious minds were corseted and constricted by familiar ways of thinking, often the opposite of what they truly believed.

Yet at this step I hesitated. There was no doubt that the children and the society would be the better for such an arrangement . . . and there was little doubt that our civilization *was* moving toward such a resolution. But there were parents who would want to retain their children and children who might be better cared for by their progenitors than by even the best-intentioned functionaries of the state. Would the state allow parents to keep their children if they wanted them? If not, it was tyrannous; if so, difficult in the extreme, for how could even the most enlightened board of analysts determine who should be allowed their children and who not? The answer, of course, was in the retraining of future generations. Let them grow up accepting as inevitable and right the surrender of babies to the state. Other cultures had done it and ours could too. But I was able to imagine, vividly, the numerous cruelties which would be perpetrated in the name of the whole, while the opportunity for tyranny in a civilization where all children were at the disposal of a government brought sharply to mind that image of the anthill society which has haunted the imagination of the thoughtful for at least a century.

I had got myself into a most gloomy state by the time Clarissa arrived, trailing across the lawn in an exotic ankle-length gown of gray which floated in yards behind her, like the diaphanous flags of some forgotten army.

"Your lawn is full of moles!" she shouted to me, pausing in her progress and scowling at a patch of turf. "And it needs cutting and more clover. *Always* more clover, remember that." She turned her back on me to stare at the river, which was as gray as her gown but, in its soft tidal motion, spangled with light like sequins on a vast train.

She had no criticism of the river when she at last turned and climbed the steps to the porch; she sat down with a gasp. "I'm boiling! Tea? Hot tea to combat the heat."

I poured her a cup. "Not a hot day at all." Actually it was very warm. "If you didn't get yourself up as a Marie Corelli heroine, you'd be much cooler."

"Not very gallant today, are we?" Clarissa looked at me over her cup. "I've had this gown for five hundred years. There used to be a wimple, but I lost it moving."

"The material seems to be holding up quite well," and now

that she had mentioned it, there *was* an archaic look to the texture of the gown, like those bits of cloth preserved under glass in museums.

"Silk lasts indefinitely, if one is tidy. Also I don't wear this much, as you can see, but with the devalued state of the dollar (an ominous sign, my dear, the beginning of the end!) I've been forced to redo a lot of old odds and ends I've kept for sentimental reasons. This is one of them and I'm very fond of it." She spoke deliberately, to forestall any further ungallantry.

"I just wondered if it was cool."

"It is cool. Ah, a letter from Iris." Clarissa had seen the letter beside my chair and, without asking permission, had seized it like a magpie and read it through quickly. "I admire a girl who types," she said, letting fall the letter. "I suppose they all do now though it seems like only yesterday that, if one did not open a tearoom, one typed, working for men, all of whom made advances. That was when we had to wear corsets and hatpins. One discouraged while the other protected." Clarissa chuckled at some obscene memory.

"I wonder if Paul can keep Cave from wandering off to some impossible place."

"I shouldn't be surprised." She picked at the tea sandwiches suspiciously, curling back the top slices of bread to see what was underneath. Tentatively, she bit into deviled ham; she chewed; she swallowed; she was not disappointed. She wolfed another sandwich, talking all the while. "Poor Cave is a captive now. His disciples are in full command. Even Mohammed, as strong-headed as he was, finally ended up a perfect pawn in the hands of Abu Bekr and the women, especially the women."

"I'm not so sure about Cave. He . . ."

"Does what they tell him, especially Iris."

"Iris? But I should have said she was the only one who ***never*** tried to influence him."

Clarissa laughed unpleasantly. A moth flew into her artificial auburn hair. Unerringly, she found it with one capable hand and quickly snuffed out its life in a puff of gray dust from broken wings. She wiped her fingers on a paper napkin. The day was full of moths, but none came near us again. "You are naïve, Eugene," she said, her little murder done. "It's your nicest quality. In theory you are remarkably aware of human character; yet, when you're confronted with the most implausible appearance, you promptly take it for the reality."

I was irritated by this and also by the business of the sandwich, not to mention the murder of the moth. I looked at Clarissa with momentary dislike. "I was not aware . . ." I began, but she interrupted me with an airy wave of her hand.

"I forgot no one likes to be called naïve. Calculating, dishonest, treacherous—people rather revel in those designations, but to be thought trusting. . ."She clapped her hands as though to punctuate her meaning; then, after a full stop, she went on more soberly. "Iris is the one to look out for. Our own sweet, self-effacing, dedicated Iris. I adore her. I always have, but she's up to no good."

"I don't know what you're talking about."

"You will. You would if you weren't entirely blind to what they used to call human nature. Iris is acquiring Cave."

"Acquiring?"

"Exactly the word. She loves him for all sorts of reasons but she cannot have him in the usual sense (I found out all about that, by the way). Therefore, the only thing left for her to do is acquire him, take his life in hers. You may think *she* may think that her slavish adoration is only humble love, but actually it's something far more significant, and dangerous."

"I don't see the danger, even accepting your hypothesis."

"It's no hypothesis and the danger is real. Iris will have him, and, through him, she'll have you all."

I did not begin to understand that day, and Clarissa, in her pythoness way, was no help, muttering vague threats and imprecations with a mouth full of bread.

After my first jealousy at Iris's preference of Cave to me, a jealousy which I knew, even at the time, was unjustified and a little ludicruous, I had come to accept her devotion to Cave as a perfectly natural state of affairs. He was an extraordinary man and though he did not fulfill her in the usual sense, he gave her more than a mere lover might. He gave her a whole life and I envied her for having been able to seize so shrewdly upon this unique way out of ordinary life and into something more grand, more strange, more engaging. Though I could not follow her, I was able to appreciate her choice and admire the completeness of her days. That she was obscurely using Cave for her own ends, subverting him, did not seem possible, and I was annoyed by Clarissa's dark warnings. I directed the conversation into other waters.

"The children. I haven't decided what to do with them."

Clarissa came to a full halt. For a moment she forgot to chew. Then, with a look of pain, she swallowed. "*Your* children?"

"Any children, all children." I pointed to the manuscript on the table.

She understood. "I'm quite sure you have abolished marriage."

"As a matter of fact, yes, this morning."

"And now you don't know what to do about the children."

"Precisely. I . . ."

"Perfectly simple." Clarissa was brisk. This, apparently, was a problem she had already solved. "The next step is controlled breeding. Only those whose blood lines seem promising should be allowed to procreate. Now that oral contraceptives are so popular no one will make babies by accident . . . in fact, it should be a serious crime if someone does."

"Quite neat, but I wonder whether, psychologically, it's simple. There's the whole business of instinct, of the natural desire of a woman to want her own child after bearing it."

"All habit . . . not innate. Children have been subordinate woman's weapon for centuries. They have had to develop certain traits which in other circumstances they would not have possessed. Rats, whom we closely resemble, though they suckle their young will, in moments of mild hunger or even exasperation, think nothing of eating an entire litter. You can condition human beings to accept any state of affairs as being perfectly natural."

"I don't doubt that. But how to break the habits of several thousand years?"

"I suppose there *are* ways. Look what Cave is doing. Of course making death popular is not so difficult since, finally, people want it to be nice.They do the real work or, rather, their terror does. In place of superstition, which they've nearly outgrown, he offers them madness."

"Now really, Clarissa . . ."

"I don't disapprove. I'm all for him, as you know. To make death preferable to life is of course utter folly but still a perfectly logical reaction for these poor bewildered savages who, having lost their old superstitions, are absolutely terrified at the prospect of nothing. They want to perpetuate their little personalities forever into space and time and now they've begun to realize the folly of that (who, after all, are they—are *we*—in creation?), they will follow desperately the first man who pulls the sting of death and Cave is that man, as I knew he would be."

"And after Cave?"

"I will not say what I see. I'm on the side of change, however, which makes me in perfect harmony with life." Clarissa chuckled. A fish leaped grayly in the river; out in the channel a barge glided by, the muffled noise of its engines like slow heartbeats.

"But you think it good for people to follow Cave? You think what he says is right?"

"Nothing is good. Nothing is right. But though Cave is wrong, it is a *new* wrong and so it is better than the old; in any case, he will keep the people amused, and boredom, finally, is the one monster the race will never conquer . . . the monster which will devour us in time. But now we're off the track. Mother love exists because we believe it exists. Believe it does not exist and it won't. That, I fear, is the general condition of the 'unchanging human heart.' Make these young girls feel that having babies is a patriotic duty as well as healthful therapy and they'll go through it blithely enough, without ever giving a second thought to the child they leave behind in the government nursery."

"But to get them to that state of acceptance . . ."

"Is the problem. I'm sure it will be solved in a few generations."

"You think I'm right to propose it?"

"Of course. It will happen anyway."

"Yet I'm disturbed at the thought of all that power in the hands of the state. They can make the children believe anything. Impose the most terrible tyranny. Blind at birth so that none might ever see anything again but what a few rulers, as ignorant as they, will want them to see. There'll be a time when all people are alike."

"Which is precisely the ideal society. No mysteries, no romantics, no discussions, no persecutions because there's no one to persecute. When all have received the same conditioning, it will be like . . ."

"Insects."

"Who have existed longer than ourselves and will outlast our race by many millennia."

"Is existence everything?"

"There is nothing else."

"Then likeness is the aim of human society?"

"Call it harmony. You think of yourself only as you are now dropped into the midst of a society of dull conformists. That's where you make your mistake. You'll not live to see it, for if you did, you would be someone else, a part of it. No one of your disposition could possibly happen in such a society. There would be no rebellion against sameness because difference would not, in any important sense, exist, even as a proposition. You think: how terrible! But think again how wonderful it would be to belong to the pack, to the tribe, to the race, without guilt or anxiety or division."

"I cannot imagine it."

"No more can they imagine you."

"This will happen?"

"Yes, and you will have been a part of it."

"Through Cave?"

"Partly, yes. There will be others after him. His work will be distorted by others, but that's to be expected."

"I don't like your future, Clarissa."

"Nor does it like *you*, my dear. The idea of someone who is irritable and at odds with society, bitter and angry, separate from others. I shouldn't wonder but that you yourself might really be used as a perfect example of the old evil days."

"Virtue dies?"

"Virtue becomes the property of the race."

"Imagination is forbidden?"

"No, only channeled for the good of all."

"And this is a desirable world, the future you describe?"

"Desirable for whom? For you, no. For me, not really. For the people in it? Well, yes and no. They will not question their estate but they will suffer from a collective boredom which . . . but my lips are sealed. Your tea was delicious though the bread was not quite fresh. But then bachelors never keep house properly. I've gone on much too long. Do forget everything I've said. I am indiscreet. I can't help it." She rose, a cloud of gray suspended above the porch. I walked her across the lawn to the driveway where her car was parked. The breeze had died for the moment and the heat prickled me unpleasantly; my temples itched as the sweat started.

"Go on with it," she said as she got into her car. "You may as well be on the side of the future as against it. Not that it much matters anyway. When your adorable President Jefferson was in Paris he said. . ." But the noise of the car starting drowned the body of her anecdote. I caught only the end: ". . . that harmony was preferable. We were all amused. I was the only one who realized that he was serious." Dust swirled and Clarissa was gone down the drive at great speed, keeping, I noticed, to the wrong side of the road. I hoped this was an omen.

FIVE

I got through an unusually sultry July without much interference from either Cave or the world. Paul paid me a quick visit to get the manuscript of the dialogues and I was reminded of those accounts of the progresses made by monarchs in other days, or rather of great ministers, for his party occupied four large cars which gleamed side by side in my driveway like glossy beasts while their contents, Paul and fourteen assistants, all strange to me save Stokharin, wandered disconsolately about the lawn until their departure.

Paul, though brisk, was cordial. "Trouble all over the map. But b-i-g t-r-o-u-b-l-e." He spelled it out with relish. Size was important, I knew, to a publicist, even to one turned evangelist.

"Is Cave disturbed by it?"

"Doesn't pay any attention. Haven't seen him but Iris keeps me posted. By the way, we're hiring a plane the first week in August to go see him, Stokharin and me. Want to come along?"

I didn't but I said I would. I had no intention of being left out of anything. There was *my* work still to do.

"I'll let you know details. Is this hot stuff?" He waved the sheaf of papers I'd given him.

"Real hot," I said but my irony was too pale; only primary colors caught Paul's eye.

"I hope so. Got any new stunts?"

I told him, briefly, about my thoughts on marriage, or rather Cave's thoughts. The literary device was for me to ask him certain questions and for him to answer them or at least to ask pointed questions in his turn. Cheerfully, I had committed Cave to my own point of view and I was somewhat nervous about his reaction, not to mention the others'. So far, only Clarissa knew and her approval was pleasant but perhaps frivolous: it carried little weight, I knew, with the rest.

Paul whistled. "You got us a tall order. I'm not sure we'll be able to handle that problem yet, if ever."

"I've done it carefully," I began.

Stokharin, who had been listening with interest, came to my aid. "In the Centers we, how you say, Paul? soft-pedal the family. We advise young boys to make love to the young girls without marrying or having babies. We speak of the family as a mere social unit, and of course society changes. I am most eager to study Mr. Luther's approach. Perhaps a little aid from those of us in clinical work . . ."

But then the dark sedans began to purr; nervous attendants whispered to Paul and I was soon left alone with the fragments of our brief conversation to examine and interpret at my leisure. I was surprised and pleased at Stokharin's unexpected support. I had thought of him as my chief antagonist. But then, my work finished, I tended roses and read Dio Cassius until the summons came in August.

SIX

The plane landed on a glare of blue water, more blinding even than the vivid sky about the sun itself, which made both elements seem to be a quivering blue fire in which was destroyed all of earth save a tiny smear of dusty faded green, the island of our destination.

The pilot maneuvered the plane against a bone-gray dock where, all alone, Iris stood, her hair tangled from the propeller's wind and her eyes hidden by dark glasses. Like explorers in a new country, Paul, Stokharin and I scrambled onto the dock, the heat closing in about us like a blue canvas, stifling, palpable. I gasped and dropped my suitcase. Iris laughed and ran forward to greet us; she came first to me, an action which, even in my dazzled, shocked state, I realized and valued.

"Gene, you must get out of that suit this minute! and get some dark glasses or you'll go blind. Paul, how are you? It's good to see you, Doctor." And, in the chatter of greetings, she escorted us off the dock and across a narrow white beach to a grove of palm trees where the cottage stood.

To our delight, the interior was cooled by machinery. I sank into a wicker chair even as Cave pumped my hand. Iris laughed, "Leave him alone, John. He's smothered by the heat."

"No hat," said Cave solemnly after the first greeting, which, in my relief, I'd not heard. "You'll get sunstroke."

Paul was now in charge. The heat which had enervated both Stokharin and me filled him with maniac energy, like one of those reptiles that absorb vitality from the sun.

"What a great little place, Cave! Had no idea there were all the comforts of home down here, none at all. Don't suppose you go out much?"

Cave, unlike Iris, was not tanned though he had, for him, a good color, unlike his usual sallowness. "I don't get too much sun," he admitted. "We go fishing sometimes, early in the morning. Most of the time I just hang around the house and look at the letters, and read some."

I noticed on the table beside me an enormous pile of travel magazines, tourist folders and atlases. I anticipated trouble.

Paul prowled restlessly about the modern living room with its shuttered sealed windows. Stokharin and I, like fish back in their own element after a brief excursion on land, gasped softly in our chairs while Iris told us of the Keys, and of their fishing trips. She was at her best here as she had been that other time in Spokane. Being out of doors, in Cave's exclusive company, brought her to life in a way the exciting busyness of New York did not. In the city she seemed like an object through which an electric current passed; here on this island, in the sun's glare, she unfolded, petal after petal, until the secret interior seemed almost exposed. I was conscious of her as a lovely woman and, without warning, I experienced desire. That sharp rare longing which, in me, can reach no climax. Always before she had been a friend, a companion whose company I had jealously valued; her attention alone had been enough to satisfy me, but on this day I saw her as a man entire might and I plummeted into despair, talking of Plato.

"Of course there are other ways of casting dialogues, such as introducing the celebrated dead brought together for a chat in Limbo. But I thought that I should keep the talk to only two. Cave and myself . . . Socrates and Alcibiades." Alcibiades was precisely the wrong parallel but I left it uncorrected, noticing how delicately the hollow at the base of Iris's throat quivered with life's blood, and although I attempted, as I often had before with bitter success, to think of her as so much mortal flesh, the body and its beauty pulp and bone, beautiful only to a human eye (hideous, no doubt, to the eye of a geometric progression), that afternoon I was lost and I could not become, even for a moment, an abstract intelligence. Though I saw the bone, the dust, I saw her existing, triumphant in the present. I cursed the flaw in my own flesh and hated life.

"We liked it very much," she said, unaware of my passion and its attendant despair.

"You don't think it's too strong, do you? All morality, not to mention the churches, will be aligned against us."

"John was worried at first . . . not that opposition frightens him and it is *his* idea. I mean you wrote the dialogue but it reflects exactly what he's always thought." Though in love's agony, I looked at her sharply to make certain she was perfectly serious. She was. This helped soothe the pain. She had been hypnotized by Cave. I wondered how Clarissa could ever have thought it was the other way around.

"In a way we're already on record," Iris looked thoughtfully across the room at Cave, who was showing Paul and Stokharin a large map of some strange country. "The Centers have helped a good many couples to adjust to one another without marriage and without guilt."

"But then there's the problem of what to do with the children when the family breaks up."

Iris sighed. "I'm afraid that's already a problem. Our Centers are taking care of a good many children already. A number, of course, go out for adoption to bored couples who need something to amuse them. I suppose we'll have to establish nurseries as a part of each Center until, finally, the government assumes the responsibility."

"*If* it becomes Cavite."

"When it becomes Cavite." She was powerful in her casualness.

"Meanwhile there are laws of adoption which vary from state to state and, if we're not careful, we're apt to come up against the law."

"Paul looks after us," she smiled. "Did you know that he has nearly a hundred lawyers on our payroll? All protecting us."

"From what?" I had not been aware of this.

"Lawsuits. Attempts by state legislatures to outlaw the Centers on the grounds of immorality and so on. The lawyers are kept busy all the time."

"Why haven't I read about any of this in the papers?"

"We've been able to keep things quiet. Paul is marvelous with the editors. Several have even joined us, by the way, secretly, of course."

"What's the membership now?"

Iris gestured. "No one knows. We have thirty Centers in the United States and each day they receive hundreds of new Cavites. I suspect there are at least four million by now."

I gasped, beginning to recover at last from the heat, from my unexpected crisis of love. "I had no idea things were going so fast."

"Too fast. We haven't enough trained people to look after the Centers, and on top of that we must set up new Centers. Paul has broken the country up into districts, all very methodical: so many Centers per district, each with a Resident in charge. Stokharin is taking care of the clinical work."

"Where's the money coming from?"

"In bushels from heaven," Iris smiled. "We leave all that to Paul. I shouldn't be surprised if he counterfeits it. Anyway, I *must* get back to New York, to the school. I shouldn't really have gone off in the middle of everything, but I was tired and John wanted company so I came."

"How is he?"

"As you see, calm. I don't believe he ever considers any of our problems, He never mentions them; never reads the reports Paul sends him; doesn't even read the attacks from the churches. We get several a day, not to mention threatening mail. We now have full-time bodyguards."

"You think people are seriously threatening him?"

"I don't know how serious they are but we can't take chances. Fortunately, almost no one knows we're here and, so far, no cranks have got through from the mainland. Our groceries and mail are brought in by boat every other day from Key Largo. Otherwise, we're perfectly isolated."

I looked about me for some sign of the guards; there was none. A Cuban woman vacuuming in the next room was the only visible stranger.

Cave abandoned his maps and atlases long enough to tell me how much the dialogues pleased him.

"I wish I could put it down like you do. I can only say it when people listen."

"Do you think I've been accurate?"

Cave nodded solemnly. "Oh, yes. It's just like I've always said it, only written down." I realized that he had already assumed full responsibility (and credit, should there be any) for my composition. I accepted his presumption with amusement. Only Stokharin seemed aware of the humor of the situation. I caught him staring at me with a shrewd expression; he looked quickly away, mouth rigid as he tried not to smile. I liked him at that moment. We were the only ones who had not been possessed by Cave. I felt like a conspirator.

For several days we talked, or rather Paul talked. He had brought with him charts and statements and statistics and, though Cave did not bother to disguise his boredom, he listened most of the time and his questions, when they did occur, were apposite. The rest of us were fascinated by the extent of what Paul referred to as the "first operational phase."

Various projects had already been undertaken; others were put up to the directors for discussion. Thanks to Paul's emphatic personality, our meetings were more like those of account executives than the pious foregathering of a messiah's apostles – and already that word had been used in the press by the curious as well as by the devout. Cave was the messiah to several million Americans. But he was not come with fire to judge the world, nor armed with the instruction of a supernatural being whose secret word had been given this favorite son. No, Cave was of another line. That of the prophets, of the teachers like Jesus before he became Christ, or Mohammed before he became Islam. In our age it was Cave's task to say the words all men awaited yet dared not speak or even attend without the overpowering authority of another who had, plausibly, assumed the guise of master. I could not help but wonder as I watched Cave in those heated conferences if the past had been like this.

Cave certainly had one advantage over his predecessors: modern communications. It took three centuries for Christianity to infect the world. It was to take Cave only three years to conquer Europe and the Americas.

But I did not have this foreknowledge in Florida. I only knew that Paul was handling an extraordinary business in a remarkable way. There was no plan so vast that he could not contemplate its execution with ease. He was exhausting in his energy and, though he did not possess much imagination, he was a splendid improviser, using whatever themes were at hand to create his own dazzling contrapuntal effects.

We decided upon a weekly magazine to be distributed gratis to the Cavites (I was appointed editor though the actual work, of which I was entirely ignorant, was to be done by a crew already at work on the first issue). We would also send abroad certain films to be shown by Cavite lecturers. We then approved the itinerary of Cave's national tour in the fall (Cave was most alive during this discussion; suggesting cities he wanted particularly to see, reveling in the euphony of such names as Tallahassee). We also planned several dinners to be held in New York with newspaper editors and political figures, and we discussed the advisability of Cave's accepting an invitation to be questioned by the House Un-American Activities Committee, which had begun to show an interest in the progress of our Centers. It was decided that Cave delay meeting the committee until the time was propitious, or until he had received a subpoena. Paul, with his instinctive sense of the theatrical, did not want to have this crucial meeting take place without a most careful build-up.

We discussed the various steps taken or about to be taken by certain state legislatures against the Centers. The states involved were those with either a predominantlyCatholic or a predominantly Baptist population. Since the Centers had been organized to conform with existing state and federal laws (the lawyers were earning their fees), Paul thought they would have a difficult time in closing any of them. The several laws which had been passed were all being appealed and he was confident of our vindication by the higher courts. Though the entrenched churches were now fighting us with every possible weapon of law and propaganda, we were fully protected, Paul felt, by the Bill of Rights even in its currently abrogated state.

Late in the afternoon after one of the day's conferences had ended, Iris and I swam in the Gulf, the water as warm as blood and the sky soft with evening. We stayed in the water for an hour, not talking, not really swimming, merely a part of the sea and the sky, two lives on a curved horizon, quite alone (for the others never ventured out). Only the bored bodyguard on the dock reminded us that the usual world had not slipped away in a sunny dream, leaving us isolated and content in that sea from which our life had come so long ago. Water to water, I thought comfortably as we crawled up on the beach like new-lunged creatures.

Iris undid her bathing cap and her hair, streaked blonde by the sun (and a little gray as well), fell about her shoulders. She sighed voluptuously. "If it would always be like this."

"If what?"

"Everything."

"Ah," I ran my hand along my legs and crystals of salt glittered and fell; we were both dusted with light. "You have your work," I added with some malice, though I was now under control; my crisis resolved after one sleepless night. I could now look at her without longing, without pain. Regret was another matter but regret was only a distant relative to anguish.

"I have that, too," she said. "The work uses everything while this is a narcotic. I float without a thought or a desire like . . . like an anemone."

"You don't know what an anemone is, do you?"

She laughed like a child. "How do you know I don't?"

"You said it like somebody reading a Latin inscription."

"What is it?"

I laughed, too. "I don't know. Perhaps something like a jellyfish. It has a lovely sound: sea anemone."

We were interrupted by a motorboat pulling into the dock. "It's the mail," said Iris. "We'd better go back to the house." While we collected towels, the guard on the dock helped the boatman unload groceries and mail.

Between a pair of palm trees, a yard from the door of the house, the bomb went off in a flash of light and gray smoke. A stinging spray of sand blinded Iris and me. The blast knocked me off balance and I fell backward onto the beach. For several minutes, I was quite blind, my eyes filled with tears, burned from the coral sand. When I was finally able to see again, Iris was already at the house trying to force open the door.

One of the palm trees looked as if it had been struck by lightning, all its fronds gone and its base smoldering. The windows of the house were broken and I recall wondering, foolishly, how the air conditioning could possibly work if the house was not sealed. The door was splintered and most of its paint had been burned off; it was also jammed, for Iris could not open it. Meanwhile, from a side door, the occupants of the house had begun to appear.

I limped toward the house, rubbing my eyes, aware that my left knee had been hurt. I was careful not to look at either the boatman or the guard, their remains strewn among tin cans and letters in the bushes.

Paul was the first to speak. A torrent of rage which jolted us all out of fear and shock. Iris, after one look at the dead men, fled into the house. I stood stupidly beside the door, rolling my eyes to dislodge the sand.

Then the other guards came with blankets and gathered up the pieces of the two men. I turned away, aware for the first time that Cave was standing slightly apart, nearest the house. He was very pale. He spoke only once, half to himself, for Paul was still ranting." Let it begin," said Cave softly. "Now, now."

NINE

ONE

It began indeed, like the first recorded shot of a war. The day after the explosion, we left the island and Cave was flown to another retreat, this time in the center of New York City where, unique in all the world, there can exist true privacy, even invisibility.

The Cavite history of the next two years is publicly known and the private aspects of it are not particularly revealing. It was a time of expansion and of battle.

The opposition closed its ranks. Several attempts were made on all our lives and, six months after our return from Florida, we were all, except the indomitable Clarissa, forced to move into the brand-new Cavite Center, a quickly built but handsome building of yellow glass on Park Avenue. Here on the top floor, in the penthouse which was itself a mansion surrounded by Babylonian gardens and a wall of glass through which the encompassing city rose like stalagmites, Cave and Paul, Stokharin, Iris and I all lived with our bodyguards, never venturing out of the building, which resembled, during that time, a military headquarters with guards and adjutants and a maze of officials through whom both strangers and familiars were forced to pass before they could meet even myself, not to mention Cave.

In spite of the unnaturalness, it was, I think, the happiest time of my life. Except for brief excursions to the Hudson, I spent the entire two years in that one building, knowing at last the sort of security and serenity which monks must have known in their monasteries. I think the others were also content, except for Cave, who eventually grew so morose and bored by his confinement that Paul not only had to promise him a world tour but for his vicarious pleasure showed, night after night in the Center's auditorium, travel films which Cave devoured with eager eyes, asking for certain films to be halted at various interesting parts so that he might examine some landscape or building (never a human being, no matter how quaint). Favorite movies were played over and over again, long after the rest of us had gone to bed, leaving Cave and the projectionist alone with the bright shadows of distant places, alone save for the ubiquitous guards.

There were a number of attacks upon the building itself, but since all incoming mail and visitors were checked by machinery for hidden weapons, there was never a repetition of that island disaster which had had such a chilling effect on all of us. Pickets of course marched daily for two years in front of the Center's door and, on four separate occasions, mobs attempted to storm the building, only to be repulsed by our guards (the police, for the most part Catholic, did not unduly exert themselves in our defense; fortunately, the building had been constructed with the idea of defense).

The life in the Center was busy. In the penthouse each of us had an office and Cave had a large suite where he spent his days watching television and pondering journeys. He did not follow with much interest the doings of the organization, though he had begun to enjoy reading the attacks which regularly appeared against him in the newspapers. Bishop Winston was the leader of the non-Catholic opposition and his apologias and anathemas inspired us with admiration. He was, I think, conscious of being the last great spokesman of the Protestant churches and he fulfilled his historic function with wit and dignity, and we admired him tremendously. By this time, of course, our victory was in sight and we could show magnanimity to those who remained loyal to ancient systems.

I was the one most concerned with answering the attacks since I was now an editor with an entire floor devoted to the *Cavite Journal* (we were not able to think up a better name). At first, as we had planned, it was published weekly and given away, but after the first year it became a daily newspaper, fat with advertising and sold on newsstands.

Besides my duties as editor, I was the official apologist and I was kept busy composing dialogues on various ethical matters, ranging from the virtues of cremation to fair business practices. Needless to say, I had a good deal of help and some of my most resounding effects were contrived by anonymous specialists. Each installment, however, of Cavite doctrine (or rationalization, as I preferred to think of my work) was received as eagerly by the expanding ranks of the faithful as it was condemned reflexively by the Catholic Church and the new league of Protestant Churches under Bishop Winston's leadership.

We sustained our most serious setback when, in the autumn of our first year in the new building, we were banned from the television networks through a series of technicalities created by Congress for our benefit and invoked without warning. It took Paul's lawyers a year to get the case through the courts, which finally reversed the government's ruling. Meanwhile, we counterattacked by creating hundreds of new Centers where films of Cave were shown regularly. Once a week he was televised for the Centers, where huge crowds gathered to see and hear him and it was always Paul's claim that the government's spiteful action had been responsible for the sudden victory of Cavesword. Not being able to listen to their idol in their own homes, the Cavites and even the merely curious were forced to visit the Centers, where in the general mood of camaraderie and delight in the same Word, they were organized quite ruthlessly. Stokharin's clinics handled their personal problems. Other departments assumed the guidance and even the support, if necessary, of their children, while free medical and educational facilities were made available to all who applied.

At the end of the second year, there were more enrolled Cavites than any other single religious denomination, including the Roman Catholic. I published this fact and the accompanying statistics with a certain guilt which, needless to say, my fellow directors did not share. The result of this revelation was a special Congressional hearing.

In spite of the usual confusion attendant upon any of the vigorous old Congress's hearteningly incompetent investigations, this event was well staged, preparing the way politically, to draw the obvious parallel, for a new Constantine.

It took place in March, and it was the only official journey any of us, excepting Paul, had made from our yellow citadel for two years. The entire proceedings were televised, a bit of unwisdom on the part of the hostile Congressmen, who in their understandable eagerness for publicity, overlooked their intended victim's complete mastery of that art. I did not go to Washington but I saw Cave and Paul and Iris off from the roof of the Center. Because of the crowds which had formed in the streets hoping for a glimpse of Cave, the original plan to fly to Washington aboard a chartered airplane was discarded at the last minute and two helicopters were ordered instead to pick up Cave and his party on the terrace in front of the penthouse, a mode of travel not then popular.

Paul saw to it that the departure was filmed. A dozen of us who were not going stood about among the trees and bushes while the helicopters hovered a few feet above the roof, their ladders dangling. Then Cave appeared with Paul and Iris while a camera crew recorded their farewell and departure. Cave looked as serene as ever, pale in his dark blue suit and white shirt, a small austere figure with downcast eyes. Iris was bright-faced from the excitement and cold, and a sharp wind tangled her hair.

"I'm terrified," she whispered fiercely in my ear as we shook hands for the camera.

"Paul seems in full command," I said, comfortingly. And Paul, not Cave, was making a short speech to the camera while Cave stood alone and still; then, in a gust of wind, they were gone and I went to my office to watch the hearings.

The official reason for the investigation was certain charges made by the various churches that the Cavites were subverting Christian morality by championing free love and publicly decrying the eternal institution of marriage. This was the burden of the complaint against Cave which the committee most wished to contemplate since it was the strongest of the numerous allegations and, in their eyes, the most dangerous to the state, as well as the one most likely to get the largest amount of publicity. For some years the realm of public morals had been a favorite excursion ground for the Congress, and their tournaments at public expense were attended delightedly by everyone. This particular one, affecting as it did the head of the largest single religious establishment in the country, would, the Congressmen were quite sure, prove an irresistible spectacle. It was.

At first there was a good deal of confusion. Newspapermen stumbled over one another; flashbulbs were dropped; Congressmen could not get through the crowd to take their seats. To fill in, while these preliminaries were arranged, the camera was trained upon the crowd which was beginning to gather in front of the Capitol; a crowd which grew, as one watched, to Inaugural size. Though it was orderly, a troop of soldiers in trucks soon arrived as though by previous design, and they formed a cordon of fixed bayonets before the various entrances to the Capitol.

Here and there, against the gusty blue sky, banners with the single word "Cave," gold on blue, snapped. *In hoc signo* indeed!

Then the commentators, who had been exclaiming at some length on the size of the crowd, excitedly announced the arrival of Cave. A roar of sound filled the plaza. The banners were waved back and forth against the sky and I saw everywhere the theatrical hand of Paul Himmell.

The scene shifted to the House of Representatives entrance to the Capitol. Cave, wearing an overcoat but bareheaded, stepped out of the limousine. He was alone. Neither Paul nor Iris was in sight. It was most effective that he should come like this, without equerries or counselors. He stood for a moment in the pillared entrance, aware of the crowd outside; even through the commentator's narrative one could hear, like the surf falling, Cave! Cave! Cave! Cave! For a moment it seemed that he might turn and go, not into the Capitol, but out onto the steps to the crowd. But then the chief of the Capitol guard, sensing perhaps that this might happen, gently steered him up the stairs.

The next shot was of the committee room where the hearings had at last begun. A somewhat phlegmatic Jesuit was testifying. His words were difficult to hear because of the noise in the committee room and the impotent shouts of the chairman. The commentator gave a brief résumé of the Jesuit's attack on Cave and then, in the midst of a particularly loud exchange between the chairman and the crowd, the clerk of the committee announced: "John Cave."

There was silence. The crowd parted to make way for him. Even the members of the committee craned to get a good look at him as he moved quietly, almost demurely, to the witness chair. The only movement in the room was that of the Papal Nuncio, who sat in the front rank of the audience. He crossed himself as Cave passed and shut his eyes.

Cave was respectful, almost inaudible. Several times he was asked to repeat his answers even though the room was remarkably still. At first Cave would answer only in monosyllables, not looking up, not meeting the gaze of his interrogators, who took heart at this, professionals themselves. Their voices, which had almost matched his for inaudibility, began to boom with confidence.

I waited for the lightning. The first intimation came when Cave looked up. For nearly five minutes he had not raised his eyes during the questioning. Suddenly I saw that he was trying to locate the camera. When at last he did, it was like a revelation. A shock went through me, and as well as I knew him, as few illusions as I had about him, I was arrested by his gaze, as if only he and I existed, as though he *were* I. All of those who watched him on television responded in the same fashion to that unique gaze.

But the committee was not aware that their intended victim had with one glance appropriated the eye of the world.

The subsequent catechism is too well known to record here. We used it as the main exposition of Cavesword, the one testament which contained the entire thing. It was almost as if the Congressmen had been given the necessary questions to ask, like those supporting actors whose roles are calculated to illuminate the genius of the star. Two of the seven members of the committee were Cavites. This was soon apparent. The other five were violent in their opposition. One as a Catholic, another as a Protestant, and two as materialistic lovers of the old order. Only one of the attackers, a Jew, made any real point. He argued the perniciousness of an organization which, if allowed to prosper, would replace the state and force all dissenters to conform; it was the Jew's contention that the state prospered most when no one system was sufficiently strong to dominate. I wanted to hear more of him but his Catholic colleague, a bull-voiced Irishman, drowned him out, winning the day for us.

Cave, to my astonishment, had memorized most of the dialogues I had written and he said my words with the same power that he said his own. I was startled by this. There had been no hint that such a thing might happen and I couldn't, for some time, determine the motive until I recalled Cave's reluctance to being quoted in print. He had apparently realized that now there would be a complete record of his testimony and so, for the sake of both literacy and consistency, he had committed to memory those words of mine which were thought to be his. At the great moment, however, the peroration (by which time there were no more questions and Cave's voice alone was heard) he became himself, and spoke Cavesword.

Then, without the committee's leave, in the dazzled silence which followed upon his last words, he rose abruptly and left the room. I switched off the television set. That week established Cavesword in the country and, except for various priests and ministers of the deserted gods, the United States was Cavite.

TWO

The desertion of the old establishments for the new resembled, at uneasy moments, revolution.

The Congressional committee, though anti-Cavite, did not dare even to censure him. Partly from the fear of the vast crowd which waited in the Capitol plaza and partly from the larger, more cogent awareness that it was political suicide for any popularly elected Representative to outrage a minority of such strength.

The hearing fizzled out after Cave's appearance, and though there were a few denunciatory speeches on the floor of Congress, no official action was taken. Shortly afterward the ban on Cave's televison appearances was lifted, but by then it was too late and millions of people had got permanently into the habit of attending weekly meetings at the various Centers to listen to Cave on film and discuss with the Residents and their staffs points of doctrine . . . and doctrine it had become.

The second year in our yellow citadel was even more active than the first. It was decided that Cave would make no personal appearances anywhere. According to Paul, the mystery would be kept intact and the legend would grow under the most auspicious circumstances. He did not reveal his actual motive in Cave's presence. But he explained himself to me late one afternoon in my office.

"Get him in front of a really hostile crowd and there'd be no telling what might happen." Paul was restlessly marching about the room in his shirtsleeves; a blunt cigar in his mouth gave him the appearance of a lower-echelon politician.

"There's never been a hostile audience yet," I reminded him. "Except for the Congressional hearings, and I thought he handled himself quite well with them."

"With your script in his head." Paul chuckled and stopped his march to the filing cabinet by way of that television set which dominated every office and home. "What I mean is, he's never been in a debate. He's never had a tough opponent, a heckler. The Congressmen were pretty mild and even though they weren't friendly they stuck to easy issues. But what would happen if Bishop Winston got him up before an audience? Winston's a lot smarter and he's nearly as good in public."

"I suppose Cave would hypnotize him, too."

"Not on your life." Paul threw himself into a chair of flimsy chrome and plastic. "Winston's been trying to arrange a debate for over two years. He issues challenges every Sunday on his program (got a big audience, too, though not close to ours. I checked the ratings.)"

"Does Cave want to give it a try?"

"He's oblivious to such things. I suppose he would if he thought about it. Anyway it's to our advantage to keep him out of sight. Let them see only a television image, hear only his recorded voice. It's wonderful copy! Big time." He was out of the chair and playing with the knob of the television set. The screen was suddenly filled with a romantic scene, a pulsating green grotto with water falling in a thin white line; so perfected had the machine become that it was actually like looking through a window, the illusion of depth quite perfect and the colors true. A warm deep voice off-screen suggested the virtues of a well-known carbonated drink. Paul turned the switch off. I was relieved since I, alone in America, was unable to think or work or even relax while the screen was bright with some other place.

"He won't like it. He expects next year, at the latest, to start his world tour."

"Perhaps then," said Paul thinly. "Anyway, the longer we put it off the better. Did you know we turn away a thousand people a day who come here just to get a glimpse of him?"

"They see him at the Center meetings."

"Only our own people, the ones in training to be Residents. I keep those sessions carefully screened. Every now and then some outsider gets in but it's rare."

I glanced at the tear-sheet of my next day's editorial. It contained, among other useful statistics, the quite incredible figures of Cavite membership in the world. Dubiously, I read off the figure which Paul had given me at a directors' meeting.

"It's about right," he said complacently, coming to a full stop at the files. "We don't actually know the figures of places without proper Centers like the Latin countries where we are undergoing a bit of persecution. But the statistics for this country are exact."

"It's hard to believe." I looked at the figure which represented so many human beings, so much diversity, all touched by one man. "Less than three years . . ."

"Three more years and we'll have most of Europe too."

"Why, I wonder?"

"Why?" Paul slammed shut the cabinet drawer which he'd been examining. He looked at me sharply. "You of all people ask why? Cavesword . . . and all your words too, did the trick. That's what. We've said what they wanted to hear. Just the opposite of my old game of publicity where we said what *we* wanted them to hear. This time it's just the other way around and it's big, ah, it's big."

I could agree with that but I pressed him further. "I know what's happened, of course, and your theory is certainly correct if only because had we said the opposite of what they wanted to hear nothing would have happened. But the question in my mind, the real 'why,' is Cave and us. Why we of all the people in the world? Cavesword, between us and any school of philosophy, is not new. Others have said it more eloquently. In the past it was a reasonably popular heresy which the early popes stamped out . . ."

"Timing! The right man at the right time saying the right thing. Remember the piece you did on Mohammed . . ."

"I stole most of it."

"So what? Most effective. You figured how only at that one moment in Arabian political history could such a man have appeared."

I smiled. "That is always the folly of the 'one unique moment.' For all I know such a man could have appeared in any of a hundred other Arab generations."

"But he never did except that one time, which proves the point."

I let it go. Paul was at best not the ideal partner in the perennial conversation. "There is no doubt that Cave's the man," I said, neutrally. "Not the last of the line but at least the most effective, considering the shortness of the mission so far."

"We have the means. The old people didn't. Every man, woman, and child in this country can see Cave for themselves, and at the same moment. I don't suppose ten thousand people saw Christ in action. It took a generation for news of him to travel from one country to the next."

"Parallels break down," I agreed. "It's the reason I wonder so continually about Cave and ourselves and what we are doing in the world."

"We're doing good. The people are losing their fear of death. Last month there were twelve hundred suicides in this country directly attributable to Cavesword. And these people didn't kil themselves just because they were unhappy, they killed themselves because he had made it easy, even desirable. Now you know there's never been anybody like that before in history, anywhere."

"Certainly not!" I was startled by the figure he had quoted. In our *Journal* we were always reporting various prominent suicides, and though I had been given orders to minimize these voluntary deaths, I had been forced every now and then to record the details of one or another of them. But I'd had no idea that there had been so many. I asked Paul if he was quite sure of the number.

"Oh yes." He was blithe. "At least that many we know of."

"I wonder if it's wise."

"Wise? What's that got to do with it? It's logical. It's the proof of Cavesword. Death is fine so why not die?"

"Why not live?"

"It's the same thing."

"I would say not."

"Well, you ought to play it up a little more anyway. I meant to talk about it at the last directors' meeting but there wasn't time."

"Does Cave know about this? About the extent . . ."

"Sure he does." Paul hea ded fo r the door. "He thinks it's fine Proves what he says and it gives other people nerve. This thing is working."

There was no doubt about that, of course. It is hard to give precisely the sense of those two years when the main work was done in a series of toppling waves which swept into history the remaining edifices of other faiths and institutions. I had few first-hand impressions of the country for I seldom stirred from our headquarters.

I had sold the house on the river. I had cut off all contacts with old friends. My life was Cave. I edited the *Journal*, or rather presided over the editors. I discussed points of doctrine with the various Residents who came to see me in the yellow tower. They were devoted men and their enthusiasm was heartening, if not always communicable to me. Each week further commentaries on Cavesword were published and I found there was no time to read them all. I contented myself, finally, with synopses prepared for me by the *Journal's* staff. I felt like a television emperor keeping abreast of contemporary letters.

Once a week we all dined with Cave. Except for that informal occasion we seldom saw him. Though he complained continually about his captivity (and it was exactly that; we were all captives to some degree), he was cheerful enough. Paul saw to it that he was kept busy all day addressing Residents and Communicators, answering their questions, inspiring them by the mere fact of his presence. It was quite common for strangers to faint upon seeing him for the first time, as a man and not as a figure on a bit of film. He was good-natured, though occasionally embarrassed by the chosen groups which were admitted to him. He seldom talked privately to any of them, however, and he showed not the faintest interest in their problems, not even bothering to learn their names. He was only interested in where they were from and Paul, aware of this, as an added inducement to keep Cave amenable, took to including in each group at least one Cavite from some far place like Malaya or Ceylon.

Iris was busiest of all. She had become, without design or preparation, the head of all the Cavite schools throughout the country where the various Communicators of Cavesword were trained, thousands of them each year, in a course which included not only Cavesword but history and psychology as well. There were also special classes in television production and acting. Television, ultimately, was the key. It was the primary instrument of communication. Later, with a subservient government and the aid of mental therapists and new drugs, television became less necessary, but in the beginning it was everything.

Clarissa's roles was, as always, enigmatic. She appeared when she pleased and she disappeared when she pleased. I discovered that her position among the directors was due to her possession of the largest single block of stock, dating back to the first days.

During the crucial two or three years, however, she was often with us merely for protection, since all our lives had been proscribed by the last remnants of the old churches, which as their dominion shrank fought more and more recklessly to destroy us.

Stokharin spent his days much like Iris, instructing the Communicators and Center therapists in psychology. His power over Paul had fortunately waned and he was far more likable. Paul was "freed," Stokharin would say with some satisfaction, by therapy . . . and a new father image.

Less than two years after the Congressional hearings, Paul, in his devious way, entered politics. In the following Congressional elections, without much overt campaigning on our part, the majority of those elected to both Houses of the Congress were either Cavite or sympathetic.

THREE

At last I have met him. Early this evening I went downstairs to see the manager about an item on my bill which was incorrect. I had thought that I should be safe, for this was the time when most of the hotel guests are bathing and preparing for dinner. Unfortunately, I encountered Butler and his newly arrived colleague in the lobby. I suddenly found myself attempting, by an effort of will, very simply to vanish into smoke like one of those magicians in a child's book. But I remained all too visible. I stopped halfway across the lobby and waited for them.

They came toward me. Butler murmuring greetings and introductions to Communicator Jessup (soon to be Resident of Luxor "when we get under way"): "And this, Jack, is the Mr. Hudson I told you about."

The Resident-to-be shook my hand firmly. He was not more than thirty, a lean, dark-eyed mulatto whose features and coloring appealed to me, used as I now am to the Arabs; beside him, Butler looked more red and gross than ever.

"Butler has told me how useful you've been to us," said Jessup. His voice was a little high, but he did not have the trick of overarticulation which used to be so common among educated

Negroes in earlier times, a peculiarity they shared with Baptist clergymen and professional poets.

"I've done what I could, little as it is," I said ceremoniously. Then, without protest, I allowed them to lead me out onto the terrace which overlooked the setting sun and the muddy river.

"We planned to see you when Jack, here, arrived," said Butler expansively as we sat down, a tray of gin and ice and tonic water set before us by a waiter who was used now to American ways. "But you had the sign on your door so I told Jack we'd better wait till Mr. Hudson is feeling better. You *are* okay now, aren't you?"

"Somewhat better," I said, enjoying the British gin. I'd had none since I left Cairo. "At my age one is either dead or all right. I seem not to be dead."

"How I envy you!" said Jessup solemnly.

"Envy me?" For a moment I did not quite understand.

"To be so near the blessed state! Not to see the sun again and feel the body quivering with corrupt life. Oh, what I should give to be as old as you!"

"You could always commit suicide," I said irritably, forgetting my role as an amiable soft-headed old cretin.

This stopped him for only the space of a single surprised breath. "Cavesway is not possible for his servants," he said at last, patiently. "You have not perhaps followed his logic as carefully as you might had you been living in the civilized world." He looked at me with bright dark eyes inscrutably focused.

Why are you here? I wanted to ask furiously, *finally*, but I only nodded my head meekly and said, "So much has changed since I came out here. I do recall, though, that Cavesway was considered desirable for all."

"It is. But not for his servants who must, through living, sacrifice their comfort. It is our humiliation, our martyrdom in his behalf. Even the humblest man or woman can avail themselves of Cavesway, unlike us his servants, who must live, disgusting as the prospect is, made bearable only by the knowledge that we are doing his work, communicating his word."

"What courage it must take to give up Cavesway!" I intoned with reverent awe.

"It is the least we can do for him."

The bright sun resembled that red-gold disc which sits on the brow of Horus. The hot wind of Numidia stirred the dry foliage about us. I could smell the metallic odor of the Nile. A muezzin called, high and toneless in the evening.

"Before I slip off into the better state," I said at last, emboldened by gin, "I should like to know as much as possible about the new world the Cavites have made. I left the United States shortly after Cave took his way. I have never been back."

"How soon after?" The question came too fast. I gripped the arms of my chair tightly.

"Two years after, I think," I said. "I came to Cairo for the digging at Sakharra."

"How could you have missed those exciting years?" Jessup's voice became zealous. "I was not even born then, and I've always cursed my bad luck. I used to go about talking to complete strangers who had been alive in those great years. Of course most were laymen and knew little about the things I had studied but they could tell me how the sky looked the day he took his way. And, every now and then, it was possible to meet someone who had seen him."

"Not many laymen ever saw him," I said. "I remember with what secrecy all his movements were enveloped. I was in New York much of the time when he was there."

"In New York!" Jessup sighed voluptuously.

"You saw him too, didn't you, Mr. Hudson?" Butler was obviously eager that I make a good impression.

"Oh yes, I saw him the day he was in Washington. One of his few public appearances! I was very devout in those days. I am now too, of course," I added hastily. "But in those days when it was all new, one was—well—exalted by Cavesword. I made a special trip to Washington just to get a glimpse of him." I played as resolutely as possible upon their passionate faith.

"Did you really see him?"

I shook my head sadly. "Only a quick blur as he drove away. The crowd was too big and the police were all around him."

"I have of course relived that moment in the library, watching the films, but actually to have been there that day," Jessup's voice trailed off as he contemplated the extent of my good fortune.

"Then, afterward, after his death, I left for Egypt and I've never been back."

"You missed great days."

"I'm sure of that. Yet I feel the best days were before, when I was in New York and each week there would be a new revelation of his wisdom."

"You are quite right," said Jessup, pouring himself more gin. "Yours was the finer time even though those of us who feel drawn to the Mother must declare that later days possessed some virtue too, on her account."

"Mother?" I knew of course before he answered what had happened.

"As Cave was the father of our knowledge, so Iris is its mother," said Jessup. He looked at Butler with a half-smile. "Of course there are some, the majority in fact, of the Communicators who deprecate our allegiance to the Mother, not realizing that it enhances rather than detracts from Cave. After all, the Word and the Way are entirely his."

Butler chuckled, "There's been a little family dispute," he said. "We keep it out of the press because it really isn't the concern of anybody but us, Cave's servants. Don't mind talking to you about it since you'll be dead soon anyway and up here we're all in the same boat, all Cavites. Anyway, some of the younger fellows, the bright ones like Jessup, have got attached to Iris, not that we don't all love her equally. It's just that they've got in the habit of talking about death being the womb again, all that kind of stuff without any real basis in Cave."

"It runs all through Cave's work, Bill. It's implicit in all that he said." Jessup was amiable but I sensed a hardness in his tone. It had come to this, I thought.

"Well, we won't argue about it," said Butler, turning to me with a smile. "You should see what these Irisians can do with a Cavite text. By the time they finish you don't know whether you're coming or going."

"Were you at all active in the Mission?" asked Jessup, abruptly changing the subject.

I shook my head. "I was one of the early admirers of Cave but I'm afraid I had very little contact with any of his people. I tried once or twice to get in to see him, when they were in the yellow tower, but it was impossible. Only the Residents and people like that ever saw him personally."

"He was busy in those days," said Jessup, nodding. "He must

have dictated nearly two million words in the last three years of his life."

"You think he wrote all those books and dialogues himself?"

"Of course he did," Jessup sounded surprised. "Haven't you read Iris's account of the way he worked? The way he would dictate for hours at a time, oblivious of everything but Cavesword."

"I supposed I missed all that," I mumbled. "In those days it was always assumed that he had a staff who did the work for him."

"The lutherists," said Jessup, nodding. "They were extremely subtle in their methods, but of course they couldn't distort the truth for very long . . ."

"Oh," said Butler. "Mr. Hudson asked me the other day if I knew what the word 'lutherist' came from and I said I didn't know. I must have forgotten, for I have a feeling it *was* taught us, back in the old days when we primitives were turned out, before you bright young fellows came along to show us how to do Caveswork."

Jessup smiled. "We're not that bumptious," he said. "As for lutherist, it's a word based on the name of one of the first followers of Cave. I don't know his other name or even much about him. As far as I remember, the episode was never even recorded. Much too disagreeable, and of course we don't like to dwell on our failures."

"I wonder what it was that he did," I asked, my voice trembling despite all efforts to control it.

"He was a noncomformist of some kind. He quarreled with Iris, they say."

"I wonder what happened to him," said Butler. "Did they send him through indoctrination?"

"No, as far as I know." Jessup paused. When he spoke again his voice was thoughtful. "According to the story I heard—legend really—he disappeared. They never found him and though we've wisely removed all record of him, his name is still used to describe our failures. Those among us, that is, who refuse Cavesword despite indoctrination. Somewhere, they say, he is living, in hiding, waiting to undo Caveswork. As Cave was the Antichrist, so Luther, or another like him, will attempt to destroy us."

"Not much chance of that." Butler's voice was confident.

'Anyway, if he was a contemporary of Cave he must be dead by now."

"Not necessarily. After all, Mr. Hudson was a contemporary and *he* is still alive." Jessup looked at me then. His eyes, in a burst of obsidian light, caught the sun's last rays. I think he knows.

FOUR

There is not much time left and I must proceed as swiftly as possible to the death of Cave and my own exile.

The year of Cave's death was not only a year of triumph but one of terror as well. The counteroffensive reached its peak in those busy months, and we were all in danger of our lives.

In the South, groups of Baptists stormed the new Centers, demolishing them and killing, in several instances, the Residents. Despite our protests and threats of reprisal, many state governments refused to protect the Cavite Centers and Paul was forced to enlist a small army to defend our establishments in those areas which were still dominated by the old religions. Several attempts were made to destroy our New York headquarters. Fortunately, they were discovered before any damage could be done, though one fanatic, a Catholic, got as far as Paul's office, where he threw a grenade into a wastebasket, killing himself and slightly scratching Paul, who as usual had been traveling nervously about the room, out of range at the proper moment.

The election of a Cavite-dominated Congress eased things for us considerably, though it made our enemies all the more desperate.

Paul fought back. Bishop Winston, the most eloquent of the Christian prelates and the most dangerous to us, had died, giving rise to the rumor, soon afterward confirmed by Cavite authority to be a fact, that he had killed himself and that, therefore, he had finally renounced Christ and taken to himself Cavesword.

Many of the clergy of the Protestant sects, aware that their parishioners and authority were falling away, became, quietly, without gloating on our part, Cavite Residents and Communicators.

The bloodiest persecutions, however, did not occur in North America. The Latin countries provided the world with a series of massacres remarkable even in that murderous century. Yet it was a fact that in the year of Cave's death, Italy was half-Cavite and France, England and Germany were nearly all Cavite. Only Spain and parts of Latin America held out, imprisoning, executing, deporting Cavites against the inevitable day when our Communicators, undismayed, proud in their martyrdom, would succeed in their assaults upon these last citadels of paganism.

On a hot day in August, our third and last autumn in the yellow tower, we dined on the terrace of Cave's penthouse overlooking the city. The bright sky shuddered with heat.

Clarissa had just come from abroad, where she had been enjoying herself hugely under the guise of an official tour of reconnaissance. She sat wearing a large picture hat beneath the striped awning that sheltered our glass-topped table from the sun's rays. Cave insisted on eating out-of-doors as often as possible, even though the rest of us preferred the cool interior where we were not disturbed by either heat or by the clouds of soot which floated above the imperial city, impartially lighting upon all who ventured out into the open.

It was our first "family dinner" in some months (Paul insisted on regarding us as a family, and the metaphors which he derived from this one conceit used even to irritate the imperturbable Cave). At one end of the table sat Clarissa, with Paul and me on either side of her; at the other end sat Cave, with Iris and Stokharin on either side of him. Early in the dinner, when the conversation was particular, Iris and I talked privately.

"I suppose we'll be leaving soon," she said. A gull missed the awning by inches.

"I haven't heard anything about it. Who's leaving . . . and why?"

"John thinks we've all been here too long; he thinks we're too remote."

"He's quite right about that." I blew soot off my plate. "But where are we to go? After all, there's a good chance that if any of us shows his head to the grateful populace someone will blow it off."

"That's a risk we have to take. But John is right. We must get out and see the people . . . talk to them direct." Her voice was urgent. I looked at her thoughtfully, seeing the change that three years of extraordinary activity had wrought. She was overweight and her face, as sometimes happens in the first access of weight, was smooth, without lines. That wonderful sharpness, her old fineness, was entirely gone and the new Iris, the busy, efficient Iris, had become like . . . like . . . I groped for the comparison, the memory of someone similar I had known in the past, but the ghost did not materialize; and so haunted, faintly distrait, I talked to the new Iris I did not really know.

"I'll be only too happy to leave," I said, helping myself to the salad which was being served us by one of the Eurasian servants whom Paul, in an exotic mood, had engaged to look after the penthouse and the person of Cave. "I don't think I've been away from here half a dozen times in two years."

"It's been awfully hard," Iris agreed. Her eyes shifted regularly to Cave, like an anxious parent's. "Of course I've had more chance than anyone to get out but I haven't seen nearly as much as I ought. It's my job, really, to look at all the Centers, to supervise in person all the schools, but of course I can't if Paul insists on turning every trip I take into a kind of pageant."

"It's for your own protection."

"I think we're much safer than Paul thinks. The country's almost entirely Cavite."

"All the more reason to be careful. The die-hards are on their last legs; they're desperate."

"Well, we must take our chances. John says he won't stay here another autumn. September is his best month, you know. It was in September that he first spoke Cavesword."

"What does Paul say?" I looked down the table at our ringmaster, who was telling Clarissa what she had seen in Europe.

Iris frowned. "He's doing everything he can to keep us here . . . I can't think why. John's greatest work has been done face to face with people, yet Paul acts as if he didn't dare let him out in public. We have quarreled about this for over a year, Paul and I."

"He's quite right. I'd be nervous to go about in public without some sort of protection. You should see the murderous letters I get at the *Journal.*"

"We've nothing to fear," said Iris flatly. "And we have everything to gain by mixing with people. We could easily grow out of touch, marooned in this tower."

"Oh, it's not that bad." To my surprise, I found myself defending our monastic life. "Everyone comes here. Cave speaks to groups of the faithful every day. I sit like some disheveled hen over a large newspaper and I couldn't be more instructed, more engaged in life, while you dash around the country almost as much as Paul does."

"But only seeing the Centers, only meeting the Cavites. I have no other life any more." I looked at her curiously. There was no bitterness in her voice, yet there was a certain wistfulness which I had never noticed before.

"Do you regret all this, Iris?" I asked. It had been three years since I had spoken to her of personal matters. We had become, in a sense, the offices which we held; our symbolic selves paralyzing all else within, true precedent achieved at a great cost. Now a fissure had suddenly appeared in the monument which Iris had become, and through the flow I heard again, briefly, the voice of the girl I had met on the bank of the Hudson in the spring of a lost year.

"I never knew it would be like this," she said almost whispering, her eyes on Cave while she spoke to me. "I never thought my life would be as alone as this, all work."

"Yet you wanted it. You *do* want it. Direction, meaning, you wanted all that and now you have it. The magic worked, Iris. Your magician was real."

"But I sometimes wonder if *I* am real anymore." The words, though softly spoken, fell between us like rounded stones, smooth and hard.

"It's too late," I said, mercilessly. "You are what you wanted to be. Live it out, Iris. There is nothing else."

"You're dead too," she said at last, her voice regaining its usual authority.

"Speaking of dead," said Cave suddenly turning toward us (I hoped he had not heard all our conversation), "Stokharin here has come up with a wonderful scheme."

Even Clarissa fell silent. We all did on those rare occasions when Cave spoke on social occasions. Cave looked cheerfully about the table for a moment. Stokharin beamed with pleasure at the accolade.

"You've probably all heard about the suicides as a result of Cavesword." Cave had very early got into the habit of speaking of himself in the third person whenever a point of doctrine was involved. "Paul's been collecting the monthly figures and each month they double. Of course they're not accurate since there are a good many deaths due to Cavesword which we don't hear about. Anyway, Stokharin has perfected a painless death by poison, a new compound which kills within an hour and is delightful to take."

"I have combined certain narcotics which together insure a highly exhilarated state before the end, as well as most pleasant fantasies." Stokharin smiled complacently.

Cave continued. "I've already worked out some of the practical details for putting this into action. There are still a lot of wrinkles, but we can iron them out in time. One of the big problems of present-day *unorganized* suicide is the mess it causes for the people unfortunate enough to be left behind. There are legal complications; there is occasionally grief in old-fashioned family groups; there is also a general social disturbance which tends to give suicide, at least among the reactionaries, a bad name.

"Our plan is simple. We will provide at each Center full facilities for those who have listened to Cavesword and have responded to it by taking the better way. There will be a number of comfortable rooms where the suicidalist may receive his friends for a last visit. We'll provide legal assistance to put his affairs in order. Not everyone of course will be worthy of us. Those who choose death merely to evade responsibility will be censured and restrained. But the deserving, those whose lives have been devoted and orderly, may come to us and receive the gift."

I was appalled. Before I could control myself I had said: "But the law! You just can't let people kill themselves . . ."

"Why not?" Cave looked at me coldly and I saw, in the eyes of the others, concern and hostility. I had anticipated something like this ever since my talk with Paul, but I had not thought it would come so swiftly or so boldly.

Paul spoke for Cave. "We've got the Congress and the Congress will make a law for us. For the time being, it *is* against the statutes, but we've been assured by our lawyers that there isn't much chance of their being invoked, except perhaps in the remaining pockets of Christianity where we'll go slow until we do have the necessary laws to protect us."

At that moment the line which from the very beginning had been visibly drawn between me and them became a wall apparent to everyone. Even Clarissa, my usual ally, fearless and sharp, did not speak out. They looked at me, all of them awaiting a sign; even Cave regarded me with curiosity.

My hand shook and I was forced to seize the edge of the table to steady myself. The sensation of cold glass and iron gave me a sudden courage. I brought Cave's life to its end.

I turned to him and said, quietly, with all the firmness I could summon: "Then you will have to die as well as they, and soon."

There was a shocked silence. Iris shut her eyes. Paul gasped and sat back abruptly in his chair. Cave turned white but he did not flinch. His eyes did not waver. They seized on mine, terrible and remote, full of power; with an effort, I looked past him. I still feared his gaze.

"What did you say?" The voice was curiously mild yet it increased rather than diminished the tension. We had reached the crisis, without a plan.

"You have removed the fear of death, for which future generations will thank you, as I do. But you have gone too far . . . all of you." I looked about me at the pale faces; a faint wisp of new moon curled in the pale sky above. "Life is to be lived until the flesh no longer supports the life within. The meaning of life, Cave, is more life, not death. The enemy of life is death, an enemy not to be feared but no less hostile for all that, no less dangerous, no less wrong when the living choose it instead of life, either for themselves or for others. You've been able to dispell our fear of the common adversary; that was your great work in the world. Now you want to go further, to make love to this enemy we no longer fear, to mate with death, and it is here that you, all of you, become enemies of life."

"Stop it!" Iris's voice was high and clear. I did not look at her. All that I could do now was to force the climax.

"But sooner or later every act of human folly creates its own opposition. This will too, more soon than late, for if one can make any generality about human beings it is that they want *not* to die. You cannot stampede them into death for long. They are enthusiastic now. They may not be soon . . . unless of course there is some supreme example before them, one which you, Cave, can alone supply. *You* will have to die by your own hand to show the virtue and the truth of all that you have said."

I had gone as far as I could. I glanced at Iris while I spoke; she had grown white and old-looking and, while I watched her, I realized whom it was she resembled, the obscure nagging memory which had disturbed me all through dinner. She was like my mother, a woman long dead, one whose gentle blurred features had been strikingly similar to that frightened face which now stared at me as though I were a murderer.

Paul was the one who answered me. "You're out of your mind, Gene," he said, when my meaning had at last penetrated to them all. "It doesn't follow in the least that Cave must die because others want to. The main work is still ahead of him. This country is only a corner of the world. There's some of Europe and most of Asia and Africa still ahead of us. How can you even suggest he quit now and die?"

"The work will be done whether he lives or not, as you certainly know. He's given it the first impetus. The rest is up to the others, to the ambitious, the inspired. We've met enough of *them* these last few years. They're quite capable of finishing the work without us."

"But it's nothing without Cave."

I shrugged. I was suddenly relieved as the restraint of three furious years went in a rush. "I am as devoted to Cave as anyone," I said (and I was, I think, honest). "I don't want him to die but all of you in your madness have made it impossible for him to live. He's gone now to the limit, to the last boundary. He is the son of death and each of you supports him. I don't, for it was my wish to make life better, not death desirable. I never really believed it would come to this. That you, Cave, would speak for death, and against life." I raised my eyes to his. To my astonishment he had lowered his lids as though to hide from me, to shut me out. His head was shaking oddly from left to right and his lips were pressed tight together.

I struck again, without mercy. "But don't stop now. You've

got your wish. By all means, build palaces if you like for those who choose to die in your name. But remember that you will be their victim, too. The victim of their passionate trust. They will force you to lead the way and *you* must be death's lover, Cave."

He opened his eyes and I was shocked to see them full of tears. "I am not afraid," he said.

TEN

ONE

A few days after our disastrous dinner, Clarissa came to me in my office. It was our first private meeting since her return from Europe. It was also my first meeting with any one of the directors for, since the scene on the penthouse terrace, none had come near me, not even Paul, whom I usually saw at least once a day.

Clarissa seemed tired. She sat down heavily in the chair beside my desk and looked at me oddly. "Recriminations?" I asked cheerfully. The recent outburst had restored me to perfect health and equanimity. I was prepared for anything, especially battle.

"You're an absolute fool and you know it," she said at last. "I suppose there are wires in here, recording everything we say."

"I shouldn't be surprised. Fortunately, I have no secrets."

"There's no doubt of that." She glared at me. "There was no need to rush things."

"You mean you anticipated this?"

"What else? Where else could it lead? The same thing happened to Jesus, you know. They kept pushing him to claim the kingdom. Finally, they pushed too hard and he was killed. It was the killing which perpetuated the legend."

"And a number of other things."

"In any case, it's gone too far. Also, I don't think you even begin to see what you've done."

"Done?" I've merely brought the whole thing into the open and put myself on record as being opposed to this . . . this passion for death."

"That of course is nonsense. Just because a few nitwits . . ."

"A few? Have you seen the statistics? Every month there are a few hundred more, and as soon as Stokharin gets going with his damned roadhouses for would-be suicides we may find that . . ."

"I always assumed Paul made up the statistics. But even if they *are* true, even if a few hundred thousand people decide to slip away every year, I am in favor of it. There are too many people as it is and most of them aren't worth the room they take up. I suspect all this is just one of nature's little devices to reduce the population, like pederasty on those Greek islands."

"You're outrageous."

"I'm perfectly rational, which is more than I can say for you. Anyway, the reason I've come to see you today is, first, to warn you and second, to say good-by."

"Good-by? You're not . . ."

"Going to kill myself?" She laughed. "Not in a hundred years! Though I must say lately I've begun to feel old. No, I'm going away. I've told Paul that I've had my fun, that you're all on your own and that I want no part of what's to come."

"Where will you go?"

"Who knows? Now for the warning. Paul of course is furious at you and so is Iris."

"Perfectly understandable. What did he say?"

"Nothing good. I talked to him this morning. I won't enrage you by repeating all the expletives. It's enough to say he's eager to get you out of the way. He feels you've been a malcontent all along."

"He'll have trouble getting me to take Stokharin's magic pill."

"He may not leave it up to you," said Clarissa significantly, and inadvertently I shuddered. I had of course wondered if they would dare go so far. I had doubted it but the matter-of-fact Clarissa enlightened me. "Watch out for him, especially if he becomes friendly. You must remember that with the country Cavite and with Paul in charge of the organization you haven't much chance."

"I'll take what I have."

Clarissa looked at me without, I could see, much hope. "What you don't know, and this is my last good deed, for in a sense I'm responsible for getting you into this, is that you accidentally gave the game away."

"What do you mean?"

"I mean that Paul has been planning for over a year to do away with Cave. He feels that Cave's usefulness is over. Also he's uneasy about letting him loose in the world. Paul wants full control of the establishment and he can't have it while Cave lives. Paul also realizes—he's much cleverer than you've ever thought, by the way—that the Cavites need a symbol, some great sacrifice, and obviously Cave's suicide is the answer. It is Paul's intention either to persuade Cave to kill himself or else to do it for him and then announce that Cave, of his own free will, chose to die."

I had the brief sensation of a man drowning. "How do you know all this?"

"I have two eyes. And Iris told me."

"She knows too?"

"Of course she knows! Why else do you think she's so anxious to get Cave away from this place? She knows Paul can have him killed at any time and no one would be the wiser."

I grunted with amazement. I understood now what it was that had happened on the terrace. I felt a perfect fool. Of them all I alone had been unaware of what was going on beneath the surface and, in my folly, I had detonated the situation without knowing it. "*He* knows too?" I asked weakly.

"Of course he does. He's on his guard every minute against Paul."

"Why has no one ever told me this?"

Clarissa shrugged. "They had no idea which side you'd take. They still don't know. Paul believes that you are with him and though he curses you for an impetuous fool, he's decided that perhaps it's a good idea now to bring all this into the open, at least among ourselves. He hopes for a majority vote in the directors' meeting to force Cave to kill himself."

"And Cave?"

"Has no wish to die, sensible man."

"I am a fool."

"What I've always told you, dear." Clarissa smiled at me. "I will say, though, that you are the only one of the lot who has acted for an impersonal reason, and certainly none of them understands you except me. I am on your side, in a way. Voluntary deaths don't alarm me the way they do you, but this obsession of Cave's, of death being preferable to life, may have ghastly consequences."

"What can I do?"

"I haven't the faintest idea. It's enough that you were warned in advance."

"What would *you* do?"

"Exactly what I'm going to do. Take a long trip."

"I mean if you were I."

She sighed. "Save your life, if possible. That's all you can do."

"I have a few weapons, you know. I have the *Journal* and I'm a director. I have friends in every Center." This was almost true. I had made a point of knowing as many Residents as possible. "I also have Iris and Cave on my side since I'm willing to do all I can to keep him alive, that he *not* become a supreme symbol."

"I wish you luck," Clarissa was most cynical. She rose. "Now that I've done my bit of informing, I'm off."

"Europe?"

"None of your business. But I *will* tell you I won't go back there. They've gone quite mad too. In Madrid I pretended to be a Catholic and I watched them put Cavites up before firing squads. Of course our people, despite persecution, are having a wonderfully exciting time with passwords and peculiar college fraternity handclasps and so on." She collected her gloves and handbag from the floor where, as usual, she had strewn them. "Well, now good-by." She gave me a kiss; then she was gone.

TWO

Events moved rapidly. I took to bolting my bedroom door at night, and during the day I was careful always to have one or another of my assistants near me. It was a strange sensation to be living in a modern city with all its police and courts and yet to fear that in a crisis there would be no succor, no one to turn to for aid and protection. We were a separate government within the nation, beyond the law.

The day after Clarissa had said good-by, Paul appeared in my office. I was surrounded by editors, but at a look from him and a gesture from me they withdrew. We had each kept our secret, evidently, for none of those close to us in that building suspected that there had been a fatal division.

"I seem to be in disgrace," I said, my forefinger delicately caressing the buzzer which I had built into the arm of my chair so that I might summon aid in the event that a visitor proved to be either a bore or a maniac, two types curiously drawn to enterprises such as ours.

"I wouldn't say that." Paul sat in a chair close to my own; I recall thinking, a little madly, that elephants are supposed to be at their most dangerous when they are perfectly still. Paul was noticeably controlled. Usually he managed to cross the room at least once for every full sentence; now he sat looking at me, his face without expression.

"I've seen no one since our dinner except Clarissa," I explained; then I added, earnestly: "I wonder where she plans to go. She didn't . . ."

"You've almost wrecked everything," he said, his voice tight, unfamiliar in its tension.

"I didn't want to," I said, inaccurately. I was at the moment more terrified than I had ever been, either before or since. I could get no real grip on him. The surface he presented me was as unyielding as a prison wall.

"Who told you? Iris? Cave? or were you spying?" Each question was fired at me like a bullet.

"Spying on whom?"

"On me, damn you!" Then it broke. The taut line of control which had held in check his anger and his fear broke all at once and the torrent flowed, reckless and overpowering: "You meddling idiot! You spied on me. You found out. You thought you'd be able to stall things by springing it like that. Well, you failed." I recall thinking, quite calmly, how much I preferred his face in the congested ugliness of rage to its ordinary banality of expression. I was relieved, too, by the storm. I could handle him when he was out of control. I considered my counteroffensive while he shouted at me, accused me of hostility to him, of deviationism from Cavesword and of numerous other crimes. He stopped, finally, for lack of breath.

"I gather," I said, my voice shaking a little from excitement, "that at some point recently you decided that Cave should apply Cavesword to himself and die, providing us with a splendid example, an undying (I mean no pun) symbol."

"You know you found out and decided to get in on the act, to force my hand. Now he'll never do it."

That was it, then. I was relieved to know. "Cave has refused to kill himself?"

"You bet your sweet life he has." Paul was beginning to recover his usual poise. "Your little scene gave him the excuse he needed: 'Gene's right.' " Paul imitated Cave's voice with startling accuracy and malice. " 'Gene's right. I never did mean for everybody to kill themselves off, where'd the world be if *that* happened? Just a few people. That's all.' And he's damned if he's going to be one of them. 'Hate to set that sort of example.' "

"Well, you'll have to try something else, then."

"Why did you do it?" Paul's voice became petulant. "Did Iris put you up to it?"

"Nobody put me up to it."

"You mean to sit there and try to make me believe that it just occurred to you, like that, to suggest Cave would have to kill himself if he encouraged suicide?"

"I mean that it occurred to me exactly like that." I looked at Paul with vivid loathing. "Can't you understand an obvious casual relationship? With this plan of Stokharin's you'll make it impossible for Cave *not* to commit suicide, and when he does, you will have an international death cult which I shall do my best to combat."

Paul's hands began nervously to play with his tie, his lapels. I wondered if he had come armed. I placed my finger lightly upon the buzzer. Implacably, we faced one another.

"You are not truly Cavesword," was all that he said.

"We won't argue about that. I'm merely explaining to you why I said what I did and why I intend to keep Cave alive as long as possible. Alive and hostile to you, to your peculiar interpretation of his Word."

Paul looked suddenly disconsolate. "I've done what I thought best. I feel Cave should show all of us the way. I feel it's both logical and necessary to the Establishment that he give back his life publicly."

"But he doesn't want to."

"That is the part I can't understand. Cavesword is that death is not to be feared but embraced, yet he, the man who has really changed the world, refuses to die."

"Perhaps he feels he has more work to do. More places to see. Perhaps, Paul, he doesn't trust you, doesn't want to leave you in control of the Establishment."

"I'm willing to get out if that's all that's stopping him." But the insincerity of this protestation was too apparent for either of us to contemplate it for long.

"I don't care what his motives are. I don't care if he himself is terrified of dying (and I have a hunch that that is the real reason for his hesitancy), but I *do* know that I don't want him dead by his own hand."

"You're quite sure of that?"

"Absolutely sure. I'm a director of the Establishement and don't forget it. Iris, Cave and I are against you and Stokharin. You may control the organization but we have Cave himself." I gathered courage in my desperation. I purposely sounded as though I were in warm concert with the others.

"I realize all that." Paul was suddenly meek, conciliatory, treacherous. "But you must allow me as much sincerity as you withhold for yourself. I want to do what's best. I think he should die and I've done everything to persuade him. He was near agreement when you upset everything."

"For which I'm happy, though it was something of an accident. Are you sure that it is only for the sake of Cavesword you want him dead?"

"What other reason?" He looked at me indignantly. I could not be sure whether he was telling the truth or not. I doubted it.

"Many other reasons. For one thing you would be his heir, in complete control of the Establishment; and that of course is something worth inheriting."

Paul shrugged convincingly. "I'm as much in charge now as I would be with him dead," he said with a certain truth. "I'm interested in Cavesword, not in Cave. If his death enhances and establishes the Word more securely then I must convince him that he must die."

"There is another way," I said, smiling at the pleasant thought.

"Another way?"

"To convince us of your dedication and sincerity to Cavesword."

"What's that?"

"You kill *yourself*, Paul."

There was a long silence. I pressed the buzzer and my secretary came in. Without a word, Paul left.

Immediately afterwards, I took the private elevator to Cave's penthouse. Two guards stopped me while I was announced by a third. After a short delay I was admitted to Cave's study, where Iris received me.

"I know what's happening," I said. "Where is he?"

"Obviously you do." Her voice was cold. She did not ask me to sit down. Awkwardly, I faced her at the room's center.

"We must stop him."

"John? Stop him from what?"

"Doing what Paul wants him to do."

"And what you want as well."

"You're mistaken. I thought I made myself clear the other night. But though my timing was apparently bad, under *no* circumstances do I want him to die."

"You made your speech to force him."

"And Paul thinks I made it to stop him." I couldn't help smiling. "I am, it seems, everyone's enemy."

"Paul has told me everything. How you and he and Stokharin all decided, without consulting us, that John should die."

I was astonished at Paul's boldness. Could he really be moving so swiftly? How else explain such a prodigious lie? I told her quickly and urgently what I had said to Paul and he to me. She heard me to the end without expressing either belief or disbelief. When I had finished she turned away from me and went to the window where, through yellow glass, the city rose upon the band of horizon.

"It's too late," she said, evenly. "I hadn't expected this. Perhaps you're telling me the truth. If you are, you've made a terrible mistake." She turned about suddenly, with a precision almost military. "He's going to do it."

The awful words fell like a weight upon a scale. I reached for a chair and sat down, all strength gone. "Stop him," I said, all that I could say. "Stop him."

"It's too late for that." She took pity on me. "I think you're telling me the truth." She came over to where I was sitting and looked down at me gently. "I'm sorry I accused you. I should have realized Paul was lying."

"*You* can stop him."

"I can't. I've tried but I can't." Her control was extraordinary. I did not then guess the reason for her calm, her strength.

"Then I must try." I stood up.

"You can't do anything. He won't see you. He won't see anyone but me."

"I thought he told Paul he agreed with me, that he didn't want to . . . to countenance all this, that he . . ."

"At first he took your side, if it is really what you feel. Then he thought about it and this morning he decided to go ahead with Paul's plan."

I was confused. "Does Paul know?"

Iris smiled wanly. "John is reserving for himself the pleasure of doing what he must do without Paul's assistance."

"Or knowledge?"

Iris shrugged. "Paul will find out about it this evening, I suppose. There will be an announcement. John's secretary is getting it ready now . . . one for the public and another for the Establishment."

"When will it happen?"

"Tomorrow. I go with him, Gene."

"You? You're not going to die too?"

"I don't see that it makes much difference what I do when John dies."

"You can't leave us now. You can't leave Paul in charge of everything. He's a dangerous man. Why, if . . ."

"You'll be able to handle him." It was perfectly apparent to me that she was no longer interested in me or in the others; not even in the fate of the work we had begun.

"It's finished, if you go too," I said bleakly. "Together we could control Paul; alone, I wouldn't last ten days. Iris, let me talk to him."

"I can't. I won't."

I contemplated pushing by her and searching the penthouse, but there were guards everywhere and I had no wish to be shot on such an errand.

She guessed my thought and said quickly, "There's no possible way for you or anyone to get through to him. Sometime tonight or tomorrow he will leave and that's the end."

"He won't do it here?" This surprised me.

She shook her head. "He wants to go off alone, away from everyone. I'm to be with him until the end. Then I'll send the body back here for burial, but he'll leave full instructions."

"You mean I'm never to see either of you again? Just like that, you both go?"

"Just like this." For the first time she displayed some warmth.

"I've cared for you, Gene," she said gently. "I even think that of us all you were the one most nearly right in your approach to John. I think you understood him better than he did himself. Try to hold on after we go. Try to keep it away from Paul."

"As if I could!" I turned from her bitterly, filled with unexpected grief. I did not want to lose her presence even though I had lost her or, rather, never possessed more of her than that one bright instant on the California coast when we had both realized with the unexpected clarity of the lovers we were not that our lives had come to the same point at the same moment. The knowledge of this confluence was the only splendor I had ever known, the single hope, the unique passion of my life.

"Don't miss me. I couldn't bear that." She put her hand on my arm. I walked away, not able to bear her touch. Then they came.

Paul and Stokharin were in the study. Iris gasped and stepped back when she saw them. I spun about just as Paul shouted, "It won't work, Iris! Give it up."

"Get out of here, Paul." Her voice was strong. "You have no right here."

"I have as much right as you. Now tell me whose idea it was. Yours? or was it John's? or Gene's? since he seems to enjoy playing both sides."

"Get out. All of you." she moved to the old-fashioned bell cord which hung beside Cave's desk.

"Don't bother," said Paul. "No one will come."

Iris, her eyes wide now with fear, tugged the cord twice. The second time it broke off in her hand. There was no response.

Paul looked grim. "I'm sorry to have to do it this way but you've left me no choice. You can't leave, either of you."

"You've read . . ."

"I saw the release. It won't work."

"Why not? It's what you've wanted all along. Everything will be yours. There'll be nobody to stop you. John will be dead and I'll be gone for good. You'll never see me again. Why must you interfere?" She spoke quickly and plausibly, but the false proportion was evident now, even to me. The desperate plan was tumbling down at Paul's assault.

"Iris, I'm not a complete fool. I know perfectly well that Cave has no intention of killing himself and that . . ."

"Why do you think I'm going with him? to send you the

body back for the ceremony which you'll perform right here, publicly. . ."

"Iris." He looked at her for a long moment. Then: "If you two leave as planned tonight (I've canceled the helicopter, by the way) there will be no body, no embalming, no ceremony. Only a mystery which might very well undo all our work. I can't allow that. Cave must die here, before morning. We might have put it off but your announcement has already leaked out. There'll be a million people out there in the street tomorrow. We'll have to show them Cave's body."

Iris swayed. I moved quickly to her side and held her arm. "It's three to two, Paul," I said. "I assume we're still directors. Three of us have agreed that Cave and Iris leave. That's final." But my bluff was humiliatingly weak; it was ignored.

"The penthouse," said Paul softly, "is empty . . . just the five of us here. The Doctor and I are armed. Take us in to him."

"No." Iris moved instinctively, fatally, to the door that led to Cave, as if to guard it with her body.

There was a brief scuffle, ending with Iris and myself considerably disheveled, facing two guns. With an apology, Stokharin pushed us through the door.

In a small sunroom we found Cave sitting before a television screen, watching the installation of a new Resident in Boston. He looked up with surprise at our entrance. "I thought I said . . ." he began, but Iris interrupted him.

"They want to kill you, John."

Cave got to his feet, face pale, eyes glaring. Even Paul was shaken by that glance. "You read my last statement?" Cave spoke sharply, without apparent fear.

"That's why we've come," said Paul. He and Stokharin moved, as though by previous accord, to opposite ends of the little room, leaving the three of us together, vulnerable at its center. "You must do it here." Paul signaled Stokharin, who produced a small metal box which he tossed to Cave.

"Some of the new pills," he said nervously. "Very nice. We use peppermint in the outer layer and . . ."

"Take it, John."

"I'll get some water," said Stokharin. But Paul waved to him to keep his place.

Cave smiled coldly. "I will not take it. Now both of you get out of here before I call the guards."

"No more guards," said Paul. "We've seen to that. Now, please, don't make it any more difficult than it is. Take the pill."

"If you read my statement you know that . . ."

"You intend to take a pleasant trip around the world incognito with Iris. Yes, I know. As your friend, I wish you could do it. But, for one thing, sooner or later you'd be recognized, and for another we must have proof . . . we must have a body."

"Iris will bring the body back," said Cave. He was still quite calm. "I choose to do it this way and there's nothing more to be said. You'll have the Establishment all to yourself and I will be a most satisfactory figure upon which to build a world religion." It was the only time in my experience with Cave that I ever heard him strike the ironic note.

"Leave us alone, Paul. You have what you want. Now let us go." Iris begged, but Paul had no eyes for anyone but Cave.

"Take it John," he repeated softly. "Take Cavesway."

"Not for you." Cave hurled the metal box at Paul's head and Stokharin fired. There was one almost bland moment when we all stood, politely, in a circle and watched Cave, a look of wonder on his face, touch his shoulder where the blood had begun to flow through a hole in the jacket.

Then Iris turned fiercely on Paul, knocking him off balance, while Cave ran to the door. Stokharin, his hand shaking and his face silver with fear, fired three times, each time hitting Cave, who quivered but did not fall; instead, he got through the door and into the study. As Stokharin hurried after him, I threw myself upon him, expecting death at any moment; but it did not come, for Stokharin had collapsed. He dropped his gun and hid his face in his hands, rocking back and forth on the floor, sobbing. Free of Iris's fierce grip, Paul got to Cave before I did.

Cave lay in the corridor only a few feet from the elevator. He had fallen on his face and lay now in his own blood, his hands working at the floor as though trying to dig himself a grave in the hard stone. I turned him on his back and he opened his eyes. "Iris?" he asked. His voice was ordinary though his breathing was harsh and uneven.

"Here I am." Iris knelt down beside him, ignoring Paul.

Cave whispered something to Iris. Then a flow of blood, like the full moon's tide, poured from his mouth. He was dead.

"Cavesway," said Paul at last when the silence had been used up. The phrase he had prepared for this moment was plainly inadequate for the reality at our feet.

"*Your* way," said Iris as she stood up. She looked at Paul calmly, as though they had only just met. "*Your* way," she repeated.

In the other room Stokharin moaned.

ELEVEN

ONE

Now the work was complete. Cavesword and Cavesway formed a perfect design and all the rest would greatly follow, or so Paul assumed. I believe if I had been he I should have killed both Iris and myself the same day, removing at one stroke witnesses and opposition. But he did not have the courage, and I also think he underestimated us, to his own future sorrow.

Iris and I were left alone in the penthouse. Paul, after shaking Stokharin into a semblance of calm, bundled Cave's body into a blanket and then, with the Doctor's help, placed it in the private elevator.

The next twenty-four hours were a grim carnival, The body of Cave, beautifully arranged and painted, lay in the central auditorium of the Center as thousands filed by to see him. Paul's speech over the corpse was telecast around the world.

Iris and I kept to our separate rooms, both by choice and from necessity, since gentle guards stood before our doors and refused, apologetically, to let us out.

I watched the services over television while my chief editors visited me one by one, unaware of what had happened and ignoring the presence of the guards. It was assumed that I was too shocked by grief to go to the office. Needless to say, I did not mention to any of them what had happened. At first I had thought it best to expose Paul as a murderer and a fraud, but on second thought (the second thought which followed all too swiftly upon the first, as Paul had no doubt assumed it would), I did not want to risk the ruin of our work. Instead, I decided to wait, to study Paul's destruction, an event which I had grimly vowed would take place as soon as possible. He could not now get rid of either Iris or me in the near future and all we needed, I was sure, was a week or two. I was convinced of this though I had no specific plan. Iris had more influence, more prestige in the Establishment, than Paul, and I figured, correctly as later events corroborated, that Cave's death would enhance her position. As for myself, I was not without influence.

I kept my lines of communication clear the next few days during what was virtually a house arrest. The editors came to me regularly and I continued to compose editorials. The explanation for my confinement was, according to a bulletin signed by Stokharin, a mild heart condition. Everyone was most kind. But I was alarmed when I heard of the diagnosis. It meant that with one of Stokharin's pellets in my food death would be ascribed to coronary occlusion, the result of strain attendant upon Cave's death. I had less time than I thought. I made plans.

Paul's funeral oration was competent though less than inspiring. The Chief Resident of Dallas, one of the great new figures of the Establishment, made an even finer speech over the corpse. I listened attentively, judging from what was said and what was not said the wind's direction. Cavesway was now the heart of the doctrine. Death was to be embraced with passion; life was the criminal, death the better reality; consciousness was an evil which, in death's oblivion, met its true fate . . . man's one perfect virtuous act was the sacrifice of his own consciousness to the pure nothing from which, by grim accident, it had come into being. The Chief Resident of Dallas was most eloquent and chilling.

Even sequestered in my room I caught some of the excitement which circled the globe like a lightning storm. Thirty-five hundred suicides were reported within forty-eight hours of Cave's death. The statisticians lost count of the number of people who fought to get inside the building to see Cave in death. From my window I could see that Park Avenue had been roped off for a dozen blocks. People swarmed like ants toward the gates of the tower.

I sent messages to Iris but received none, nor, for that matter, did I have any assurance that she had got mine. I followed Paul's adventures on television and from the reports of my editors who visited me regularly, despite Stokharin's orders.

On the third day, I was allowed to go to my office, Paul having decided that it would be thought odd if I were to die so soon after Cave. No doubt he was also relieved to discover that I had not revealed to my friends what had happened. Now that he had established the fact of my weak heart, my death could be engineered most plausibly at any time.

I did not see him face to face until the fourth day, when John

Cave's ashes were to be distributed over the United States. Stokharin, Paul and I sat in the back seat of a limousine at the head of a motorcade which, beginning at the tower, terminated at the airport where the jet plane which would sprinkle the ashes over New York, Seattle, Chicago and Los Angeles was waiting, along with a vast crowd and the President of the United States, an official Christian but known to incline, as Presidents do, toward the majority. Cavites were the majority and had been for almost two years.

I was startled to find Paul and Stokharin in the same automobile. It had been my understanding that we were to travel separately in the motorcade. They were most cordial.

"Sorry to hear you've been sick, Gene," Paul said with an ingenuous grin. "Mustn't strain the old ticker."

"I'm sure the good Doctor will be able to cure me," I said cheerfully.

They both laughed loudly. The car pulled away from the tower and drove down Park Avenue at the head of a long procession. Crowds lined the street as we drove slowly by. They were curiously still, as though they hardly knew how to react. This was a funeral, yet Cavesway was glorious. Some cheered. Most simply stared and pointed at our car, recognizing Paul. I suddenly realized why they were so interested in this particular car. On the floor, at Paul's feet, was what looked like a large flowerpot covered with gold foil.

"Are those the ashes?"

Paul nodded. "Did an extra quick job, too, I'm glad to say. We didn't want any slipup."

"Where's Iris?"

"I was going to ask *you* that." Paul looked at me sharply. "She disappeared yesterday and it's very embarrassing for all of us, very inconsiderate too. She knew I especially wanted her at the ceremony. She knows that everyone will expect to see her."

"I think she took the idea of Cavesway most illogically," said Stokharin. His usual sang-froid had returned, the breakdown forgotten. "She should be grateful to us for making all this possible, despite Cave's weakness."

I ignored Stokharin. I looked at Paul, who was beaming at the crowd, acknowledging their waves with nods of his head. "What will you do now?"

"You heard the ceremony?"

"Yes."

"Well, just that. Cavesway has become universal. Even the economists in Washington have privately thanked us for what we're doing to reduce the population. There's a theory that by numerous voluntary deaths wars might decrease since—or so the proposition goes—they are nature's way of checking population."

"Perhaps you're right." I assumed a troubled expression as I made the first move of my counteroffensive.

Paul looked away from the crowd to regard me shrewdly. "You don't think I trust you, do you?"

I shrugged. "Why not? I can't change Cavesway now."

Paul grunted. I could see that he did not credit this spurious *volte-face*; nevertheless, an end to my active opposition would force him to revise his plans. This would, I hoped, give me the time I needed. I pressed on. "I think we can compromise. Short of rigging my death, which would cause suspicion, you must continue to put up with me for a while. You've nothing to fear from me since you control the Establishment and since the one weapon I have against you I will not use."

"You mean . . ."

"My having witnessed the murder of Cave. If I had wanted to I could have revealed this before the cremation. An autopsy would certainly have ruined everything for you."

"Why didn't you?" I could see that Paul was genuinely interested in my motives.

"Because it would have meant the end of the work. I saw no reason to avenge Cave at such a cost. You must remember he was not a god to me, any more than you are."

This twist of a blunt knife had the calculated effect. "What a cold devil you are!" said Paul, almost admiringly. "I wish I could believe you."

"There's no reason not to. I was opposed to the principle of suicide. It is now firmly established. We must go on from there."

"Then tell me where Iris is."

"I haven't any idea. As you know, I've been trying to get in touch with her for days. Your people intercepted everything. How *did* she manage to get away?"

"One of the guards let her out. I thought he was one of our

boys but it seems she worked on him and he left with her. I've alerted all the Centers; so far no one's seen her."

Just before Grand Central Terminal, the crowd began to roar with excitement and Paul held up the jar of ashes. The crowd went wild and tried to break through the police lines. The cortege drove a bit faster and Paul set the ashes down. He looked triumphant but tired, as though he'd not slept in a month. One eyelid, I saw, was twitching with fatigue.

"When are we to have a directors' meeting?" I asked as we crossed the bridge which spanned the river. We're still legally a company. We must elect a new board chairman."

"As soon as we find Iris," said Paul. "I think we should all be there, don't you? Two to two."

"Perhaps three to one on the main things," I said, allowing this to penetrate, aware that his quick mind would study all the possibilities and arrive at a position so subtle and unexpected as to be of use to me if I, in turn, were quick enough to seize my opportunity.

At the airport, a detachment of airborne troops was drawn up before a festooned reviewing stand. Nearby the Marine Band played incongruous marches, while in the center of the stand, surrounded by cameras and dignitaries, stood the smiling President of the United States.

TWO

The next day while I was examining the various accounts of the last ceremony, the chief editor came into my office, his face blazing with excitement. "Iris Mortimer!" was all he could say.

"Iris? Where?"

"Dallas." He exploded the name in exhalation. Apparently, word had come from our office there that Iris had, a few hours before, denounced Paul for having ignored Cave's last wishes to be embalmed and that, as a result of this and other infidelities to Cavesword, she, as ranking director and with the full concurrence of the Chief Resident of Dallas, was calling a Council of Residents to be held the following week at Dallas to determine the future course of the Establishment.

I almost laughed aloud with pleasure. I had not believed she would show such vigor and daring. I had feared that she might choose to vanish into obscurity, her life ended with Cave. Even at my most optimistic, I had not dreamed she would act so boldly, exploiting a rivalry between Paul and the Chief Resident of Dallas, the premier member of the Council of Residents, a group that until now had existed for purely ceremonial reasons, exerting no influence upon the board of directors which, while Cave lived, was directed by Paul.

I moved swiftly. The *Journal* was at that moment going to press. I scribbled a brief announcement of the approaching Council of Residents, and I referred to Iris as Cave's spiritual heir. By telephone, I ordered a box to be cut out of the first page. I had not acted a moment too soon, for a few minutes after my telephone call to the compositor, Paul came to my office, furious. He slammed the door behind him.

"You knew this was going to happen."

"I wish I had."

He paced the floor quickly, eyes shining. "I've sent out an order countermanding Iris. I've also removed the Resident at Dallas. I'm still in charge of the Establishment. I control the funds and I've told every damned Resident in this country that if he goes to Dallas I'll cut off his Center without a penny."

"It won't work." I smiled amiably at Paul. "Your only hold over the Establishment is legal. You are the vice president of the corporation and now, at least for the interim, you're in charge. Fine. But since you've become so devoted to the letter of the law you can't act without consulting your directors and two of them will be in Dallas, reorganizing."

He cursed me for some minutes. Then abruptly he stopped. "You won't go to Dallas. You're going to be here for the directors' meeting that will cut off every Resident who attends that circus. We own the damned Centers. We can appoint whom we like. You're going to help ratify my new appointments."

I pressed the buzzer in my chair. A secretary came in. I told her to get me a reservation on the next plane to Dallas; then, before she had closed the door behind her, I was halfway through it. I turned to look back at Paul, who now stood quite alone in the office. "You had better come too," I said. "It's all over."

THREE

The new Establishment was many months in the making. The Council of seven hundred Residents from all parts of the world sat in general session once a week and in various committees the rest of the time. Iris was everywhere at once, advising, encouraging, proposing. We had adjoining suites in the huge white marble Center, which had now become (and was to remain) the capitol of the Cavite Establishment.

The Residents were an extraordinary crew, ranging from wild-eyed zealots to urbane, thoughtful men. None had been in the least disturbed by Paul's threats, and with Iris and myself as chief stockholders (Clarissa had turned her voting shares over to Iris, I discovered), we dissolved the old company and a new organization was fashioned, one governed by the Council of Residents, who in turn chose an heir to Cave and an administrative assistant to direct the affairs of the Establishment. Iris was unanimously appointed Guardian of Cavesword, while the Chief Resident of Dallas undertook Paul's old administrative duties. From a constitutional point of view the Council was in perfect agreement, accepting Iris's guidance without demur.

I myself was something of a hero for having committed the *Journal* at a crucial moment to the Dallas synod. I was made an honorary Resident (Poughkeepsie was given to me as a titular Center) and appointed to the Executive Committee, which was composed of Iris, Dallas, two elected Residents and myself.

We worked harmoniously for some weeks. Each day we would issue bulletins to the news services which had congregated in the city, reporting our progress devotedly.

Paul arrived in the second week. He came secretly and unannounced. I have no idea what it was that he said to Iris or what she said to him; all I know is that a few hours after their meeting in the Center, he took Cavesway of his own free will and to my astonishment.

I had not believed it possible, I said, when Iris told me, shortly after the Center announced the presence of Paul Himmell among the dead for that week (regular lists were published of those who had used the Center's facilities to take Cavesway); in fact, so quietly was it handled that very little was made of it in the press, which did not even report the event until ten days after it had taken place.

"We may have misunderstood Paul." Iris was serene. In the last year her figure had become thick and maternal, while her hair was streaked with premature white. We were alone in the Committee Room, waiting for our fellow committeemen who were not due for some minutes. The August sun shone gold upon the mahogany table, illuminating like a Byzantine mosaic the painting of Cave that hung behind her chair.

"He really did do it himself?" I looked at her suspiciously. She smiled softly, with amusement.

"He was persuaded," she said. "But he did it himself, of his own free will."

"Not forced?"

"I swear not. He was more sincere than I'd ever thought. He believed in Cavesway." How naturally she said that word which she had so desperately tried to keep from ever existing.

"Had you really planned to go away?" I asked. "The two of you?"

Iris looked at me, suddenly alert, impersonal. "That's all finished, Gene. We must keep on in the present. I never think now of anything but Cavesword and Cavesway. It does no good to think of what might have been."

And that was the most we were ever to say to one another about the crisis in our lives. We talked of the present and made plans. Stokharin had disappeared at the same time Paul flew to Dallas and we both decided it was wisest to forget him. Certainly he would not trouble us again. There was no talk of vengeance.

The committee members, important and proud, joined us and we took up the day's problem, which by some irony was the standardization of facilities for Cavesway in the different Centers, Quietly, without raising our voices, in a most goodhumored way. we broke neatly in half on Cavesway. I and one other Resident objected to the emphasis on death. Dallas and the fourth member were in favor of expanding the facilities, both physically and psychologically, until every Cavite could take Cavesway at the moment when he felt his social usefulness ebbing. We argued reasonably with one another until it became apparent that there was no possible ground for compromise.

It was put to a vote and Iris broke the tie by endorsing Cavesway.

FOUR

This morning as I finished the lines above I suffered a mild stroke . . . a particularly unusual one since I did not become, as far as I know, unconscious. I was rereading my somewhat telescoped account of the Council of Dallas when, without warning, the blow fell. A capillary burst in my brain and I felt as though I were losing my mind in one last fantastic burst of images. The pain was negligible, no worse than a headache, but the sensation of letting go one's conscious mind was terrifying. I tried to call for help, but I was too weak. For one long giddy moment I thought: I am dying; this is the way it is. Even in my anguish I was curious, waiting for that approach of winged darkness which years ago I once experienced when I fainted and which I have always since imagined to be like death's swift entrance.

But then my body recovered from the assault. The wall was breached, the enemy is in the city, but the citadel is still intact and I live.

Weakly I got up, poured myself a jigger of brandy and then, having drunk it all at once, fell across my bed and slept and did not dream, a rare blessing in these feverish last days.

I was awakened by the sensation of being watched. I opened my eyes and saw Jessup above me, looking like a bronze figure of Anubis. "I'm sorry . . . didn't meant to disturb you. Your door was open."

"Perfectly all right," I said, as smoothly as I could, drugged with sleep. I pulled myself up against the pillows. "Excuse me for not getting up, but I'm still a little weak from my illness."

"I wanted to see you," said Jessup, sitting down in the chair beside the bed. "I hope you don't mind my coming in like this."

"Not at all. How do you find Luxor?" I wanted to delay as long as possible the questions which I was quite sure he would want to ask me.

"The people are not so fixed in error as we'd been warned. There's a great curiosity about Cavesword." His eyes had been taking in the details of the room with some interest; to my horror I recalled that I had left the manuscript of my work on the table instead of hiding it as usual in the washstand. He saw it. "Your . . . memoirs?" He looked at me with a polite interest which I was sure disguised foreknowledge.

"A record of my excavations," I said, in a voice which descended the scale to a whisper. "I do it for my own amusement, to pass the time."

"I should enjoy reading it."

"You exaggerate, in your kindness," I said, pushing myself higher on the bed, preparing if necessary for a sudden spring.

"Not at all. If it is about Egypt, I should read it. There are no contemporary accounts of this country . . . by one of us."

"I'm afraid the details of findings in the valley yonder," I gestured toward Libya and the last acres of the kings, "won't be of much use to you. I avoid all mention of people less than two millennia dead."

"Even so," But Jessup did not pursue the subject. I relaxed a little.

"I must tell you," he said suddenly, "that I was suspicious of you."

Now I thought, now it comes; then I was amused. Right at the end they arrive, when it was too late for them, or for me. "What form did your suspicions take?" My fear left me in one last flurry, like a bird departing in a cold wind for another latitude, leaving the branch which held it all summer through to freeze.

"I thought you might be the one we have so often heard of . . . in legend, that is. The enemy of Cave."

"Which enemy?"

"The nameless one, or at least we know a part of his name if lutherist is derived from it."

"What made you suspect me?"

"Because were I an enemy of Cave and were I forced to disappear, I should come to just such a town in just such a country as this."

"Perfectly logical," I agreed. "But there are many towns in the Arab League, in Asia too. Why suppose one old man to be this mythical villain?"

Jessup smiled. "Intuition, I'm afraid. A terrible admission from one who has been trained in the logic of Cavesword. It seemed exactly right. You're the right age, the right nationality. In any case, I telephoned Dallas about you."

I took this calmly. "You talked to the Chief Resident himself?"

"Of course not." Jessup was surprised at my suggestion. "One just doesn't call the Chief Resident like that. Only senior Residents *ever* talk to him personally. No, I talked to an old friend of mine who is one of the five principal assistants to the Historian General. We were in school together and his speciality is the deviationists of the early days."

"And what did you learn from this scholar?"

Jessup gave me a most charming smile. "Nothing at all. There was no such person as I thought existed, as a number of people thought existed. It was all a legend, a perfectly natural one for gossip to invent. There was a good deal of trouble at the beginning, especially over Cavesway. There was even a minority at Dallas that refused to accept the principle of Cavesway, without which of course there could be no Establishment. According to the stories one heard as recently as my university days, ten years ago, the original lutherist had led the opposition to Iris, in Council and out. For a time it looked as though the Establishment might be broken in two (this you must remember since you were contemporary to it; fortunately, our Historical Office has tended more and more to view it in the long perspective, and popular works on Cave now make no reference to it); in any case, there was an open break and the minority was soon absorbed by the majority."

"Painlessly?" I mocked him. Could he be telling the truth? or was this a trap?

Jessup shrugged. "These things are never without pain. It is said that an attempt was made on our Mother Iris's life during the ceremony of Cave's ashes. We still continue it, you know."

"Continue what?"

"The symbolic gathering of the ashes. But of course you know the origin of all that. There was a grave misinterpretation of Cave's last wishes. His ashes were scattered over the United

States when it was his wish to be embalmed and preserved. Every year, Iris would travel to the four cities over which the ashes had been distributed and collect a bit of dust in each city to symbolize her obedience to Cavesword in all things. At Seattle, during this annual ceremony, a group of lutherists tried to assassinate her."

"I remember," I said. I had had no hand in that dark episode, but it provided the Establishment with the excuse they needed. My partisans were thrown in prison all over the country. The government, which by then was entirely Cavite, handed several thousand over to the Centers, where they were indoctrinated, ending the heresy for good. Iris herself had secretly arranged for my escape . . . but Jessup could know nothing of this.

"Of course you know these things, perhaps even better than I since you were alive then. Forgive me. I have got into the bad Residential habit of explaining the obvious. An occupational disease." He was disarming. "The point I'm trying to make is that my suspicions of you were unworthy and unfounded since there was no leader of the lutherists to escape; all involved responded nicely to indoctrination and that was the end of it. The story I heard in school was a popular one. The sort that often evolves, like Lucifer and the old Christian God, for instance. For white there must be black, that kind of thing. Except that Cave never had a major antagonist, other than in legend."

"I see. Tell me, then, if there was no real leader to the lutherists, how did they come by their name?"

His answer was prompt. "Martin Luther. My friend in the H.O. told me this morning over the telephone. Someone tried to make an analogy, that's all, and the name stuck, though as a rule the use of any words or concepts derived from the dead religions is frowned upon. You know the story of Martin Luther? It seems that he . . ."

"I know the story of Martin Luther," I answered, more sharply than I intended.

"Now I've tired you." Jessup was sympathetic. He got to his feet. "I just wanted to tell you about my suspicions, that's all. I thought it might amuse you and perhaps bring us closer together, for I'd very much like to be your friend, not only for the help you can give me here but also because of your memories of the old days when Cave and Iris, his Mother, still lived."

"Iris was at least five years younger than Cave."

"Everyone knows that, my friend. She was his *spiritual* Mother, as she is ours. 'From the dark womb of unbeing we emerge in the awful light of consciousness from which the only virtuous escape is Cavesway.' I quote from Iris's last testament. It was found among her papers after her death."

"Did *she* take Cavesway?"

Jessup frowned. "It is said that she died of pneumonia, but had death *not* come upon her unexpectedly it was well known that she would have taken Cavesway. There has been considerable debate over this at Dallas. I hear from highly placed people that before many years have passed they will promulgate a new interpretation, applying only to Iris, which will establish that intent and fact are the same, that though she died of pneumonia she *intended* to take Cavesway and, therefore, took Cavesway in spirit and therefore in fact."

"A most inspiring definition."

"It is beautifully clear, though perhaps difficult for an untrained mind. May I read your memoir?" His eyes strayed curiously to the table.

"When it's finished," I said. "I should be most curious to see how it strikes you."

"Well, I won't take up any more of your time. I hope you'll let me come to see you."

"Nothing could give me more pleasure." And then, with a pat on my shoulder and a kind suggestion that should I choose Cavesway he would be willing to adminster the latest drug, Jessup departed.

I remained very still for some minutes, holding my breath for long intervals, trying to die. Then, in a sudden rage, I hurled my pillow across the room and beat the mattress with my fists; it was over. All was at an end except my own miserable life, which will be gone soon enough. My name erased; my work subverted; all that I most detested regnant in the world. I could have wept had there been one tear left in me. Now there is nothing I can do but finish this narrative . . . for its own sake since it will be thought, I know, the ravings of a madman when Jessup reads it, as he surely will after I am dead.

I have tried now for several hours to describe my last meeting with Iris but I find that my memory is at last seriously impaired, the result, no doubt, of that tiny vein's eruption this morning in my brain. It is all a jumble. I think there were several years in which I was in opposition. I think that I had considerable support and I am almost sure that, until the attempted assassination of Iris at Seattle, I was close to dominating the Council of Residents. But the idiotic attempt on her life ruined everything. She knew of course that I had had nothing to do with it, but she was a resolute leader and she took this opportunity to annihilate my party. I believe we met for the last time in a garden. A garden very like the one where we first met in California. No, on the banks of the Hudson . . . I must reread what I have written to refresh my memory. It is all beginning to fade rapidly.

In any case, we met in a garden in the late autumn when all the trees were bare. She was white-haired then, though neither of us was much over forty.

I believe that she wept a little. After all, we were the last who had been close to Cave, heirs become adversaries, she victrix and I vanquished. I never loved her more than at that last moment. Of this I am sure. We talked of possible places of exile. She had arranged for my passage on a ship to Alexandria under the name of Richard Hudson (yes, she who erased my name, in her compassion, gave me a new one). She did not want, however, to know where I intended to go from there.

"It would be a temptation to the others," she said. I remember that one sentence and I do remember the appearance of the garden, though its location I have quite forgotten: there was a high wall around it and the smell of moldering leaves was acrid. From the mouth of a satyr no water fell in a mossy pool.

Ah yes! the question and the answer. That's it, of course. The key. I had nearly lost it. Before I left, I asked her what it was that Cave had said to her when he was dying, the words the rest of us had not heard. At first she hesitated but then, secure in her power and confident of her own course, she told me: "He said: 'Gene was right.' " I remember looking at her with shock, waiting for her to continue, to make some apology for her reckless falsification of Cave's life and death. But she said no more. There was, I suppose, no explanation she might have made. Without a word, I left the garden. My real life had ended.

There's more to it than this but I cannot get it straight. Something has happened to my memory. I wonder if perhaps I have not dreamed all this: a long nightmare drawing to its bitter close among the dry ruins of an ancient world.

It is late now. I still live, though I am exhausted and indifferent to everything except that violent living sun whose morning light has just this moment begun to strike upon the western hills across the river: all that is left, all that ever was, the red fire.

I shall not take Cavesway even though I die in pain and confusion. Anubis must wait for me in the valley until the last, and even then I shall struggle in his arms, for I know now that life, *my* life, was more valuable than I knew, more significant and virtuous than the other's was in her bleak victory.

Though my memory is going from me rapidly, the meaning is clear and unmistakable and I see the pattern whole at last, marked in giant strokes upon the air: I was he whom the world awaited. I was that figure, that messiah whose work might have been the world's delight and liberation. But the villain death once more undid me, and to *him* belongs the moment's triumph. Yet life continues, though I do not. Time bends upon itself. The morning breaks. Now I will stop, for it is day.

Other Panthers For Your Enjoyment

Man and Woman

☐ **Gore Vidal** **MYRA BRECKINRIDGE** **40p**

The elegantly outrageous novel that demolishes lots of American sexual myths. Vidal's piercing invention is at its most dazzling in this story of Hollywood sex-changes.

☐ **Martin Seymour-Smith** **FALLEN WOMEN** **40p**

The strumpet in literature – from the Old Testament right up to today's highly professional porn. The author does it with insight, sympathy and wit, and his conclusions are controversial – or, as the *New Statesman* puts it, 'Provocative'.

☐ **Trans. Charles Plumb** **THE SATIRES OF JUVENAL** **42p**

The vices – and what vices! – of Imperial Rome by one who was there. A translation for the 1970's – direct, witty, lewd.

☐ **Jean Genet** **QUERELLE OF BREST** **60p**

The criminal-homosexual world so sensuously evoked by Genet is a taboo subject in suburbia. Elsewhere, Genet is 'Matchless . . . any comment at once becomes presumptuous' – Terry Southern

☐ **Jean Genet** **OUR LADY OF THE FLOWERS** **40p**

The great sensual novel about the criminal-homosexual world with which Genet overturned middle class values.

☐ **John Rechy** **CITY OF NIGHT** **40p**

Rechy's city of dreadful night is any downtown American city after dark, when lonely homosexuals begin their frantic prowl in search of companionship.

The Underground Man

'A hugely charming book, the duke is an unusually lovable protagonist'
Robert Hanks, *Independent on Sunday*

'What Jackson evokes with invention is the play of energy within His Grace's lonely self-absorption: the strange comedy and bravery of a self-diagnosis attempted with inadequate means'
Francis Spufford, *Independent*

'A strange, imaginative, rich and ultimately sad novel'
Andrew Roberts, *Spectator*

'What this unorthodox and remarkable novel amounts to is an elegaic, engaging and labyrinthine portrait of an aristocrat'
Andrew Biswell, *Daily Telegraph*

'An enjoyable and successful first novel, colourful and serious'
Philip Hensher, *Mail on Sunday*

'An intriguing and satisfying first novel about fantasy, identity and the reliability of perception'
John Burnside, *Scotsman*

'The writing is poised, clear and concise . . . it has an accomplished finesse and a thrilling sense of ambition. This is an intriguing debut'
Peter Whitebrook, *Scotland on Sunday*

MICK JACKSON was born in Great Harwood, Lancashire in 1960. He has written and directed several short films and lives in Brighton.

MICK JACKSON

The Underground Man

PICADOR

First published 1997 by Picador

This edition published 1998 by Picador
an imprint of Macmillan Publishers Ltd
25 Eccleston Place, London SW1W 9NF
and Basingstoke

Associated companies throughout the world

ISBN 0 330 34956 2

3 5 7 9 8 6 4

A CIP catalogue record for this book is available from the British Library.

Typeset by SetSystems Ltd, Saffron Walden, Essex
Printed and bound in Great Britain by
Mackays of Chatham plc, Chatham, Kent

The Underground Man

From His Grace's Journal

September 30th

*

I have no idea how an apple tree works. The quiet machine beneath the bark is quite beyond my ken. But, like the next man along, I find Imagination always willing to leap into Ignorance's breach . . .

The tree roots, I imagine, play a major part – managing somehow to soak up the richness of the earth. I picture this richness drawn slowly up the trunk, pumped out along every branch.

No doubt the sun and rain are also involved, their warmth and moisture in some way being essential to the constitution of the tree. But how the richness of the earth, the sun and the rain come together to produce (i) a perfect blossom, then (ii) a small apple-bud – well, that remains a mystery to me.

*

Locate a local apple tree. Visit it daily through the summer months. Note how the bud slowly puffs itself up into apple-shape. See how it slowly takes a breath. The weeks roll by until its own increasing weight finally forces the fruit to fall. You will find it on the ground, all ready to eat. This whole process is utterly dependable; has a beginning, a middle and an end. But I am not satisfied. Far from it. Plain baffled is what I am. All sorts of questions remain unanswered. Such as

... who taught the tree its apple-conjuring? And ... where does the fruit's flavour come from?

*

I have on my estate one of the largest orchards in the whole of England. My Bramleys and Orange Pippins bring home trophies and silver cups. Each year, as the summer grinds to a close, I watch the carts being led down the drive. Their wheels creak and judder under the weight of the baskets. Every one is packed to the brim. I sometimes stand at the gate to the orchard and watch them dreamily trundle by. Sooner or later, an apple takes a tumble. I pick it up. I study it. But am never any closer to understanding how it came about.

O, how wonderful to be an apple tree – to know one's place in the world. To be both fixed and fruitful. To know what one is about.

*

Woke at dawn this morning, after a wearying night's sleep. Blew down to Clement to fetch a sack of corn and twenty minutes later we were both of us striding out along the Sloswick path to feed the deer. The day was bright and fresh enough, certainly, but had about it a brittleness, as if it had been wrought from glass, and though the sky was perfectly cloudless I sensed a chill in the air which rang silently all about me and warned that autumn was on its way. This proceeded to fill me with such foreboding that I became quite distracted and had to leave Clement to attend the deer alone.

As a young man I imagined growing old would be something like the feeling one has at the close of a long and satisfying day: a not unpleasant lassitude, always remedied by a good night's sleep. But I now know it to be the gradual revelation of one's body as nothing more than a bag of unshakeable aches. Old age is but the reduced capacity of a failing machine. Even my sleep – that beautiful oblivion always relied upon for replenishment – now seems to founder, has somehow lost its step. My fingers and toes are cold the whole year round, as if my fire is slowly going out.

Made my way home via Cow-close Wood where I spotted the lazy dipping flight of a single magpie. Spat twice, raised my hat, said, 'Good morning, Mr Magpie,' then looked around to make sure my little ritual had not been observed by anyone. I do believe I grow more superstitious with every passing year. Once upon a time, I would have thrown a stone after the bird. Now I cower like a frightened child.

A hundred yards further down the lane, rounding the corner by Horses' Graveyard, I came suddenly upon a huge and tatty crow, perched on a rotting tree stump, with his little legs apart. I was less than ten foot from him before I registered him and the shock of it brought me skidding to a halt. He eyed me, I thought, most malevolently, like some squatting devil in his black raggedy cloak. I distinctly felt my sphincter slacken, my testicles shuffle in their sack.

That awful crow stared right at me; its gaze seemed to penetrate my skull. By now, my mind was furiously sending out instructions – to turn and run, to get well away from that bird – but my body, I discovered, was weirdly stuck, as if caught in a spell. (As I sit here at my desk with my feet in my slippers I can muse over how but a minute before I had dealt quite satisfactorily with the single magpie . . . had known how to counteract its little load of bad luck. But with the crow I was utterly defenceless. I had no antidote for that bird at all.)

Coming so dramatically upon it had left me breathless. My mind's slate was rubbed quite clean. And yet my own voice whispered distantly to me, insisting that if some effort were not soon made to remove me the crow might hold me in those woods until the end of time. So I did all I could to encourage my legs into action and found that some blood still shifted weakly in my veins. I inched my foot out along the ground until, at last, it became a tiny step; tentatively put some weight on it, then began the whole interminable process again. All the while, that damned bird kept his evil eye on me. But by concentrating my mind on my own creeping feet and doing my utmost to block out his vicious gaze I began slowly to edge my way past him until, in time, I had put between us an extra yard . . . two yards . . . finally, three.

Now I have never been especially athletic (and, even if I had, those days would now be long gone), but as soon as I was a dozen steps past that bird I broke into a frantic, rickety trot. I turned only once – to be certain the little winged monster wasn't after me – and as I did so he let out a terrible 'Caw' from his throne. Then he spread his oily wings and pumped them; rose, banked and disappeared into the trees.

I would not claim to be especially mindful of bird lore and the symbolic meaning attributed to each one but I am in no doubt that that crow most assuredly meant me harm. It had created around it an almost paralysing field of malignity; I am sure any other man would have felt it just the same. Such a small and common creature, yet its evil filled the whole wood up.

When I got home I found that Mrs Pledger had grilled for me my favourite smoked bacon and she looked most put out when I failed to raise a forkful to my mouth, but it was all I could do to get a cup of sweet tea down me and make my way back up to my rooms. I was deeply shaken by my crow-encounter and reckoned I might have caught a headchill along the way. When he returned, I asked Clement to be good enough to dig out my old beaver hat and give it a brushing down – a sure sign that summer is at an end.

*

*

Slept right through till eleven when I was woken by Clement as he tended the fire. Felt much improved on yesterday, if a little muddled. Bathed, put on my thick tweed trousers and a brand-new Norfolk jacket. Strapped myself into my good brown boots and tried to comb some sense into what remains of my hair.

I have been going bald now for well over thirty years; was still quite a young fellow when I first found a little nest of hair in the lining of my deerstalker after a particularly vigorous stroll. Thereafter, I brushed my hair less frequently (and with a good deal more care), vainly hoping to slow the whole terrifying process down. I thought perhaps my strolls' exertion might somehow be to blame or, more specifically, the heat they generated under my hat. I don't mind admitting it took me quite a while to come to terms with the facts before me, one day managing to convince myself how it was all in my imagination and that I wasn't going bald at all, the next day suddenly certain I would be an egghead by a week Friday and that my life was not worth carrying on.

But there are, it seems, a hundred different ways of losing one's hair and I should perhaps be grateful that the manner handed out to me was one which takes a good long while. My hair made a slow, almost imperceptible retreat from my forehead, while at my crown a small circle of exposed scalp gradually grew. Two carefully positioned mirrors were required for me to observe the decay as, year by year, these two clearings made their way towards each other. Eventually, a thin channel of flesh connected them up, which then widened from generous parting to a broad pink trough, until, at last, all that remained was an occasional startled baby-hair on my otherwise bare cranium.

Even now, there are days when I am sure it is all over, that the damage is finally done. But closer inspection always obliges me to concede that new corners of my scalp continue to come to light and that the spread of flesh goes on. It is not an unbearable burden. My days of real vanity are gone. I no longer fret about it. There is simply more face to wash, less hair to comb.

The hair which still clings to the sides of my head is white, like lambswool. It sprouts out around my ears and in a rude manner behind. In order to scotch the inevitable comparisons with the proverbial coot, I have long sported a full moustache and beard, also white but a good deal more muttony, which seems to me to restore some much-needed equilibrium.

After five minutes' oiling and tinkering my head looked little different to when I started out. To perk me up I undertook twenty gentle knee-bends and trimmed my moustache then had a glance in the full-length mirror.

I have heard me described as a wiry man, which I interpret as meaning 'held together with wires' and seems altogether quite fitting and fair. Now, whether I have more wires in my body than the next man or whether it is just that mine are more on display, I could not say, but they are clearly at work at every junction of my frame – most noticeable in my arms, legs and neck. When I walk or bend or even grimace they can be seen twitching under the skin like tense lengths of twine.

Where my neck and torso come together is usually a regular network of root and vein. Of late, however, I have become uncertain whether all these wires are properly attached. Some appear to have grown quite slack; one or two to have come away from their housing altogether. On a bad day I worry that somewhere inside of me an essential spring might have snapped, to dangle and rattle about in me for the rest of my days.

I have also recently noticed how, in wet weather, I have a tendency to creak – there's no denying it, it's plain for all to hear – so on damp days I stay in by the fire and play Patience or Bagatelle. All the same, I think 'wiry' still just about does the job – even if the wires are not as taut as they once were.

*

October 5th

*

I was returning down the West avenue this morning, with autumn's grim carnage all around, when I came across one of my gamekeepers walking the most gargantuan dog. A terrific beast, it was – some sort of long-haired pepper-and-salt mongrel with a two-foot tail and an insolent gait. A donkey of a dog. Well, the keeper and I struck up a conversation about the weather and suchlike. Meanwhile the dog appeared to listen most intelligently, furrowing its brows as we carried on, so that I half expected it to share with us its own considered opinions and maybe put us right on the odd point or two. I complimented the keeper on his fine creature and asked what he fed it on and I recall him saying how, as a matter of fact, it belonged to his wife's brother and thrived on Lancashire hotpot – a large bowl, three times a day. Well, I was most impressed; especially after hearing how the keeper's young niece and nephew often went riding on its back with never a grumble from the dog.

I stroked its huge head – as big as a bison's! – and felt a lovely warmth spread across the palm of my hand from the thick rolls of dogflesh. I could have happily spent the entire morning marvelling at the beast but the keeper seemed eager to be about his business so we drew our brief exchange to a close. He raised his cap, made a clicking noise from out the side of his mouth and gently tugged on the dog's leather lead and that great solemn creature seemed also to nod its heavy head at me before turning and ambling away.

Once the dog had picked up a bit of momentum I saw how the keeper had trouble keeping up, and in no time they were fifty yards away and apparently still gathering speed when a thought occurred to me. I called after them, which sent them into something of a spin, and I hurried over to where they had come to rest. It took me I should say maybe three or four attempts to properly get the idea out – I tend to become tongue-tied when my mind is all fired up – but managed finally to articulate my offer of having a saddle made up in the dog's measurements so that the keeper's niece and nephew might sit upon it without fear of falling off. Personally, I thought this a first-class idea – a dog in a saddle, very good! – but the keeper kept his eyes pinned to the ground and politely declined. So we said our goodbyes all over again and I let them carry on their way.

I have always been very fond of dogs. Cats have much too high an opinion of themselves and generally make for poor company. Are, on the whole, utterly humourless and always wrapped up in their own thoughts. Some days I reckon all cats are spies. Dogs, on the other hand, are reassuringly foolish and always game for a roll-around. Over the years I should say I have owned several dozen dogs – of all temperaments and shapes and sizes – and while I retain a good deal of affection for each of them it is fair to say I have been besotted only with one.

About twenty years ago, on my birthday, good Lord Galway of Serlby presented me with a beautiful basset-hound pup. At that time his was the only pack in the country (brought over from France, I believe) so that they were valuable and unusual to boot. Immediately recognizable by their stout little legs, concave back and baggy ears, something about their appearance suggests that they have been knocked together out of odd bits of various other dog. The simplest task – such as walking – can prove very troublesome for a basset-hound. It is as if they have been poorly designed. Their coat is always most generously tailored and none more so than on the pup handed me that day. He had on him enough flesh to adequately clothe another two or three dogs besides – the majority of it hanging off his face – and though he was, at the time, no more than a few months old he wore the immutable basset expression of Lifelong Woe.

His eyes were all red and rheumy, as if he had tried washing away his miseries with port wine, but his tail stood to attention like the handle on a water pump and the look of utter disgust with which he regarded my dinner guests enamoured him to me straight away. Being presented with a great ribbon around his neck, to the accompaniment of whoops and cheers, was, apparently, a humiliation almost too great for him to bear. It was his doleful expression, his deep disdain which first stole my heart away, whilst simultaneously, and so vividly, calling to mind my father's long-departed brother, Leonard.

(Uncle Leonard was some sort of military man. My one abiding memory is of him sitting alone in the Games Room, quaffing great quantities of Scotch whisky while his cigar smoke slowly filled the room. The little finger on his right hand was missing, which he once told me was from his having bitten his fingernails as a boy. He died at Balaclava in '54, kicked in the head by a horse.)

The likeness between dog and dead uncle was so startling that I wondered if there was not, after all, some grain of truth in this notion of reincarnation – the upshot being that I named the dog Uncle on the spot, which seemed as acceptable to him as it did to me.

From that day forward we got along famously, were constant companions, and I don't doubt we made quite a spectacle as we took our daily constitutional: me in my brightly coloured waistcoats, which I favoured at the time, and proud Uncle in matching collar and coat, zigzagging beside me and scouring the ground with his plum of a nose.

I can only hope that he was happy, for he never lost that forlorn and put-upon look, but he was animated enough and most affectionate, which I took as signs of contentment, and when he slept he did not kick or twitch as many dogs do. On our cross-country walks his great flapping ears would gather up all kinds of rubbish, and I would like nothing more than to be picking them clean today. But one spring morning he spotted a rabbit in a nearby field, chased it into its burrow and got himself stuck. I ran back to the house like a madman, stood in the hall calling for servants and spades, but by the time we had returned and dug down to him the poor fellow had suffocated. I carried him home, with all the servants trailing behind and buried him in a quiet corner of the Italian gardens the following day.

Out strolling years later I would find myself idly talking to him, as if he were right there by my side and us still the best of friends. Even now, if I have grown sleepy in a fireside chair and decide I must go to bed, I might whisper, 'Come, Uncle,' without thinking, as I rise.

Some essential part of him stays with me; persists down all the years. Somewhere deep inside me his tail still wags. He never seems to tire.

*

OCTOBER 10TH

*

The last tunnel is all but completed – heady days indeed.

When Mr Bird entered the dining room this morning, a roll of papers tucked under his arm, he had about him his usual unassuming attitude but his features were all aglow. I noticed how he was a little ... *nervy* ... and how his eyes flashed about the place, which was enough to get me quite giddy with anticipation myself. Down the years Mr Bird and I have got to know each other very well and he is fully familiar with my love of maps and charts, but as he rolled out onto the table his latest set of plans I would be hard pushed to say which of us had more difficulty standing still. A mustard pot, a cup and a saucer were employed to hold down the curling corners of the map. Then Mr B. and I stepped back a foot or two to take the whole picture in.

In the very centre of the map stood the house in miniature (a good likeness, I have to say, done in pen and ink) accompanied by all the stables and outhouses – each clearly labelled in italic script. The whole estate was etched out around the house, with the woods and drives all carefully marked in. As we both stood there looking dumbly down at the map Mr Bird discreetly produced from his breast pocket a small pencil stub. He raised it to his mouth, gave the lead a little lick and, with a precision any surgeon would be proud of, marked out the first tunnel, as I looked anxiously on. The squat little pencil travelled east from the house, coolly dissected the lake, crept right up the Pudding Hill and came to rest in the outskirts of Worksop town.

Mr Bird pushed himself back on an elbow and looked up at me. I nodded back at him, encouragingly. A faint whiff of sweat hung in the air between us and it occurred to me how our hushed exhilaration had somehow managed to evoke the rare stench of horse-heat in that large cool room.

In the minutes which followed Mr Bird proceeded to pencil in a further three tunnels, which left the house and headed north, south and west. At times they swung slightly to left or right but, on the whole, kept pretty much to the straight line. Mr Bird's pencil lead advanced through the forests and fields at quite a rate and when it reached the end of each tunnel I distinctly heard a sticky sound as it was plucked from the map. The mark it left was nothing more than a full stop at the close of a sentence, but in that tiny speck I saw quite clearly the tunnel entrance, as craggy as a cave.

A small gatehouse stood where each underground thoroughfare emerged, each with the word *Lodge* as a foundation. The map informed me how these lodges are currently occupied by Digby, Harris, Stoodle and Pyke, whose job it will be to lock and unlock the gates as necessary, to light the gaslights down their tunnel if word is received that they are to be used after dark and to ensure that no children get in.

The chart now consisted of four simple pencil-paths, of roughly equal length. A house with four roots sprouting from it, perhaps, or something vaguely akin to a compass face. But when Mr Bird had got his breath back and wet his pencil a fifth time the set of tunnels he brought into being caused the image to change most radically. Expertly, he fitted a second cross over the cross already on the map. The pie which had previously been quartered was now divided into eighths, so that when he had done with his pencilling the whole arrangement of tunnels was no longer compass-like and more like the spokes of a rimless wheel. For a second I had trouble swallowing and I felt myself come over quite faint. It had never previously occurred to me – a Wheel, with my house as its hub!

Mr Bird looked down at the map with evident satisfaction,

as if he had just conjured the tunnels into existence with a wave of his modest wand. He rested one hand on the table and pushed his spectacles back up his nose with the other. Out of the corner of my eye I felt him sneak a glance at me. Then for a minute or two we did nothing but gaze down and drink in every last detail, until all my pleasure and gratitude finally welled up inside me and overflowed.

'Sterling work, Mr Bird,' I said.

Mr Bird's Account

I should say His Grace first made contact with me a good year and a half before the work was begun. He had me travel up to Welbeck for a meeting where he told me all about his tunnelling plans. In some shape or form he had already worked out in his head what he wanted – he always had quite firm ideas – though he never mentioned to me what purpose they were to serve. Well, to be honest, tunnels weren't what we were normally about and, when the opportunity arose, I told the Duke as much. Garden landscaping, the occasional lake or ha-ha was much more our line. The previous year we had done a little something at the back of His Grace's London residence which, I was informed at that first meeting, had pleased him very much. As I recall, he was greatly taken with the wrought-iron fancywork on the frame of a sunk glass walkway. And so, right from the start, he was eager to impress on me the notion that my company was right for the job.

I remember how he had with him a small wooden box full of sketches which he emptied out onto the table. All sorts of drawings and diagrams, all jumbled up together. Then there were the plans he had never got around to putting on paper, some of which took a long while coming back to him and even longer to explain. But the basic idea was that there was to be a whole series of tunnels leaving the house and going out under the estate in all directions. Most were to emerge by gatehouses; only two were unattended, as I recall. But it would be fair to say that if you didn't know about these last two you would not easily trip over them.

Of the eight tunnels we eventually built on His Grace's estate – a good twelve miles of them in all – half were twenty foot wide, reaching fifteen foot in height and big enough for two carriages to pass without much difficulty, and the rest about half that size. I can't say that they were very elegant to look at: plain red brick in a horseshoe arch, with vaulted roofs where they met under the house and tiled passageways off to the stables. But they were sound and did the job they were built to do and I've no doubt they'll be standing a hundred years from now.

Once we were clear of the house and out into the gardens and surrounding fields most of the tunnel-laying was done by what is commonly called 'cut and cover', which simply means digging a deep ditch directly into the ground and, when the brickwork is completed, putting the earth back over the roof. Consequently, most of the tunnels on the estate are no more than a couple of feet beneath ground level. They were lit in the daytime by skylights – two foot in diameter and four inches thick – at regular intervals of twenty feet or so and each one requiring its own 'chimney', which is probably what slowed us down the most. Each tunnel had a line of gas jets plumbed in, both left and right, for use at night. I heard there were over five thousand such lamps put in place down there but am glad to say that particular task fell to someone else.

All in all, as you can imagine, this amounted to a great deal of work which took us some time to carry out. We employed, on average, a gang of about two hundred men – each on a shilling a day. The Duke insisted that every two men should have between them the use of a donkey for riding to and from the camp and that each man be given an umbrella. Well, you can picture the scene yourself, I'm sure. In the summer it was as gay as the seaside, but in the rain it was very grim.

On top of the tunnels we had stairwells and passages to put in, which went up into the house itself. He was very fond of trapdoors and suchlike, was the Duke. That was what got him going the most.

While I think about it, one thing does come back to me. On only the second or third meeting, I think it was, when we were still at a very early stage, His Grace came in looking highly vexed and asked me straight out, 'What about tree roots, Mr Bird? What about damage to the roots?' When I was quite sure I had grasped what it was he was asking, I did my best to assure him how the roots of the trees on the estate would be in no danger and that if there were any chance of us coming up against the roots of a great oak, for example, then it was quite within our means to steer a course round the thing. This seemed to put his mind at rest.

Anyhow, I don't mind saying that I think we made a good job of it. It was the largest commission my company undertook. We were up there so long that by the time I left I felt like a proper Nottinghamshire man. I was sad to say goodbye.

There were stories, as you know, regarding the Duke's appearance – how he was said to be deformed and dreadful to look upon. But the people who go about saying such things are nothing but gossip-merchants. Anyone who ever met the man will tell you just the same. I saw him a hundred times if I saw him once and the worst I could say was that on a bad day he could look a little ashen. A touch under the weather is all.

I'm afraid our tunnel-building did nothing but encourage the wild stories. When a man starts acting eccentrically and hiding himself away, people feel at liberty to give their imaginations some slack. By the time they'd finished they'd made him into a right monster, but it was all in their own minds.

The whole time we worked on the tunnels – and we were

up there five years in all – I don't believe I ever asked His Grace directly just what the tunnels were for. It quickly ceased to matter. In the end I suspect I was just as wrapped up in the project as the old man himself. From time to time some of the lads would quiz me about it or make up a little gossip of their own. People like to let themselves get carried away. It comes, I think, from idleness, or envy, maybe. But then His Grace would come out to the site and have a look around and that would nip it in the bud, right there.

There are times when I wonder if he did not simply suffer from shyness. Shyness in the extreme. But then it's not my place to say. Most of us, at some time, have peculiar ideas we'd like to carry out but have not the money to put them in place. That was not the case with the old Duke.

Yes, I was sorry to see the back of him. He was a most gentle man.

From His Grace's Journal

October 14th

*

Woke with a decidedly sour stomach, after a third consecutive disturbed night's sleep. Had intended, this morning, to pay a visit on my old gardener, Mr Snow, who, I hear, has been very ill, but when I peered out at the day from my window the wind was stripping the leaves right off the trees and the barometer tower on the West wing promised more unsettled stuff to come. Resolved to stay indoors, at least until the rain had cleared. Dug out a clean nainsook handkerchief and dipped it in lavender oil. Blew down the pipe for some news on my Balbriggan socks but got no response from any quarter so, like some slippered nomad, trekked down the stairs to see what was going on.

Finally located Mrs Pledger in a steaming laundry-room, her sleeves rolled up to her elbows as she set about a mound of wet washing. She nodded in my direction but continued to pummel away. Today, it transpired, is the day allocated for the washing of bedsheets and it was a moment or two before I was able to fully take in the industrious scene before me. Stone sinks overflowed with hot water, soapsuds slid and drifted everywhere. The piercing aroma of cleaning agent made a powerful impression on the eyes and nose. Damp sheets hung down from wooden slats which were suspended from the ceiling on a web of pulleys and ropes, and this huge expanse of wet linen and the frantic activity beneath encouraged in me the notion that I had stumbled aboard some many-masted cutter as it weathered some terrible storm.

Four girls helped Mrs Pledger with her laundry and as I am in the habit of constantly forgetting the names of those in her employ (they are always coming and going, it seems, or turning into women overnight) I had her introduce me to them. Thus, I learned that the house staff currently includes at least 'two Annies, an Anne and a Sarah' and while they persevered with their scrubbing and rinsing I leaned against one of the vast sinks and repeated their names under my breath, finding the phrase to have a strangely calming quality to it.

With everyone so thoroughly immersed in their business I was left very much to myself, so to pass the time I stared into some temporarily abandoned sink, where I observed on the water's cooling surface the quiet collapse of soapy-suds. Very interesting indeed. What began life as a gently frying pancake of lather gradually changed its appearance as its tiny bubbles gave out, one by one. By exercising my mind on it I found that, with a little effort, the suds took on a shape not unlike the British Isles (a very frothy fellow he was, as if recently covered by a fall of snow). He wore an angular hat for Scotland, stretched his toes out at Penzance, had Wales for a belly and the Home Counties for a sit-upon. This little discovery rather pleased me, although, in all honesty, I could not say for certain how much was in the beholder's eye and how much was in the suds.

Well, those abandoned bubbles continued popping and my suddy Briton duly stretched and shrank, until I saw that he was, in fact, metamorphosing into – yes! – Italy's high-heeled boot. Britain turning into Italy – what confusion that would cause! What kind of weather would we have, I wonder? And what language? We should all have to speak in Latin. (*Amo, amas, amat* . . .) Excellent!

I was still happily ruminating in this manner when Italy's centre suddenly came apart and what had just now appeared to be solid land split into four or five smaller isles. Well, this came as quite a shock, and I had to fairly pump my imagination to come up with another port of call (my geography has always been very poor). Japan, perhaps, or the Philippines. I had to hurry . . . the islands were shrinking like ice-floes in the sun. I just about managed to bring into focus one final archipelago of froth but it was the briefest vision and in a second it had shimmered and gone, leaving nothing behind but a flat pool of dirty water, as if some aquatic apocalypse had run its course.

The whole process, I found, had quite tired me out. All the same, I offered to roll up my sleeves and lend a hand, thinking I would quite like to stir up some suds of my own. Mrs Pledger, however, was adamant that she and the girls were best left to do the work themselves so I loitered quietly in the corner and did my best to keep myself occupied.

Seeing all the sheets having the dirt drubbed out of them reminded me of a theory I have recently been entertaining. One which, on reflection, I was perhaps rather foolish in presenting to Mrs Pledger. Namely, might it not be possible for a bad night's sleep to somehow leave a trace of itself on one's sheets? A remnant of melancholy, perhaps, which the linen could in some way absorb. Is it not in any way plausible, I continued, that my recent disturbed sleep might be the result of some ill feeling, previously sweated out, which, when rewarmed by my body, is made potent once again?

I could tell straight away that my seeds had been cast on the stoniest of grounds. It is, I admit, an unusual theory and still somewhat underdone. But Mrs Pledger has never had much time for progressive thinking. Her long thin lips became even longer and thinner – became, in fact, little more than a crinkly line. She filled her great chest, emptied it in a single great sigh then went back to wrestling with her heap of washing.

All the same, as I left, I asked her to be sure and have one of the girls strip the linen from my bed and give it an especially ruthless scrub.

Mr Grimshaw's Account

It was getting on towards sunset when I received orders to prepare a carriage for His Grace, in order to take him and his valet, Clement, on a visit to see old Mr Snow. That day is fixed most firmly in my memory, seeing as how our return journey was set to be the first one underground and there being quite some excitement at the prospect. So I brought the carriage around to the front of the house and sat and watched the sun go down with a chew of tobacco in my mouth. And I sat and I chewed and I waited, as I seem to have done half my life.

Now, I'd be dishonest if I didn't come straight out and say how that big house hasn't, on more than the odd occasion, made me most uncomfortable just by looking it over, so that I might find myself shifting in my seat, if you take my meaning, and I'm not usually the fidgety type. It is a many pinnacled affair – to my eyes, very ugly – spires and towers all over the place and a roof needing constant repair. There's no doubt that it is large and impressive. A mountain of stone, with who knows how many windows. But I couldn't call it pretty. No. It never seemed to me a jolly place to live.

In olden days, I am told, it was a monastery where many monks would creep about in sackcloth and eat naught but nuts. It was them who built the first underground tunnels, in fear of ... now, would I be right in saying the boys of Henry the Eighth? Well, whoever's boys they were, they were dreadful enough to scare the monks into having escape tunnels dug. Two or three of them, I believe, and very narrow, which, in emergency, they would run along to come up out of the ground in the woods.

So I imagine I must have sat there the usual quarter-hour before they finally emerged . . . His Grace with his famous beaver hat on and Clement close behind. I shall always think of His Grace as a pointy little man, with his trowel of a beard and his sharp blue eyes. To my mind, he was always a collection of angles – all elbows and knuckles and knees. Generally speaking, Clement accompanied His Grace on such trips and together they made a curious pair, what with Clement being so very large and silent and His Grace so small and always chattering on.

I might also just say here, if I may, that while I have always myself been very fond of the horses, it's my opinion His Grace went too far in giving them a graveyard of their own. I was brought up Christian and I have to say it seemed somehow unholy to me. I believe they should have gone to the knacker's yard and been got rid of in the usual way. Not given headstones with their names carved on 'em and poetry quotations and all.

Sometimes, like that evening, when the light was all but gone and we left the estate by Horses' Graveyard, my mind would take it upon itself to dwell most morbidly on all the horse corpses resting there. The thought of those tired old nags all a-mouldering would end up giving me a most sickly feeling inside. Would make me grip the reins extra tightly and get my living horses to gee-up, double quick.

From His Grace's Journal

October 15th

*

Old Mrs Snow had been staring at me through her spectacles for what seemed like a good long while. She had yet to make any utterance, being so wholly taken up with observing me standing on her doorstep in the dark. Her right hand clung tightly to the door latch, as if I might be a robber and it a tiny pistol, and as the silence deepened I could feel the warmth of the cottage seeping slowly past me and out into the night.

Clement stood close behind me and I heard him take a breath to introduce us a second time when, at last, some connection registered in Mrs Snow's bespectacled eyes and she opened up her neat little mouth.

'It's the Duke,' she said.

'It is,' I replied, and bowed my bare head towards her. She nodded back at me – three or four times, maybe more. Then, just as I feared we might be in for a further period of standing about, she embarked on a series of shuffled backward steps, dragging the heavy door with her, then asked why we did not come in.

With Clement's aid, she managed to hang our coats on a hook behind the door. Then the three of us organized ourselves into a caravan, with Mrs Snow at the head and Clement at the rear, and we all set off at a funereal marching pace towards the parlour's orange light.

I'm afraid I could not help but notice the poor state of Mrs Snow's legs – bandier even than mine – and as we processed through the cottage I saw how her hand took support from, first, a stair banister, then the jamb of a door. At the threshold to the parlour Mrs Snow halted, in order to gather her wits, which gave me ample opportunity to look over her shoulder and take in the tiny room. A great deal of space was given over to a thickly-varnished sideboard, laden with all manner of gaudy crockery and assorted ornaments. Both the proportions and shining timber of the thing called to mind a small steamer on Lake Windermere. A dining table and various sitting chairs took up most of the remaining space.

Having herded all her thoughts together, Mrs Snow announced, 'It's the Duke,' again (this time, I assumed, for her husband's benefit rather than mine) then stooped off towards a stool which allowed me to catch my first glimpse of old Mr Snow, held in place by a great many cushions in an armchair by the fire. He smiled a curious half-smile and tried vainly to raise himself up, so I hurried over, took his hand in mine and Clement brought me over an upright chair.

The John Snow before me, packed all around with cushions, was a very different man to the one I had last come across. For one thing, and I can say this without fear of contradiction, the man had visibly shrunk. Yes, indeed. His body had been emptied like a sack. And though he had never been particularly portly his skull now seemed to push at the flesh of his face. The tuft of hair sticking up at the back of his head, his greatly bewildered air, his elbows pinned to his ribs with cushions all put me in mind of a nest-bound, flightless chick waiting to be fed.

'How are you, my friend?' I asked him, pulling my chair right up close to him.

The room was perfectly quiet but for the middle finger of Mr Snow's left hand, which drummed out a complicated rhythm on the arm of the chair which kept him captive. He nodded his head at me, just as his wife had done, but with Mr Snow it seemed not so much an attempt at communication as a man attempting to balance the weight of his head on his neck. He blinked at me – once, twice, three times – and then he nodded some more.

'Mr Snow has suffered a stroke,' announced Mrs Snow.

'So I hear,' I replied over my shoulder, before returning my attention to her husband, saying, 'We are all at sixes and sevens since you left, you know. Not nearly so many blooms.'

I waited for him to take up the conversation but he simply smiled his half-smile again. I went on, 'You remember your lovely gardens?'

His middle finger continued to tap out its frantic message. It was as if he had found a spot on the chair arm and was desperate to scratch it away.

At long last his dry lips parted. He said, 'I am not quite sure.'

Well, this knocked the wind right out of me. Forgotten the gardens? Impossible. How could a man not remember the place he had spent his every working day? I was hurt – I don't mind admitting it – as if the old fellow had actually landed a blow on me. His failure to retrieve any memory of the gardens seemed almost wilful. But I did my best to hide my disappointment and hung on to his withered hand.

I told him how we now had three men doing his job and how they were not doing half so well. I reminded him of his trip to the parks at Battersea and Kew and Crystal Palace after new combinations of bedding plants. I talked of tulips and crocuses and other spring bulbs, hoping to cast some healing light into the dark corners of his mind. And in the same way, perhaps, that a fly fisherman attempts to lure his catch with brightly coloured twists of feathers, so I attempted to reel in my frail old gardener with talk of blossoms and exotic fruit. 'You remember the black muscat grapes you grew me? The pineapples and the peaches?'

I smiled a full, broad smile for the both of us but felt the ground beneath me crack and part. I had an awful need for anchorage. Felt myself slipping away. And I found that I was soon talking ten to the dozen about any old thing that came to mind, while John Snow wore on his face an expression of utter perplexity, broken only by an apologetic raising of the brows. His eyes were terribly distant and though they once or twice flickered with what I hoped might be some sign of revelation, they remained lost and as cold as a pair of pebbles and revelation refused to come. 'The glasshouses are still there,' I told him.

'The glasshouses . . . Yes,' he replied.

This small affirmation reassured me. Gave me some small hope to hang on to. In time, I reasoned, his memory might restore itself; like a damaged muscle which requires gentle exercise before it will properly function again. Then he leaned awkwardly over towards me and whispered in my ear.

'Much of it is gone,' he confided, and gripped me weakly on my arm. 'It's all there,' and here he took another bewildered breath, '. . . but there's no getting at it.'

I stared back at him, quietly horrified. His face had buckled into a scowl. His eyes looked anxiously at me as if over some abyss.

Only two years ago I had trouble getting a word in edgeways with John Snow. Forever marching up and down his garden paths he was, picking at every plant along the way. But some awful event inside him, some tiny blockage or severage or flaw, had caused the man's entire capacity to be irreparably reduced. He had been halved; had been more than halved. A lifetime's memory all but gone. Great expanses now underwater, whole continents washed away.

'Mr Snow has suffered a stroke,' said Mrs Snow, and this

time I turned and properly took her in. Two small flames shone in her spectacle lenses – reflections of the lamp's yellow light – but the face itself was as blank as a sheet. The only vitality about the poor woman was her tiny chest which pumped laboriously in and out and trawled the room for air. And in that single moment I became aware how both the Snows had suffered the stroke. How, one way or another, they had both been swept away.

*

We returned home in silence, save for my asking Clement to be sure the Snows' supply of food and fuel be kept in order and to ask Dr Cox to pay them a visit and give me a full report. I was so upset by the whole affair I was obliged to postpone the tunnels' christening and had Grimshaw take us home down the Eastern avenue, though from what little I could make out through the carriage window and with my state of mind being so black we might as well have been travelling a mile or two beneath the ground.

*

October 16th

*

To the north of the house and clearly visible from my bedroom is a row of lime trees, each about fifty feet tall, which hum and fizz right through the summer with their own colony of bees. In June and July and August when the sun is at its peak they fairly work themselves up into a frenzy and the trees become lost in a blur. I suppose they are simply making honey. One cannot blame them for that. All the same, one has trouble thinking straight above their interminable noise.

The bees are perfectly silent now. All dead or deeply asleep. Their eggs secreted in the branches until the world grows warm again. Somewhere in those limes there must be the makings of an entire bee population. Locked away till spring.

The leaves are deserting those lime trees just as they desert every tree across the estate and this stirs in me a most dismal disposition. The walnuts and chestnuts, the ashes and oaks – all now close to naked in the cold and damp autumn air.

As the fall of leaves gradually reveals each tree's wooden skeleton I can sometimes detect how it has been marginally altered since it last stood bare. One tree in particular – an unrecognizable variety on the other side of the lake – looks even more peculiar this year than it did last wintertime. Some folk on the estate reckon it was once struck by lightning – a theory which makes a good deal of sense – yet, though some parts of the tree are certainly stunted, each year it just about manages to force out the odd flourish of sickly leaves. I recall how, several years ago, it looked to me very much like the hanging carcass of a pig. Last autumn it was no more than a monster, a great mass of carbuncles and sores. But this morning, as I strolled past it, I felt sure I saw a horse through its thinning veil of leaves. A wild horse raised right up on its hind legs, with its head and neck thrown back.

*

All day I kept myself busy. Before lunch, Clement helped me shift my bed around so that the headboard now faces due north. I have heard that positioning a bed in this manner encourages a body to sleep more soundly, so I dug out my old brass compass and we aligned the bed right along the old north–south. Inevitably, Clement did the lion's share of the work while I fussed about and contributed nothing but the odd grunt or two. But when we were done and I lay down on the bed to recover I thought I registered a distinct improvement. A greater calmness of the mind.

Rearranged the tunnels' christening for nine o'clock tomorrow; returned a dozen shirts to Batt and Sons (they are three ounces overweight and the collars much too wide); had luncheon – a spicy celery soup – with young Mr Bowen, the stonemason, who is finishing the tunnel entrances and such-like, then inspected the stables and the riding school. In this way I managed to plough an idle furrow right through the day and did not once give myself the opportunity to dwell on my recent visit to the Snows. From the moment I woke I kept myself occupied with the most trivial of tasks, but at the very back of my mind, I have no doubt, some part of me meditated wholeheartedly on the devastation I had seen.

By four o'clock – always my most miserable part of the day – I had run right out of steam and found myself in the upstairs study. Just me and the old tick-tock.

I sat there in the emptiness. I became aware of a slow wave of horror, all set to crash over me. I waited. I listened. And, in time, the wave came crashing down.

It raced to fill every corner of me. An awful boiling and thrashing in my head which, now I have had time to make some sense of it, I can articulate in the following way . . .

> Our life experience is kept safe and sound in the strongroom of our Memory. It is here that we store our pasts. We keep no other record, save the odd souvenir, of life's small successes, its staggering failures, of those whom we have loved and (if we are fortunate) the ones who have loved us in return. The only assurance we have that our life has been well spent – or, for that matter, spent at all – is the proof delicately held in our Memory, in those great ledgers of the mind.
>
> But what if the door to that room is broken? What if the rain and the wind get in? If they do, then we are in grave danger of becoming hopelessly and eternally lost.

And if such a havoc-wreaking illness should befall us our only solace would be that we might at least remain ignorant of what we had lost, and be left to live out our feeble days in a childlike ignorance. Yet, from what John Snow said, it seems he has been denied even that crumb of comfort. 'It's all there,' I distinctly recall him whispering to me, 'but there's no getting at it.'

Deprived of our memories we are deprived of our very selves. Without our histories we are vacated. We may walk and talk and eat and sleep but, in truth, we are nobody.

I sat here at my bureau for close on an hour with my hot head in my hands. Felt the darkness moving about me. A fearful inner darkness, it was.

*

October 17th

*

The sun was up and out this morning and the whole world looked as sharp as a pin which, one way or another, encouraged a little brightness in myself. Wore my thick beige shirt, poplin waistcoat and Cossack trousers and had a fine breakfast of smoked haddock and eggs, lightly poached. But while cheered by the prospect of the tunnels' christening, found my body still very much at odds with itself and several thundering cups of strong Assam failed to set in motion my morning evacuation.

Asked Clement to round up Grimshaw, a coach and horses and a couple of stable lads then tracked down my new carriage coat and deerstalker. Picked out a yellow scarf along the way.

I now have a choice of four routes to the basement – by which I mean the tunnels – and two dumb waiters besides.

There's the original stone stairwell, via a small doorway beneath the staircase in the Great Hall, then what used to be known as the 'service stairs' which I have had fitted out with new flags and banisters. I have also added a wrought-iron spiral stairwell which leads from a door by my bedroom fireplace directly down to the tunnels (and may be picked up by a tidy little door set into the panelling of the dining room) and, finally, a narrow passageway which wanders all about the house before descending by several flights of stone steps (and whose construction, I might add, caused a great number of complaints from all quarters of the house, to do with dust and general disturbance).

This morning I chose the spiral stairs, so my descent was accompanied by the clanking of my boots on the steps, their echo ringing eerily back at me from high above and far below. The coldness of the tunnels first introduced itself at my ankles then crept slowly up me, in the same way a bather's body is coldly embraced by the sea. As requested, the gas jets in the lower reaches of the house had all been lit. I passed the entrance to the original monastery passages (all gated and bolted now), the underground chapel and the family vaults and came out, at last, behind the landing stage where Clement and two stable lads waited, with their shadows splashing on the walls behind them like great inky cloaks.

I am proud to say that, broadly speaking, the design for the new tunnels was very much my own but put in place, of course, by the ingenuity of Mr Bird and his men. An inner circle, roughly two hundred yards in circumference, links the entrances to all eight tunnels and the passages which lead off to the stables and so forth. The stairways come out at a grotto by the staging platform and it was here that the four of us gathered, to wait for Mr Grimshaw and his carriage.

Standing around on that stone landing stage was a rather chilly affair, due in part to the cold earth all around us but also from the stiff breezes which came sweeping down the tunnels – a problem I admit I had not foreseen. But, looking down one of them, I was pleased to see how the skylights lit the way admirably and made it appear altogether quite inviting. I reckoned that only on the most overcast days would it be necessary to light the gas jets much before dusk. To my eye, the tunnel nearest us looked like the inside of a flute, with the skylights representing the finger holes where columns of daylight streamed through. So it was quite fitting that as we stood there in our quiet little gang, different-pitched whistles slowly made themselves known. Very weird to hear them washing in from the tunnels and stairwells and have them mingle around our feet.

Asked Clement if he would mind fetching me an extra frock coat and my Inverness cape as the carriage coat would clearly not suffice, and suggested he perhaps go up in one of the dumb waiters, to give it a try-out. He was most reluctant, worrying I think that his being so large might cause the lift to fall, but I assured him that it was built with a mind to taking a load many times his weight and, after some concerted cajoling from myself and the stable lads, he rather timidly squeezed himself into its compact little compartment. What an excellent sport! The lads took turns pulling on the rope and the wooden box in which he huddled slowly ascended into the belly of the house. I stuck my head out into the shaft and kept up a reassuring conversation with him which bounced all about the place. 'I shall keep my head in the shaft, so that if you fall we shall both of us be killed. How's that, Clement?' I called.

The lifts were originally installed to save lugging baggage up and down the stairs, but I see now how they might prove to be a source of entertainment in themselves.

Clement had returned (by the stairs, I might add) and we

were all beginning to wonder what was up with Grimshaw when a distant rumble came at us down the inner circle which started up reverberations down all the other passageways. Seconds later, the horses and carriage came crashing round the corner with Grimshaw, very flustered, clinging to the reins. It was a long while after the carriage had ground to a halt that its clattering quit swimming up and down the place and the dust settled to reveal Grimshaw, who was apologizing most profusely, saying how he had got himself first a little confused and then hopelessly lost. He promised to properly acquaint himself with all the turnings and linking passages at the soonest opportunity. Then Clement and I clambered in and made ourselves comfortable and I tied my deerstalker firmly under my chin.

Grimshaw, high up on his driver's seat, pulled back his little hatch and presented his head to us upside-down and framed by his boots, saying, 'First off, Your Grace. You're quite sure there's no danger of me banging my head on owt?'

I told him there was not. He nodded gravely at us, obviously not the least bit convinced. He then asked, 'Which tunnel is it I am to take, Your Grace?'

I gave it a little thought. 'North,' I announced. 'North towards the Pole ... And with a little spice, if you don't mind.'

Grimshaw nodded again, still grim and upside-down, then closed his little hatch. I heard him let out a sigh as he settled himself in his seat. Then, with a crack of the whip and a call of, 'Gee-up, there ... I say, gee-up,' we moved off, past the stable lads who were waving their caps in the air. They appeared to be heartily cheering us – I can only assume so for I could not hear a thing above the wheels and the hoofs. I had no inkling there would be such an intense din and might have considered plugging my ears with my handkerchief had I not been so busy shouting up at Grimshaw, who had missed the North tunnel entrance, forcing us to take an extra run of the inner circle and pick it out next time round.

When we raced past the stable lads again they looked mightily confused but, to their credit, raised their caps a second time and set up another bout of muted cheering. Then, at last, Grimshaw found the right entrance (I made a mental note to have each one clearly signposted) and we went haring down the North tunnel with the horses champing at the bit.

All morning we raced up and down the tunnels – first North, then North-east and so on. The noise was unimaginable; like shouting down a well. The skylights flew by at regular intervals, which had the effect of a constantly flashing light. This initially proved a little sickening, along with the almighty noise, but, in time, became quite exhilarating, with the smell of the heaving horses and Grimshaw's exhortations adding to the drama.

With my precious pocket watch I timed the duration of each journey (both away from the house and returning, as some of the tunnels are on a gradient). I had brought with me a notebook and recorded all my findings, at both *trot* and *full gallop*.

By midmorning we were in need of a change of horses and the lads took the first two off to give them a brushing down and soon after I sent a message to Mrs Pledger asking her to put together some refreshment, which we picked up when we next went by the landing stage and ate as we went along.

I was disturbed to hear from Grimshaw how as we emerged from the tunnels into the light the horses were sometimes dazzled, but it was his opinion that blinkers would remedy the problem. I made a note of this in my book.

Both Mr Pyke and Mr Harris stood to attention by their

respective lodges and were plainly most intrigued, so I invited them to join us for a trip to the house and back. Mr Harris (one of our best dog men) seemed to enjoy himself but Mr Pyke needed more encouragement to come along and looked decidedly shaky when we dropped him off.

From the expression on the faces of the stable lads I saw that they had lost a good deal of their punch and each time we passed them I noted how it had waned a little more. So, as a treat, I allowed them a ride on the luggage shelf which cheered them up no end and by the time we were done they were grinning at each other like a pair of gormless fools.

It was close to two o'clock when I finally drew proceedings to a close. A sticky heat filled the tunnels. We had exhausted three sets of horses and Mr Grimshaw needed some help getting down from his seat. Gave him the rest of the day off and had the young lads lead the carriage away. My coats were powdered all over with dust and my ears rang like church bells.

As Clement and I made our way towards the spiral stairwell and passed the door to the underground chapel my eyes lit upon a rather unusual carving. One I felt sure I had not seen before. The design could not have been simpler: on a circle of stone, six inches wide, an infant's face stared out through a screen of grasses or reeds. I stared back at him. Something about his gaze deeply disturbed me, though I couldn't say just what.

I quizzed Clement about it but he claimed to have no more knowledge of it than I did myself. Wondered if Bowen might have knocked it up, though I must say it did not look new, just unfamiliar. I found myself coming over a little sick.

This behaviour, this constant vacillation of mood, is becoming something of a habit with me. One minute I am triumphing over a depressive fit and feeling positively tip-top.

The next, for no good reason, I feel myself start to sink again and spend the rest of the day mooning all about the place.

*

I have nothing but admiration for the engineers of this world. Scientists, mechanics, inventors . . . I take my hat off to them all. How I envy their ability to comprehend how a thing is put together without their head getting in the way. To be able to fix that which was broken, to make the apparently irreparable sound again. I should very much like to have that knack.

But I'm afraid such a faculty is something one is blessed with either at birth or not at all and however one might try quantifying it there is no doubt I have always been short on the stuff. At age ten I was still having difficulty tying my bootlaces, and even now the whole fiddly business can get me in a state. Anything remotely technical, such as distinguishing right from left, has, for me, always necessitated a great deal of mental stress and strain, so that my first tutor, a Mr Cocker, perhaps misinterpreting these inadequacies as slovenliness and, worse, something of a challenge, took it upon himself to set me straight. Every day for a whole month a piece of paper was tied with string to each of my wrists – one with the letter R on it for right, the other with L for left. But if he had asked me I could have told him how they were helping me not a jot and at the end of each day when they were taken off I was as lost as when I'd begun. They only made me feel very foolish and tended to get in my soup until, at last, Mr Cocker threw his hands in the air, made a strange sound through his nose and admitted defeat. I remember very well my holding my hands out like a chained prisoner about to be granted his liberty. It was a relief of no small magnitude for I was still spending half an hour every morning guessing which piece of paper went on which wrist.

But I am not happy in my ignorance. Far from it. I like to

think I have the same curiosity as the chemist or the architect; it is simply their talent I lack. Believe me when I say that my backwardness has never stopped me taking things apart, merely putting them back together again.

*

Since I was a boy I have periodically suffered from the irrational fear that I am on the verge of fatal collapse. I think I am right in saying it is my mind which is chiefly to blame. Left to its own devices my body appears to function reasonably well, requiring feeding and watering and a good deal of rest but being for the most part a quite contented and smooth-running apparatus. Yet the moment I begin considering some particular pump or piston – the lungs being a prime example – an alarum goes off inside me and suddenly all hell is let loose.

My mind panics, tries to wrest from my body the breathing controls and before long I am in a fit of difficulty, not knowing whether to breathe out or in. And once I am started I find there is no way back. All that's left is to try and get me to think of something else. So, to distract myself, I might have to recite poetry or skip madly around the room.

But are we not all of us ignoramuses when it comes to our own bodyworks? I somehow doubt that even those who claim to understand every fleshy connection – every last valve and gland – actually regard themselves with such sophistication as they go about their day. For it is my opinion that we all tend to rely upon the simplest mind-pictures which represent for us the functions of our body's various parts. For example, I have one for my lungs, which is as follows . . .

> Each lung is in fact a tiny inverted tree with the base of the trunk coming out at my throat. When I breathe in, leaves appear on the branches. When I exhale, the leaves disappear.

Thus, the seasons are constantly shifting in my ribcage. They come around every second or two. If I am to stay alive it is vitally important that these little trees do not stay barren for long.

I believe I first conjured up this image when I was still quite small but must have since spent several hundred hours of my life (including a good many as an adult) endeavouring to keep my lung-trees sufficiently leafy. As an infant I would often lie in bed too terrified to fall asleep lest my body forget to keep me breathing through the long dark night ahead.

I would claim that, in fact, the majority of us know next to nothing about our bodies and how they really work. Yet surely such information is essential; should be available to us without having to read it in books. When we are delivered into this world the very least we might expect is to come complete with a comprehensive manual to ourselves.

'Why no manual?'

That is my plea.

'Why no instructions?'

Mr Bowen's Account

My work for His Grace was my first proper job after finishing my apprenticeship so, as you can imagine, I was altogether very pleased with myself and walked about the place with a few inches added to my stride. I was on the estate about six months in all. Was paid and treated very well. I had a room in the servants' quarters and it was left to me to get myself up and out first thing. I would take with me a little bread and cheese wrapped in linen, which I would eat while I was on the job, and my dinner would be keeping warm for me in the kitchens when I came in around seven or eight.

After meeting with His Grace a time or two I was left very much to myself. I'd go to him with my designs and he might sometimes slip me one or two sketches of his own. Odd little drawings, they were, on bits of paper. I would pin them on my workshop wall. But His Grace was not much of a draughtsman, so I would take care to listen to his ideas and work from what he said. Once in a while he might drop by to see how I was faring but on the whole he left me alone.

I was given some of the finishing touches to do on the tunnels, such as the gateposts and so forth. Well, I assumed that what would be required would be an obelisk or a Grecian urn. The usual sort of thing. But when I was ready to get on with them and went to ask His Grace what he had in mind, he asked me how I felt about onions. Onions about a foot and a half wide.

Well, it took me a while to come up with an onion we both

felt happy about. They caused me a bit of a headache. To be honest, I was worried I might become something of a laughing-stock. What I eventually came up with was something quite similar to a traditional stone orb, but fatter in the middle and with a stalk coming out the top. But there was no mistaking it for anything else – it was an onion from top to toe. His Grace told me that he thought it was just the job. Once it was erected folk would come up and ask me about it. Most of them thought it first rate. It was my own design, so of course I was very pleased to be asked if I was the onion-man. Quite proud, I was. So we had onions by the lodge at Norton and cauliflowers on the gateposts out at Belph.

My largest undertaking was what the Duke always referred to as 'the Grotto', which was down where all Mr Bird's tunnels came in above the landing platform. Well, I was instructed to cover the ceiling with plaster – easily thirty feet high – then carve out of it the likenesses of various 'natural' things. His Grace gave me a list of suitable subjects for me to bear in mind, such as pineapples, grapes and fish-heads. I remember he asked if I could do a seashell and maybe some barleycorn.

Well, just like the onion and the cauliflower before it, I had no training in such things and I was a little hesitant at the start. But His Grace asked me if I had an imagination and when I replied that I believed I had, he told me I had better get on and make some use of it. I was told I could include more or less anything which took my fancy, just as long as they were 'natural'.

Well, I gave it a go. Did some fruit to start off and then some creatures . . . snakes and snails and so forth . . . and soon found I'd fairly got the hang of it. After a day or two I didn't worry at all. A bird's head here, an acorn there. Perhaps a fern leaf alongside a feather.

In the evenings I would occasionally nip out for a drink –

the Vault in Whitwell or the old Bird's Nest – and, of course, I would come across all the stories about the Duke which were doing the rounds at the time. As a stranger to the area and with my being a good bit younger than the other drinking men, I sometimes found it hard to go against what they said. If I am honest, I will say that after a couple of jars I found I could spin a tale or two myself. I am most ashamed of that now.

In my last week on the estate I was called in to see His Grace and the first thought I had was that I must have done something wrong. I thought perhaps something I'd said in the pub had got back to him and that I was going to get a dressing down or even dismissed. But he only asked me about a roundel he'd seen by the underground chapel. Wondered if it was anything to do with me. He took me down there and I had a look at it. Very simple it was – just a face peering through a bush. At a guess I'd say fourteenth century, though I'm no historian. Probably put in when the chapel was first built. The stonemasons, of course, wouldn't have shared the beliefs of the monks who paid them so it was maybe just a little pagan symbol which they tucked away. I've heard that they would often do that. At a guess I'd say it was just old Jack in the Green.

From His Grace's Journal

OCTOBER 22ND

*

What a treat! This morning, as I stared out of the dining room window and wondered what to do with the day, Clement came in with a large tube-like package, bound together with string.

I immediately took control of the situation, saying, 'We are going to need scissors, Clement. Scissors, as quick as you can.'

In a minute we had cut the twine away, removed several square yards of brown paper and were unrolling onto the table the most exquisitely coloured map. Tears welled up in my blinking eyes – such a baby! – so that I worried they might spill onto the map and spoil it. I took out a handkerchief, gave my nose a good blow and tried to pull myself together.

Clement handed me an accompanying note, which read,

My Lord Duke,

Here is the map I once spoke about, rendered by a local surveyor, Mr George Sanderson. Please accept it as a small token of my company's thanks for work so generously commissioned and as a personal gift to mark the end of a most pleasurable stay.

I remain Your Grace's Obedient Servant,

Gordon S. Bird

P.S. I believe it is meant to be hung.

'Mr Bird says it is meant to be hung,' I announced, between gulps. 'We shall need help to hold it up.'

So while Clement went off to drum up some support I took the opportunity of examining the map alone.

Mr Bird and I discovered very early on we shared a passion for cartography. I showed him my modest collection of maps of the North of England and I remember well him mentioning to me a large-scale local map, executed in the shape of a disk. In my usual vague way I promised to make enquiries after it, but never got around to the task. But here I was, years later, standing before the very thing and I was quite overcome with joy. Like most of life's more potent pleasures, it came strangely tinged with melancholy.

I had barely begun taking in all the pinks and greens and blues when Clement returned with a couple of maids who, under his careful instruction, held the thing up so that it could be properly viewed.

Well, the effect was quite staggering. The map is so big that the girls had to stand on chairs. It is easily six foot in diameter. Maybe more.

It is the shape of the map which makes the biggest impression – an apparently perfect circle – so that one is inclined to imagine one stands before a map of the entire world. Here are oranges and purples and yellows, all come together in a beautifully bruised fruit. Yet it is only when one looks a good deal closer and reads the names of the principalities these colours so delicately adorn that one realizes what a very small world this is, with Mansfield as its capital, as if the rest of England has been trimmed away with a palette knife like so much overhanging pastry on an uncooked pie.

Roadways and rivers are clearly visible: the prominent veins of an exerted man. They creep up and down and all about the place, tying the whole peculiar ball together. Every township, village and ox pasture is given its rightful name, every church represented in miniature form, each wood by a caricature plane or oak perching in its own neat pool of shade. The names of each district and county sweep across the map in sizeable script, so that one's heart goes out to those unfortunate enough to live in the shadows of the huge A or O of WARSOP PARISH.

Every gradation is delineated by the bunched scratches of Mr Sanderson's pen. Indeed, the cross-hatching of a sudden incline looks like the grubby thumbprint of the artist himself. It is as if Mr Sanderson has had the pleasure to sit up at God's right hand. To take in the view from our Creator's perspective and sketch it for us mortal men.

But all is not well! On closer inspection, one notes that where many roads come together and many buildings stand the effect is most unwelcoming – like a tumour or a spill of ink. A city of Sheffield's proportions, for example, appears very dark and people-congested; an ugly blockage in the circulation of this little world.

Looking closer still, one sees that, in order to squeeze some peripheral town on to the edge of his map, Mr Sanderson has occasionally lost the circumference's lovely line. Rotherham protrudes from the planet like a boil fit to burst. Bakewell hangs off it like a scab.

So I drew my eyes away from the cankerous towns and cities, to go in search of my own bucolic abode. Whitwell is found easily enough, therefore I must be just a little to the *East*. There is Clumber, so I must have gone too far. I go back – slowly, slowly now. Then, of a sudden – hurrah! – there we are! My house, my lake, my own front drive! Even the ice house is named, and *Greendale* and *The Seven Sisters* – my grand old oaks. This gives me no end of the most profound pleasure. I am located. Verified.

I put my nose right up to my own house, as if I might see me waving from a window. And, no doubt to the great amusement of my young housemaids, I gently plant my forefinger on the map at that very spot.

'I am here,' I say.

*

October 27th

*

Yet another disturbed night's sleep. Woke not knowing where on earth I was. It was as if I had been plucked from sleep's great ocean and flung on some unfamiliar shore.

There is no shortage of fanciful notions which seek to explain the mysteries of sleep. Personally I have always favoured that which proposes that the souls of the sleeping ascend to another plane, so that while our bodies sleep under worldly sheets our spirits play among the stars.

It is my opinion that the finest of threads connects the spirit with the vacated body, the latter acting as an anchor, and that down this line come the vibrations of the spirit's starry gallivanting, which the dormant body perceives as dreams. Thus when we sleep we go kite-flying, yet we are both flyer and the kite.

But if all the world flies kites at night it follows that the sky must be filled with threads. Very dangerous. Question– What happens when two lines become tangled? – for it must be easily done. Might a soul not return down the wrong string by accident and wake to find itself inhabiting a stranger's body? This has concerned me, on and off, for quite a while and was more or less how I felt this morning. It was getting on for lunchtime before I had properly straightened myself out.

This afternoon we took the West tunnel out to Creswell to inspect the damage done by a fire to the cottage of a Mr Kendal, who wandered aimlessly up and down the place in floods of tears, despite my many assurances that everything would be taken care of. I am told he has something to do with the infant school, or the kennels – either way he is lucky to be alive. A dreadful acrid stench still filled the house; every wall and ceiling was blackened by smoke. After five minutes I decided I had seen enough and told Clement to return in the carriage so I might walk back through Tile Kiln and Cow-close Wood.

When a man falls asleep in his armchair with his pipe still lit, the transformation by fire to his surroundings is truly something to behold. Every surface changes texture. Familiar objects – a kettle, a stool, a mirror – are made unrecognizable. But all this is nothing when put alongside the carnage wrought upon woodland by the seasons' change and as I strolled through the estate today I was confronted with destruction of the most comprehensive kind.

The entire scene was drained of colour; every tree and bush quivered leaflessly. The slimmest fraction of the spectrum had been left to them – from an ash-grey to the faintest brown. The rest had been sucked back into the hardening ground or washed away by the rain. The smaller trees stretched out their branches like young beggars, but I could not do a thing for them.

The only life on show was a single rabbit which, sensing my approach, made a mad dash for its burrow. My footsteps produced a painful racket as they came down on the dried leaves and twigs and this crashing was cast back at me by the dumb timber all around. Every tree seemed ... *humiliated.* Hushed and resentful, like a struck child. The only other sound I heard all afternoon was a gun's report (one of my own men, I trust) which twice came up from the Wilderness with the grim finality of a slammed door.

I reckon I am very much like the leafless trees. Autumn scares the life right out of me. Every year I worry I will not survive it, that this may be my last. Sometimes I fear a malevolent hand has cut spring and summer from the calendar and, for a cruel joke, stitched winter straight onto the following autumn. There is never much rest from autumn. Always autumn, it seems.

I must have stopped to catch my breath. I cannot walk as far as I might like these days without the occasional breather which, in company, I attempt to conceal by making a show of taking in the view. Certainly it did not seem to me that I fell asleep but I must have somehow slipped from consciousness for when I came to, slumped on a boulder, the sky had grown quite dark. At first, I felt only a modicum of concern, but when I looked about and found myself deep in the woods with no recollection of how I had got there I suffered the most profound shock. It was as if I had become utterly dislocated from time.

Like my father before me I have suffered from occasional 'absences' – seconds, even minutes when my mind seems to completely switch itself off. In my youth, without the slightest warning, I would become entirely detached from everything going on around me. Friends who witnessed these episodes said only that I seemed to go into a brown study of the deepest introspection. (My father, incidentally, claimed they were the result of a diet lacking iron, which is why he ate so much liver.) So whilst finding myself in such confusion is not entirely new to me I cannot honestly recall being so thoroughly absent and for so long a time. When I came to my throat was dreadfully dry and my whole body was icy-cold.

Getting to my feet cost me a tremendous amount of pain. The blood which had slowed to a near standstill now took to raging round my limbs. A thoroughly unpleasant sensation, which only served to exhaust me more. My feet felt as if they had been filled with twice their proper capacity of blood and might burst at any moment and fill my boots.

The wood was no longer silent. Nearby, an owl hooted in a plaintive tone – perhaps he had stirred me? – and a stiff breeze was intent on rattling the branches of the trees. I had the idea they now crawled with all manner of tiny insects. Night had brought the whole wood to life.

I set off without being at all sure of my bearings. After a few strides a whey-faced moon popped out from behind a tree and followed me along. For a minute or two I was glad of the company – his brightness lit my way. But after turning and watching him keeping up with me a time or two I soon thought I would very much like to be rid of him. The moon is very knowing and he looked down at me as if he understood exactly what I was about. I picked up some speed, but the faster I went the faster he swept through the branches and when I slowed my pace a little he followed suit. 'Damn him!' I thought, 'he will not let me go.' Then, 'If he is going to follow me all the way home I may as well get it over with,' and I broke into a ferocious trot. At some point I think a cloud must have blocked him out and I was able to return at a more civilized pace.

Clement met me on the drive, a lamp illuminating his anxious face. He said nothing, simply wrapped a blanket around my shoulders and escorted me back to the house.

*

Fanny Adelaide had a voice like an angel. When she left the stage after the final curtain she could barely walk for all the bouquets. But when I think of her – and I still think of her all too frequently – it is not her voice that leaps into my mind uninvited, but the neck which gave it life.

She had come up from London on one of her visits and the journey had evidently worn her out for when I returned to the Swan Drawing Room after calling down for tea I found her fast asleep on the chaise. Her gloved hand was tucked under her tilted head, a shoe had slipped from a foot. Her dress swam out around her. Beautifully capsized, she was. Her hair, I recall, was a great labyrinth of stacked curls held together in a manner which was a mystery to me. I watched as she lay there, dozing, breathing through a minutely-opened mouth.

I interpreted her falling asleep as somehow flattering, thinking it showed how safe she felt in my company. So I perched myself on a leather footstool and quietly drank her in. Would have continued to do so had not the jangle of tea things in the hall sent me hurrying out to head off the maid.

But as I gently set the tray down she came to, and in an instant had decided she had no stomach for tea after all, but wished to take a turn around the gardens and breathe in some country air. So I led her out through the French windows and we did a tour of the flower beds and the lawns. And though she contributed very little to the conversation I was pleased just to have her at my side with her hand resting on my arm.

I wanted to show off every corner of the gardens. I started talking spiritedly about a dozen different things – a gabbling fool, I was. But under a cherry blossom she stopped, turned and raised a finger to my lips. Cocked her head as if she had picked out some exotic birdsong, when all I heard were my own foolish words still rushing round my head. Then she looked me in the eyes and said she had given proper consideration to my proposal and that now it was her turn to speak.

O, I would have given anything. Anything. I would have died for her.

When she had finished, she slipped a hand inside her purse, removed a fancy box and held it out to me. I was not to open it until she had gone, she said. She caught the next train back to London. Left me standing there in the gardens, all tangled up and undone.

The following year she married her agent, Peter Nicolson,

and retired from the stage for good. They had two children, George and Charles, who, by all accounts, were as beautiful and intelligent as one could wish for and very well behaved. Every morning the whole family climbed up Parliament Hill. Then, a week after her thirtieth birthday, she ate a piece of fish which she thought did not agree with her and by the following day she was dead. She was buried in Highgate Cemetery. It was in the newspapers, but I did not attend.

The case she presented to me under the cherry blossom contained a gold timepiece. An old-fashioned Hobson and Burroughs fob watch. In its lid a delicately scrolled inscription declared her lasting affection for me.

I have opened up that watch ten thousand times. On its face I have seen countless New Years come about; each one, it seems, in less company and to fewer whistles and cheers. Even now I must open it up twenty or thirty times each day, to count the hours until the next meal or fresh pot of tea. Ten days ago I used it to time our carriage as Clement and I raced up and down my tunnels. But what that watch has measured most precisely is the unwinding of the slow decades since Fanny Adelaide refused my hand in marriage and was laid in the ground by a bad piece of fish.

It is a beautiful watch, and perhaps ironic that such a fine example of craftsmanship should sit in my waistcoat pocket and be a neighbour to my heart which, being merely human, has functioned so poorly since the two were introduced.

*

October 28th

*

Last night I had my first sound night's sleep in a fortnight. I drifted happily in the ether until I was woke by the crackle of the fire. Clement is a wizard with a few twists of paper and the odd dry stick and his broad back was still bent over the hearth when I opened up my eyes. The firelight gave the room a rosy glow which helped chase off some of the chill I acquired from my spell in the woods. Clement strolled purposefully from the room and while I coaxed myself closer towards consciousness the fire's crackle was joined by the gush and splutter of hot water from my bathroom next door. Then Clement re-entered very grandly in his own small cloud of steam, which slowly evaporated about him as he swept over towards my wardrobe. (He's as big as a bear, is Clement, but his step is as light as a kitten's.)

My dressing gown was held open for me and as I snaked my arms into the sleeves' deep recesses I became aware of the extent to which my body ached. Those lost hours spent crouched on the boulder last night appear to have left their mark.

I followed Clement into the bathroom like a faithful old dog. Picked up a hand mirror from a dressing table and found a wicker chair while I waited for my bath.

I should know better than rest a mirror in my lap. It makes the bags under my eyes look like pastries and my face-flesh hang down all over the show. But it is quite likely that this morning a mirror from any angle would have returned an equally awful aspect. So, doing my best to ignore the general prospect of collapse and decay, I concentrated my efforts on those corners of my head where a little repairwork might still do some good.

With nail scissors I carefully clipped at my nostril hairs. Ditto, eyebrows. Then hacked back the bracken sprouting from my ears – my ears, for pity's sake! – and which make them look more like the verdant openings to forgotten caves than the ears of a civilized man. The hairs from all three regions of my head look surprisingly similar – all are dark and disturbingly thick. All grow in a most anarchic manner and at a tremendous rate. I am sure if I did not keep at them with the scissors I should one day look in the mirror and see a wildman staring back.

Just as there is an art to starting a fire, so there is an art to running a bath, and it would perhaps be too much to hope that everyone could master it. Some years ago, when Clement's sister was poorly and he took a week's leave to look after her, Mrs Pledger had one of her girls take over the running of my baths. To be fair, her first effort was not so bad – a little too quickly run and not properly stirred up but, all in all, a not altogether unpleasant experience. Her second attempt, however, was a disaster. An insult to bath and bather alike. It seemed she'd put the hot and cold in back to front and at completely the wrong speed. The whole thing was utterly ruined and had to be thrown away. I sent her back to the kitchens, post-haste, to spoil the potatoes no doubt, and for the rest of the week had to wrestle with the damned taps myself.

Clement cleared his throat. My bath was ready. I blew the trimmings off the mirror and, with my hand clamped on Clement's forearm for support, got first one foot then the other up and into the bath, with my gown and nightshirt still on. Stood there until I was sure I had my footing, then let Clement carefully lift my clothes over my head (which he did with his usual politely-averted gaze, as if he had just that moment noticed a speck of dust on the shoulder of his jacket and was considering how best to get shut of it). Then I gingerly lowered my old bones into the water.

Something is certainly up inside of me. I am in no doubt about that. Organs which, only a month ago, pushed and pulled in a businesslike manner seem to have slowed their undulations to a near halt. But as the hot water crept over my goosepimpled flesh and searched out armpits and frozen toes

I felt that at least some vital heat was being restored. I let myself slide slowly down into the bath until the tip of my beard dipped into the water like some riverside bush, wondering how on earth mankind ever managed to properly relax before hot water was invented. (Apparently, in his declining years, Napoleon rarely left his bath. And the Minoans, I have heard, were so fond of theirs they would often be buried in them.)

As I say, Clement is a Master Bath-Runner and likes to give every bath its own unique character – usually a combination of depth and temperature along with other, less easily identifiable qualities – in order to satisfy what he reckons to be my most pressing needs. I am never consulted on the matter; I leave it entirely up to him. But when a bath is in the offing I sometimes feel his big brown eyes looking me over as he makes his calculations.

This one was hot and deep and soapy. My head lay in a high collar of suds. My kneecaps remained an inch or two clear of the water and were soon the only part of me not turned an impressive lobster-red. My ribcage is like a scrubbing board and as it rose and fell the bathwater crept up and down it like the ebb and flow of rapid tides. As I lay there I wondered if the great to-ing and fro-ing of the world's oceans might not, in fact, be the result of the swelling and shrinking of continents instead of some weird relationship between the sea and a distant moon. It was very much an idle theory, weakly held, and in a minute had drifted off, along with all other coherent thoughts.

This was one of Clement's deeper varieties and the water came right up to the overflow beneath the bold brass taps. As I sank deeper into the suds I set in motion a small wave of water which momentarily covered the overflow's circled sieve before returning up the bath. Then, as the water level gradually resettled, I could clearly hear the gargle of the released water as it went racing down the pipe.

Somewhere above me I heard the distant creaks and wheezes of the hot-water tank restoring itself. A minute later, the turning of a tap somewhere else in the house – the kitchen, perhaps – sent a new chorus of whines and screeches juddering up and down the pipes. I listened most intently, picking out ever-more subtle sounds, until at last I began to see myself as a conductor in charge of an orchestra whose concerts consisted of nothing but watery whistles and groans. I lay there quietly contemplating all the pipes in the house – hidden beneath the floorboards, winding in the walls – and found myself strangely cheered by them. I thought of the fountains out in the gardens and their own small water systems. I thought of all the guttering and the miles of drainpipes. The water closet's violent flush. And for a moment I felt that by simply lying there in my warm bathwater I was part of the house's complex circulation which, despite its whole range of rattles and shudders, continued to function in a most admirable way.

I was still lying in this happy stupor when I heard a tap-tap-tapping come down the corridor. I recognized it straight away as the footfalls of some long-lost loved one – of some errant friend. Emotions which had lain dormant for many years rose up in me, filled me and I was altogether very glad. The footsteps came closer and closer and with each one I became gladder still. Then they were right outside the bathroom door and on the verge of entering. With a full heart I waited, breathless, but they simply would not come in. They fell insistently – tap . . . tap . . . tap . . .

'Open the door,' I think I said.

I opened my eyes and watched as the footsteps slowly transformed themselves into the sound of a dripping tap. As each drop hit the water it rang out, and sent a series of ripples sweeping across the surface. I clambered from the bath, still groggy, and all but threw myself at the door, but before my hand had even reached the handle I knew I would find nobody there.

Returned to my bath and sat stewing in it for quite a while, tearful at my failure to be reunited with the owner of the footsteps, yet curious to know whose they might have been.

*

November 2nd

*

All morning we rolled up and down the tunnels, checking no birds had got in. Went down one after another until I was absolutely sure. Had a fine jugged hare for lunch.

Following my recent disappearance, Clement insists I do not wander too far from the house, so this afternoon I took a gentle stroll out to Norton village and had a scout around. Called in on Miss Whittle at the Post Office and told her all about the jugged hare. We exchanged our views on various broths and sauces until another customer interrupted us and I set off home again.

The climate of late has been not the least bit kind so I was all wrapped around with scarves. Had on my famous beaver, two frock coats and carried a third one over my arm, so I was a little put out when I came across two infants playing on the common in nothing but their shorts and vests.

I stood at a discreet distance, trying to make sense of their game, which appeared to involve a great deal of running and shouting and the occasional violent shove, but after two minutes' intense observation any rule or clear objective had still to make itself known to me. The whole thing seemed utterly lawless, but the two boys kept relentlessly at it and would have probably gone on all day had one of them not spotted me as I attempted to sneak by.

The other lad continued running and shouting until he became aware that the game had been held up. Then both the boys simply stood and stared at me, their mouths hanging slightly ajar. Their play, with all its tupping and skipping, had made me think of mountain goats, so I greeted them with a hearty,

'Hallo, young goats,' which was met with a stony silence. The young goats continued to stare.

One was much larger than the other but it was his little friend who finally spoke up. He had recognized me, apparently, and bade me a very good day, so I bade him a very good day in return. He then asked me what it was I had on my head and when I introduced it as my beaver their eyes fairly lit up. The larger and quieter of the two asked me how I had caught it and I explained that I had not been present and therefore could not say for sure, but supposed that most likely it was caught with a trap.

The three of us then proceeded to have the most stimulating conversation, in which I was quizzed with disarming ingenuousness on my appearance, wealth and newly completed tunnels. The smaller boy earnestly informed me how it was his intention to one day own a beaver very much like mine and we soon found ourselves agreeing on the many virtues of tunnels and beaver hats.

As we chatted the boys became a good deal more relaxed and did not stand so rigidly. The quieter of the two showed me a trick with a piece of string and the other tried to teach me how to whistle by inserting my forefingers in my mouth. At last I got round to the game I had just seen them playing and asked what the rules of it were. Well, they looked at one another, quite baffled, standing there in their tatty vests and shorts, and the small boy looked up at me and said, 'It wasn't the kind of game which has rules, sir.'

Feeling altogether old and foolish, I thanked them for a most pleasant conversation and said that I must be getting along, else my valet would start worrying. They both nodded, as if they too had trouble with worried valets, and I gave them each a penny and a pat on the head.

I was a hundred yards down the road when I thought to myself, 'How hot their little heads were.' If an adult's head were half as hot, he'd be put to bed and a doctor called for straight away. I turned to find them already fully re-immersed in their unruly game and for a second I stood there and thought how like little furnaces children are. Little engines – that's how one might see them – with their own enviable reservoirs of power.

This got me thinking about how, sometime last year, as I was walking along the Cow-close path I found a dead sparrow lying on the ground. It appeared not to have a mark on it, so there was no knowing how it might have died. I picked up the motionless creature and held it in my hand, half expecting it to suddenly revive itself and fly off in a flurry. 'How little a sparrow weighs,' I remarked to myself at the time, and, 'How unconvincingly dead it seems.'

But I knew in my heart that it was indeed dead, for it felt cold in the palm of my hand. Its tiny feathers were finely frosted and its colour was all gone. I thought at the time how all creatures are just vessels of heat and how this one's small quota had been used up or had somehow leaked away.

So, perhaps every creature carries inside it a living flame – a modest candlepower. If, for some reason, the flame falters the creature's existence is put at risk. But if our inner flame flares up and engulfs us, madness is the result. I think that makes some sense.

But there are so many different creatures in the world –

from flitting insects to great lumbering beasts: it is inconceivable they all possess the same candlepower. It stands to reason that the twitching sparrow lives at a speed wholly different to the worm it drags from the ground, and that the inner flame of the cat which slowly stalks the bird must burn at a rate wholly different again.

Perhaps the variety in speed-of-life from one creature to another is common knowledge and recorded in the great science books. But do they also record the difference in candlepower between the young and old of a single species? For who would deny that a child lives at a rate nothing like that of an old fellow like myself? In a child's eye each day lasts for ever; to an old man the years fly by.

Time's back is bent on the candle flame. For each one of us the sun arcs through the sky at a different speed. For some creatures life must be but a series of shooting suns. Others must have but the one sun which takes a lifetime to rise and fall.

*

November 6th

*

First thing this morning I had a boy run into town with a message for Dr Cox, telling him to come at once. I had woken with an uncomfortable nagging sensation in the small of my back and pain all about my waist. Needed Clement's help just to sit me up in bed.

My belly is quite distended – a most distressing sight. If I were any more distracted I might imagine I was in the latter stages of some unnatural pregnancy.

It was well past lunchtime when Mrs Pledger knocked on my bedroom door. Dr Cox came marching in. He had his 'I am a very busy man' written all over his face. That was clearly what was on his tongue's mind, so I swiftly countered with, 'And I am very sick.'

This knocked the cocky beggar off his perch and before he had hoisted himself back onto it, I followed up with, 'So what are you to do about it?'

He stuffed his hands deep into his trouser pockets and puffed out his waistcoat, as if I might like to admire its buttons. He held his breath for a couple of seconds, then let the air out noisily through his nose.

'Clement tells me you've been getting yourself lost in the woods,' he said.

Clement was noticeable by his absence.

'Something's up with my stomach,' I replied. 'Now get your stethoscope on the job.'

He turned away and trundled over to his little black bag. Opened it up, gazed inside it for a second or two before removing a large, soiled handkerchief and snapping it shut again. He sauntered back over to my bedside, blowing his nose in a series of short blasts, and deposited his vast, tightly-trousered behind on the edge of my bed so that its springs creaked and groaned with the strain.

'Did the scrofula clear up all right?' he asked, a coy little smile playing on his lips.

'Thankfully, it passed of its own accord,' I replied. 'Must have been a mild attack.'

He made a wide-eyed face at me and nodded. 'Very good,' he said, unbuttoning my nightshirt and slipping a freezing hand inside. 'And the lockjaw?'

'I found it eventually eased with time,' I was obliged to concede.

'And the meningitis?'

'That too.'

'I see,' he announced. Then, having warmed his hand on

my chest, he retrieved it and heaved himself off my mattress to leave me bouncing in his wake. He gestured for me to button up my nightshirt, then threw an arm round Mrs Pledger and marched her off to a corner of the room, where the two of them stood in secret conference with their backs towards me – Dr Cox doing a good deal of whispering while Mrs Pledger nodded her head along. At last, Dr Cox sprang out of their little knot. He seemed to be making for the door.

'Is that it?' I shouted at him, exasperated.

'It is, Your Grace,' he said, and was gone.

I was left staring at Mrs Pledger who remembered some soup she had to take care of and scuttled away herself, pulling the door to behind her.

'He didn't even take his hat off!' I cried.

*

Later, when I asked Mrs Pledger about her tête-à-tête with Cox, she said he had offered her no diagnosis and when I asked her what in the world all their muttering and nodding had been about she said he had been telling her how best to stew fruit.

'Stew fruit!' I yelled at the woman. 'A man lies on his death-bed and the doctor gives his cook tips on stewing fruit!'

Unfortunately, Mrs Pledger is not the least bit afraid of me. I only wish she was. She squared up her ample shoulders as if contemplating charging at me and knocking me out of my bed.

'He said it will do you good,' she trumpeted and made a grand exit, which involved her slamming the door as she went.

What is the matter with everybody? They keep slamming my bedroom door.

Information is being kept from me. I am being left to die like a dog.

*

Clement poked his head round the door; rather sheepishly, I thought. He had with him some soup in a small tureen. It smelt fair enough but when I'd taken a mouthful of the stuff it was all I could do not to spit it back into the bowl.

'Is there fruit in this soup?' I asked him but he just shrugged his shoulders and spooned up some more.

*

All afternoon I lounged uncomfortably in my bed, bedraggled, like a shipwrecked sailor on his raft. Memories of childhood illnesses came back to me – those unending days of feverish tedium. I remember a stuffed bear which I clung to throughout one particular sickly bout. When, at last, I began to improve a little he was taken from me and put on the fire. Mother reckoned he was full of germs. Quite naturally I assumed that he had caught these germs from me and I was riddled with guilt for weeks afterwards. How many days of my childhood did I spend in a bedroom with the curtains closed, I wonder? *Poorly* . . . the very word fills the room with its sickly-sweet smell.

The sheets made me sweat which made me restless. They got all tied up in my feet. A crumb somehow found its way in to me and I simply had to get it out. It was trying to penetrate my very skin. Neither properly awake nor properly asleep I lumbered through the day in an irritable stupor. Once in a while I would stir, sit up and glance under my nightshirt but the sight of my swollen belly did nothing but make me feel worse.

*

I don't mind admitting that after this morning's fiasco with that blasted Cox I feel some essential trust between doctor and patient has been broken beyond repair. Traditionally, when one feels ill one consults a doctor who identifies what is wrong. Isn't that the way it goes? When the doctor gives a name to one's previously nameless malaise is that not the first step towards recovery? The doctor informs the patient that he is right to say he is sick. The problem is located, some term or title dispensed (*You have a chill, sir*, for instance or, *I believe you have broke your toe*), then one has something to hold on to and can set about being ill in earnest. The doctor gives permission to act out a specific sick-man's role. It is a small but integral part of the drama of being ill.

But if a fellow's complaints are simply dismissed with a wave of the hand, if he is not even properly consulted, then the whole relationship is in danger of completely falling apart.

I mean to say the man didn't even get out his stethoscope! His bowler stayed on his head like it had been glued there. The only thing he took out of his bag the whole time he was here was a damned handkerchief! How is one supposed to have faith in a man like that?

Well, there's an end to it right there. I am done with the medical world!

*

The only thing to cast some light on an otherwise dismal day was the return of the Sanderson map from Watson and Blakelock, the framers. They've done a first-rate job and I had them hang it on the wall right beside my bed. Now, *there* is order, *there* is sense, *there* is reason. There is observation put to use.

*

I've been blowing down the tube like an elephant. I want some food which tastes of something other than stewed fruit.

*

*

By six o'clock this morning I was wide awake, my stomach filled to bursting with the most incredible ache. It has hardly let up the whole day, like a steel plate strapped tight around me – a cummerbund of pain.

Words fail me. I *hurt*. That is established easily enough. And I can immediately locate the discomfort all around my waist. But in no time at all, it seems, words disappoint me. I may endeavour to dream up more cummerbunds, more steel plate – and knives and spears, come to that – but none conveys the sensation sufficiently to diminish it in any way. Words, evidently, aren't up to sharing pain out. They fall well short of the mark.

Dozed off again and slept fitfully until around midday. Blew down to Mrs Pledger for some tea with honey and asked her to bring up a quantity of hot towels. These I placed across my distended belly and they gave me some small relief.

For my distraction and entertainment this afternoon kind Clement rounded up various members of staff to play a game of Association football. He has heard that Worksop have started up a team and thinks it might be an idea for the estate to do the same. The lawns were nowhere near long enough so they were obliged to use the cricket pitch. Unfortunately, it is several hundred yards from the house and as I had no intention of venturing out in my present state it was through the cold lens of a telescope that I watched my cooks and keepers and stable lads congregating for the match.

They were quite a collection of shapes and sizes, I must say, and practised kicking the leather ball between them with tremendous apathy, managing to waste a further five minutes arguing over how they were to divide themselves into two teams. But once these shenanigans were finally settled and the ball had been passed around for inspection they began stretching and warming up a little more earnestly. Makeshift goals were marked out on the ground with piles of discarded jackets and one forlorn chap from each team delegated to stand in between them as last defence. Then, when Clement, who was umpiring the match, peeped on his whistle and the football was finally placed and kicked, every man – about sixteen in all – set upon it like a pack of wolves.

They ran from one end of the pitch to the other. They ran in one great screaming and kicking mob, while I surveyed the whole bloody battle through my telescope, like a general up on a hill.

After ten minutes or so the older men had grown tired of running around and tried to compensate by resting strategically about the field, so that if a colleague happened to win possession of the ball they shouted that he should kick it over into their acre of space. Thus the game was gradually transformed from a scene of outright pandemonium to one involving at least a modicum of skill, as members of each team attempted to pass the ball without the intervention of their counterparts. As time went by and weariness took a firmer hold it became apparent which of the men had some talent and which of the men had none. Once or twice some unspoken manoeuvre would develop between fellow players and a pleasing piece of kick-about would result. Lobbed balls and passes wove cat's cradles. Angles slowly unfolded and were a minor joy to behold.

Keeping my telescope firmly on the action, I began to anticipate possible feints and runs from my vantage point. Several times I was obliged to shout out some advice, little minding that none of the footballers were likely to hear. At some point, the leather ball was kicked high into the air and the game slipped briefly into limbo as one brave young gardener positioned himself right under it so that his head would interrupt its descent. But with the ball having gone so far up in the first place it picked up a good deal of velocity on its way back down and when it finally made contact with the gardener's head he was knocked to the ground in a crumpled heap. He seemed about to change his mind at the very last moment. But by then it was too late. The other players all flinched in horror and a great chorus of 'Oh' went up as he was felled. Needless to say, the lad's foolishness was well heeded and after he had been carted off the field there were no more acrobatics of that sort.

All in all, though, the ball was given a sound kicking and by the time the last man had run himself into the ground and a truce had been agreed, everyone looked very proud of the fact that they had covered themselves from head to foot in mud. Even as a spectator I found it a pleasant way to waste an hour, although I can't say I remember the score.

When they had all trooped off to wash and have their lunch I took to wondering about the young boy who was hit on the head with the ball. I wondered what particular pain he suffered, what sensations currently addled his mind. But, try as I might, I was forced to acknowledge that I could not summon them up. A ball on the head, that's a nasty thing. I had no trouble picturing him but whichever way I came at it could not quite manage to climb into his boots. Perhaps I had enough on my plate with my own discomfort – mine is certainly much more vivid and real to me. His fellow-gardeners had probably dumped the chap in some darkened room to recuperate. That is usually the way. It was with a certain glumness that I concluded that all pain-sufferers are doomed to be shut away in quiet, shadowy places and that each one of us must suffer our pain alone.

*

Spent the rest of the day in near agony, rifling through an old medical dictionary after a label for my malady. At first I had suspected appendicitis and spleen trouble later on, but under closer examination both hypotheses proved somewhat unsustainable. Then, around five o'clock when I was deep into the dictionary and the sun had all but given up on the day, my finger came to rest by some odd-looking entry and the next moment I was exclaiming a small 'Eureka!' to myself.

Under *Stones* I found a whole range of fascinating information. It appears that given half a chance, these stones will make a home for themselves in just about any organ in the body of the unsuspecting man. And when I came down to *Stones, of the kidney* I saw at once what Dr Cox had chosen to ignore. My symptoms correspond exactly with those in the medical book. 'A band of pain extending from the base of the spinal column, towards the groin' . . . and so forth. Well, that is me all over. My symptoms were tailor-made for 'kidney stones'.

But my joy very soon grew muted, after a moment's reflection made me realize that these stones would likely require surgery of some sort. For once a stone gets itself inside a man, one cannot imagine it being easily shaken out. Presumably big knives would be necessary and my belly would need completely opening up.

Question – How did these stones get inside of me to begin with? In my bread? In my soup?

Whichever way they got in, the dictionary seemed to suggest that, by now, they had most likely set off on a journey through my insides, which is apparently what causes the pain. I pictured great boulders . . . stationary at first . . . then slowly starting to roll . . . and gathering some unstoppable speed as they went along.

They made a terrible rumbling. I lay there listening for a full hour, not knowing what to do.

*

When I woke I was all in a lather, having dreamed how a tiny carriage had got inside me and how its progress through my personal tunnels was making my stomach ache. I was, if I remember rightly, the man in the carriage as well as the man whose innards I journeyed through.

It was seven o'clock when Clement brought me some fruity-tasting game pie. I insisted he check no carriages were missing and that none of the tunnels were in use.

Tomorrow I will get me another doctor. Not some ape in a waistcoat, but one who really knows his stuff. I will get me a qualified surgeon and tell him about the stones.

*

November 9th

*

My head is a barometer. Has been all my life. And though blood, not mercury, creeps through my veins and my face lacks a needle to point at *Fair* or *Change* the anticipation of the shifts in climate are registered there just the same. So when I was woken last night in the pitch-dark by a sickening pressure behind the eyes and my scalp a nest of shooting pains I knew before I was properly conscious that some tempest was on its way. If there had been a hint of daylight I could have looked out of the window, consulted the barometer tower and had my findings verified. But I was marooned in the depths of night-time and everything was as black as could be.

Pains in my head I am used to – I have twinges every week

or two – but these were not the familiar forebodings of a downpour or the premonition of a blustery day. A storm of colossal proportions was coming, for my head felt completely pumped full of air and my skull was about ready to crack. Yet the discomforts up top were nothing compared with the stresses and strains I was experiencing down below. My belly was so bloated I was having trouble breathing. I was ridden with pain. It had rendered me awake.

I leant out of bed and lit a candle to try and calm me down, but its flame barely dented the dark. It merely slunk back a foot or two and continued to study me. I sat myself up, blinking, in my big four-poster. Looked out from my small corner of candlelight, still reeling from dreams. The shadows swung lazily to and fro as if the whole house pitched in the night, while the pains in my head and stomach squeezed me like a vice.

The bedsheets had fallen from me to reveal a stomach straining at my nightshirt's seams. I stared down at it – at my own unrecognizable stomach. What, in God's name, was I full of? If it were indeed a stone then it was growing at an incredible speed, must now be a good ten inches wide. Fearfully, I slipped my fingers under my nightshirt and peeled it back over my spherical belly. The flesh, usually slack, was now tight as a drum. My belly button, an aperture normally capable of swallowing half my thumb, had been forced out into a tight, bulging knot – a wildly staring eye. Some little monster had picked me as its place of refuge. Some evil had made me its home.

The storm kept on advancing. 'God help me,' I heard me say.

The thick curtains at the windows danced a little, twitching in the gusts from the cracks. Outside, a gate rattled madly on its latch, as if the wind shook it with its very own hands.

I thought I heard the creaking of an ancient ship: ropes and timbers straining to hold it all together. An awful chorus of discordant screeching and scraping, it was, before some final coming-apart. But the sound came not from beyond the windows, nor even the bed where I failed to sleep. I was sickened to discover that the sound came from me, and that I was that creaking ship.

Something heavy lurched inside of me. Turned and slid to one side. Whatever creature had recently taken up in me stirred. What was in me had come alive.

A tear crept out from the corner of my eye and hurried down my cheek. Such *pain*! I had never known such pain. The monster inside me forced my legs apart and began to burrow its way out. I grabbed the candle from the bedside table. Held it between my legs and peered into the light. One hand gripped a bedpost behind me while the other tried to keep the candle in place. And the next moment I was seized by the most incredible agony, as if I was being ripped in two. A mountain moved inside me; the first raindrop dashed itself against the window-pane.

A high-pitched rasping noise came out of me, like the tearing of a sail. It caught the candle and transformed itself into a blinding, billowing flame. Purple-blue, it was, and six foot long, lighting up the entire room. The flash came back from the mirrors and bounced from wall to wall and that dreadful noise continued to launch itself from me as I clung to the bedposts with both hands. But just as my own great flame began to dwindle and the pain had begun to abate I became aware of other, new flames in the room. The netting round my bed had been caught up in it and my sheets were all alight.

I leapt from the bed, dancing madly. Tripped and fell. Got to my feet. Tripped again. The flames swept up the muslin with an evil crackle and multiplied themselves.

'Fire!' I shouted, as if to wake me. 'Fire!'

I continued running frantically around the room and caught sight of me in a mirror. A small flame clung to the tail of my nightshirt, like some evil party game. I leapt back, aghast, and when I looked again, saw how the flame had spread; now crept around me in a cruel embrace.

'Fire!' I yelled, louder this time. 'Fire!'

I hopped from one foot to the other, slapping my flaming nightshirt with bare hands. I was like some demented person, like some injured bird. One second the flame went out – O, blessed relief! – the next it had returned. I patted it out at my shoulder only to see it reappear at my waist. I must have put that same flame out a dozen times – I was beating myself like an African drum – until at long last the blasted thing went down and did not come back up and, with a sudden inexplicable charge in my blood, I set about extinguishing those larger, wilder flames which were consuming my aged bed. 'Off my bed!' I shouted at them. It was as if a different part of me took over – a brighter and much braver man. I looked around the room. I could not say what for. Then, in a flash, I had dived under the flaming four-poster and come out with my china pot. Almost full. Excellent. I took aim and threw its contents in an ever-widening arc.

There was a moment when the chaos seemed to hang in the air and wait for instruction. The next moment, all the flames were out.

The room was pitch-black again and suddenly silent. I stood listening, gulping in the smoky air. The door swung open and there was Clement, with his lamp held high. The room slid back into the light. The bedsheets were wet and blackened, the muslin hung in tatters everywhere. A thick pall of smoke crowded the ceiling and huddled over the whole sorry scene. I opened a window to let the smoke out, but the rain and the wind came in instead. A handful of leaves entered, formed themselves into a whirlpool, then skipped like infants around an invisible maypole.

In the long mirror, I caught sight of somebody. An old beggar of a man, he was – all singed and smudged. The charred remains of a nightshirt hung from him and his pale body showed through here and there. I tried to stand a little straighter, but it did no good. Did not improve my opinion of him at all.

Clement looked on from the doorway in his leather slippers and freshly-laundered robe. He had a puzzled expression on his face.

'Gas,' I explained.

*

November 10th

*

The hairs on my legs are all singed away but my stomach is flat as a pancake. All that talk of stones and my being opened-up like an oyster is done with. I shall sleep in one of the guest rooms until my own is redecorated.

*

The sky had been lardy all day long – or, at least, since I first set eyes on it around eleven o'clock. I had resolved to get out for my constitutional at some point and charge my lungs but kept putting it off in the vain hope of a little sun and by late afternoon the same grey veil hung over the world so I settled on a swift twenty-minute circular, then getting myself back indoors. I took with me one of the stable dogs – a whippet called Julius, who is blind in one eye – and, all things considered, we were having a quite agreeable time, with Julius nearly catching a rabbit and me finding a handsome stick. But as we were heading over towards the Deer Park a mist came up around us with all the opacity of a Turkish bath.

It was thickest on the ground, up to a height of about three feet, so that we were able to wade through it like a shallow milky lake. Very strange and quite intriguing at first, but when the great oak towards which we were headed was swallowed up in the fog I began to find myself somewhat at sea. Poor Julius, with only his one good eye, was in right over his head, so I quickly put a leash on him, for he had got into the habit of standing stock-still and I am quite sure I would have lost him if he hadn't been making such a row with all his whimpering.

We had wandered around the meadows long enough for me to go beyond being merely irritated and to start to feel a little troubled, so I thought it best to stop and make some firm decision about which way to go. In the mist the world had lost all its edges; had become vague and unreliable. I searched for some familiar landmark – a copse or fence or stream – without success. Dusk was beginning to slip in all around us and we were neither of us dressed to spend much time out in the cold, but were in no immediate danger, when the most peculiar thing came to pass. Without warning, I recoiled – quite violently – as if I had been stung by a wasp. It was as if some crumb of a dream stirred in me – the smallest fragment, from long ago. Some nightmare, which had haunted my earliest years; no more than an itch to begin with, but I scratched at it and there developed in me the most convincing scene . . .

I am in a carriage with my mother and father. I am in my travelling clothes. It is an old-style carriage with the hard bench seats. I am very small, I am in my travelling clothes and I can smell the sea.

I can see no others in the carriage. There is no one, I think, except Mother, Father and myself. The wheels make a sort of 'whishing' sound; the horses' hoofs are somehow dampened down. We trundle along quite slowly, and out of the window I see sand thrown up by the wheels.

We are on a beach somewhere. That is it. The wheels are making a 'whishing' sound for we are travelling across a beach.

A shout.

I hear a shout . . .

Then I have lost it. I lose the carriage at the shout. I think too hard on that particular shout and the carriage disappears.

So I try a different sort of remembering. I dwell on the travelling clothes I wore with such pride. Encourage myself to recall the smell of the sea and look for the sand as it is thrown up by the wheels.

And the carriage gradually re-emerges. Comes up slowly out of the sand. Then . . .

I am in my travelling clothes. Mother . . . Father . . . the whole family is here. A shout. The driver shouts a 'Whoa!' to the horses, and the sand is no longer thrown up by the wheels. The carriage has come to a standstill, which grieves me, for I was enjoying watching the sand fly.

I hear the driver put the brake on. I become frightened. We do not move and this frightens me.

Father opens a window and leans out. The cold smell of the sea sweeps in. He has words with the driver, the two of them conversing in a way which is incomprehensible to me. I am very young and hear nothing but an exchange between grown men, so I get to my feet and look out of my own window, where the sand is no longer thrown up.

A thick mist has come up all around us. The mist has brought us to a halt.

But here I lose it again. The thing slips from me. It is very hard to hold. When the mist came up it escaped me. So I tell myself to think of the voices. Think of Father's voice . . .

And I am back among the voices. There are three of them. My father's, the driver's and another one. I do not understand what they are saying but understand that something is wrong. My father does not get angry. He is quiet and smokes a pipe. But I hear anger ringing in my father's voice and see anxiety on my mother's face. These elements ... along with the mist and the halting ... have stirred all the fear up in me.

I can feel it brimming.

In a minute it will fill the whole carriage up ...

Then the dream stops in its tracks and collapses, and I find myself back in the Deer Park with Julius, in a lake of mist.

I set off at quite a pace, dragging the half-blind dog behind me. I worry I may be cut off from the house.

How strange. Not five minutes' walk from my own front door and I am frightened that it is out of reach.

*

November 11th

*

As a boy I had great difficulty sleeping; was often troubled by dreams of abandonment. Time and again I would wake sobbing deep in the night and have to wrench my fearful body from the bedclothes to go barefoot down the hallways of the house. For an age, it seemed, I would run the gauntlet of my own ghouls and demons towards the sanctuary of my parents' room.

I remember heaving against their heavy door and standing trembling in my nightshirt on the cold stone floor, only vaguely able to make them out in the half light, sleeping on the altar of their bed. Yet something would hold me back from calling out. Perhaps the fear of stirring up more monsters in the dark. I only know that in those endless moments before I finally summoned up the courage to call I would look upon the bodies of Mother and Father and think to myself, 'Far from me . . . far from me . . . They are far, far away.'

And it was true, they were indeed far from me; their bodies vacant, minds drifting on a distant plane. Together they had slipped away and lay wrapped in the winding sheets of dreams. Side by side they quietly drifted. Mother and Father at sea in sleep.

And though, in time, they would always groggily return to me, for those moments while I shivered in their doorway I would convince myself that this time they were gone for good. I listened for their breathing, watched to see if their bodies rose and fell, until finally fear itself squeezed out of me a squeak loud enough to bring them home. Then one or the other would turn momentarily from their dreams to say, 'What? . . . What is it, son?'

It was a question, of course, I could not properly answer. I might have said I had a stomach-ache or was in need of a glass of water. But now that I am older and wiser and understand myself a little more, I can answer truthfully. 'I woke from a bad dream and ran here for safety,' I should have said, or even, 'I feared the two of you had slipped away.'

*

This morning, as I made my way down to the mausoleum, I remembered a song my father used to sing to me, which was entitled (if my memory serves me right) 'Every Wingèd Thing', or something similar. A curious little piece it is, with each verse given over to a different bird. No real chorus to speak of, but a few bars where one whistles in the manner of each verse's bird. So as I descended the back stairs and felt the temperature around me fall I filled the whole well with echoes of all sort of birdsong and made believe I was the keeper of some underground aviary.

I tend not to visit my parents' tomb more than two or three times a year, but have lately felt a growing need to impart a small prayer in their presence. To make some attempt at communion.

The mausoleum was the first thing I commissioned. I was twenty-two at the time. I see now how I was still too tender in years to properly run a house, but I had no option. Both parents were gone and I was the only child. So I took charge and did my best to run things in a manner worthy of their memory. Got up bright and early, ate my breakfast and spent the day marching manfully about the estate. First thing I did was have a resting place built for them, on the grandest scale. In other words, I jumped right in.

One enters through a huge wooden portal, where two dozen musicians reside – each in his own small compartment. A great gang of frozen troubadours . . . pipers piping, harpists plucking and so forth. In the mausoleum proper, six carved pillars support the ceiling, with a stone figure brooding at the base of each one. Beneath one pillar an aged scholar reads from an open book, beneath another a naked boy blows on a conch shell. At first they quite enchanted me, these stone inhabitants of my own small underworld, but when I now go down to lay a wreath or reflect awhile I find myself saddened by the old man studying the same blank page or the melancholy boy still failing to produce a sound from his shell.

The roof is crowded with cherubs and angels. Once, they looked down on my parents' tomb with a benign attitude and generally cast their love around. But no one warned me that the air down there is very damp and that in time it would eat away at the stone. So the cherubs now seem to contemplate only their own disfigurement and the angels are more kin to the gargoyles who gape from the house's guttering.

The trimmings up and down all the archways, so lovingly fashioned by the mason's chisel, were pocked and perforated within the year. A braided maiden's torso remains miraculously untouched, unaged by the atmosphere, but where her slender arms once offered grapes and flowers she now offers nothing but her breasts, has only chipped stumps jutting out below both shoulders. I came down one day to find her stone fruit lying shattered on the ground, as if she had had enough of holding them year in, year out and had cast them down.

Only last year, one of the gryphons which had perched on a ledge by the ceiling with never a murmur of complaint decided to try and leap across the vault to spend some time with his crusty twin. No doubt he had squatted for so long with his pounce all tightly-sprung that he felt he could clear the distance in a single bound but discovered that he was stiff from all that sitting and as things turned out covered hardly any space at all. He simply fell, hit the floor and exploded, trimming the nose from a woman with babe-in-arms on his way down.

It is as if the entire population of that vast damp room has returned from the same strange battlefield. It is like some hospital for fractured statues. Every month I have the floor swept from one end to the other but there is always the crunch of fresh grit underfoot.

This morning I bowed my head by the effigies of Mother and Father, who lie side by side just as they did in their sleep all those years ago. The stone angels continue to crumble all around them, but the figures of my parents remain pristine, carved as they are from Carrara marble and wiped clear of debris by a housemaid every second week. Their features, though beautifully shone, are in fact poor representations. My father looks more concerned in death than he did alive. My mother is almost softened by the stone. The marble has given them a sallow glow, as if they had been cut from candlewax, though there is no denying that my parents' flames went out long ago.

Strange that their faces are now younger than mine. In their absence their only son has grown old. When I think of them I am always a bright young boy. Not the bald and bent old man I have become.

After I had said a prayer for my mother and father, I said a prayer for myself. I find I am troubled by that half-remembered memory, that fragment of some distant dream. Something very far back demands my attention.

I asked my parents, 'What is it I cannot remember?' but received no reply.

They are not telling. Their lips are firmly closed. In the end, of course, they did indeed slip away from me.

*

November 12th

*

A day spent around the house, recuperating. Still a little pain in my stomach region. I think the skin must have become stretched while accommodating all that mysteriously-accumulated wind. Otherwise I am feeling much improved, if a trifle tired.

Took a mint bath first thing and dressed in velvet trousers and smoking jacket. Wrote a letter of thanks to Miss Whittle at the Norton Post Office from whom I received today a package containing one tin of 'Essence of Beef'. An accompanying note explains how she has heard I have been suffering from 'difficulties with stomach' and that 'the enclosed beef essence', which is entirely new to me, 'is a guaranteed remedy for the unsteady gut'. She goes on to say how it is frequently employed in her household as a pick-me-up and comes with her heartiest recommendation.

An odd little tin, I must say. No more than four-inch square, but quite a weight. On the underside a printed label, announcing . . .

> This essence consists solely of the juice of the finest beef, extracted by a gentle heat, without the addition of water or of any other substance whatever, by a process first discovered by ourselves in conjunction with a celebrated physician . . . best taken cold.

It seems not a single item finds its way onto the chemist's shelf these days without some physician, celebrated or otherwise, putting his name to it (and for a tidy remuneration, no doubt). Every razor blade, bunion cream or hair-restoring device now carries the enthusiastic personal approval of some much-respected Expert. Yet I note how a good many of these revolutionary remedies, hailed on the inside page of magazines one month, are seldom there the next. It would be too much to hope that their manufacturers had gone bankrupt and been hauled up before some humourless judge, so I must assume instead that these fellows are constantly transferring their energies on to other, ever more miraculous cures.

Which is not intended as any slight towards dear Miss Whittle and her tin of essence of beef. She concluded her note by suggesting I take half the tin at lunchtime with a brandy and water, and as I put such store in the woman's opinions I resolved to do just that. The odd whine and whinny still came up from my stomach and it seemed that beef essence might be just the stuff to quieten them down.

Noontime found me in my dining room, looking nervously down at the tin which I had placed on the tablecloth. Its case had moulded on it a strange bas-relief and I mused awhile on how the lid's lovely rounded lip and exotic design might lead one to suppose it contained not beef but some flavoursome Turkish tobacco. In this way I managed to dally for several minutes before getting around to removing the box's lid with my penknife. It was quite a struggle to get the blade into the nick between the lid and base and, having got some purchase, even more of an effort to prise the two apart. The knife seemed to push in vain against a vacuum until at last the lid sprung off with a mighty 'pop'. Beneath was a muslin cover, very sticky to the touch, and, having peeled back its corners, I found beneath a solid leathery block, like a shrunken pocket Bible, set in a thick film of gelatine.

The knife went through the stiff jelly and into the beef substance with no trouble at all, but as soon as the skin of the latter had been punctured the most rancorous smell leapt out. My whole body reeled back as if I had been struck on the chest and it was all I could do to hold the tin away from me while trying to keep my balance and shake some sense back into my head. So pungent and pervasive was the odour, it was as though a living beast had appeared right there in my dining room. I had to wipe my eyes with a handkerchief until I recovered myself sufficiently to open some windows and let some breathable air in.

I was amazed and, quite frankly, more than a little impressed that such a potent odour could be contained in such a tiny tin. I edged my way back up to it and tentatively peeked inside. 'Who on earth would actually eat the stuff?' I thought to myself, giving the beef a little prod with a fork. It had the same texture as the dirt packed around a horse's shoe.

About then I saw me put my head round the door at the Post Office and Miss Whittle asking how her medication had gone down. I have never been much good at lying. She would see right through me at a glance. I would simply have to bypass the Post Office for six months – or a year, maybe. The last thing I would wish to do is hurt Miss W.'s feelings but only a fool of the highest order would insert into his body something which smelt so convincingly of living cow.

It was a good five or ten minutes before I finally lunged at the tin with my little fork and wolfed down a chunk without a single chew. I then grabbed the brandy decanter by its delicate neck and took a couple of swigs, paused, then took a couple more.

I must have sat in the chair for quite a while, waiting to see what happened next. When Mrs Pledger came in to announce lunch I doubt if I had moved a muscle; was not sure if the essence of beef was happy where it was or might suddenly reappear. She stepped into the room, filled her lungs to speak, then paused, with her mouth hanging open. A look of consternation quickly spread across her face, causing both eyebrows to bunch up together above the bridge of her nose. She took a second, more discriminatory sniff of the air, her eyes flashed left and right before settling on me in her most withering glare. Then she span her great weight around and exited, without having uttered a single word.

It is now a good eight hours later. Thankfully I am still alive. And though my stomach is a little queasy and my breath much beefier than before I comfort myself by thinking how I can at least now face Miss Whittle with my conscience clear.

*

November 18th

*

Afternoon spent catching up on accounts and correspondence. Wrote a note to Dr Cox expressly refusing to pay his bill and telling him, in plain English, how I want nothing more to do with the fellow. Blew down to Clement and had a boy take it round to him straight away.

I learn from his letter this morning that the Reverend Mellor has been excavating the caves at Creswell – something I apparently gave my consent to several years ago – and now seeks my permission to stage a lecture there. Yesterday I received a tearful epistle from one Sarah Swales, appealing for the continued use of a cottage, following her mother's recent death. Gave the Reverend Mellor permission for his lecture (he can stage a circus there if he can fit all the animals in) and dear Sarah, who I am told works out at Norton, appears to have wrongly assumed I am about to throw her out. This is, of course, absolute nonsense and I wrote to assure her of the fact.

Sitting quietly at my bureau, fiddling with papers and pens, brings me no end of pleasure. It is here I fancy some order is restored into my cock-eyed life. I am told it is a Dutch 'cylinder-front' bureau – by now well over a hundred years old – previously belonging to my father and his father before him. In a house packed with ancient furniture which long ago set to sagging and spewing their stuffing all over the floor my bureau is one of the few remaining upright pieces in the place.

Inlays and veneers cover about every inch of it: a kaleidoscope of fine marquetry. Weird birds and butterflies flutter up and down its sides, leafy vines creep across its drawers and dangle down its belly. The whole thing glows warmly from a thousand French polishes – ten thousand! – so that an idle caress evokes an exquisite squeal.

Three solid drawers make up the bulk of it, curving most seductively, as if they may have melted in the sun. And when the ribbed lid is rolled back, to disappear into its own slim cavity, a heady aroma is released – not just of lovely woods and varnishes but also inks and pencil shavings, old manuscripts and book-binding glues. A neat little row of sentry boxes stands at the back, housing tilted notebooks, ragged letters, miniature ledgers and suchlike. In the middle of them sits a small stack of drawers, six inches wide, where odd bits of wax and blotting paper, nibs and pens are tucked away. These worthless but oft-sought odds and ends are what my paper-sentries so nonchalantly guard.

Golden hinges and handles and brackets are cold to the touch the whole year round. Every corner and moulding and edging is hewn from the finest woods. One chap said he had never seen so much amboyna lavished on a single piece. But when one's eyes have done feasting on the bureau's beauty and one's nose has drawn in the many elements of its complex bouquet, when one's fingers are sure they have found out and fiddled in every last nook and cranny, a dozen secret drawers and compartments will still have eluded one's eager grasp.

For the whole cabinet is riddled with hidey-holes which only give themselves up to the most intimate acquaintance. Pick the right panel to press or the right latch to twist and some swivelling chamber will reveal itself. Pull the top drawer out altogether and another drawer comes into view. A whole series of springs and levers are sunk deep in the carpentry so that a handle tugged here releases a catch over there and what appeared just now to be solid becomes a tiny sliding door. The whole thing is a great hive of recesses which rarely see the light of day. I only wish I had more valuables which needed hiding, with so many little places they could be hid. Some old coins, a few private letters and documents are tucked away here and there, but more for the clandestine fun of it than necessity truly demands.

*

Whilst making this entry I have paused several times to look out on the day. The grounds seem utterly deserted, as if humanity has been erased from the face of the earth. Now that the trees are bare I can see in every direction, but whichever way I look there seems not to be a single soul about. Contrary to popular wisdom, I believe winter actually greases the world's wheels. When the weather is kind we are more inclined to stop and have a chat, for in the summer it is pleasant to let the sun warm us, so we take our time between one thing and the next. But when the weather turns cold and the frost comes we want to be back indoors as quick as we can so we hurry through the landscape, leaving it altogether barren and sad.

*

November 21st

*

The frequency of my evacuations is returning to normal, though the stools are quite painful to expel. I have heard (or perhaps just imagined) that consumption of eggs may impede one's movements and have a tendency to generally clog up the works. So, no eggs – at least for a fortnight – to see if this does any good. After a breakfast of kippers, toast and marmalade, washed down with a tablespoon of cod-liver oil, I felt nothing if not lubricated. So much so that as I sat there letting it all settle I felt as if I might slip right off my chair.

Though every tree on the estate looks haggard and wretched, the sun shone all around and as the morning unfolded I found myself tempted out of doors. Dressed myself in a lime double-breasted frock coat with fur collar and a knee-length burgundy cape. At the door I picked out a grey, wide-brimmed top hat, a pair of goatskin gloves, cream lambswool scarf and a cane.

I had planned to go as far as Creswell but was not a hundred yards from the house when I felt some sort of fearful shudder pass through me, as if someone had stepped over my grave. For that fraction of a second I felt utterly vulnerable – was almost quaking in my boots. An awful, anxious moment which came from I know not where. Then it was gone. The sky was clear, a slight breeze blew. Most perplexing. Perhaps I have been holed up in the house for too long.

Creswell suddenly seemed a long way away so I changed course and aimed for the lake, thinking I might go on after toward Wallingbrook and march some circulation back into my frame. I reached the lake in a matter of minutes and stood on the old landing bay, looking out over the water which was perfectly solid and still. At that corner of the water's edge stand plenty of horse chestnuts and sweet chestnuts and I bent down to pick up one or two of their rotting leaves. I might have derived some pleasure from their splendid colours if I had not so wished that they were still up in the trees. I held one sad specimen up to the cold sun. 'Did you jump?' I asked him.

His thin veins seemed to map a river's tributaries. I thought to myself, 'You have fingers like me. You are just a flat hand.'

And then, 'A tree is a many-handed man.'

I was dwelling on the precise impracticabilities of one year sticking all the fallen leaves back into the trees when a noise, close by, broke the silence and caused me to look up.

A fish had leapt out of the water. Its silver back caught the sun. But before I had begun to properly grasp the situation it was back in the water and gone. How shockingly odd. The lake, which but a minute before had seemed so dull and lifeless, had thrown a fish up into the air, then swallowed it again. I looked about me, stupidly – as if needing confirmation from someone else. But I was the only witness. The fish had jumped only for me.

From the spot where it had re-entered the water – and a fair-sized fish it was, too – a dozen ripples gently spread across the lake's oily skin. And like those circles rolling over the water and now delicately reaching the shore, the picture of the fish – the sheer surprise of it – kept recurring in my head.

It was a few minutes before I recovered myself and, even then, the splash and glint of the creature would suddenly leap back into my mind. I found myself looking out at the water, half expecting it to jump a second time. But nothing stirred. The lake was flat and solid again.

Several minutes passed, full of the lake's silence and punctuated by my memory of the jumping fish, before I slowly began to make sense of what I had seen. In my pocket I found a scrap of paper and a pencil and noted down my thoughts . . .

> When considered against the backdrop of eternity the period between our birth and death is the shortest of trajectories. From the moment we first feel the smack of life to that moment when we re-enter the deep, black pool is but one breath. We are no sooner aloft than we begin to feel gravity's inevitable pull. We hang there but for a second in all our twisting glory. We feel the air on our bodies, our cold eye snatches at the light. We turn a little, as if on a spit. Then we start to fall.

I concluded with a thick full stop. Listened to my thoughts a second and found myself apparently not the least bit alarmed by what I had just jotted down. On the contrary, I felt quite exhilarated. I returned the paper and pencil to my pocket and set off back home.

*

*

After lunch I became increasingly listless, which is by no means exceptional for me this time of year. I do sometimes wonder if we human beings are not meant to hibernate in the dark months, along with the squirrels.

My stomach is not yet sorted out and my lower back has been uncomfortable the whole day and I thought a good walk this afternoon might do me the power of good.

It occurred to me, not for the first time, that perhaps the autumn air is bad for me. So I decided to walk to Creswell, as I had originally planned to yesterday, but to do so underground. I forwent the lime frock coat for a light-coloured paletot and took a fur muff instead of gloves. Otherwise I was dressed much the same as yesterday when, around two o'clock, I set off down the Western tunnel. The coach rode twenty yards behind me, with both Grimshaw and Clement aboard. Clement insisted he come along, bringing with him blankets, sweet biscuits and a pot of cold rice pudding in case I required sustenance on the way.

A grand walk it was, too. I had not examined the tunnels so closely since they were finished and I must say I was very pleased with what I saw. The brickwork is quite magnificent and the Western tunnel in particular runs about as straight as an arrow. One problem which neither Mr Bird nor I had reckoned on was that the tops of some of the skylights have got covered over with fallen leaves. I made a mental note to have some lads sent out and sweep them clean as soon as we returned.

Felt altogether quite bright and cheery as I headed underground towards Creswell village, so I set up a little singing session, starting off with 'Johnnie Sands' – an old favourite of mine – then on to a few rounds of 'I Am Ninety-Nine'. The many echoes at first interfered with my performance and made me lose my place but in time I managed to gauge their duration and incorporate them into the song, so that I was able, after a fashion, to duet with myself. I broke the song up, line by line – one harmony placed carefully upon another – until at last the whole tunnel rang with a chorus of my voices. I sang the lead and I sang the alto, had a stab at treble and a breathy 'profundo' bass. Like a military man I marched along and opened my lungs right up, once or twice even managing to knock together some semblance of a descant on the top.

Reached Creswell in next to no time. As I emerged from the tunnel the sun did indeed dazzle me and a light breeze goosepimpled my flesh. Mrs Digby was hanging out her washing so I raised my hat to her and asked after her cats. But by the time the carriage had come out of the tunnel and pulled up alongside of me, our chit-chat was drawing to a close and I was having trouble remembering why Creswell had seemed such an attractive prospect. Came up with no good answers so I cancelled the rest of the expedition on the spot. Turned, waved goodbye to Mrs Digby and set up another singing session as I passed through the tunnel gates.

Sang mainly ballads returning home – my father's bird song and an old sea shanty. Most of the shanty's verses had slipped my mind, which rather obliged me to fill in with some of my own. Amused myself with the thought of the cows above, lazily munching in an empty field, and the sound of some old fellow coming up from the ground, roaring on about the rolling waves and the hunt for the great white whale.

All in all, a most satisfactory day. I am sure tonight I will sleep like a top. But something has been troubling me. As I looked back just now on the day's events and saw me striding down the Western tunnel, I saw not a man who strode along on his own. I had the impression that . . . how can I put it . . . that I had *company* with me. Not entirely visible, perhaps, but company just the same.

A very young fellow – that is all I can come up with. A young fellow who generally hangs about.

I have often wondered if the chap I engage in conversation when I debate some issue with myself is within me or without. Maybe this is my man? What's more, now that I turn my attention to it I rather think he has been there for a very long time.

*

November 24th

*

Not quite right yet, by any means. The discomfort comes and goes. Gave myself a dry-rub with a bath towel to invigorate me (what my father used to call an 'Aberdeen bath') but succeeded only in adding exhaustion to my list of ills. What was last week most definitely a twinge has developed into more of a throb. Very strange – the damned thing appears to move about. I feel sure it is deeper inside me today and further up toward the ribs.

At lunch I had just drunk the last of an excellent oxtail soup and was chewing on a piece of bread when my teeth clamped down onto something which they had difficulty getting through. 'A bit of gristle?' I thought, and fished about with my tongue. The matter had lodged itself between my teeth. Then, with finger and thumb, I picked out what proved to be, on closer examination, a tightly-packed papery wad.

'Paper in my bread,' I said.

With a good deal of effort I managed to unravel the scrap

which, when flattened out on the table, measured some two inches by half an inch. I could just about make out on it a message of some sort, written in pencil. The paper was damp from its short stay in my mouth but, in time, I was able to decipher the following words:

> '... *for the bread we there eat is one bread, and the wine we drink*...'

Well, this meant absolutely nothing to me – rang no bells at all – and I soon concluded that it must be but a fragment of a longer piece. Quite frankly, I found the whole thing more than a little disturbing, partly due to the text's declamatory tone. Someone is sending me messages, I thought. Messages to do with bread and wine. And if I was in possession of only a fragment of what I took to be a much longer tract, then who was to say I had not swallowed the rest, which would be sure to upset my digestion even more? I called Mrs Pledger in.

'Mrs Pledger,' I explained, calmly, 'I have found some words in my bread.'

After the situation had been laid out before her she asked to see the scrap of paper. Her eyes swept over the handwriting and she gave a knowing nod. 'Ignatius Peak,' she said.

The name was completely new to me. It conjured up some craggy mountain-top. But, as Mrs Pledger informed me, Ignatius Peak is an employee in our bakery. Then, lowering her voice to a whisper, said she believed him to be '... an overly-religious man'.

Twenty minutes later he stood before me in my study, still dressed in his apron and white cap and dusted all over with flour, as if he had been put in a cellar and forgotten about. The robustness evoked by the fellow's name was decidedly lacking in the man himself. He stood there and did not say a word. I had, I think, expected an apology without his needing a prompt. He was a small man, with well-trimmed whiskers, but when he spoke he fairly brimmed with God.

'I believe you put some words in my bread, Mr Peak.'

'Not just words, Your Grace, but religious words. They are from the Bible, which means they are sacred. They are holy words, Your Grace.'

As he spoke his short arms waved all about the place, causing a gentle avalanche of flour to fall down his jacket and settle on the floor.

'And why were these holy words put in my bread, Mr Peak?' I asked.

'Well now,' he said, staring in to the distance, 'I believe that this morning, while I was about my baking, I got the sudden inspiration to do so, sir. It happens on occasion ... the inspiration to spread God's Word.'

This confounded me somewhat. He smiled most beatifically, which did not help at all.

'Just *my* bread, Mr Peak, or everybody's bread?'

'O, everybody's, Your Grace. Every loaf in sight.'

He stretched out both arms as far as they would go, so that his tiny wrists protruded from his jacket cuffs and he swept his hands backwards and forwards to draw my attention to acre upon acre of holy bread. Throughout our conversation he had a tendency to gesticulate, as if he were preaching from some lofty pulpit. Once or twice he went so far as to clench his fists and raise them above his head, as if summoning his own thunderbolts and lightning. There appeared, however, to be little correlation between these grand gestures and the actual words as they came hurtling from his mouth.

'What is the quotation I found in my mouth just now?' I asked, and handed him the scrap of paper.

He barely glanced at it before rolling his head back on his shoulders, screwing up his eyes and addressing the ceiling in such a calamitous tone I nearly jumped right out of my skin.

'"*We are joined together into one mystical body, and declare ourselves to be so, by our fellowship together in the ordinance of the Lord's supper; for the bread we there eat is one bread, and the wine we drink is one wine; though the one be composed of many grains of corn, and the other made up of many particular grapes . . .*" One Corinthians, ten, seventeen.'

His eyes stayed tightly shut the whole time but his arms flapped wildly about, continuing to flap for several seconds after his recital had reached an end. Then, quite suddenly, they foundered, as if they had been shot out of the sky, and fell dramatically to his side, where they knocked two new clouds of flour down his trouser legs

'And what does it mean?' I asked him.

'Fellowship through the Lord, Your Grace,' he replied.

I considered this for a moment, watched keenly by my baker-man. Then I asked if his bits of paper did not burn in the ovens, but was informed that the quotations were, in fact, inserted after the loaves had been baked.

'I just makes a little cut with a palette knife and slides the fellows right in.'

I nodded at him, finding myself in something of a quandary. I had originally called Mr Peak in to see me in order to reprimand the man but I was having difficulty finding suitable grounds on which to do such a thing. 'You don't worry you might choke someone?' I asked, rather hopefully, thinking that if I could locate somewhere in him the smallest kernel of guilt I would at least have made a start.

'None have choked so far, sir,' he said, smiling. 'They are only short quotations, after all.'

'And do you always use quotations that are to do with bread?'

'In the main, sir. Yes, I do, sir . . . It seems appropriate somehow.'

I agreed that it did. I was completely at a loss as to what to do with the fellow. Clearly he had done nothing gravely wrong (or, more to the point, nothing which *he* thought was wrong). A heavy sigh rose up in me. The pain in my ribcage gnawed away. On a whim, I asked, 'I don't suppose you happen to heal, do you, Mr Peak?'

He looked at me for a moment, before launching into, 'The *Lord* heals, sir. "*Lest they see, and convert and be healed.*"'

'Yes, I'm sure. But it is healing of the body I'm after, Mr Peak, not healing of the soul.'

'He heals the body too, Your Grace. "*I will heal thee of thy wounds, saith the Lord.*"'

He was quiet for a second and I felt a deep despondency creeping through my bones. Here was a man who was utterly and happily immersed in his faith. He knew his way around it (or at least its vocabulary) like the back of his hand; seemed to have no doubts at all about the world and his place in it. This depressed me mightily. I think perhaps I envied him more than any other man I have ever come across. He stood before me with bowed head – busy, I felt sure, digging ever deeper into his memory for other, more impressive passages from the Good Book. At last he looked up and asked,

'Have you ever seen the Oakleys, sir?'

Now, if the name of the man before me had conjured up a craggy mountain-top, the Oakleys put me in mind of a range of low hills, such as the Malverns, or some other lush terrain. But, as Ignatius Peak informed me, the Oakleys are in fact two sisters living out at Whitwell who are said to have the rare ability 'to look deep inside a man'.

'Are you poorly, Your Grace?' he asked me. I told him I thought perhaps I was. 'Well, they're the women you're after. They are the best diagnosers in the county, those two. They'll diagnose where all others fail.'

So I thanked him and wished him well with his quotations. Then, as an afterthought, suggested he might consider attaching them to the loaves with string. That way they would tend to remain intact, would not risk being eaten and could be read by the recipient at their leisure.

'O, no, sir. That would be no good. You see, the surprise of the discovery is what makes the sinner stop and think. That is how we win him over.'

'I see,' I said.

He smiled broadly, gave me a brisk little bow and marched off towards the door.

It was a second or two after his departure, while I was wondering if I should chase these two weird sisters up, that I noticed on the rug where Mr Peak had stood two perfect footprints in a small heap of flour.

*

November 25th

*

Straight after breakfast I had Clement go out to the Oakleys' and by ten o'clock he was back with news that they would be happy to receive me this afternoon. A price, agreeable to both parties, had been arranged and by two o'clock we were clear of the North-west tunnel and making our way through the village of Whitwell. We had especially taken the fly to tackle the steep hill but Grimshaw soon found it difficult to keep the horse moving and it became necessary for Clement and me to alight and walk the last few hundred yards.

The dull throb in my ribcage had rather been keeping its head low and I was worried I might reach the Oakleys' with no discomfort to speak of at all, but as we reached the crown of the hill and stopped to admire the cold corner of Nottinghamshire spread out below, the throbbing suddenly returned and I drank in the view before me, strangely relieved to have relocated my malaise.

What little I knew of the Oakleys I had picked up from Mr Peak – namely that they were middle-aged sisters with a reputation for possessing some peculiar spiritual power which enables them to see right inside a man. It was said they could observe a functioning organ as if it sat before them twitching on a plate. As we stood there, looking out over the fields and woods, I asked Clement what he reckoned to such claims of visionary powers, but he politely declined to comment. I don't mind saying that there are times when his unflagging diplomacy can be more than a little irritating.

Five minutes later we had reached the Oakleys' and Clement went off to take tea with Grimshaw, whose cousin lives nearby, and I found myself before a modest stone cottage on the top of the hill, with an overgrown garden and a marvellous view all round. As I rapped on the knocker I noticed how all the curtains were drawn and wondered if perhaps the sisters were taking an afternoon nap. Then I heard the clatter of the latch and the door swung back to reveal two splendid women – in their late forties, I should say – with jet-black hair down to their shoulders and both dressed in starched white pinafore. Mr Peak had failed to mention that they were, in fact, twins and made a most striking combination. Not quite identical-looking, but plainly cut from the same stone.

One of the two raised her eyebrows and smiled at me. The other whispered, 'Won't you please come in?'

I was shown into the front parlour, the room which had all the curtains pulled to. It was very sparse, the ceiling so low it almost grazed the ladies' heads. The only ornamentation was two framed pictures on the mantelpiece – one of a Russet apple in cross-section, the other of the same fruit hanging on the bough. I accepted their offer of tea and, a few minutes later, all three of us sat round the table with only the squeak and rattle of our cups and saucers to disturb the growing silence. I eventually felt obliged to venture a little polite conversation. 'I'm an apple-grower myself,' I announced gaily, nodding towards the pictures. But the sisters simply smiled their tiny smiles and continued to sip at their tea.

After another lengthy silence I expressed some enthusiasm for their brew of tea, saying how it was 'very fine indeed'. But my words hardly seemed to register with the women, who kept their gaze firmly fixed on the table top, both apparently wrapped up in some profound and unspoken exchange.

I was wondering what other trifles I might be obliged to bring to their attention (the weather perhaps, or the tablecloth) when they rose simultaneously from their chairs without the slightest warning.

One said, 'Would you care to follow us, Your Grace?'

I rather hurriedly returned my cup to its saucer, catching the teaspoon in the process and causing quite a fuss, by which time both sisters were over by the door and gently beckoning me towards the neighbouring room.

Like the parlour, heavy curtains shut out the daylight. The whole place was lit by a pair of ceiling lamps which between them effused a good deal of warm and amber light. Two longcase clocks faced each other across the floor and knocked the seconds between one another like a tennis ball. Both sisters waited patiently by the door for me, standing so still and silent that as I entered the only movement in that warm, velvety room seemed to be the pendulums in the bellies of the clocks. The atmosphere was so altogether slow and syrupy that I found myself becoming quite alarmed. It was as if I was being invited to jump into a very deep pool. My breathing quickened, my head began to spin.

One of the sisters took me by the hand. The other said, 'It is all right, you know?'

And with that, I have to say, all my fear evaporated and I

felt only embarrassment at the beads of sweat on my brow. I can only imagine that some animal instinct had momentarily surfaced, prompting in me the irrational urge to run right from the place. But the sisters had recognized my anxiety and, in an instant, had soothed it away. They had said, 'It is all right, you know,' and, just like a child, I was assured that it was.

One sister helped me off with my jacket, the other asked me to lift my shirt. And there I stood, in the middle of that honey-warm room with my shirt pulled up around my chest.

The sisters began to slowly circle me. The clocks ticked and tocked in counterpoint. Every pendulum swing sliced away another moment of time. One called, the other replied.

'What a strange little world,' I thought to myself, feeling buoyed-up and beginning to float. I felt increasingly calmed as, one by one, the years of my life slipped away and from deep, deep inside a child's voice whispered to me, 'I have a tummy ache.'

'Where is the ache, Your Grace?' asked a sister.

I touched my stomach, just below my ribs. I pressed, to show how deep it was. Then one of the sisters took my hand, moved it aside and positioned herself in front of me. She settled herself there and proceeded to stare at me. The other positioned herself behind. And as the seconds slowly unfolded and the twins dwelt on me I felt myself sway a fraction of an inch from side to side. But I never feared I might take a tumble, for I was pinned securely in place by the sisters' powerful gaze.

And the room had become perfectly quiet now. One sister nodded her head before me, the other hummed in agreement behind. The whole place was awash with the most unusual atmosphere. Unseen currents shifted everywhere. And it dawned on me, in the most agreeable way, that the sisters were, in fact, observing the tea inside of me. Were following it as it steadily made its way. They had given me a cup of tea to sip at and now watched to see how my organs dealt with it.

I felt not the least bit troubled by their penetrating eyes. In fact, for the first time in my life, became quietly conscious of the independent existence of each organ as they worked away. The sisters' nods and gentle 'ums' and 'ahs' flew back and forth and I nodded forward and looked into the lovely redness of my lids. And, gradually, I came to picture, in quite vivid detail . . . my liver, my heart, my lungs. I had no idea of their size or their colour, or the tubes which connected them up. Had no idea what stopped them slipping from their separate shelves. But they were no longer raw, anonymous entities but individual beings with their own characters and important duties to perform. *Fishes* . . . that is how they seemed to me. Fish, nestling at different levels of my pool. Like the trout I had once seen just beneath the water, sleeping by a stone, their whole bodies gently swelling and contracting inside of me.

'Finished, Your Grace,' one of the sisters whispered.

The clocks' tick-tock suddenly returned to fill the room.

Both sisters now stood before me. It was a while before I recovered myself. And by the time my feet felt the earth beneath them one of the sisters was indicating towards the door. The other was smiling.

'Shall we?' she said.

As I followed along behind them, tucking my shirt back in, I noticed how my gums ached, as they do when I have dozed off in the afternoon. We each took our place around the table and both sisters looked across at me.

'If you don't mind me coming straight to the point,' I said, '. . . what exactly did you see?'

They looked at one other while they decided which one was to speak.

'You have been eating beef,' she said. It was more of a statement than a question.

I thought for a second, before spluttering out, 'Yes. Essence of beef, I ate . . . and very foul stuff it was too.'

'Beef does not agree with you,' said the sister.

'Good Lord, and oxtail, too,' I went on, excited. 'I had an oxtail soup just yesterday.'

'Beef does not agree with you,' she repeated.

This time I heard her and conceded, 'Very well. I'll steer clear of beef from now on.'

Then the two of them exchanged further meaningful glances before the other sister said, in an even quieter voice, 'When you first came in . . . we noticed . . .'

I nodded at her, to help her along.

'We noticed that your aura is not right.'

Well, I must say, this rather stumped me. I had not the first idea what my aura was. Had been ignorant of the fact I even owned one until that very moment.

'It is the light which emanates from a person,' the other sister said. 'Yours is incomplete.'

Well, as you can imagine, this was highly distressing news. Who would want an aura which is incomplete?

'Then how do I make it whole again?' I asked.

'Perhaps you are lacking something,' the quieter sister said, and gave me a second to digest this. 'You must make it your business to find the gap and fill it in.'

*

I handed them their fee in the hallway, shook their hands and thanked them for their time. When they opened the door the daylight flooded into the hall. I paused on the doorstep for a moment or two.

'I'm sorry,' I said, 'but if you don't mind my asking . . . what exactly do you see when you look at a man?'

'We see inside him,' said one.

The other added, 'We see how he is put together.'

*

Clement met me at the garden gate and escorted me back to the carriage. 'They're not fakers, Clement. Honestly,' I told him. 'They saw the essence of beef.'

Clement nodded appreciatively as we carried on down the hill. At some point I turned and looked back at the sisters' cottage and thought I glimpsed a white face peering out between the velvet curtains, but when I looked again a second later the face was gone.

*

November 26th

*

A long while ago, when I was still a socializing man and drank brandy and smoked cigars, I heard the most curious anecdote from my friend, the good Lord Galway.

While we sat gazing into the coals of a roaring fire, coming to terms with the enormous dinner we had just packed away, he told me about an old friend of his who had come bounding up to him at a function the previous spring with 'the most wonderful news'. And indeed it was good news for, after many a barren year, his wife had just been told she was pregnant and, not surprisingly, Lord Galway's friend was as pleased as Punch, not least because he might finally father a son who would one day take over his affairs.

Well, for several months after these glad tidings Lord Galway was kept very busy and when the two of them next met up he straight away detected the most solemn attitude about his friend. Fearing his wife had perhaps lost the child, he decided, as he put it, to 'act the diplomat' and kept up his end of the conversation until his friend got around to saying what was on his mind. Apparently, he was very worried about his wife's mental state; indeed feared she had already gone some way down the road towards insanity. Lord Galway trod ever more carefully – the grave look on his friend's face told him this was wise – but, bit by bit, managed to draw the fellow out.

It transpired that the man's wife was a coal-eater . . . was always at the stuff. He first discovered her sucking a small chunk of it crouched under the desk in his study. Then, at lunch a few days later, he noticed a piece which she had hid in her napkin and was crumbling into her soup. As the weeks went by he found coal all over the house: tucked in her muffler, wrapped in silk handkerchiefs, even a piece in her very best bonnet. At night-time, after the light went out, he could hear her munching under the bedclothes, for she even kept a piece in her pillowcase to suck on till she fell asleep. In the morning, apparently, the sheets were filthy and her lips and teeth jet-black.

Well, all this upset her husband no end. He shouted at her and stamped about the place and confiscated every bit he could find. He forbade her from going near the stuff and made his staff act like prison guards but, of course, there was no way he could keep an eye on her all day long, and he knew full well that as soon as his back was turned she would sneak down to the cellar to get herself a fresh supply.

Now it was unfortunate for Galway's old friend that he had kept to himself for so long what he felt sure were the first signs of his wife's creeping lunacy, for if he had earlier shared out the information he might have been earlier put at ease. For Galway is very worldly-wise and had heard tell how a woman who is carrying a child becomes susceptible to a whole dynasty of inner-change which, in some instances, may result in cravings of the most irrational kind. It has been suggested that the craving of coal – in fact, not at all uncommon – may be nothing more than the mother-to-be's need for iron.

Anyhow, Lord Galway swiftly passed all this information on to his friend, who went on his way with a terrific lightening of his load. A few months later his wife gave birth to a beautiful son, her passion for coal having passed just as quickly as it came about, and as the years went by her husband was relieved to note that it was a habit not inherited by their child.

I think this tale must have been lingering somewhere at the back of my mind as I walked around the grounds some months ago. It was a beautiful morning in June or July and the sun was pouring down. Mr Bird directed a gang of men in the construction of the new bridge across the lake and with the weather being so warm and humid some of the lads had stripped to the waist. I had already raised my hat to Mr Bird and was intent on quietly passing by when one of his men turned away to mop his brow and I noticed that he had on his back a huge tattoo of Ireland.

It was livid-red in colour and reached from his shoulders right down to his waist. Of course, the amateur-cartographer in me became most excited and I hurried over to get a better look. As I drew near I saw that the map-tattoo had been somehow effected in relief form, which really rather baffled me, and it was only when I was a couple of yards from the fellow that I realized that what I had taken to be the work of a tattooist was, in fact, a huge expanse of scab.

He must have seen me recoil a little for, without my having uttered a word, he announced, in a matter-of-fact way, 'Psoriasis, sir.'

'Psoriasis,' I echoed dumbly.

Fortunately, he was a bright chap and, seeing that I was in the dark, added, 'It is a skin complaint, Your Grace.'

'Aha,' I said and moved back in on him.

Well, I have to say, he was most accommodating and let me scrutinize the magnificent scab without seeming to mind a bit. It was all very much of a solid piece, with a surface like burnt jam. The shape of the scab, to my mind still very much like Ireland, was a little flaky round the coastline and had, here and there, come away from the skin. It occurred to me, I remember, that I should very much like to slide my fingernails under it and rip the whole thing up. Luckily, it was an urge I managed to keep reined in, for he was a broad fellow, used to heaving a pick and would, I'm sure, have been greatly upset by any interference with his scab.

I asked him if the scab always took the shape of Ireland or if it ever resembled other countries of the world and he replied that while the scab was constantly on the move – sometimes shrinking, sometimes spreading – the similarity between it and a map of any country had, frankly, never crossed his mind.

Still, I found our encounter most fascinating. I gave the good fellow sixpence and thanked him for his time and was in the process of taking my leave when another question popped into my head.

'I was wondering . . .' I said, 'how you treat it.'

And, again without the least inhibition, he told me how a physician had recently recommended exposing the scab to the sun's rays whenever possible, which is why he had his shirt off today.

I was still absorbing this information, when he added, 'And coal tar, sir.'

Now, as I have already mentioned, I must have still had drifting at the back of my mind the wife of Lord Galway's acquaintance gorging herself on coal for, before I had properly got my thoughts in order, the words

'You drink *coal tar*, man?' had popped out of me, in a voice so loud and clear that the fellows who had recently returned to their digging immediately stopped again and stared.

The big chap looked me over very coolly, his eyes narrowing to two tiny slits. When he spoke it was as if he was addressing a backward child.

'Not *drinks* it, sir. Wipes it on.'

In the circumstances it seemed like an easy mistake to make, but would have been impossible to explain.

'Of course, of course,' I said. Then I bade him good day and left the scene just as fast as my legs would carry me away.

It is one of those awful moments that I know will haunt me for many years to come. (When I was a child I used the seeds of dried rose-hip as 'itching powder' and, for want of some other child to 'itch', would put them down my own back. I mention this because it seems to me that the two sensations are somehow similar.)

No doubt while I sit here recording the embarrassing event that same labourer holds court in some nearby alehouse, telling anyone who cares to listen all about the mad old Duke who suggested drinking coal tar to cure his psoriatic scabs.

*

November 27th

*

Taking to heart the advice of the Oakley sisters I have ordered that, henceforth, no beef be included in my meals. Mrs Pledger has risen to the occasion and presented me this lunchtime with a delicious croquette of Stilton and asparagus which fairly sent my tongue into raptures. The croquette – about six inches in length and beautifully breadcrumbed –

was accompanied by honeyed carrots and a light, spicy gravy. Tonight, I am told, we are to have devilled lobster. At this rate I think it will be no great effort to forgo the dreaded beef. I only hope the benefits will soon make themselves felt.

The repairwork required by my damaged 'aura', however, may not be so easily carried out. The sisters' description left me with the impression of something like a warm glow around a lamp. That picture, I think, is a good one. A warm glow will do very well. But when I try to imagine this glow as 'incomplete' or broken, I run immediately into problems. If I had been asked to imagine the aura as a cloak, for example, I would be as right as rain. The cloak – let us say, a large tweed redingote – has a small rip in it somewhere. Perhaps I snagged it on a nail. Clearly then, what is needed is for me to lay my hands on a needle and thread and stitch it up where it has been rent. But a *glow* – how does one go about mending a hole in a glow?

I repeatedly put my mind to the problem but end up neither here nor there, wavering constantly between a warm glow in the one hand and a redingote in the other.

*

I am certain the little fist of malevolence last located below my ribcage is on the move again. It is higher up in me than it has been and seems inclined towards my spine. As my lungs are always susceptible to infection I worry it might get at them and give me a nasty cough, so last night I had Clement light a camphor candle to keep the blasted thing at bay and when I woke I felt sure it had smelt the camphor and promptly doubled back. I conclude that it is shrewd and conniving but also cowardly; still heading in a northerly direction, but by some different route.

*

Received another remedy this afternoon – this one from the Reverend Mellor. Convinced that I suffer from 'rheumatics', his note contained a recipe which he insists I should have made up. It came to him from a sister-in-law in Whitby where, apparently, the trawlermen take it right through the winter months. The recipe is as follows . . .

Stone brimstone
turkey rhubarb
powdered guaiacum
powdered nitre
. . . of each a quatre of an oz.,
made into pills of 6 grains each
. . . take two every night at bed time.

Well, I must say the ingredients put me more in mind of gunpowder than any medicine, but I duly sent a boy off to mix the concoction up. When he returned, proudly showing the pills off on a plate, they looked very much like tiny cannonballs – all pocked and dangerous. I had him put them on my bedside table. If I am feeling especially brave tonight I might fire a couple into me.

I might admit to being old and creaky, my body racked with innumerable twitches and unnameable pains, but I feel sure it is not plain rheumatism that I suffer from. The word simply doesn't fit.

As I sat at my bureau this afternoon, keeping warm by a well-stacked fire, I came around to wondering how the news of my ill health had reached the Reverend Mellor. Certainly, I did not mention it in my letter and, as far as I know, he hasn't called round to the house.

It is fascinating to speculate, is it not, on how the word generally gets about. Miss Whittle at the Post Office may, on occasion, dispense a little more than postage stamps but one would never seriously accuse her of being the village gossip.

And yet between Miss Whittle and the Reverend Mellor I'll wager there exists an intricate web, along which the news of my unstable health has merrily worked its way. Perhaps I am mistaken. Could be that the Reverend was in the Post Office and happened to mention me. Then Miss Whittle might have countered by saying how she sent a tin of beef essence up to the house, upon hearing I was unwell. But then I turn up another question. How was it Miss Whittle first came by that information? How did word get to her?

Well now, I have dozens of employees spread all over the estate. On a slow day I suppose it not inconceivable for two of them to exchange news which, at a pinch, might include their master's health. There need be no malice in it; just the common verbal barter of one man with the next. And if the result of that chain is that one or two acquaintances show their concern by sending me remedies, then I'm sure I should be nothing but flattered and pleased. But once or twice I have overheard men talking, where the exchange of information has been driven not by benevolence but the profoundest spite. Nothing in the world moves at half the speed as a rumour with the scent of scandal to it. Have we not all been guilty, at one time or another, of repeating the words a better man would have kept to himself? Yet, to some people news of another's misfortune – whether true or purely speculative – is their bread and butter, and they like nothing more than to squander their days whipping that wheel on its way.

Just now I attempted to draw a map on which the journey of some item of interest might be laid out. Using my illness as an example, I began by writing the name of Miss Whittle on one side and the Reverend Mellor's on the other. I estimated that between these two people it might have taken perhaps two or three others to unwittingly act as the stepping stones for the news. But, just when I was feeling very pleased with my little diagram and thinking how easy it was proving to be, it occurred to me that those two or three nameless individuals between dear Miss Whittle and Mellor would hardly be likely to tell a story just the once. No, if a tale is remotely worth telling then one might tell it a dozen times. So suddenly every line on my simple map is multiplied by twelve and they go shooting off all over the place. And, of course, each of the twelve who are told the story may pass it on to a dozen more. This process continues and in no time one winds up with nothing but a ball of twine.

I quickly saw how I was about to give myself a headache so I thought about something else for a while (a flowering bud, a pot of jam). Then I wondered if perhaps a better way of setting it out might be in the form of a family tree. At the top of the page would be the name of the pair who first exchanged the story (or *conceived* it, as it were) while below, in an ever-expanding fan, would be the many generations which followed on. As in any family, one might expect the features of the later generations of the story to have some, but by no means all, the characteristics of the first. Yes, very good.

Encouraged by this, I tried to dream-up other unusual journey-maps and recalled one I have often thought I would like to commission, which is the route taken by an ordinary postal letter. How many pairs of hands must the envelope pass through between the moment it is first dropped in the post box and the moment it lands on the mat? No doubt along the way the letter must spend many tedious hours waiting in various bags and piles. Perhaps not so interesting, after all. But how wonderful to at last be sorted and carried down the lane in the postman's sack. How wonderful to be plucked open and read!

A Local Woman's Account

It is well known round here how the Duke was deformed very bad as a result of the syphilis. His old body was riddled with it, right from top to toe. This is what led him to have all those miles of tunnels made, so he could hide his terrible face from view and pop up out of the ground at will.

My husband knows a man who saw the old Duke face to face, just as close as I stand here next to you. He says his left eye was a good two inches higher than the right one and that he dribbled from the corner of his mouth the whole time. A terrible sight to behold, he was. The children would run a mile from him or be struck dumb on the spot. And there's plenty others round here that'll back me up on that score. You knock on any door. Shocking, that's the old Duke for you. A shocking sight all round.

From His Grace's Journal

November 28th

*

Annoyed with myself all day today. Could not get anything done.

By all accounts my aura is in tatters and I have not the first idea how to put it right. I feel as if I have sprung a leak somewhere. Look for signs of me listing to port.

The pain which has been travelling up my body has emerged between my shoulder blades, which now clench together like pincers to try to squeeze the life out of it (an action over which I have not the slightest control). Last night I took a couple of the Reverend Mellor's rheumatism pills. They looked and smelt like rabbit pellets and I imagine they did me about as much good.

What with the concern for the state of my aura and the twisting dagger in my back, I have felt highly agitated right through the day and just about ready to snap. Hardly the best condition for introspection, but that was just what Fate had in store. There are few enough days when one's resilience is up to taking a cold hard look at oneself, to ask 'What have I made of my life?', but it seems the days we undertake such assessments are often the days we are least likely to be satisfied.

I have never composed a work of art. I have invented nothing, discovered nothing. The land and wealth which were left to me, though hardly squandered, were not employed as fruitfully as they might. And while I may have built the odd row of almshouses and a cottage hospital out near Belph, there will be no statues unveiled in homage to my benefaction, no great weeping when I go. I did not even manage to marry the woman I loved – a feat most men manage to carry off. No, all I've done with my life is take countless melancholy constitutionals and grow apples by the ton. Even the credit for the apple-growing belongs elsewhere. As things stand I will be remembered as the Duke who built the tunnels and kept himself to himself. Otherwise I am eminently forgettable – but half a man.

If Fanny had married me instead of Nicolson she would not have been poisoned by a bad piece of fish. She would still be alive today. I would have fed her on the finest titbits, would have tested every spoonful myself. She would have come up to live with me in the country and brought this sad old house to life. Her bright dresses and her songs and laughter would have chased misery from every last corner. I can see her now in her great sweeping dresses going from one darkened room to another, pulling back the shutters and letting the sunlight in. She throws the dustcovers off the divans and armchairs, orders windows to be opened wide. The fresh air rushes in and every room in the house is brightened by her good cheer.

By now we would have grown-up children. Grandchildren most likely, too. I would teach them how to whistle and let them climb all over me as if I were a tree. If I had been loved by her I would be a stronger man and my flame would not now be going out. But there are no children, there are no grandchildren. There are covers on the divans. I live in three or four rooms in total and leave the others empty and unused and when a maid comes in to open a window I scuttle away like a crab.

No doubt I should count myself lucky to have such a fine staff waiting on me. Indeed I should. When the sun shines I can have a horse saddled up in a minute and spend the whole day trotting round my estate. If I wished, I could waste my worthless time in one of a thousand different ways. But every happy moment has the brake put on it, for I know it will be recalled alone.

There are men who in years to come will explore the world's furthest corners, who will think up great philosophies. But when it comes to real creation men are of little use. We are not gifted in that way, have not the machinery. All we can do is stand by and wonder – and perhaps offer to lend a hand. For, in reality, there is but one set of true makers and the men are not among them. At best, men are the midwives of this world.

*

All day I have been in this stupor, like a dog which has forgotten where it buried its bone. So agitated and uneasy with myself that I simply had to get up and move around.

When I am restless, I find I have a proclivity for going in search of the past. A territory which is, I suppose, more familiar – more solid and safe. Which is probably how I came to find myself on the tiny flight of steps leading up to the attic. The door was firmly locked up and I had to blow down for some help. It was only when Clement finally came puffing up the stairs with his big bunch of keys that I was able to make my way in.

As a boy I imagined that heaven would be something like an attic – for no other reason, I suspect, than it was right at the top of the house and full of discarded things. I assumed that when a man died and became redundant he would be taken up to the attic of the world.

But if memory served me right my previous trips had been

to a warm, even humid place, whereas today it was frightfully cold. My breath was visible before me and a lamp was required to illuminate the rooms. Clement was anxious to stay with me in case I set the place afire but my spirits were so low that even his benign company was too much for me to bear and I shooed him down the stairs.

Spent over an hour rifling through the chests and trunks – mostly rubbish, of course. The debris of five generations washed up on the bare floor, each forming its own musty little isle. Folded clothes – ancient and reeking of mothballs. Once-fashionable furniture. Trinkets, hatstands, framed paintings and broken bits and pieces whose purpose I could not ascertain. Then box upon box of decaying papers – many of them rotted right through, my fingers gradually growing so utterly numb that I was unable to continue picking through them and gladly returned to the civilized world.

If I had been unknowingly searching for some lost treasure I am sure I did not turn it up. The only trophy I came away with was a wind-up monkey which now perches on my bureau (originally purchased, I believe, from Hamley's toy-shop in Regent Street, back in God-knows-when). Not so much a toy as a conversation-piece but I'm sure a child would like it just the same. There is a key in its back to wind it up. The monkey nods its head and lifts its little top hat. Most dignified. But it is tatty now from sitting in the attic and its wheels and cogs are all clogged with dust. In the middle of lifting its hat for me just now it paused, as if distracted. That is all I have to show for the day . . . a wind-up monkey whose thoughts, like mine, are elsewhere.

*

*

Woke with a shout of 'Information!' which quite shook poor Clement up. He was standing right by my bed at the time and very nearly dropped his tray.

The stiffness in my neck was incredible. I had never known the like. It was as if six-inch nails had been driven between my skull and my collarbone. Clement had to carry me to the bathroom and lower me into one of his specially-prepareds. The night had been bitter-cold, which might have contributed to my freezing up, but I now had not the slightest doubt that some evil little fist was at work in me. It had dug its fingernails right in.

The heat of the bathwater gradually found its way through to me and began to thaw me out. I tried to nod my head up and down a little, then slowly side to side until, in time, it was just about moving independently of my shoulders. Even so, the merest twist beyond these axes brought about a blinding pain, which was accompanied by a most disconcerting noise and put me in mind of the rubbing-together of many small stones. 'My body is at war with itself!' I announced from my bathtub. 'Civil war is what it is!'

I have tried to be calm, tried to be steadfast, have even tried to befriend that craven pain. I have run the whole mad gamut of emotion while it took a merry jaunt around my shaky frame. But this morning I was just plain angry. I had had enough and resolved to take it on. As I lay hunched and twisted in my steaming tub I swore I would locate it and put a stick right through it. I would crack its miserable skull.

Took breakfast in my bedroom. Tomatoes and mushrooms sprinkled with ground peppercorn. The accompanying rasher of bacon looked not the least bit appetizing as it lounged in its shallow lake of grease, but I am nothing if not resourceful, so I unbuttoned my shirt and placed it flat against my neck. The fat was still warm and I found that rubbing it against the affected area afforded me some small relief.

When I had done with breakfast I searched for some paper – where is the paper in this house! – and having at last tracked down a notepad wrote myself out a plan, while my spare hand held the cooling bacon in place.

I made a heading . . .

<u>Information</u>

which I expanded to . . .

<u>Information Required</u>

and composed a short list beneath it . . .

Drawings;
Photographs;
Maps;
Writing of any sort – regarding bodies, necks in particular.

Blew down to Mrs Pledger, Clement and Mr Grimshaw, announcing, 'Information required.'

'What information, Your Grace?' said Mrs Pledger.

'Body information,' I told her. 'Information on neck-bones.'

By lunchtime no information had surfaced and I found myself dozing off before the fire.

When I woke the fist had its grip on me again. My upper body was completely seized, so that I could not turn my head without the rest of me coming along. I felt like an automaton.

'Damn you!' I yelled at my body.

Called down to Mrs Pledger, asking for more bacon – as hot and greasy as it would come.

When Clement arrived with the bacon I grabbed the plate and slid the rashers straight under my shirt. Buttoned it back up to keep the fellows in place. Told Clement to round up reinforcements as I intended to carry out a daylight attack on the library, and in no time I was joined by a clutch of housemaids and a couple of lads from the plumbery. Once briefed, we all set off down the corridor: Clement silent and cautious, the boys and girls falling in behind while I marched at the front, proud and barefoot, my bacon-epaulettes now showing through my shirt.

We made the library in no time. The door was open. If it had been locked I would have broken it down. 'Books on bodies is what we want,' I announced to my company, and ran through the list again.

We spread out, taking a dozen or so shelves apiece. Only one ladder between us so I ordered the rest to pair up and help one another to climb the shelves. The room was much bigger than I remembered. A chap could get lost in there. Many of the books brought down a thick layer of dust with them and we were soon enveloped in great clouds of the stuff. We had to cover our mouths and noses with handkerchiefs to stop us choking. Could barely see my hand before my face.

By the time we pulled back we each had our own small booty – medical books, atlases, sketches, daguerreotype collections and so on, which included . . .

Anatomy, Descriptive and Surgical by Henry Gray;
Chambers Journal of Sciences (1860–65);
The Anatomy of Melancholy by Robert Burton;
and several collections of sketches by Leonardo da Vinci.

Had the whole lot dropped off in my bedroom beneath Mr Sanderson's map. Thanked my comrades and shooed them away. Searched out my medical dictionary and added it to the heap. Sat my wind-up monkey on top. Remembered Mr Peak's short quotation. Located it in a jacket pocket and pinned it to the wall.

In a book called *Ancient Chinese Healing* I found a peculiar diagram. A man whose body was fairly coursing with a complex system of interconnecting streams. They ran up and down his arms and legs and filled his torso, as if he had consumed a great deal of string. I ripped the map right out of the book and pinned that to the wall as well.

I have created in a corner of my bedroom a kind of shrine. I am quite sure that somewhere within it is the key to my current distress.

*

I became tired. Sat by the fire, dozing and stirring, right through the afternoon.

At some point I wrote on my notepad . . .

> Add to previous entry on gossip, postal letter, etc. . . .
>
> Coins – circulation of. A penny, for instance. Might well be in circulation for many years. How many miles does an average coin travel in its lifetime? How would map of same look? All the purses it resides in. Number of palms.
>
> Consider – is it likely a man would be in possession of same coin twice? How would he know? Would have to make a recognizable mark on it.
>
> Consider – when I have a penny in my purse, do I not think of it always as the same penny?
>
> Also – consider heat in coin. Miss Whittle's habit of holding change in her hand while she is talking, so that when she eventually hands them over, the coins are very warm. How might this connect with previous ideas on heat, etc.?

*

When I woke again it was dark. Clement brought me some soup, but I could do nothing with it. Woke again to find him stoking up the fire.

The next time I came around the house was perfectly still and the fire was almost out.

Clement helped me change into my nightshirt and put me to bed. I slept but there was no rest in it. It was an exhausting sleep. Had a dream . . .

> I am at the reins of a two-horse brougham, endlessly circling a leafy wood – desperate to find a way into its secret world of bramble and brush. All night I wrestle with the reins and steer that carriage around. I shout 'Ho!' and 'Come up there!' at the horses until my throat is raw. I circle and recircle for hour upon hour, longing to land and lie down and close my eyes. But the wood keeps me locked out, forcing me to go around again, until at last I am delirious from the torments of sleeplessness.

It was early morning when I next opened my eyes. I knew straight away there was something wrong. There was no newness to the day. That was the problem.

I stumbled over to the mirror above the mantelpiece. My hair stuck out in the usual places but my eyes were wild. My head looked as if someone had removed it and glued it back on. An absolutely shoddy job. My neck had twisted right round and got lodged there. I had to turn my body sideways to get a proper look at me. My mouth was all agape with pain.

I remember Clement coming in. And me collapsing. This happened very slowly. Seemed to take an age.

I have the vaguest memory of Clement carrying me down the back stairs to the tunnels. I remember the sound of his huge feet on the old stone steps.

When I next came to my head was in the crook of his

elbow. He cradled me as we went along. Out of the carriage window I saw a blur of red brick as we sped down the tunnels.

'I am in pain,' I told him.

He looked down at me and gave me a grave nod.

'Where are we going, Clement?' I asked him.

'We have found you a neck-man, Your Grace,' he replied.

*

December 2nd

*

When I next opened my eyes we were pulling up outside an unfamiliar row of cottages, with me propped up in the carriage like a broken doll and still swimming in a dream. I saw Clement stroll up one of the garden paths and knock at a low gabled door. Saw him turn and walk back towards me. I recall the carriage door opening, him leaning over me and the cold morning air coming in. Then I was heft up into his arms again and gently carried towards the tiny house.

I leaned my head against Clement's shoulder and gazed up at his large round face as he marched me up the narrow path and ducked his head under the lintel. Then I found myself in a plain white room, warmed by a modest coal fire. My shirt was unbuttoned for me and pulled over my spinning head and I recall being eased back onto a trestle table, which was covered with a single sheet. Being naked amongst so much whiteness made me feel like a corpse on a mortuary slab.

'Good morning, Your Grace,' said a kind voice above me. 'My name is Conner.'

'Good morning, Conner,' I croaked back at him. 'And what is it you do?'

'I'm a bone-setter,' he said.

'A neck-man?'

'In a manner of speaking, yes. So tell me, Your Grace, how are your bones this morning?'

'O, they are old bones, Conner, and in very poor shape. My back is all locked-up.'

'Well, then,' said Conner, 'I shall do my best to unlock you.'

'O, I wish you would,' I said.

I was in such discomfort I had hardly opened my eyes, but as he turned me onto my stomach I caught a glimpse of the chap. He was youngish, stout and florid, with dark brown curly hair and a neat moustache. He wore a clean white apron over his daily clothes and had his shirt sleeves rolled up past his elbows, revealing an impressive pair of forearms.

As I lay my cheek on a lavender-scented pillow, I felt a large warm hand rest on my shoulder. 'A little oil,' he whispered, '. . . for lubrication.'

And in the gully between my shoulder blades I felt a sudden liquid heat. My mind, at first, was thrown into terrible confusion, not sure if the sensation was pleasurable or adding to my distress. Meanwhile, tiny harbingers of ecstasy shot out in every direction beneath my back's cold flesh, as the warm oil crept confidently along the shallow valley of my spine.

'You have had breakfast, Your Grace?' he asked me, easing the oil into my shoulders with neat circular movements of fingers and thumbs.

'I have not, Conner – no,' I wheezed from under his mighty hands. 'Clement brought me straight from my bed.'

'I thought I smelt bacon,' said Conner.

'That would be yesterday's bacon,' I replied.

'Ah,' he said, his thumb-circles now expanding. 'Strange how a smell can linger.'

And he kept up this gentle banter as his hands encouraged the oil into my flesh. Most of our conversation was of little significance and evaporated as soon as it was out, but I found an underlying kindness to it which gradually put me at my ease so that in a few minutes I was able to admit, 'I think I have been a little agitated this last day or two.'

To which Conner replied, 'That is understandable, Your Grace. A body does not like to be tied up in knots.'

And now his fingertips pressed deeper into me, tracing precise symmetrical eddies down either side of my spine. 'And how does a body come to have so many knots in it?' I enquired.

'O, a hundred different ways, Your Grace. I should say accumulation of tenseness is most common. Or a sudden twist of the head, perhaps. Sleeping badly is another ... too many pillows, too few ...'

And blow me down if, as he spoke, he wasn't working his magic on me. His fingers seemed to draw the pain right out of me, like a spell. And looking back I see how, unlike the ignorant Dr Cox, Conner actually encouraged me to voice my anxieties, dealing with each one of them there and then – smoothing them away with his fingertips and the soothing flow of his voice.

'Tell me, Conner,' I said, 'do you not worry that some of the bad feeling you draw from a patient might come to rest in you?'

He bent down and whispered in my ear, 'What I do, Your Grace, is think of myself as a chimney ... that way, any ill feeling just passes right through.'

'A chimney,' I said. 'Yes. Very good.'

Then he turned me onto my back and moved round to the head of the table, taking care to keep a hand on me all the while. I must say, having my chest exposed to the room made me feel decidedly vulnerable, but I was quickly reassured by Conner's trusty fingers as they gently slid under my neck. He raised my head an inch or two off the table and held it there in the cradle of his hands and for the first time I felt able to open my eyes and briefly survey the scene. Like an infant I looked all about me. In a far corner of the ceiling I spotted a cobweb, slowly waving above an otherwise spotless room. And now Conner had my head in the palm of one hand while the other slowly worked its way down my neck, his fingers checking the condition of each vertebra before moving on to the next. I noticed that the walls of the surgery were completely bare. Not a picture or a chart in sight.

'Give me the full weight of your head, Your Grace,' he told me. 'I will not let you drop.'

Then, by almost imperceptible degrees, he began to rotate my head – a most peculiar sensation, which initially induced in me near-vertigo, so that it was all I could do to resist an urge to lock my muscles up and bring the whole process to a halt. I felt like someone's puppet, not to say a little foolish. The room shifted around me mechanically. But after a minute or two of having my head eased this way and that, I felt myself becoming, first, unspeakably comfortable, then mercifully heavy-lidded. I recall drowsily dwelling on the complexity of the joints which could accommodate such a complicated manoeuvre and wondered at the many muscles being called into play as my skull swung slowly through space.

Conner's voice came to me from a great distance, saying, 'I think I might make a small manipulation, Your Grace.'

From the cradle of his huge hands I dreamily concurred.

I was asked to take a deep breath and to slowly let it out. So I filled my old lungs right to the top and began exhaling into that small white room and began to feel for the first time in many weeks that I had located a quiet corner in which to meditate. The world was slowing-up most pleasingly.

Then Conner suddenly yanked my head eastward with such incredible power and violence that an almighty *crack* went bouncing between the room's bare walls.

I was absolutely horrified, not least because I feared my head had just been pulled clean off my neck. I feared also that some small but important bones had just been rendered useless. I pictured me lying in my own cottage hospital, in a bed with all manner of devices strapped around my head. My anxiety must have been evident, for Conner said wistfully, 'It is a dramatic sound, sir, is it not.'

I agreed that it was and asked, rather sheepishly, 'Are there more?'

'There are,' he replied.

After checking the whereabouts of another vertebra or two (which were, by now, most definitely on the move) he calmly asked me to fill my lungs up and to let the air out, as before. Well, I did as I was told and was exhaling (more self-consciously this time round) when my head was suddenly jerked over to the west, emitting another great bony crack.

'Now take a minute or two to recover yourself, Your Grace,' said Conner. 'And when you are ready, I would like you on your front.'

Well, to be quite honest, I was worried that when I rolled over my head might stay behind on the pillow. The sound produced by Conner's manipulations was like a full tray of crockery being dropped on a stone floor and continued to ring in my ears. So when I finally dared to lift myself off the table I was much relieved to find my head was still attached to the rest of me – if not quite as surely as before.

Now my cheek was back on the lavender-scented pillow, with Conner's fingers inching methodically up and down my spine, searching for clues. When they came across something suspicious they halted and, while one hand crept out along a rib to the left, the other went off to the right. On the odd occasion when the fingers came upon some nexus of painful muscle they would rub, quite firmly, for half a minute then gently check over the surrounding terrain and, when they were satisfied that all was in order, would return to the trail. My back felt as if it was a human puzzle which Conner was intent on solving, joint by aching joint. 'I'm all over the place,' I confided.

'O, you're going back together just fine,' he replied.

'How on earth does a man's back become so higgledy-piggledy?' I asked.

'When one bone goes astray,' Conner informed me, 'others will tend to follow. The body tries to restore some balance but sometimes can do more damage than good.'

'So one might end up a little like ... a Chinese puzzle,' I suggested.

'Exactly, Your Grace,' he replied.

Then he rolled me onto my side so that I faced away from him, tucked one of my arms right under me and brought my left leg up to my chest, all accomplished with such facility I was inclined to congratulate the man. He simply tapped me gently behind a kneecap and the leg folded obediently into place. Seemed intimately acquainted with every spring and joint inside me; to have as much command over my body as I had myself. Not since I was a young lad playing with my father had I been so ably thrown around.

He pulled my raised hip gently towards him with one hand, while his other eased my shoulder toward the table top. He held me there a second, leaned closer and asked, 'Are you ready, Your Grace?'

I must have whispered some sort of tentative assent; in truth, I had not the first idea what terrible contract had just been agreed.

My shoulder went down into the table. My pelvis went the other way. Between these two opposing forces my spine had no choice but to surrender. Every vertebra in my back made a popping sound – one after the other – like the rasp of a fresh pack of playing cards. Who would have thought one's body could be made an instrument to produce such exotic sounds? I was grateful I had on my baggy trousers for a tighter pair might not have come through the experience intact. This occurred to me as I was rolled over onto my other side and my head buried deep in Conner's apron (which had about it a faint whiff of carbolic), whereupon the whole noisy business was repeated, my spine now arching in the opposite direction but producing the same startling sound.

Then I was left to lie on my back to recover, and consider how, when I eventually came to take my leave of Conner, I should anticipate doing so a much taller man. I took a deep breath to reassure myself that it would not always be followed by the crunching of my spine. My bone-setter, meanwhile, had gone over to a bowl of water and was now busy soaping his hands. 'Tell me, Conner,' I called over to him, 'do you believe in auras?'

A moment's silence. Then, 'Well, I would have to know what such a thing was before I could say if I believed in it.'

'It is a light or a heat which emanates from a man.'

'Well, I wouldn't know about light, Your Grace, but there is certainly heat. That I know for sure.'

I chewed this over. 'Do you believe in spirits, Conner?' I went on.

'Why do you ask?' he replied.

And so I explained about my general state of mind and the moon in the woods and the boy who has been following me around. 'Do you see the boy?' was his only question.

'I suppose I must do, yes.'

'Then surely you believe in him, Your Grace?'

'Well, that may be true ... but I cannot tell if he belongs in the real world or in my imagination.'

'With respect, Your Grace, how much does it matter which world he inhabits, if he is real enough to be seen?'

'I take your point,' I said.

Conner swung my legs off the table and helped me get to my feet. Told me to let both my hands hang loose by my sides. He stood behind me and, when I had found my balance, moved his fingers slowly up and down my spine.

'That's a little less higgledy-piggledy, Your Grace. In fact, not a bad arrangement at all.'

Then he came round and stood before me, placed a hand on either shoulder and generally took me in.

'Shoulders roughly the same altitude,' he said.

And for the first time I looked him full in the face. He was as kind and handsome as I had imagined, but while his voice was full of purpose I thought I detected about him some remoteness ... an almost unanchored air. As he spoke his eyes seemed to wander, as if they could not concentrate and preferred to cast about for cobwebs up above. Perhaps he is just a trifle shy, I thought to myself, and has difficulty looking another man in the eye – that is sometimes the case. It was another moment or two before I realized that Conner was, in fact, blind.

'How is that now?' he asked me.

'That is much better, Conner. Thank you,' I replied.

He nodded and smiled so that his moustache extended another inch or so at either end. 'In case you wondered,' he told me, 'I have been blind since the day I was born.'

I was flabbergasted. 'How in the world did you know what was on my mind?' I asked.

'Well, to be fair, I should think this must be your first chance to have a good look at me. But, just now, you paused a moment before answering my question. And when you did answer there was a hint of hesitancy there.'

'You're quite right, Conner,' I told him, ashamed of myself. 'Please accept my apologies.'

'Not at all, Your Grace.' He shook his head. 'No need. No, not at all.'

I studied him for a second, as if the man had just appeared before me in a puff of smoke – how peculiar and intriguing he was – before realizing I was staring at him as if he was some sort of circus freak. I had allowed a silence to grow between us, so I spoke up and brought it down.

'Forgive me saying this, Conner, but you must notice all manner of sounds and noises which pass most people by.'

'I may well do, Your Grace,' he replied. Then added, 'But they're there for everyone to hear.'

'Quite so,' I said. 'Quite so.'

And I looked around that tiny room as if it too had just been brought into being. The door and the shelves and the spartan walls all came to me anew. I considered the contents, hidden in darkness and found by measured steps. The jars of oil, the water jug, the coal tongs – all had transformed themselves into a blind man's things. Had become suddenly weightier. More palpable somehow.

Conner helped me get my shirt back over my head and I watched as he reached my jacket off a hook. He returned and held it open for me, then led me gracefully through the cottage towards the door.

'You must excuse my sudden silence, Conner. I have not come across a man such as yourself before.'

'Well, I should say we all have our little qualities which are not apparent at first. But I assure you, Your Grace, I'm the same man as the one you met an hour ago.'

When he opened the front door Clement was already waiting there, ready to escort me back to the carriage. As I shook Conner's hand it seemed my own palm was newly-charged, and for the briefest moment I sensed something of a whole other world which was lost to me.

'You have set me straight, Conner,' I said, 'and I very much appreciate it.'

He smiled, then leaned towards me and whispered, 'If this spirit of yours keeps pestering you you might do well to have words with him.'

'I will, Conner,' I said. 'Goodbye. And thanks again.'

'Goodbye, Your Grace,' said Conner. Then, 'Goodbye Clement,' though Clement had not said a word.

*

December 4th

*

Since Conner's recent treatment I have had not the least inclination to eat, my body perhaps regarding a reconstituted backbone as quite enough on its plate without being troubled with digestion's stresses and strains. Around lunchtime yesterday I managed a sliver of toast spread with a mushroom pâté, but that has been about the only solid food to pass my lips.

Mrs Pledger, however, is adamant I should at least maintain my consumption of liquids and boiled up for me a big pot of camomile and lemon-balm tea. This, I was assured, would calm me down after the recent hectic days and encourage in me a more tranquil frame of mind. I must admit that, while the aroma (and indeed flavour) are reminiscent of some damp corner of the garden, I found I had soon developed quite a taste for it. A fondness which rapidly developed into a fierce, almost unquenchable thirst. It seemed the more I drank of the strange yellow brew the more desiccated I became. Perhaps I have recently misplaced some vital inner juice. Perhaps my body recognized in the tea some mineral which I currently lack. What ever, my original request for Mrs Pledger to boil up a second pot was swiftly followed by ever more frequent and desperate appeals. I felt thoroughly parched, like some poor wretch lost on a desert's sands and, like a human sponge, I soaked up every last sip.

By early evening, however, the prodigious tea-drinking

had caught up with me and the constant trips to the water closet were becoming tedious. I was awash with camomile and lemon-balm. If I shifted too quickly in my armchair I could feel pints of the stuff splashing around inside, so that when Mrs Pledger put her head round the door around seven she found me beached in my armchair, utterly (if naturally) intoxicated and having difficulty staying awake. At which point Clement was called to help put me to bed.

To cap it all I slept remarkably well – without interruption or a single bad dream. The most satisfying sleep I have had in many a month. When I woke, a good fourteen hours after my head first hit the pillow, I felt myself thoroughly rested and quite a new man, although when I opened my mouth to let out a yawn found my breath still had about it the faint reek of scented grass.

*

December 5th

*

I do not think I have left my rooms all day and I can't say I feel any the worse for it. When Clement had finished drying me after one of his soapier baths, I simply changed into a clean nightshirt and took my breakfast by the fire. Managed some coddled eggs and a cup or two of Assam but resolved to spend the whole day very quiet and give my bones a chance to settle themselves. Had Clement dig out my old satin skullcap and a pair of thick knee-socks, so that with my dressing gown pulled tight around me I was almost completely insulated against the outside world.

My session with blind Conner has given me a new perspective on my body and to consolidate some of the issues raised by it I took my *Gray's Anatomy* down from the shrine and opened the old chap up.

Much of the day spent in my armchair with that weighty tome in my lap, idly picking over the pages and pausing only to heap more coal on the fire. Though I must have spent several hours in the book's learned company I cannot claim to have 'read' it as such. It is much too crammed with technical terms for me to pick up any speed. Rather, I would pore over each pen and ink drawing which took my fancy, then move on to the next.

Many of the illustrations depict some specific visceral valve or bone-corner and, in truth, these are of little interest to me. I prefer the pictures with slightly broader scope, where one can more readily identify the whole locale as part of the human form (such as a sectioned arm or leg). Each time I turned the page to cast my eye over some new junction of muscle and bone I always sought out the hand or toe or eyeball which might help me get my bearings, but if, after half a minute, I could still not tell north from south, I would simply turn to the next page and begin the whole process again.

The 'subject' of the drawings appears to be the same poor fellow throughout and it was not long before I found myself pitying him for having undergone such torture on my behalf – for assenting to be so thoroughly taken apart. His face, where it is visible, wears an attitude of weary resignation, which is commendable to say the least, considering that half his face has been crudely ripped away to show the network of nerves and veins beneath.

On one page the brave chap stands with outstretched arms, his bare back turned toward the reader and not a single scrap of flesh left on him. One looks upon a truly naked man. The only stuff covering his poor bones and organs are the ribbons of muscle, wrapped around him in fibrous swaths . . . pulled tautly over the shoulders, under armpits and seeming to glisten on the page.

Amidst this sea of twisting muscle I noticed the bone causeway of the spine – an unhooked necklace of numbered pearls, beautifully bisecting his back. And as I peered at them I found myself moved a little, recognizing them as the same tiny bones which had so recently been checked and shifted by the knowing fingers of kind, blind Conner.

I studied every string of this body's bow and still he refused to flinch. In fact, so convincingly was his skinlessness mapped out for me that I had to suppress an urge to go in search of a blanket to cover up his sticky form.

On one page hand-bones were laid out like rows of flint, every knuckle and joint labelled and given its proper Latin name. How many small bones there are in one hand – as complicated an organization as the bones of a bird! – and so convincingly represented that when I next turned the page I found myself half-listening for their rattle.

The rack of ribs seemed not so much an aspect of the human form and more some butcher's shop window display. Or some bleached-out sheep-relic one stumbles across while walking upon a fell.

Then, at last, the skull! – that constant grinner – a likeness all faces gradually acquire. Each time I confront the mirror I see a little more of him peering through.

Once my cheeks were full of pie but they have slowly become hollowed-out and every year now my forehead has about it a greater determination.

Strange to think that we each carry inside us a functioning skeleton; that buried deep within the meat of me my own bone-tree patiently waits.

*

Not surprisingly, this morbid reading did nothing for my appetite so that when word came up that it was boiled gammon for lunch I called down and asked to skip straight to the pudding.

By the end of the afternoon I was still happily reading and jotting down the odd note, when I felt a dismal and lethargic cloud begin to slowly settle all around. This is not in itself unusual, for when the light first fails on a winter's day I often experience a corresponding dwindling of spirit, which can tend towards melancholy. On this occasion, however, I decided to try and counteract it with a quick bout of standing-on-my-head. As a boy, this was a favourite pastime and could be more or less relied upon to induce an agreeable light-headedness. Fortunately, I took the precaution of locking the bedroom door, for no sooner were my legs up against the wall than my nightshirt fell down around my ears.

With a thick cushion on the floor to protect my head I managed to maintain the position for several minutes, feeling refreshed and then reflective and finally a little faint. When I was upright again I could feel blood cascading through me like so many mountain streams. I was altogether much invigorated and promised myself from now on to spend at least five minutes a day upside-down.

*

Some time ago I found a small briar pipe at the back of a desk drawer which had once belonged to my father. It is carved in the shape of a Dutch clog and fits snugly in the fist of my hand. When I came upon it I saw how it had in the bottom of its bowl a scrap of ancient tobacco and it seemed not unreasonable to suppose that this tiny strand helped make up my father's last smoke.

Sometimes I think I am nothing but a foolish old man, for tonight when it was dark and the fire roared in the grate I took a twist of some new tobacco mixture (which claims to be beneficial for the heart and lungs) and filled up that briar pipe. I took care to keep in place the ancient string of tobacco and, after tamping and tucking the bowl of the pipe in the way I fancied a smoker might, I lit her up.

With an old coat around my shoulders I went out on to the balcony and in the cold night air allowed myself to imagine I inhaled the same smoke my father drew into his lungs all those years ago. I pictured it slowly wafting through my innermost caverns and felt myself much calmed. I stared up at the stars, scattered between the horizons, and added the modest glow of my pipe to their sombre display.

While I stood there in my own small cloud of smoke, thinking all manner of dreamy thoughts, I became aware how, not more than a couple of yards over my shoulder, there floated the mysterious boy. If I had reached out I could have touched him. But he would not have liked that and most likely would have disappeared. So I continued to puff quietly on my father's Dutch clog pipe and gaze up at the stars, while the floating boy kept me company in the vast, near-silent night.

*

December 7th

*

Lassitude continues. Perhaps I have drunk too much of the camomile. The whole day amounted to little more than a series of yawns and stretching of arms. Strange to report that at each yawn's peak I hear the sound of church bells ringing. Have never noticed them before.

Mrs Pledger continues her herbal assault on me. No plant on the estate is safe. Now I am quite happy to drink a little sarsaparilla to purify my blood. But one minute she is bringing me crushed mugwort (to stimulate the appetite) and the next it is elderflower and peppercorn (to clear my cloudy head). I only wish I had it in me to tell her that my head might not be so cloudy in the second place if it hadn't been for the mugwort in the first. But such talk would not go down well with her and I shudder to think how she might react. All the same, I would get along much better with all these concoctions if they didn't taste and smell like so much boiled-up bark and root. There must be a limit to how much folk-medicine a man's constitution can take. At times it is like taking a swig from a stagnant pool.

All day it has been Mrs Pledger's objective to get my appetite up so at midday, in order to show willing, I announced how I quite fancied an apple (something we are never short of in this house) and made a show of smacking my lips. Ten minutes later I was presented with a platter stacked with half a dozen varieties, from which I picked my favourite, a beautiful Russet – coarse, tanned skin; tender, creamy flesh with a rich and smoky flavour.

I rolled its lovely roughness in my palm before cutting it cleanly in half, the knife ringing out as it struck the plate. The two halves separated perfectly, flat and white, and as I took one up and bit into it watched a single pip, which had leapt from the apple's split core, gently spinning on the plate.

Such colossal potential in the humble pip! How pleasing that locked away in the very heart of the fruit there nestles a tight cluster of its eager seed. And that in each dark little teardrop is the makings of a tree.

But we do not like to eat them. They are bitter! We spit the fellows out. Yet, when spilt or planted (or even spat) onto fertile soil, that little pip will set about its ambitions of one day becoming a sapling, one day a tree. In its tough little shell are all the elements required to throw up a tree – bizarre . . . a tree from a pip! – which one day, many years hence, may produce pippy apples of its own.

*

Around two o'clock I decided that if I did not make some effort to move about I might expire right there in my chair. So I called down for my long sable coat and beaver and laced up a pair of brown ankle boots. I already had on my moleskin trousers and knitted waistcoat and when I added my coat and hat and stood before the mirror I thought myself very smart indeed. As he picked the odd speck of dust from my shoulders Clement expressed concern at the prospect of my walking out alone, but once he understood I merely intended to take a stroll around the house he was greatly put at ease.

I checked my supplies before departing – compass, handkerchief and a pencil and paper in case I needed to make some notes – and had removed my sable while I limbered up when, out of the corner of my eye, I spotted Clement slipping a large oatmeal biscuit into my coat pocket. Made no mention of it.

Stood at my bedroom doorway, having difficulty recalling whether there was still a stairway at the end of the West wing or if it had been removed after becoming riddled with worm. By and by, however, I satisfied myself that it was the East wing not the West which had suffered the worm and that the stairs had most definitely been replaced ... a good fifteen years ago, most likely. No, twenty. (Or even twenty-five.)

Clement was still most eager to accompany me but I insisted (quite forthrightly I thought) to be allowed to go on my own. We both stood by the door for a minute, rather stuck for something to say. Then I patted him on his shoulder and set off, feeling like a soldier marching off to war. When I looked over my shoulder a few seconds later I found

Clement still standing there, so we waved to one another and I carried on my way.

I was right at the end of the corridor before I realized I was headed eastward instead of west. What an idiot! Thankfully, Clement had surrendered his post at my bedroom door and was busy tending the fire so I was able to retrace my steps and creep past on tiptoe. Cantered quietly down the corridor until I had reached the bend.

I was completely lost within five minutes, but not altogether troubled. It was quite exciting to meander from room to room, taking in some which were quite foreign to me and others which I found I knew quite well. So, here was a study crammed with furniture and a ten-foot marble fireplace that might as well have belonged in a neighbour's house. But here was a room I remembered very fondly, for I had planned to decorate it and name it the Bachelors' Hall, where all the single men in Nottinghamshire could meet and socialize. I had envisaged indoor sport and much singing and manly camaraderie, but the long tables stood bare and dusty, without ever having had a single port or pastry set down on them. It is disturbing sometimes to find one's old dreams half alive and shabby-looking when, in truth, one would prefer them dead and six foot underground.

I strolled down one corridor after another, exploring every new avenue I came upon. One was carpeted with rugs from the Orient, the next had a plain parquet floor. Down one curving hall I ran the gauntlet of my whole glum ancestry, who glared down at me from their portraits. Another was lined with the mounted heads of deer. The walls of one room were covered with oil paintings of horses whose legs were too big for their bodies. And round the next corner I found my mother's old Sewing Room, which I had always thought to be in another part of the house.

When I became hopelessly disorientated I consulted my trusty compass. It was a minute or two before it dawned on me that finding North was not necessarily going to help me out. But by wiping the grime from a pane of glass and squinting out at the cold, damp world I found I could roughly calculate my whereabouts in the house by my relationship to one of the trees.

Eventually found myself down in the kitchens. Two girls were peeling the vegetables and quite taken by surprise. I think they mistook me in my sable coat for a bear which had wandered in from the woods. So I swiftly removed my beaver and introduced myself and their screaming died down in no time at all.

I was pleased to inform them that my walk had stimulated in me a healthy appetite and asked them to pass this news on to Mrs Pledger. As I turned to go I noticed two chickens stretched out on the table, waiting to be plucked. They looked rather pathetic lying there, with their heads dangling off the deck, so I put in a request for a little parsnip soup instead, then scurried away before Mrs Pledger had a chance to show her face.

I was out of the door and halfway down a cream-painted corridor before I realized my predicament. Had to return to the kitchens and ask the girls for directions back to my rooms.

*

Stood on my head for a good ten minutes, which left me seeing stars for about half an hour. After dinner I put on my sable and went out on to the balcony to puff on my father's pipe. The white smoke went down into me and filled me up and soothed me from top to toe. Few men, I think, could manage to fill a pipe and smoke it without becoming more philosophical by several degrees. There is something in the very nature of pipe-smoking which demands it.

As the smoke curled all about me I took in the icy moon through my old telescope. They say it has its own seas, just like ours. So, for a while, I dwelt on those distant waters and wondered what drove their tides. I studied the same stars I have studied a hundred times before and in my own modest way considered my Maker. Think I might have hit upon something, namely . . .

> . . . that perhaps we have a God up in the heavens to give us some perspective on our lives. And that the search we each undertake for a partner in life might work along similar lines, i.e.: that by establishing a point outside of ourselves we seek some much-needed objectivity. In other words, by regarding ourselves through the eyes of another we are momentarily relieved of the burden of inhabiting ourselves.

I am no clearer now, an hour later, if any of this makes sense. It may have just been the tobacco talking. However, of one thing I am certain, which is that as I stood out there on the balcony grappling with such grand and hefty thoughts, I again sensed, very close to me, the presence of the floating boy.

He was silent – just hung there in the near distance, looking down at me. He is a nervous boy, so I took great care not to frighten him off, and managed to find a way of looking up at the moon through the telescope whilst observing him in the periphery of my other eye. In doing so I began to make out something of his form. He is very young. There is a milkiness about him. He is a most blurred and milky young boy.

*

*

I had just finished breakfast this morning and was admiring Sanderson's map when Mrs Pledger knocked at my door and came striding in, full of bustle, with her mouth firmly set.

'What can I do for you, Mrs Pledger?' I asked.

'I have some bad news, Your Grace,' she replied.

In that case, I told her, she had better come right out with it, double-quick. So she filled her chest and raised her head and, in what sounded suspiciously like a well-rehearsed tone, informed me that Mr Snow, my old gardener, had recently passed away.

Well, this knocked the stuffing right out of me. I must have slumped down in a chair. All sorts of emotion began to bubble up inside me and I was still waiting to see how they might manifest themselves, when Mrs Pledger raised her hand to regain my attention, then proceeded to tell me how Mr Snow had passed away quite peacefully in his sleep but that ... and here she faltered ... but that Mrs Snow had died soon after.

Well, by now I had more than enough to cope with, but Mrs P. had her tap turned full on and words continued to pour from her ... how it was 'a most dreadful thing, to be sure', but how Dr Cox reckoned 'the shock of losing her husband had almost certainly contributed to the death of his wife' until, with her left hand twisting her apron pocket, Mrs Pledger finally drew her speech to a close by saying how Mrs Snow was 'nearly as old and infirm as Mr Snow and how it was hardly any surprise at all'.

By now I was altogether swamped and baffled. I may have nodded my head and murmured, 'Quite so,' once or twice but, in truth, this represented little comprehension on my part. Several conflicting thoughts fought for my attention, like sheep all squeezing through a gate. One was grief at the loss of my old gardener and it whispered in my ear, 'Mr Snow, your old gardener ... gone.' A second was more concerned with that dependency between Mr Snow and his wife which I had witnessed on my recent visit, and it whispered, 'Here is confirmation, as plain as your nose – one flame is extinguished and it takes another one with it when it goes.'

Other thoughts gnawed away at me – all of them murky and half-formed – by far the loudest being a nagging voice of doubt, which wondered at the peculiar manner Mrs Pledger had divulged her story and why, at that very moment, she refused to look me in the eye.

'How long between the death of Mr Snow and his wife?' I asked Mrs Pledger.

Her fingers screwed her apron pocket tighter still. 'Three days, Your Grace,' she said.

And now a new voice leapt into the chorus. 'Three days!' it shouted. 'John Snow dead three days!' And yet another voice, more distant, began ranting, 'All that contemplation last week on the circulation of gossip, yet no one thought to put you in the picture ... Three full days since John Snow died!'

And an anxious, bilious ball rose in me. I was not as strong as I had been a minute before, but I staggered to my feet and, though there was barely room for it, drew in a breath and looked my housekeeper full in the face.

'When is their funeral, Mrs Pledger?' I asked and heard the stitching of her apron pocket coming apart in her hand.

'Their funeral was two days ago, Your Grace.'

I buckled beneath an impossible weight. The whole house folded up around me. My ears had in them a high-pitched ringing, so that I barely heard Mrs Pledger as words continued to fly out of her. 'You have not been well, Your Grace,' was in there somewhere. As was, 'Dr Cox said it would only upset you more.'

And now the growing ball of anxiety pushed right up into my throat. My whole body brimmed with emotional pain. I thought, 'My staff and Dr Cox have decided between them that I am weak. They have kept the Snows' death to themselves.'

I saw the cortège carrying their bodies, laden with wreaths and not a single petal from me. 'Have I not the right to grieve?' I thought to myself. 'I am a grown man – why not let me grieve?' The horses leaned forward into their harnesses and the cortège began to pull away.

'He was my friend,' I told Mrs Pledger. 'I should have liked to have said goodbye to my old friend.'

She nodded at me, then mercifully turned and left me to suffer my distress alone. And as the door closed behind her I felt the bubble finally burst and I fell, as if my legs had been kicked from under me. I fell and continued falling and was at long last engulfed in my own tears.

I wept for my old and much-loved gardener and his faithful wife who had followed him to the grave. I wept for my absence at their funeral; their being seen off without my being there. I wept from the shame of my own staff thinking me weak and mad and not to be trusted with the truth. And I wept because of that damned pain which climbed the ladder of my ribcage and might have strangled me had it not been for kind Conner. And somewhere in my tears I believe I wept for Mrs Pledger – for having picked the shortest straw and having to wend her way up to me, to own up to my staff's deceit.

With one hand I rubbed at my streaming eyes while the other clawed at the rug on which I sprawled. I think my fingers would have liked to unpick the whole carpet, thread by thread. I shook and shuddered, as if some pump had broken free inside me; had to snatch my breath in great wet gulps until my shoulders ached. But when my eyes ran dry and my sobs subsided, I got to my feet and stumbled over to the mirror on the mantelpiece. There was the old man looking back at me, his pink little mouth all twisted and limp. His brows were knitted together above a pair of marbly eyes and his whole visage looked thoroughly beaten and bruised.

But I was in no position to be of any use to him, for I was too busy enjoying the show. How perverse that at such moments I am still fascinated by my every twitch and tremble, by my tear's slow journey down my cheek. That even as I moulder in a pit of misery some part of me still coolly observes my every move.

*

I did no headstands this evening. No pipe-smoking, no gazing at the stars. I did not leave my rooms at all. I simply lay on my bed and stared into space.

I had lost a friend and missed his funeral, and suffered the indignity of not being the master in my own house.

I was tempted to get on the mouthpiece and blow down to every last one of them and ask if they'd prefer me to be the black-hearted tyrant instead of the whimsical old fool that I am.

At last, I took down my wind-up monkey and gave him a turn or two and watched him go through the effort of raising his little hat for me.

*

December 11th

*

Although the sun had barely risen, enough of it filtered through the skylights for me to make my way along the tunnel without incident. When I emerged near Holbeck village I still had no idea where my destination lay and it was only my seeing a curl of smoke from the Reverend Mellor's chimney which prompted me to pay him a visit.

After a restless night's sleep I had woken early, with just one thought on my mind – that I must get out of the wretched house or risk being suffocated by it. I dressed quickly in a blue cotton morning suit and took the main stairs down into a deserted hall; called in at the cloakroom where I picked up my beaver, a burgundy frock coat and matching cape. Took the door under the Great Stair Way down to the tunnels and, without any particular forethought, set off down the South-west passage to find myself, within the hour, on the doorstep of Reverend Mellor's vicarage.

The Reverend himself opened the door to me looking somewhat muddled and badly organized; shirt and waistcoat were all asunder, as if his seams had finally given out. His neck and cheeks were covered with shaving soap and he clutched a razor, rather menacingly, in one hand. As he stood there blinking at me a bead of blood slowly seeped into the soap.

'You have cut yourself, Reverend,' I told him.

There was another moment or two's squinting, before his face gave way to a smile.

'Your Grace,' he said. 'I am not used to such early callers.' Then, 'Come in, come in, come in.'

I was led into a parlour-cum-study where he turned and squinted at me again. Mellor is a solid, plump sort of fellow who, by some freak of nature, has only a young lad's legs to support his considerable weight, which jut out from under him at acute angles like the legs on a milkmaid's stool. His tiny feet had on a pair of Oriental slippers and were positioned 'ten-to-two' on the rug, as if they were about to launch him into some great balletic leap.

'I must apologize for not recognizing you, Your Grace,' he said, 'but I am without my spectacles.'

He leaned towards me and squinted at full strength, as if assessing what the situation required.

'Cup of tea?' he said, raising his eyebrows.

'A cup of tea would be just the thing,' I replied.

He smiled and nodded towards the hearth. 'Kettle's on,' he said.

Then he waved his razor in the air again. 'Now, if you don't mind, I must complete my ablutions,' and he skipped off up the stairs, leaving me to make myself at home.

Finding a path through the room was no easy matter, for it was packed with so much clutter and stuff. Bookshelves heaved on almost every inch of wall and framed watercolours and sketches and yellowing prints all jostled for the remaining space. There must have been close to a dozen tables, all different sizes, scattered around the room, each one piled with papers and boxes and stacks of threadbare books. Half-naked statuettes thrust their swords into the air and some teetering vase or fancy lamp jangled with my every step. Even the narrow window sills were crowded with glass ornaments and the sunlight took their pinks and turquoises and sent them shimmering on the floor.

I advanced carefully through this jungle of bric-à-brac, nervous of catching some table corner or protruding text and bringing about some dreadful calamity. But at last the fire-place swung into view and I found myself in a clearing before a sagging mantelpiece with a pair of armchairs standing by and so I set about removing my coats. A fresh fire was settling into the day's business and I don't mind admitting I felt a twinge of jealousy for the master of such a hearty little room.

I was idly picking over the shelves of books when the Reverend reappeared. He was now all brushed-down and buttoned-up and his eyes swam happily in his spectacles. As he nodded, gently priming himself for speech, it occurred to me that he had about him not a fraction of Ignatius Peak's zeal. The Reverend Mellor, I decided, keeps his God very much under his hat.

'Now, Your Grace,' he said, eyeing me closely, 'I assume you have had your breakfast?'

When I told him that, in fact, I had not his eyes grew very wide indeed, almost filling his spectacle lenses. A small, incredulous smile played upon his lips.

'Your Grace, I believe you have run away from home,' he said.

Counselling the bereaved and distraught members of his parish has clearly made him an expert in getting quickly to the bottom of things.

'I needed to get out of the house for a while,' I told him and added, 'I left a note for Clement.'

'Well, in that case, he shall not be worrying. Tell me, would you like me to toast your muffin or would you care to toast your own?'

And we soon were leaning forward on our armchairs like boys around a campfire, each holding out a toasting-fork with a muffin skewered to the end. The Reverend brewed up a pot of smoky-flavoured tea and opened a new jar of quince jelly (a gift, I assumed, from some grateful parishioner). The muffins and the tea were excellent and, finding no good reason to call the proceedings to a halt, we continued to stuff ourselves for getting on an hour until at last the sheer volume of bread and tea inside us forced us to sit back in our chairs. As we rested I felt about as round and breathless as Mellor himself and wondered if it wasn't perhaps muffins and quince jelly which had given him his distinctive shape. Sitting side by side I thought the two of us must look like a pair of Toby jugs.

The Reverend said how sorry he was that I had missed the Snows' funeral service and I assured him that there was no man sorrier than myself. I thanked him for his recipe for his rheumatism pills and he asked if they had done me any good.

'In all honesty, I don't think so,' I told him.

He nodded. 'It was the same with me,' he replied.

We were still meditating on this when, quite suddenly, Mellor sat up in his chair, made a weird, muted exclamation and pressed a forefinger to the side of his head. He leapt to his feet and with admirable alacrity picked his way between the heaped tables and dangling plants, reached a bank of drawers, drew a couple of them straight out from their cases and returned with one under each arm and a large magnifying glass clenched in his teeth.

He rolled back into his armchair with the drawers in his lap. His head disappeared into them. There was the sound of much scuffling and rattling about. When he re-emerged he looked much invigorated and held up a curious looking object which he passed to me, saying,

'What do you make of that, Your Grace?'

Well, it was flat and fairly heavy – about eight inches by four. White and smooth, like something which had been washed up on a beach.

'Is it a bone?' I asked.

'Full marks,' announced Mellor. 'Now, Your Grace, any idea what beast?'

I must have stared at that cold old bone for getting on a minute, as if it might whisper me a clue, but at last I was forced to admit that I was completely in the dark.

'It is the jawbone . . .' said the Reverend, with eyes widening, 'of a hyena. And a big fellow he was, too.'

He held both hands out in front of him, a foot apart.

'Head about so big,' he assured me, raising his eyebrows. Then he gazed down at the space between his hands, so utterly engrossed in his hyena-thoughts that I feared he might suddenly throw back his head and let out a terrible howl.

'Found just over a year ago, in your own caves up at Creswell.'

'Well, well,' I said, noting how he had got me nodding along with him.

Another fragment of bone was tossed over to me, about the same size as the razor Mellor had been waving about. I turned the thing over in my hands. It was considerably lighter than the previous one and smelt, I thought, vaguely of mutton.

'Take a closer look,' said the Reverend, handing me the magnifying glass. So I held it over the narrow bone and through the swell of the lens managed to make out several rows of tiny scratches along the bone's edge, not unlike the fractions of an inch on a ruler, or the cross-hatching on Mr Sanderson's map.

'What are they for?' I asked.

'Decoration, maybe . . . Art of some sort. Who can say?'

I must admit I was a little taken aback by the Reverend's rather dismissive tone and, of course, he picked up on this straight away.

'You'd be surprised, Your Grace, how that which we are in the habit of referring to as "historical fact" is often little more than speculation. A thousand years from now some chap might come across an ornament of our day. He might identify it as such in no time. But when he comes to decide what it is *for*, exactly . . . well, that is going to be guesswork, wouldn't you say?'

I conceded the point while privately vowing to give more thought to it later on. And like a truffling pig the Reverend went back to rooting in his drawers of bone. One specimen after another was turned up and offered to me and while I examined one he was furiously digging out the next, so that my lap was soon heaped with them. All, the Reverend assured me, had once belonged to some creature who stalked the local countryside, many centuries ago. Bison, reindeer, mammoth, wild horse . . . they were beginning to weigh me down. As I shifted in my chair they ground against one another and made an eerie scraping noise but the Reverend was much too deeply immersed in the past to notice any discomfort I was presently suffering.

At some point I asked what tools he used to unearth these relics. 'Oh, just a teaspoon and a small brush,' he told me, still foraging. 'The cave floors are nothing but silt, you see? Perfect for preservation. But we would never have had an inkling what was down there if the farmer who used one of the caves to shelter his cattle hadn't tripped over a fossil or two.'

He stopped for a second, raised his head and peered over his drawers at me. 'Have you not seen the caves since they were tidied-up, Your Grace?'

I told him that I had not and admitted being unable to recall ever having been right inside them, though I drive past them often enough.

'And you being such an underground man,' he said. 'Well, we must go. Yes, of course we must,' and he began nodding. 'We must go this very minute.'

He paused for me to nod along with him. 'How splendid. I shall show you round your own caves.'

He was now nodding his head so violently the two drawers in his lap had begun to bounce about. But all of a sudden he stopped and raised a finger, for us both to hold our horses. 'Before we go,' he said gravely, 'one final bone.'

And, with considerable care, he presented me with an almost circular piece of bone. Quite small, but heavy as a rock.

'And who is this?' I asked the Reverend.

'The woolly rhino,' he replied with evident pride. 'Very rare.'

'A rhino in Nottinghamshire?' I asked him.

He gave me his surest, wisest nod.

I was most impressed. 'If you don't mind my asking, Reverend, how do you know it is a woolly rhino?'

He indicated a row of books. 'It's all in there,' he said, and sighed a little, as if recalling every weary hour of reading, the many months spent with his head in a book. 'But, you know, one must also employ a little bit of this,' and he tapped the side of his round head.

'Naturally,' I said, less certain with every second just what it was we were talking about. 'And in your opinion how might a woolly rhino actually look?'

'Well, now . . .' The Reverend took his time chewing over this one. He gazed into the far distance, as if down all the centuries. 'I would say he looks much the same as the modern rhino . . . but with a little more hair.'

I am sorry to admit that at this point my estimation of archaeologists plummeted somewhat. So much so that I wondered if, with the aid of the odd book or two, Mrs Pledger and I might not prove as proficient an archaeologist as Mellor himself.

*

It took us less than half an hour to trek across the fields to the caves, the Reverend setting an impressive pace. A strapped-up five-barred gate was the only thing that caused us any real delay.

The cave entrances are about fifty feet up a huge craggy slab and, from a distance, look like the gaps in an idiot's grin. We paused at the bottom of the sharp incline which leads up to them. The Reverend raised his nose and sniffed the air. 'Chilly . . .' he said.

I was still considering this when he went charging off up the sandy slope, leaving a trail of dust behind. Well, there was little else to do but chase after him, so I set off at my own bow-legged trot. I soon caught him up on the incline and was becoming closely acquainted with his vast behind, having good reason, all of a sudden, to hope that his momentum did not suddenly give out on him.

We were both of us well wrapped-up in overcoats and our brief gallop generated a fair amount of heat, and when we had scrambled up the last of the steep path we sat ourselves down on a rocky ledge by the cave entrance to look down at the river below and try to recompose ourselves.

We were too breathless to make any conversation and the perspiration was still drying on my brow when the Reverend reached into his rucksack and brought out a small oil lamp.

'Let us have a little look-see, shall we?' he said and placed the lamp on the ground between us. Then he produced from his waistcoat pocket a porcelain matchbox, in the shape of a cherub, whose head bent back on a hinge to reveal the matches hidden inside. Mellor took one out and struck it on the underside of the box.

'Show us the way, young fellow,' he said, as the match burst into life.

We advanced down a damp, narrow passage which went straight into the rock. The second we had set foot in it I felt the temperature dramatically drop and every breath was immediately transformed into a shocking blast to the chest.

'No wonder the bones keep so well,' I remarked to Mellor. 'It is like an ice-house in here.'

With his lamp held out before him the Reverend led the way, our footfalls coming right back at us from the cold and stinking rock. We had covered hardly any distance when the tunnel began to shrink around us. A most unpleasant feeling. But we kept on, creeping deeper into the earth, one tentative step after another, until Mellor's breadth prevented all but the faintest flicker coming back to light my way and I was forced to stumble in his dismal wake. In no time my hands were out in front of me, lest I be struck by some protruding rock, my fingers fussing over the stone around me – sometimes dry, sometimes greasy with moss. I was utterly lost in the darkness and bumbling along so clumsily that when Mellor suddenly stopped to catch his breath, I walked straight into him.

Our faltering journey had advanced maybe thirty yards in all when the tunnel's roof dropped by a couple more feet. Originally, it had cleared our heads by several inches but now pressed right down on top of us, so that we were obliged to walk bent-double in order to avoid cracking our heads. I found I kept looking keenly back over my shoulder, towards the entrance's ragged circle of light, each time noticing how it had diminished a little, until it was nothing more than a distant, fading sun.

I could not say I had so far taken much pleasure from our little underground hike, but any hope of such a thing was trounced entirely when I found myself taken over by a quite irrational but profoundly-rooted fear. Without warning, I became utterly convinced that I was about to be cut off from my precious circle of light. In an instant my breath quickened to the pant of an exhausted dog, my heart pounding frantically at the walls of my chest. Some imminent rockfall was about to cut us off. Some faceless adversary was plotting to shut us in. The same awful fear possessed me which I had felt as I entered the Oakleys' front room, but I had not now the sisters' kind words to soothe me, their quiet confidence to calm me down. I was filled up with trepidation; it animated every fibre of me painfully. My own infant's voice pleaded with me to abandon the journey, to dash back down the passage. 'Danger!' the voice insisted. 'Run for the light, before it disappears!'

Well, I did everything in my power to silence that voice. I blocked my ears and clenched my jaw. I did my damnedest to bring my breathing under control, telling myself again and again, 'You are all right, man. You are all right.' It was a desperate and pathetic struggle but I was determined that Reason should win the day. When, at last, I managed to recover myself a little, managed to reach some momentary plateau of near-calm, I found I had lagged several yards behind Mellor and his oil lamp. My mouth and throat were completely parched. I swallowed hard and pushed on into the dark.

I continued to walk with my hands out in front of me (more like the antennae of an insect than appendages of a man). Every half-dozen or so steps I would halt and spread my fingers on the tunnel walls to sense how much space I had around me in which to breathe. It seemed that this futile gesture – of my palms pressing against the rock – was all that kept it from closing in on me and crushing me to death.

Twice the Reverend stumbled. Both times he called out, 'Careful here.' The words skittered down the tunnel, returning first as a single echo, then a second and third and fourth, until they all ganged-up together in a deafening, lunatic roar. When I heard him slip a third time and call out, 'Careful here,' again, I very nearly lost my head. There was little enough room in the tunnel, without his demented voices flying everywhere.

The tunnel roof had now sunk to such a miserable height it was right down on our backs and the two of us all but crawling on our blessed hands and knees. Time and again I told myself, 'I shall turn and get out of here in a second,' while becoming less and less certain there was space enough to execute such a manoeuvre. The pressure in my head was close to bursting and both my shoulders were grazing against the rock when I thought I felt the hint of a cool breeze sweep across my face.

The next minute Mellor and I were clambering free of the tunnel, were standing upright and stretching and stamping our feet. We had come out into some sort of cavern, perhaps thirty foot at its highest point, and when the Reverend lifted the lamp above his head its amber light filled the entire dome. The cave walls hung over us like great ocean waves, frozen at that last moment before crashing down.

I must have stood there, entranced, for several minutes, trying to make some sense of the place. It had about it an ochre glow which seemed to emanate from the very rock. Tiny rivulets had eaten away at the chamber walls and made rocky fingers out of them so that one felt almost as if one was caught in a giant's cupped hands.

The Reverend found himself a boulder on the cave floor and daintily lowered himself onto it. He placed the oil lamp on the ground beside him and folded his arms in a proprietorial way while I proceeded to silently circle him and take in every aspect of this weird subterranean place.

The lamp's flame momentarily flickered and I saw my own shadow shudder on the wall and this had on me a powerful, almost hypnotic effect, as if the shadow was not mine but some distant ancestor's who was feinting this way and that. I thought to myself, 'He is trying to mesmerize me with some ancient dance.'

The light in that cavern was at such a premium and the darkness so eager to return that the shadow which stretched and shrank before me seemed a good deal more at home there and had a presence at least as convincing as my own.

The Reverend clasped his hands round his knees, leaned back on his rock and stared up at the ceiling. 'What do you make of it, Your Grace?' I heard him whisper, before the words were taken up by the cave walls and tossed about the place. My reply lodged itself deep in my throat, fearful of what the cave's acoustics might do with it. A word here too harshly spoken might let loose a whole Bedlam of broken voices. But I was also silent because the peculiar beauty of the cavern had all but robbed me of my speech.

High up, where the Reverend had fixed his gaze, were minerals, embedded in the rock. They crackled silently in the light. The cold air now began to find its way through to me, investigating every cranny of my boots and coats, and I began to feel a little unwelcome among all the smooth formlessness of the cave.

At last I said, 'It is somehow similar to how I imagine the surface of the moon to be.'

The Reverend smiled and nodded back at me from his stone seat. 'I have often thought the same thing myself,' he said.

I asked if all the other caves were as grand and the Reverend told me that this was by far the largest and queerest but that, at one time, all would have offered shelter to some creature or other.

'And was it only animals that used them?' I asked.

'O, no,' said the Reverend. 'Primitive Man once lived here. There's no doubting that.'

I tried to picture Primitive Man, dressed in nothing but a few rags of hide, as he went about his Primitive Life . . . creeping out into the valleys of ancient Nottinghamshire to hunt wild bison and reindeer (and the woolly rhino) and spending his nights in the cold, damp dark. For a second I even fancied I saw the carcasses of those beasts laid out on the cave floor and the crude implements which my primitive ancestor might have used to rip their flesh apart.

Well, I could not have chosen a worse time for such a reverie. These gruesome pictures of brute gore were still most vivid in my mind when the Reverend drew me to him with his finger and gave up half his boulder for me. I perched myself down beside him and was still wondering what his enigmatic expression meant when he reached over to his oil lamp and whispered, 'Watch carefully, Your Grace.'

And the flame on the lamp's wick began to hesitate; gave out as it was slowly choked of air. All around us the light slowly drained from the cave and seeped back into the ground. The lamp's tiny flame shrank and spluttered to a single ounce of light and the cave quietly reasserted its awful power over us. Every second of its thousands of years of darkness returned to it. The brief moments of light we had brought in with us were erased. Horrified, I watched the flame dwindle, and with a final flicker, die.

I was alone, deep in the rock. There was no light. No memory of it. Only the darkness pressing down.

'What is this?' I hissed at Mellor and a thousand snaking voices sprang to life.

He said nothing. He was no longer next to me. I could not move for the rock.

'That is enough, Mellor,' I insisted, but my tongue was thick with fear. 'For God's sake, man, strike a match.'

My own voice jabbered back at me in chorus before slowly consuming itself. Then there was nothing but the darkness and the silence. Nothing but the deep, dead rock.

At last, I heard the Reverend say, 'Hold tight. Just one more minute . . . Ah now, look up, Your Grace.'

Well, I did as I was told. At first, nothing. Blindness. No sound, except my own mouth, gasping for air. Then somewhere up above, out of the corner of my eye, I saw the glitter of the very first star. Then it was gone again but as I tried to retrieve it I found another, further over. Then another. All the stars were coming out. They twinkled mercifully up in the heavens, each one its own small message of hope. And, slowly, the faint moon revealed itself, calmly filled itself with ghostly light and took its place among the stars.

‘Can you see it now?’ Mellor asked me.

‘Yes. Yes, I see it,’ I said. ‘It is beautiful . . . Very beautiful indeed.’

From our shared stone seat we continued to look up at the stars until at last I said, ‘I’m afraid I don’t understand.’

‘It is a hole,’ he said. ‘A natural chimney. Which is why this cave is called the Pin Hole Cave. Only a small hole but big enough to let in the light which picks out the crystal in the rock.’

So was there mercy or was there not? I was still trying to make sense of it and staring up at the moon and the stars when the Reverend struck a match. The brightness was too much for me and I had to cover my eyes against its terrible glare. And when the lamp was relit I found myself back in the cave’s strange ochre glow. The heavens above had been turned to stone. The stars had been washed away.

‘Time to go?’ said the Reverend, nodding. ‘Hup. Hup.’ And he helped me to my feet.

It was as if the hands on my mind’s clock had been frozen, then released by the match’s flame. Time suddenly flooded back in and exhausted me.

The Reverend lifted his lamp, smiled and made towards the tunnel and I had no choice but to stagger after him and prepare for the long trek back. But as Mellor squeezed himself into the tunnel and stole the light away I had one last glance at the place.

I felt as if I had come within an inch of Primitive Man. Spent a fraction of a second in his skull.

The journey back down the passage was, thankfully, without incident and as we made our way along it I managed more or less to allay my fears that the Reverend might somehow contrive to get himself wedged between the tunnel walls. In time, the tunnel began to open itself up to us and the light from the entrance formed a gentle halo around the Reverend. And in what seemed like half the time it took us to get in there we were walking out into the day.

The view from the cave entrance, though frosty and wintry, was a marvel to behold – full of colour and distance and depth. I looked up and down the valley and drew in its rich air, wondering how it might look with a huge glacier to fill it up. I imagined that massive slab of ice as a vast silvery ship, sitting on a slipway, calmly awaiting its launch. Slowly, century by century, it inched towards the sea.

I looked at my watch – barely midmorning, though I seemed to have crammed in enough experience to last me the whole of the year. Mellor was busy packing his lamp away and I thought perhaps I should be getting back or Clement might start sending out search parties again.

So the two of us shook hands and I thanked him for his hospitality and for showing me the caves.

'You must drop by again, Your Grace,' he said.

'I will,' I assured him and set off across the fields.

*

December 13th

*

I seem to find the less I eat the livelier I become. Each rejected savoury gives me an extra charge of vim. All these years I have thought it was food which kept me going – the fuel for my body's fire. Now I am not so sure. Recently I went for a whole day without eating a single thing and when I woke the following morning felt just as bright as a button. Mealtimes have begun to slip by without even a hint of appetite stirring in me. Some days the thought of a sandwich is enough to make me sick.

But it is not as if I am starving myself. Yesterday I ate a pear and two dry scones. Today I have already had an onion pastry and shall not be in the least surprised if I have something else before I retire. Have vowed to forgo meat of all kinds and must say I am feeling better for it. Mental faculties are a deal sharper. Each day now there are moments when I become so altogether pure I begin to float away.

*

Have been forced to discontinue my custom of standing-on-my-head, which is a bitter disappointment as I am certain that gravity is the natural way to encourage extra blood to the brain. I recently immersed myself so successfully in meditation that I dozed off for a moment or two. When I came round I was out by ninety degrees – had gone from vertical to horizontal, bringing a curtain and an Elgin vase down with me. Mrs Pledger was quite insistent I give the whole thing up there and then.

So, as an alternative means of invigoration, I have taken up what my father used to call 'the hot and cold treatment', which, in plain English, is simply the practice of jumping straight out of a hot bath and into a cold. It does wonders for the complexion, giving a body the ruddiest glow. Clement is not keen on the idea – I suppose it rather rubs up against his own philosophies – but I am proud to say that in my old age I am learning to dig my heels in and so every day now he fills one bath for me with scalding water and another with ice-cold. Unfortunately, there is only the one tub in my own bathroom so we have to draw the cold one in a bathroom down the hall.

Now, I cannot pretend that leaping into a cold bath is an altogether relaxing experience, especially when one has been stewing-in-a-pot only seconds before, but there is no denying that it wakes the body up with an almighty jolt. My heart sometimes takes twenty minutes to return to its pedestrian plod.

From one bathroom to the other is a good fifty- or sixty-yard trot and it has become necessary to seal off the whole landing by hanging up blankets at both ends. This follows an unfortunate incident when a housemaid happened to come round the corner with a pile of towels as I was going down the corridor at full-pelt. The poor girl almost leapt down the stairs in fright and had to be carted to my study by Clement and given a brandy to bring her round. We had to send her home. But the sight of a naked old man must be very alarming to one of such tender years. Especially when he is haring towards you for all he is worth.

So, as I say, we now take the precaution of hanging up blankets. And, in order to clear the area, Clement strikes a small gong just before I go.

*

This afternoon I went on another walkabout, setting out along the East wing and then venturing off down other corridors. By some deft little twisting and turning I came across an unfamiliar flight of stairs and, following them, found a tiny storeroom which I had not come across before. It was no more than ten foot by twenty, in what used to be the servants' quarters, and with nothing in it but a stack of chests and boxes and a collapsed bedstead. The contents of the boxes were mostly broken or in poor condition. In one was an ancient rug, stored in peppercorns; in another, a hammock and several pairs of flattened shoes. There was an ivory chess set with two pieces missing, a dented sports cup and a Chinaman's hat.

I cannot honestly say I know what I am after on these little expeditions of mine, but have convinced myself that in some forgotten corner of the house there sits an item which will make sense of my recent spiritual hurly-burly.

Whatever form this enigmatic object might take, I can safely say it was not unearthed today, though I did come across a rather curious wooden microscope, wrapped in linen, and three boxes of glass slides. No idea who they belonged to. I do not recall acquiring them myself. All the same, I brought the whole lot back to my bedroom, feeling quite pleased with my little find.

Sat myself down at my table and took the slides from their neat little tins but as I removed the tissue paper found that most were cracked or shattered and only one set was intact. The box was marked

HYMENOPTERA
Honey Bee
Apis mellifica
– DRONE –

Each slide was individually labelled, indicating the part of the bee it contained . . . 'third leg', 'mandible', 'hind wing' and so forth.

I held one of the slides up and, even without the microscope, could make out the tiny fragment of the long-dead bee. Each slide was, in fact, two identical glass wafers with the bee-part sandwiched in between, held in what looked to me like a flattened drop of the bee's own amber honey.

I gave the microscope a quick dusting-down and moved the table over to the window where there was a little more light.

The scope itself is no more than ten inches tall and turned from a beautiful dark wood – walnut, perhaps – squat but curvaceous, like a tiny stair banister, and fitted at one end with three crooked brass legs. Each leg is welded onto a thick brass ring which, when turned, effectively raises or lowers the height of the microscope, thereby allowing the operator to bring the object into focus.

I placed a sheet of paper on the table top, selected a slide and slipped it under the lens. The microscope was cold against the bag of flesh beneath my eye – a sensation which stirred in me memories of my old telescope. But with this instrument I looked not up, up, up at the distant stars, but down, very deeply down, and found myself suddenly in the troubling company of gargantuan insect limbs.

A single wing was veined like a leaf – more a construction of glass and steel than a part of a once-living thing.

The 'first leg' became bristly and muscular under the microscope . . . gnarled with all manner of knots and joints. A massive spring for his alighting, for flicking the fellow up in the air . . .

In this manner I examined each tiny component of the dismembered honey bee. Scrutinized him; made him whole again, limb by furry limb. When he was restored he was a frightening creature. He sat hugely in my mind and seemed much angered as he licked his scalpel wounds.

There is something about him I do not care for. He is not the friendly type. After peering at him down the scope for five or ten minutes I had to jog around the room to shake him from my head.

When I eventually returned the slides to their little box I added it and the microscope to my slowly-growing shrine. At present it consists of:

Sanderson's map;
Peak's note;
the *Ancient Chinese Healing* man;
Gray's Anatomy (and various other books);
a wind-up monkey;
my father's clog-shaped pipe.

Mr Hendley's Account

It must have been quite early in the morning, for I was only out at the Pykes, which is the gatehouse just this side of Clumber near the top of my round. I had dropped them off a letter and was climbing back on my bicycle when I saw him at the entrance to the tunnel, standing and watching and not saying a word. His not talking made me a bit uncomfortable, so I said, 'Morning,' to him to try and bring him round. He nodded at me then he slowly come over. He come right over and started inspecting my bike. Asking all sorts of questions, like if the saddle was especially comfortable and what sort of speed the thing could make.

I remember him looking up at me, excited all of a sudden, and asking what I reckoned to a cycle down the tunnel. Said we could take it in turns or I could sit on the saddle and he could do the pedalling. Well, I didn't want to get myself in trouble, but I said no, because I never did like tunnels, nor any dark place come to that, so there was no way he was going to get me down there without a fuss. Besides, I had my whole round in front of me and I didn't have the time to be loaning out my bike.

Well, of course, he wasn't altogether happy with my answer. He went very quiet again. Then he asked if he could just sit on the thing for a minute, to see what it felt like. To be honest, I was still a mite suspicious. Thought he might try and pedal off with it. But I thought who am I to stop a Duke from sitting on my bike? So I let him have a go.

He sat there with his hands on the handlebars and nodded to himself and said it seemed very good indeed. Said he had always fancied being a postman and looked rather enviously over at my sack. He seemed to get a little melancholy, which, I have to say, rather baffled me. I should have thought a man with his money could be just about whatever he chose to be.

Anyway, I told him I really should be getting on my way again and he eventually climbed off the bike and handed it back. He said goodbye and turned and went on his way. He didn't hang about, by any means. Last time I saw him he was disappearing down his tunnel. That was the only time I came across him. He did seem a bit of a rum old chap.

From His Grace's Journal

December 15th

*

He is all root and branch and foliage, with bright red berry-eyes. He creaks and crackles as he creeps along and frightens the birds away. He has stalked the Wilderness as long as I can remember, sneaking from tree to tree the whole year round, waiting for a small boy to wander close enough to be dragged back into the undergrowth.

A man of scratches and of tangled bramble, he is, all in a nasty knot. But when he wishes, the Berry Man can scatter himself into a hundred disparate parts and a prying eye would see nothing but the same leaves and twigs as lie on any woodland floor. But once the prying eye has passed on the Berry Man draws himself back in. The scraps of bark slowly shift along the ground and are reintroduced to each other; the chill wind shuffles him into shape. The vines wind around him and bind him up until he stands broad and tall again.

Sometimes he wears the antlers of a broken branch, sometimes he wears a thorny crown. Some days he is a skinny man, made up of nothing but bark-stripped twigs. Other days he has an ivy belly, packed with wriggling worms. One day he has mossy eyebrows, the next a hornet's nest hat. Ever changing, always insecty, made from whatever comes to hand.

But you'll not hear a whisper out of him. The Berry Man has no tongue in his head. When he is angry he just takes to spinning. Spins so fast he pulls the whole wood in. He spins until the whole world is nothing but a whirling dervish of rattling leaves.

*

All my life the Berry Man has occupied the Wilderness. He is as much a part of the place as the trees. Mother and Father believed in him with a passion. They introduced me to him when I was very small. I remember them saying how if I strayed into his territory he would take me off and whip me with the switches of his arms. A year or two later I believe I suggested that perhaps the Berry Man was only make-believe after all, but they both looked at me most gravely and slowly shook their heads.

A child is expert at frightening himself, his mind primed to imagine the most terrible things, and I cannot now say for certain how much of my Berry Man was inherited from my parents and how much I conceived myself. Certainly I have retained a particularly vivid picture of a little boy (who looks very much like me) running through the Wilderness. The boy has no flesh left on his body for he has been caught and thrashed by the flailing arms of the Berry Man. Right through my childhood this picture served as a warning to keep well clear of that wood.

I was so convinced of the awful creature's existence that once or twice I thought I saw him, squatting among the bushes at the edge of the wood, watching me as I hurried by. All these years later, I still find myself walking half a mile out of my way to avoid that dreadful place. I do not really expect to be confronted by some leafy creature, yet always find some dim excuse to take a different route. The ghouls which haunt our childhood are not easily shaken off.

*

I was out on my constitutional this morning, with a young terrier who had repeatedly misbehaved. So much so that I had lost all my patience and put him on a leash. I must have been cold or damp and heading home in something of a hurry, for I had chosen to return by way of the Wilderness.

We were thirty yards or so from the old wood and I was keeping my mind busy with as many trifling thoughts as I could think up, when I became convinced that a pair of eyes were trained on me. Felt their gaze wash up and down my spine. I turned and scanned the woods from one end to the other. Most of the trees were leafless and they were all a winter-grey and I had just about assured myself that I was mistaken when I caught sight of a face, peering grimly from a bush. I leapt back and almost tripped over the dog, which started him barking and jumping all around.

The face in the bushes looked left and right. The leaves around him twitched. Then all at once, with a swish, the branches parted and he came racing out of the woods. He was nothing but a blur of thrashing limbs and I would have run myself had I not been all tied up with the blasted dog. The Berry Man scythed through the high grass towards me. His steps made a terrible whipping sound. After all these years, I thought, the Berry Man has grown tired of waiting and broken cover to come and snatch me away.

I was frantically trying to untangle myself when I saw how the Berry Man was, in fact, not headed for me at all but was running down the hill towards the lake. I saw also how there was something troublesome in his gait; some hindrance, as if one leg was shorter than the other. And in that instant, when I realized that this was not the Berry Man but some fleeing, limping lad, I found all my courage restored to me; found I had a sudden abundance of it.

'Ho!' I shouted after him. 'Ho, there!'

But he continued limping hastily away from me and in a

minute he was hobbling onto the bridge across the lake with me and the barking dog quite a way behind. Now, I am not overly fond of running and would most likely have given up the chase if I had not that moment spotted one of my keepers coming along the track on the far side of the lake. He was a big fellow and very familiar but his name had momentarily slipped my mind, so I called out,

'Ho, there! Keeper! Stop the boy!'

And in a thrice he had dropped his shoulder bag and was barging his way through the iron gates and came running onto the bridge at such a pitch that the hobbling boy found himself trapped between the two of us. I slowed my pace a little and pulled on the leash to try and quieten the dog. And now the boy was all in a fluster, glancing first towards the keeper, who continued to bore down on him on one side, and then right back at me. And for a moment I thought he recognized just how old and bandy I was and how easily he might knock me down and I felt all my courage drain away again and I wished I had let him go. The lad was turning one way, then the other, and working himself up into a right old state. Then, to my horror, I saw how he had started scrambling up the low wall which runs along the length of the bridge.

'No, boy!' I shouted at him, but he was like a rabbit, and carried on clambering for all he was worth. He dragged his lame leg up onto the wall beside him, stood and hurled himself at the lake. But the keeper had come along behind him, made a lunge and grabbed him by his arm.

By the time I caught them up the keeper had dragged the boy down from the wall and dumped him on the ground, where he now thrashed his arms and legs about and made an awful grunting sound.

'Calm down, boy. Calm yourself!' I shouted, but it did not the slightest good.

The dog was still barking and baring his teeth and the poor boy had his hands up in front of his face as if the keeper and I were all set to give him the stick. The whole scene was so chaotic that I was obliged to give the dog a smack to shut him up, and it was another minute after he had swallowed his bark before the lad finally drew his terrible sobbing to a close. When he drew his fingers down from his face I saw that there was indeed something wrong with him. His head seemed to have too much jawbone about it, if that makes any sense. It was as if his eyes and nose and mouth had been put together not quite right.

'Nobody is going to hurt you,' I told him, but he stared nervously down at the keeper's grip on him. When it was released the boy's moans just about abated and the three of us were able to lean, panting, against the wall of the bridge while the dog looked stupidly on and, not knowing how best to deal with the situation, I suggested the boy come up to the house.

It was a maid who recognized him as one of the Linklater sons. They apparently live out near Cuckney village, so I sent a footman to their cottage, post-haste. While we were waiting on him I had Mrs Pledger make us a pot of tea and a few rounds of cinnamon toast and asked Clement if he would join us, as the man's very presence can soothe the most agitated scene. So the whole gang of us trooped into the downstairs study and sat around in silence while the poor lad drank his tea. He was very thirsty and supped it up most lustily and I was sure his fumbling grip would crack the china cup, or that his huge jaw would take a bite out of it. He looked to me no more than twelve years old but his hands and forearms were as thick as a thatcher's. One of his shoulders was a little hunched-up so that he appeared not to be able to turn his head as easily as he might have liked. And the sole on his left shoe, I noticed, was built up an extra inch or two, so that the whole leg tended to hang rather sorrily from his hip.

If there were no more tears then there were no words either. He must have sat there without a whisper for getting on half an hour, taking self-conscious sips from his cup of tea until I thought it must be freezing-cold. The rest of us made some attempt at conversation while snatching occasional glances at him across the room, until at last I got word that my footman had returned with another of the Linklater boys.

I dismissed Clement and the keeper and once they were out of the way asked our guest to be shown in. As he entered the room I kept an eye on his younger brother, to see how he would react, and though he remained seated and stared most fixedly at the dregs in the bottom of his cup, I could see that he had clearly registered his brother and, I thought, begun to tremble a little. The lad who came in had only a year or two on his brother – was no more than fifteen years old himself. The same mousy coloured hair sprang from his head. He even had a few whiskers on his chin. I suppose I was expecting some sort of introduction, but he simply nodded in my direction and marched straight past me towards his kin, taking his hand from his jacket pocket as he did so, and moving with such determination and velocity I wondered what humiliating punishment I was about to be a witness to. By now the lame brother had got up from his chair and stood with his big head hanging down and his cup and saucer still clutched in his hand. He was panting now and I thought his shoulders had begun to shake up and down again. Yet when the older boy reached him he simply took his cup and saucer, set them down on a table, put his arms around his brother's shoulders and pulled him to him in a loving embrace.

Straight away the young thatcher started sobbing like a

baby, while his brother gently stroked his head and I must say that as I stood there observing them it was all I could do to stop myself joining in.

'I must apologize for my brother,' said the older boy. 'He must have wandered onto your estate.'

I nodded my head then shook it once or twice and waved my hands vaguely in the air.

'You see, he likes to look around, sir. Always has done. His curiosity sometimes gets the better of him.'

I told him not to mention it and that no harm had been done, and that I only hoped we had not frightened the boy too much with all our carrying-on. To try and put us at our ease I introduced myself. The older brother told me his name was Duncan and, easing his damp-eyed brother off his shoulder, added, 'And this is Doctor.'

'Doctor ... Ah.' I tried digesting the information, but I simply couldn't keep it down. 'He is a doctor, you say?'

'He is the seventh son of a seventh son, you see, sir, so that is his given name. It is an old tradition. Sevens being lucky. It makes him special, you see.'

All this was announced most matter-of-factly, as if it were common knowledge, but I felt sure I detected also a note of pride in his being the bearer of such exotic news.

The whole idea was, of course, quite fantastic. I was obliged to ask Duncan how his brother's special qualities manifested themselves and was informed (in a most ingenuous tone) how he was frequently consulted by local people, as an oracle or prophet might have been in ancient times. I found all this rather hard to imagine as I had yet to hear the boy utter a single word and when he referred again to Doctor's 'rare faculties' I felt compelled to ask for an example of them.

'Well, for instance, if you give him the date and the month and the year you were born he can tell you which day of the week it was.' He then added, 'It doesn't matter how many years ago it was.'

I allowed the implication of this last comment to sink in a little and was about to furnish young Doctor with the required information and generally try him out when he sort of shuddered, took a gulp of air and spluttered out,

'Wednesday,' then was silent again.

Incredible! I stared at one brother, then the other. I had *indeed* been born on a Wednesday. I remember my mother saying so. I was trying to work out how on earth he might have guessed it, when he added in a whisper,

'March 12th, 1828.'

I was absolutely dumbstruck. His brother turned and saw from my expression that the young prophet was right on the mark again.

'Now then . . .' he said to himself. 'He's never done that before.'

*

I ordered more toast from Mrs Pledger and the pair of them stayed on for a good half hour, Duncan proving to be very good company but Doctor, unfortunately, having nothing more to say. At some point in the conversation I discovered that Duncan is, in fact, the younger of the two.

'It's a common mistake,' he told me. 'He is very boyish-looking, is he not?'

We were all gathered at the front door and the two of them were just about on their way when Doctor hesitated and ground to a halt halfway down the steps. He stared anxiously at his boots for a few seconds and grimaced and shifted from foot to foot. Duncan went over, put an arm round his shoulder and asked him what was wrong. Doctor chewed on his cheek a little before finally surrendering a solitary, mangled word.

'Underwood,' he muttered in my direction.

I begged the young fellow's pardon.

'Underwood,' he said again.

Well, neither Duncan nor myself had heard of any such fellow and after we had stood around in silence for a minute were obliged to leave it at that. But as they set off down the driveway Doctor turned briefly back to me and with his good arm pointed towards the Wilderness, where I had first mistaken him for The Berry Man.

*

December 19th

*

The weather this month has been very bad. We have had just about everything thrown our way. These last few days especially have been some of the coldest for a long while, with a great deal of frost and snow. Icicles, some of them six foot long, have been hanging off all the gutters and Clement has had to lean from the windows with a broom to knock them down, which was a shame for they were most impressive but necessary, lest they fall and cleave some unfortunate chap in two.

Every pipe in the house is frozen-up – the staff have had to fetch water from the well – and when the thaw eventually comes around I have no doubt we shall have a hundred leaks on our hands. But what the cold weather has also brought with it is the freezing-up of the lake. Very rare. It is nothing but one great crystal slab with a surface as smooth as glass.

The day it first froze over there were children knocking at the back door at dawn, after permission to skate. Now it would be the meanest of old men who would deny folk a pleasure which came so cheaply to him, and once word got round that the lake was open people came from all over, with their ice-skates tucked under their arm. From first light until last thing at night any number have been out on the ice, all of them slowly spinning in a giant human wheel. Courting couples, their arms crossed before them, glide gently left then right; whole families make chains, each member holding on to the waist of the one in front, as their many-headed, many-legged creatures go snaking over the solid lake.

All this I have observed from an upstairs study and this very afternoon I watched musicians troop across the snow and set up on the benches at the ice's edge. They played their fiddles and whistles and squeeze-boxes until their fingers must have been numb from the cold. But while they played I caught the odd half-familiar fragment of a tune, which was brought to me on the breeze.

I stood there for a while this evening with the window open an inch or two to let the music in. The moon was up and around the lake several dozen lamps were hung on poles. They formed a glowing oasis in the night which I was admiring when Clement appeared at my side. We both stood there quietly for a moment, watching the distant figures swinging under the stars.

'The lake is very busy tonight,' I said.

Clement nodded. A distant cheer found its way through to us.

'O, yes,' I said, 'they are having a gay old time.'

As I turned to face him I noticed how Clement stood rather strangely – almost Napoleon-like – with one arm tucked inside the front of his jacket. For a second I thought he had perhaps burnt his arm and had it bandaged, but as I watched he slowly withdrew it and there, in his hand, were a pair of ancient skates.

When the penny finally dropped I stepped back, aghast,

saying, 'O no, Clement, I couldn't possibly. No, I really don't think I could.'

But old Clement deposited the skates into my outstretched hands, which had the effect of momentarily silencing me.

I turned them over.

'I mean to say, Clement, that a skate would be very pleasant,' I went on, 'but you know how I am not one for the crowds.'

Well, he swept out of the room at such speed that if I had not known him better I might have thought he had taken offence. I made a closer examination of the old skates. A most unsophisticated pair they were. Very heavy. Little more than a pair of old bread knives bound together with straps. I was still looking them over when Clement swept back through the door with a heap of clothes in his arms. These he dumped on the rug before me and proceeded to pick out various jackets and mittens and woollen caps.

Then Clement dragged from the heap a ten-foot huckaback scarf and set about winding it around my neck, so that when he had finally done wrapping and tucking only my old man's eyes were left peeping out.

I looked at my reflection and, in a muffled voice, said, 'If I fall, Clement, I shall bounce back up,' and padded my prodigious girth with mittened hands.

It was in this state of woolly incognito that Clement sent me out into the night, a lantern clamped in one hand, my ancient ice-skates in the other.

It must have been several days since I last ventured outside, for the fresh air made me come over quite giddy. The world had been charmed by snow and ice and all the trees were whitely gowned. Every fold in the land glowed in the moonlight, as if the clouds had given in to gravity and tumbled from the sky.

My boots made a fresh path towards the lake, each footfall

packing down the snow with a creak. The voices grew steadily louder and the distant figures slowly took shape and in time I found myself at the edge of the frozen lake, hanging my lantern with the others on an alder branch. The hearty babble of all the skating strangers washed around me, their dreamy locomotion drew me in.

As I strapped my skates to the soles of my boots I leant against a rowing boat, which was half in and half out of the ice. It was a second before I spotted on its bench a young child, every inch of him swaddled in coats and scarves, just like me. I assumed he had been put there by his parents while they were both out on the ice, being too much of a mite to skate himself. To his credit, he seemed to wait most patiently. I nodded my bandaged head at him and he nodded back.

'Are mother and father out taking a spin?' I asked.

From his jacket pocket he produced a half-eaten apple.

'App-le,' he said, as if offering me a bite.

'Good boy,' I answered and patted him on the head, then I turned, drew in a draught of chilly air and cast myself out onto the ice.

I had not skated for many a year and my arms were rather inclined to flail about. But after a while I began to find my balance, then some confidence and quite soon felt I was making some modest contribution to that great turning, stirring mass.

As everyone swept round in the circle a space was left in the middle of the lake where, now and then, an especially gifted skater would show off his skating skills. A man in a balaclava executed an impressive figure of eight, the blades of his skates making a hissing sound as they cut into the ice. Then a young girl – no more than fourteen years old – took the stage and slowly wound herself up into a tight little spin, gradually drawing her arms and feet into her so that she was soon spinning on a sixpence and sending out a fine white spray. Her audience gave her a round of applause but she continued to spin furiously on, until I feared she would cut right through the ice and disappear into the lake below. Then she suddenly cast a leg out and with a graceful backward slide emerged from the blur and in no time had rejoined her more sedate skating companions.

But though I am old and bow-legged I did not envy her. For I was brimming with the simple pleasure of skating with my fellow man. O, we swung and we sang and we gathered speed, did so many anticlockwise circuits I thought we had escaped the grasp of Time. I was lost in a skating-ceilidh. It was Fellowship, without a doubt.

You see, I have been thinking about my baker, Ignatius Peak, and his enviable religious zeal. I recall how 'Fellowship' was the biggest bee in his bonnet. And, indeed, what could be a worthier pursuit than harmony with one's fellow man? But out on the ice tonight I felt as if I had found my own version of it. It rather crept up on me. I was a stranger, skating among other strangers. Nobody said a word. Yet between us we seemed to stir up enough fellowship for the whole wide world.

*

December 21st

*

I believe I may have found what I have been looking for – Mr Fowler's head. As I write this he stares blindly across the study, in meditation many leagues deep. If the tortured fellow in *Gray's Anatomy* had attained an air of resignation then it is indifference – profound indifference – Mr Fowler's creamy head personifies. How can I put it? He is passive yet full of prospect. Silent, but like an unstruck bell.

These past few weeks I have undertaken several house-safaris and on a number of occasions climbed the stairs to fumble in the attic's airless gloom, but my only trophies so far have been the odd book, a wind-up monkey and a bee in several parts. Sensing a fresh approach was necessary if I was to succeed where I had previously failed, I gave my tactics a thorough review: rather than wander up and down the corridors, I decided to pull back from the problem and come at it more objectively.

Rigged myself out, as usual, in beaver and sable coat then strode purposefully down the Great Stairs to sally forth into the frosty morn. On the porch I did a bit of marching on the spot to warm me up, then weighed anchor, swung to starboard and took the narrow gravel path which skirts the house. For it was my intention this morning to circumambulate the place; a task which, I believe I am right in saying, I have never previously carried out. One tends always to approach one's home or leave it, rather than go around and around. But there is something magical about a circle and the act of circling itself seems to generate all sorts of powerful stuff.

Once I had embarked on this mission, however, I discovered that keeping close to the house would not be as easily executed as I might have hoped. I was constantly finding walls and hedges and flower beds in my way. But by some mindful orienteering and a little clambering here and there I managed to go some way towards accomplishing the task I had set myself.

How instructive to look *at* my house instead of *from* it. I did not immediately recognize the balcony where I have recently taken to stargazing and smoking my pipe, nor the bay window of my bathroom, come to that. It demands, I now see, a special sort of thinking to match up the picture one has of the inside of a room with how it might look from *without*. The same might be said about journeys to and from a place ... that when one travels in each direction one might sometimes just as well be covering different ground.

My aim today, however, was to turn up some room or annexe which had previously eluded me, so as I tramped along the path and scaled the occasional wall I continually scanned the house. I was approaching the barometer tower and beginning to puff and pant and wonder, frankly, if I had not dreamt up for myself another fool's errand when I rounded a corner and came upon a place which had entirely slipped my mind.

There are times when I am quietly impressed by my powers of forgetfulness. In this instance they had brought about the disappearance of a whole host of bricks and mortar. A sizeable building, so no mean feat. But as I stood there staring at it, its mental equivalent slowly re-emerged in my mind. Wasn't this the place my grandfather once whistled for me his favourite tunes? I believe it was. The longer I stared at the outhouse the more my memory's muscle was restored, so that in time I could recall with some certainty how it had originally served as a stable block before the riding school went up. It was like bumping into an old acquaintance.

The building is not connected to the house and stands, I should say, a good twenty yards clear of it. Over the years it has become ivy-covered and introverted-looking. A sapling now sprouts from its roof. I spotted an old gardener nearby, pushing a creaking barrow towards a smouldering fire, and called out to him. He gave not the slightest hint that he had heard me and seemed to carry on his way undisturbed. But as I continued to observe the fellow I saw how he leaned a little to the left, slowly swung his barrow over a few degrees and, in his own time, wheeled his pile of rotting leaves in my direction.

He pulled up and let his barrow down. He had an unlit pipe in his mouth. I asked if he knew anything about the old stables, which obliged him to push his cap back on his bald head.

'I believe they are used for storage, Your Grace,' he said.

Well, the door was bolted but was not padlocked. Its wooden stalls were all intact. Not much effort had been made to clean the place up for the floor was still strewn with strawdust and the sweet pungency of horses seemed still to hang in the air, though the only evidence of the building's former use was a pair of cobwebbed cartwheels which leant against the far wall.

Like a policeman I investigated, my breath making their own small clouds, until I came across an aged staircase, tucked away in a corner. I went up it with considerable caution, each step creaking painfully as it bore my weight, to come out in a low loft, beneath the naked tiles of the roof. Somewhere, behind a rafter, a bird rustled in its nest.

The room was bare but for a few tea chests which huddled together in a corner. Of these, two were empty, the others containing old tools, a broken sundial and a coil of stinking rope. But sliding the cover off the last one I found myself face to face with Fowler's porcelain head. I imagine he had been packed away in a bed of springy straw but the intervening years had withered it and only a few blackened strands of the stuff now clung to his eyes and mouth. I peered down at him in his wooden box. He stared back at me with his strange sightless eyes.

'I remember you,' I said.

All through my childhood that head sat on a mahogany chest of drawers in the corner of my father's study and I had no reason to doubt it had rested there since the very dawn of time. The bust utterly fascinated me, with his bald, inscribed cranium and his vacant gaze. Once, while my father sat at his desk, writing, I silently climbed the chair next to the cabinet and slowly reached out a hand. My finger was hardly an inch from the porcelain when my father said,

'You must not touch him, boy.'

I froze right there on tiptoe with my finger in midair.

'Touching is forbidden,' he added, then returned to his paperwork.

And now, all these years later, that same head stared up at me from a damp old crate and stirred in me a whole world of forgotten thoughts. The head was identical in every detail – except size, for it seemed strangely diminished, as if the years had worn it away. He nestled uncomfortably in the old straw, like a creature in cold hibernation.

His skull was covered with the same curious inscriptions. The porcelain was as inviting as it had always been. But my father was no longer there to scold me and I was no longer a worried young boy and I found myself reaching a hand into the crate . . . tentatively, as if towards a cornered animal.

When my fingertips were less than an inch from the porcelain they froze. I listened for the voice of my father, booming down the years. But he was quiet and too distant. And my finger touched the skull.

'Cold,' I whispered into the cold air.

With the cuff of my sable I wiped the window pane and located my gardener, fifty feet away. Managed to open the window without it coming away from its hinges and called down to him, to ask if he might lend a hand. Again, there was nothing in his attitude to suggest he had heard me – he did not look up, there was no discernible shift in direction or speed – so that I was considering calling out a second time when I saw how he was, in fact, banking slightly to the left and, in a roundabout way, wheeling his creaking barrow towards the stable door below.

The bust is no more than a foot and a half tall, but I was anxious no harm should come to it and did not trust myself to carry it all the way round to the front of the house. So when we were safely down the stable stairs my gardener (whose name, I discovered, was George) suggested I place it in his barrow with his decomposing leaves. Then he wheeled it gently around the network of paths, with me walking by his side.

'Is it heavy, George?' I asked him as we went along.

'No, Your Grace,' said George. 'It is just right.'

When we reached the front steps George lowered his barrow and offered to carry the head into the house for me. I thanked him for the offer but told him I thought I should be able to manage the rest of the way, took the head up in my arms like a baby from a perambulator and went carefully back up to my rooms.

*

The plinth is inscribed . . .

'PHRENOLOGY'

BY

L. N. FOWLER

From the base I note that he hails from Staffordshire.

A damp cloth cleaned the dirt and rotten straw from his face. He is about as good as new. He sits in his shadowy corner, pondering the same intractable puzzles he has always pondered.

Nothing seems to come or go between him and the world. His thoughts are buried deep in the pot. He might almost be a member of some shaven-headed tribe who communicate silently and on a different plane. But what lends his appearance such peculiarity are the lines which map out his skull. His face is blank but his cranium is parcelled and labelled like so many cuts of meat. Friendship, Approbativeness, Mirthfulness. All the things which fail to register on his face.

I wonder if this is the fellow. My long-lost phrenological man.

*

December 22nd

*

First thing this morning I sent a note to Mellor.

> Mellor,
> PHRENOLOGY
> – information required.

And in no time the reply came back . . .

> Your Grace,
> Information available
> – you are always welcome.

So after a lunch of buttered comfrey greens and a slice of seedie-cake I called down to Grimshaw, had him hitch up a coach and bring it round to the tunnels' landing stage.

My sable has become a little damp, lately. Smelt a bit mouldy when I put it on today, so swapped it for a redingote and cape and even forwent the beaver (I found I was in no mood for hats). Then, with one hand on the banister and the other round Fowler's head, I slowly made my way down the back staircase to the tunnels below. Clement roped a rug or two down in the dumb waiter and we were still sorting ourselves out when Grimshaw came trundling around the bend, looking very smart in knee boots, gauntlets and goggles.

Clement sat with his back to the horses and I settled Fowler's head down next to me among the tartan rugs. Then, with Grimshaw under strict instruction to avoid every pothole along the way, we set off for Holbeck village.

The floating boy grows in confidence. He came along for the ride, for most of the journey quite content to hover at the same speed as us just outside the carriage door. Like the moon on a crystal-clear night, he was, keeping up with us and peeping in. But when we neared the end of the tunnel he decided to slip inside the coach. He is a sly fellow and no mistake – always receding from view. Like the eye-detritus of hair and such which obscures my vision on sunny days. Always skimming off into the periphery and impossible to pin down.

I did manage to snatch a glimpse of him today before he ducked out of sight. He is a tiny fellow, not much more than a babe-in-arms. His flesh is the same colour as Fowler's head – luminous-white, like the clouds – which made such an impression on me that, without meaning to, I blurted out, 'Both so very white,' which caused Clement to give me a most quizzical look. I had to pretend I had nodded off for a second and was talking in my sleep.

When we reached Holbeck I asked Clement and Grimshaw to wait in the carriage and assured them I would not be long. Gingerly made my way up Mellor's garden path with Fowler's head peeping over one shoulder and the boy-in-the-moon floating on the other. The Reverend, clean shaven this time, opened the door straight away, saying, 'I see you have brought a friend along,' and I was stumped for a second as to which of my creamy companions he referred to.

At the edge of the sea of knick-knack laden tables I became worried lest I trip and smash my phrenology head. Asked Mellor if he would mind playing St Christopher.

'Not at all, Your Grace,' he said, and took him from me

with admirable sureness (which I attributed to his many christenings) then he was off, gracefully weaving his rotund little body through the maze of book-towers and fragile glassware towards the fireside, while I did my best to stay on his tail. As we picked our way through the debris, Fowler's head peered back at me over Mellor's shoulder and a song of wonderful whiteness composed itself in my mind.

When we were seated and had cups of tea in our hands, Mellor allowed himself a closer look at the head. He seemed very pleased.

'So what's your knowledge of Phrenology, Your Grace?' he asked.

'Of the philosophy, next to nothing,' I admitted, but went on to tell him how, as a child, my head had been measured (very roughly, I might add) by some old gent with bony fingers, while my mother and father looked concernedly on. I recalled the phrenologist taking from his case a huge pair of callipers which he proceeded to place over my skull. I can still see me perching on my wobbly stool, overflowing with apprehension, convinced that at any moment the old fellow was going to plunge the tips of those callipers right into my temples.

'Very fashionable at one time,' said Mellor. 'You will have heard, perhaps, that Her Majesty had a phrenologist measure each of her offspring's heads?'

He is a regular treasure-chest of information, is Mellor. A walking, talking book. And, without the least bit of prompting on my part, I found myself the recipient of what turned out to be a great torrent of the stuff. This particular torrent was all to do with the science of Phrenology – the chap who had originally come up with it (named *suchandsuch*) and how the science had first spread across Europe (by two other fellows) then across the Atlantic (by some other chap). Names and dates swept all around me, as well as the marching feet of large committees of medical men – some of whom were in favour of phrenology, but most of whom were decidedly against – until finally it was all I could do to hang on to the arms of my chair and try and keep myself from being washed away.

How much of this impressive oration was spontaneous and how much had been prepared I could not say. It is quite possible the Reverend had been cramming from some text-book right up until the moment I knocked at his front door. On the other hand, it might simply be that his is one of those minds which drinks up every drop of information it is offered and has no trouble in later pouring it back out. Either way, I just about managed to withstand Mellor's assault on me without either falling asleep or falling off my chair and came out clutching what I reckon to be the gist of the matter ... namely, that phrenology was an attempt to gauge an individual's character by recording the various bumps and hollows on that person's head. Each bump, depending on its whereabouts, suggests a predominance of a particular quality – Hope, Spirituality, Firmness, etc. – so that by consulting a map (or a model, like Fowler's head) the phrenologist can assess the head in hand.

'Not many of the old fellows left kicking about, Your Grace,' said Mellor. 'The whole caboodle fell out of favour some years ago.'

Then he paused and looked me squarely in the eyes.

'Beg your pardon in asking, Your Grace, but where does this sudden interest in phrenology spring from?'

Fowler's head sat coyly in Mellor's lap. The pair of them stared silently at me. If I had not known and trusted them both so well I might have imagined they were ganging-up on me.

The silence spread across the prickly room. I took the opportunity to look around for my boy-in-the-moon. I searched every last inch of my periphery but found he had slipped away.

'I have given the matter a good deal of thought,' I heard me say, 'and have concluded that what I need is a good head-man.'

The Reverend nodded slowly at me, gently placed Fowler on the rug and hupped himself out of his chair. He then proceeded to spend the next five minutes clinging to the rock face of his bookshelves, picking over their spines with a tilted head. He hum-hummed to himself and ground his teeth and paused only to draw out some huge leathery slab. As the minutes crept by and the book-hunt pressed on I thought I saw him grow increasingly discouraged, until at last he stepped back from one shelf with an expression of great suspicion on his face – as if the books had been guilty of conspiring against him. He turned slowly, slowly . . . listening, it seemed, for the scurrying footfalls of his prey's retreat.

'Ah-ha,' he said, and pounced upon a seemingly-innocent table. He wrestled briefly with its pile of papers, whipped out a cardboard folder from its base and left the whole precarious structure swaying from side to side.

He returned, removing a single sheet from the file.

'Here she is,' he said, and dropped it in my lap.

The paper was all yellowed with age and eaten away at the edges, but the illustration was perfectly intact. And what a strange and exotic picture, to be sure – a cross-section of a head, much like Fowler's, but nothing like as mundanely numbered or named. At first I thought it was some sort of head-hotel, for in each compartment miniature folk posed, in representation of all the characteristics of Man. Here in tableau-form were Self-Esteem (a proud couple strolling in the country) and Suavity (some slippery-looking fellow, drawing the reader in with a crooked finger). Here was

Combativeness, personified by two boxers ... in fact, all the human qualities, good and bad, with a man or woman acting them out in their own little cell.

'Wonderful,' I told the Reverend.

'A gift,' he replied, before adding, 'Not very rare.'

I thanked him all the same and was already planning how it might fit into my shrine. I continued to examine the picture while I got around to asking if he might know where I might find a good head-man.

I waited a second before looking up. When I did so I found he had fixed me with a wry expression.

'A head-man? Well, as I said, Your Grace – phrenologists are very much a dying breed. But, if pressed, I would have to say Edinburgh. That's where the last of them retreated to.'

'Edinburgh,' I said.

'I know a professor there. An old friend of mine ... I could introduce you. I'm sure he'd see you straight.'

'And are there tunnels to Edinburgh?' I asked.

He shook his head.

'Not yet, Your Grace.'

This was a big disappointment. I rather hoped there might have been.

'Edinburgh,' I said. 'Very well.'

I was making ready to leave when the Reverend caught me by my coat sleeve and whispered excitedly in my ear.

'Before you go, I must show you my latest acquisition.'

And he trotted off to burrow in some corner, returning with what I first took to be a pair of thick spectacles which had a strip of card attached. He was fairly beaming as he handed the strange contraption over.

'Try them on,' he said.

Well, I slipped the things over my nose and as I did so, a photograph came into view. But – how extraordinary! – one with lifelike depth of field. A young boy sat with an open book in his lap, yet the table in the foreground and the wall behind seemed to exist on quite separate planes. Remarkable! As I moved my head from side to side I could even sense some parallax. For the sake of it I peeped over the glasses at the piece of card and saw two identical photographs, side by side, but when I looked back through the glasses they merged into a single, startling image with all dimensions accounted for.

'Stereoscopic,' announced Mellor over my shoulder.

'Very good,' I said. 'And what is the scene?'

'"A boy, reflecting",' he told me. 'What do you say to that?'

When I left I had my new phrenology head-map under one arm, all rolled up and tied with string, and Fowler's porcelain head under the other. Clement and Grimshaw sat stiffly in the carriage, wrapped in the tartan rugs. I must say, they looked quite cold.

Mrs Pledger's Account

It has long been a tradition at Welbeck that on Christmas Eve every employee of the House and estate drop by with their families in the afternoon. Nothing much, just a stand-up buffet in the ballroom and some games for the little ones. But mainly just an excuse for a get-together and the opportunity to wish each other well.

So, around three o'clock His Grace comes down for ten minutes or so, to help ladle out the punch. He was never one to make a speech or draw attention to himself and it is not as if anyone expected it. But when one year he joined in a game of dominoes with some of the children it was talked about for weeks on end. Just a little thing like that, you see, but it goes a very long way.

Well, me and the girls had put some effort into it the last time round. We'd made a big potato salad, brought up some smoked hams and laid it all out on the best tablecloths. But it had got to three o'clock, then quarter past and half past with nobody having seen hide nor hair of His Grace. So Clement goes off and searches for him and eventually tracks him down in some corner of his rooms with his books and charts. Tries to get him down, to show his face just for a second, but His Grace says that he is busy and to leave him alone.

Well, some of us see him every day of our lives but for others it might be the only time they will see him from one year to the next and when it becomes clear His Grace is not to make an appearance people begin to drift away. And all this time he was upstairs reading. What is one to make of that?

It was later on that His Grace came down and apologized. Said he had not realized that it was Christmas Eve and was quite upset. But when a fellow forgets it's Christmas something is definitely wrong. It's not just the effort. It's people's feelings I'm talking about.

From His Grace's Journal

Edinburgh, January 6th

*

By eight o'clock this morning we were on the platform at Worksop station with time enough to stand and watch the train come rolling in. There was an unholy commotion of steam and brakes before it juddered to a halt and blocked out what little light had previously illuminated the place. I was helped up into my carriage by Clement, who then heaved himself and the baggage in after me; he swung my cases easily up onto the racks and generally fussed about the place. I must say I had not expected the carriage to be so luxuriously fitted-out. The last time I travelled by train it was little more than a wooden box with a leaking roof, but now there are curtains and cushions and carpets and even a mirror in which to comb one's hair.

I had on my William IV coat with its high moon pockets and deep collar and a letter of introduction from Mellor tucked away somewhere. On the seat beside me I placed my knapsack which had in it a vegetable pie, some fruit and pastries and a flask of hot sweet tea. It had been my intention to travel to Edinburgh alone and to stand on my own two feet, but I had come under pressure from various quarters to allow Clement to come along. It was Mrs Pledger who pointed out that my shirts and trousers would need pressing after spending the best part of a day crammed in their cases, and that though there may be no end of boot-cleaners in our hotel there is slim chance they will know one end of a boot from the other. So I relented, on the strict understanding that he travel up in a separate carriage and generally keep out of sight, so that anyone coming upon me these next few days might think me a regular and independent man about town.

Clement was now back on the platform, checking departure times with various railwaymen and working himself up into a right old state. And now he was back in the carriage and checking me for the journey and now very reluctant to close the door.

I shooed him away with my cane until he finally relinquished the door. Then a guard came along and slammed it shut and Clement loped off to his own carriage. Then somewhere down the platform a whistle was blown and a second later the whole contraption made an awful lurch, followed by a series of smaller, more frequent lurches until my tiny, fancily-furnished room began to carry me away. I poked my head out of the window to watch the station slide by and saw Clement two carriages back down the train, looking anxiously up at me. I shouted at him to put his head in and eventually he did as he was told. I suppose he just wants to be sure of me. But he needn't have worried for I had my floating boy for company.

The engine dragged us through the town, coughing and spluttering most unhealthily, but gradually managed to clear its lungs and soon we were out of Worksop and generally flying along. The wheels squealed on the tracks beneath me like little pigs and through the window the hills took to rising and falling in great earthy waves and, what with farms and cows slipping past as if on greased wheels, I must admit I began to feel a little sick. Drew the curtains to try and quell the queasiness and took deep breaths until some composure had been regained.

Clement had taken the precaution of fixing a sign to my door which read

ESPECIALLY RESERVED

so that passengers waiting to board at stations along the way would be discouraged from barging in on me.

Well, we seemed to call in on just about every town and village in the North of England; forever pulling to or pulling away. There was a little porthole by the curtained window and at the first few stations I stood on the seat and peered out to watch the people come and go. Huge trunks were being wheeled in every direction and there were kisses and handshakes and embraces and much waving of handkerchiefs as we set off. But I soon tired of spying on these anonymous leave-takings and as the stations grew steadily further apart I slipped slowly into a not unpleasant torpor.

An hour or two later, I ate some pie.

Although I was very nicely curtained-away and cordoned-off, at every stop the station's noises still bundled their way in. Countless calls of 'Take care!' and 'Write . . . Promise to write!' came through to me, along with 'Give my love to suchandsuch . . .' – all punctuated by the shrill comma of the guard's whistle and the clatter of slamming doors.

I found myself unintentionally eavesdropping on these hurried farewells and began to note how, mingling with the voices of the returning Scots, one could make out the local accents and how, as we ventured further north, these slowly shifted from one brogue to the next.

The boy in the bubble floated up by the luggage rack with his back turned most defiantly towards me. I thought perhaps he bore me a grudge of some sort; an idea which I proposed to him, but which received no reply. He is not a very talkative chap.

We had been travelling for several hours and I was

beginning to feel thoroughly bored. So bored, in fact, that while I knew we were still a good way from Edinburgh, I resolved to leave the curtains open at the next stop and as we sped across a viaduct I slipped my arm out of the open window and removed the sign which Clement had fixed to the door. I told myself that if Fate decides that I should have travelling companions then so be it. I had a sudden desire to be in the company of my fellow man.

By Newcastle my fellow man had taken the shape of a young mother and her twins (a boy and girl, aged about five years old) and a severe-looking chap in his fifties with an over-waxed moustache. My hopes of some camaraderie between fellow travellers were dashed immediately: the young woman was almost too exhausted to lift her children up onto the seats and the attitude of the gentleman who sat down next to me made it quite plain that conversation was the last thing on his mind. After our initial greetings I think not a single word was exchanged. The children were the epitome of good behaviour, only piping up once or twice, but each time met by a vicious glance from the evil Moustache Man. So imposing was his presence that I became aware how my own gaze had rationed itself to the smallest plot of carpeted floor, my eyes barely daring to stray from it. At the time I wondered (as indeed I wonder now) how we can allow one person to get away with so wilfully and malevolently imposing himself on a situation and generally poisoning the atmosphere. Perhaps it is the strangeness of modern travel which cultivates such dismal isolation in its human freight.

The train brought us right alongside the North Sea, which was a wonderful brackeny-brown and so utterly sharp and shiny it looked to have been hacked out of flint. If I had been on my own I might have opened up the window and drawn great draughts of the sea air into me. As it was, all five of us stared rather balefully at it before returning our gazes to their prison cells.

Soon after, one of the twins let out a terrific yawn, totally debilitating its little owner. It was then a wonder to see the speed at which the same condition struck down the rest of us, though we adults hid ours behind raised palms and subjected them to such terrible compression as to squeeze all the pleasure out of them. Even so, the young one's yawn swept round the carriage like a contagious infection, bouncing from seat to seat just like a ball. And very soon, we all found ourselves vacant-eyed and full of sighs, as we surrendered to the motion of the train. And we adults were all slowly reduced to infants, each one of us rocked in our mother's arms, so that while we failed to come together in conversation in the first place we found ourselves united in sleep at the last.

*

Edinburgh, January 7th

*

A free day before visiting Professor Bannister so Clement and I spent the morning touring the town. As we trailed up and down the windy streets, going from tea-house on to tailor, I noticed how strangely everybody appears to be dressing these days – hats and collars so meanly cut. Felt quite old-fashioned and over-fancy in my burnous and tall hat and my shirt with its double frill.

After lunch, on Mellor's recommendation, we visited the famous Camera Obscura, which is right at the top of the High Street just outside the Castle gates. It is a chubby sort of tower, a little like a lighthouse, but has a half-timbered air about it and a wholly wooden hat.

Mellor had become highly animated when telling me about the place, saying how he never visited Edinburgh without calling in at the Camera. So, having located it, we went straight in and up to a tiny counter where I paid our pennies to a woman dressed from head to toe in tweed. She congratulated us on choosing such a breezy day for our visit as all the morning cloud had been blown away, thereby guaranteeing, she insisted, a particularly spectacular show. Heartened by this news we set off up the stone steps – hundreds of them, there were, like marching to the top of the world – to emerge, at last, on a high terrace where three other gentlemen stood, smoking and taking in the view. And what a prospect! – so grand and gratifying it alone was worth the effort and the entrance fee.

The Camera shares the Castle's great chunk of rock, so we had an almost perfect panorama of the vertiginous city below.

'So many spires,' I said to Clement, who nodded vaguely in reply.

Indeed, there looked to be one on just about every street corner, puncturing the firmament. The nearest clouds were banked up on the horizon several miles away and the sky was a most heavenly hue, lending all the roofs and churches an even frostier sharpness and making one's eyes prickle with delight. I had counted well over a dozen spires and steeples and had plenty more to go, when the woman in tweed (and a magnificent pair of brogues, I might add) came puffing up the steps.

'This way, gentlemen, if you please,' she announced.

She opened up a door off the terrace and waved us into a wooden room, which from the outside looked like a tall windowless gazebo or a bathing-machine with the wheels removed.

Now, I must admit that as we were herded towards that tiny room I had not the least idea what to expect. The Reverend Mellor, whilst heartily promoting the Camera

Obscura and even endeavouring to describe the mechanics involved, had left me with no abiding notion as to what the occasion might actually entail. So, finding myself in a small round room with only a high ceiling to distinguish it, I will admit I was a trifle disappointed. If we were to bear witness to a visual demonstration of the magnitude and beauty which the Reverend had led me to expect, then surely, I mused, some major gadgetry would have to be drafted in.

As these thoughts drifted around my head the woman in tweed closed the door behind her, then took a minute or two to introduce us to the basic principles of the Camera. I was not overly impressed and took some satisfaction from seeing another chap stifle a yawn. But when she reached over and began to dim the lamps I was suddenly all eyes and ears as it dawned on me I might be about to endure another session as claustrophobic as the one in Mellor's cave. So in those last moments before we were completely engulfed in darkness I made quite sure I had located the door's precise whereabouts, in case I was gripped by another fearful attack and had to make a sudden and embarrassing dash for it. 'Small wonder this is such a favourite of Mellor's,' I thought to myself, as my stomach tied itself in a familiar panicky knot and the darkness swept up from the corners and covered the room and its inhabitants with its gloomy cloak.

But, as in the cave, one moment I was on the verge of absolute terror, with my own child's voice screaming in my ear, and the next I found myself landed on the other side of the abyss. Somehow the knot in my stomach had been magically undone and I was keen and lucid again.

Like my co-spectators I rested my hands on a circular railing and looked down on a broad concave table – perfectly smooth and white – whilst the woman in tweed pressed on with her practised intonation about the room in which we stood. With one hand she had hold of a long wooden rod which hung down from the high ceiling and as our eyes accustomed themselves to the dark she gradually became more visible. Her hands and face had about them a ghostly luminosity. She twisted the rod, saying, '. . . the same principle as the camera. A tiny aperture in the roof allows an image to be cast on the dish below . . .'

And indeed, as her incantation washed over me I saw the first outlines of a picture take shape. I saw trees – the trees of the nearby gardens, their branches slowly coming into focus, whilst behind, the whole length of Princes Street was emerging from the mist. It was as if we were witnessing, from a bird's-eye view, the very making of Edinburgh. For a minute I was quite overcome with emotion and when I snatched a glance at my fellows found my own astonishment reflected there. Like characters in a Rembrandt their faces shone with the dish's milky light.

I looked back to the dish just in time to see the whole picture suddenly slip on its axis, accompanied by the creaking of the tweedy woman's rod as it was twisted in her grip. The castle swung into view.

'Hurrah,' cried one of the other gentlemen.

'The Fortress,' announced our guide.

Every detail was sharp as a pin now and I was thinking how remarkably like a photograph this image was – a very round and colourful one at that – when a seagull sailed right across the shallow bowl and the scene was suddenly brought to life. Well, the whole company burst into startled laughter. One or two started chattering excitedly.

'What we see,' announced our guide, as if to calm us, 'is not fixed but a living image of the world outside.'

So there we stood, in the belly of a breathing camera, as the whole city leaked into us through a single beam of light. Yet the vision it cast among us was not in any way frozen but as real and vivid as could be.

As we watched that white dish and clung to our railing we were transported through each of the city's three hundred and sixty degrees. Here were horse-drawn trolleys inching up the High Street, past street pedlars with their baskets laid out – all the trade and transport of a working city, with the deep sea standing by.

The whole of Edinburgh was poured into the bowl before us, as if we were ringside angels, yet was conjured out of nothing more than a couple of lenses and a small hole in the roof.

*

When we emerged blinking into the daylight I honestly felt as if I had sat in the lap of the gods. And for the rest of the day, as we carried on with our sightseeing, I found I had to keep the odd giggle from slipping out.

*

Edinburgh, January 8th

*

'Professor Bannister,' I say, holding out my hand.

'Come, come,' says the tall fellow, and waves a finger in my face like a metronome. 'William, if you please.'

I was in the very bowels of the University's Anatomy Department, meeting the man around whom this whole trip had been arranged and, judging by the deference bestowed upon him by his students and colleagues outside his office and the capaciousness within, he must be a singularly important chap, for he had sofas and armchairs and an aged chaise, not to mention a vast writing desk with a green leather top.

The Professor set about impressing upon me what old friends he and Mellor were. And, for a while, we juggled between us the pleasantries such occasions demand, regarding train journeys and the dampness of Edinburgh, before we returned to our mutual friend.

'Is he still round?' asked Bannister.

'Very round,' I replied, which seemed to please him no end.

'Excellent,' he said most earnestly, and ushered me into a chair.

I should, I think, make some reference to my host's extraordinary height, as this greatly occupied my mind at the time, in that having taken his own seat he proceeded to cross his long legs with such far-reaching swiftness I worried he might inadvertently cut me down.

'Heads, is it?' said William Bannister, waving my letter of introduction at me. 'Mellor says it's heads you want.'

'Information, rather than the heads themselves,' I replied, rather lamely. 'I am . . . working on a project to do with heads.'

He smiled at me, slid down into his chair a foot or two, made a church and steeple with his fingers and perched his chin on top. In retrospect, I appreciate that his silence most likely denoted a man who was ordering his thoughts (for I soon discovered he had no shortage of them), but at the time I wondered if he hadn't simply drawn a blank. The only animation about the man was the huge foot which balanced on the kneecap and waggled madly, as if all his energy had congregated there. He sized me up for another minute, pursed his lips, then finally let loose.

And I must say he turned out to be about as full of head-information as a man could possibly wish: how a head might be judged and measured, for example, or how it might be broken and repaired. In fact, it soon became clear that, like his old friend Mellor, Professor Bannister was a wordy fount and once his tongue had properly got into its stride it left me struggling far behind.

Unfortunately, his monologue seemed to me quite tedious, being marred in two different ways. Firstly, the *tone*, which was academic and totally humourless (no anecdotes, which will often keep my interest up). Secondly, the *sheer magnitude* of the thing for, stored in his skull, he seemed to have information equivalent to several dozen regular headfuls and in no time my own rather small, unacademic head was filled right to the brim.

After twenty minutes I was so thoroughly saturated I began to wonder if he did not perhaps have some work he should be returning to and my only participation had been whittled right down to the odd nod or grunt, to signify I was still awake. Then, right in the middle of this very erudite and thoroughly boring flood of words, my ear caught hold of a vaguely familiar term. A phrase I must have come across in one of my medical dictionaries.

'Trepanning?' I said (putting something of a stick in the Professor's spokes). 'Now what is that all about?'

Well, at first he was quite floored by my interruption. He looked like a man who had just been snapped out of an hypnotic trance.

'A hole in the head, Your Grace,' he said. 'A man-made hole.'

And an arm reached out to a distant desk, scrabbled among the papers for a second or two, before scissoring back and dropping into my lap a yellowed, jawless skull.

'Well held, sir,' said Bannister.

I turned the thing cautiously in my hands. I was beginning to understand why Bannister and Mellor are such firm friends – both are such wordy fellows and both enjoy sporting with bones.

Having a dead man's head rolling in my hands made me feel a little strange, but I was determined not to be outdone and managed to gamely ask, 'And who is this fellow, then?'

'That is *Homo erectus amazonas*, Your Grace. We found him down in Brazil.'

I had a good long look at what was left of him – I had never met a Brazilian before – and gently ran a finger along the fine fissures where the different continents of the skull had merged.

'If you care to look at the crown,' Bannister told me from the depths of his chair, 'you'll find a hole about three-quarters of an inch wide.'

Indeed I did.

'Now, while we medical men find these holes very handy for carrying old skulls about the place – one's middle finger fitting so snugly inside – there are a good many in our profession who claim that such holes are, in fact, the result of primitive surgery . . .'

'But why would a Brazilian consent to having a hole made in his skull?' I asked.

'Well now, Your Grace, that's a fair question, for there's no evidence that the fellow consented to any such thing. But it is commonly held that such operations were undertaken in order to release Evil Spirits.'

I looked down at the dried old husk in my hands. Whatever once possessed it had long since upped and gone.

'Tell me, William,' I said, continuing to look down at the skull, 'are men still trepanned today?'

'O, plenty. Plenty of them. I should say there are several hundred people currently walking about with some sort of hole-in-the-head. Though not for spiritual reasons, of course, but to relieve a haemorrhage perhaps or to allow us to have a poke around. But, to answer your question . . . Yes, Your Grace. We still like to make the odd hole or two.'

Bannister was now so far down in his armchair he was practically horizontal, with his legs stretched out before him and his feet crossed neatly at the ankles. I was anticipating another verbal onslaught when, quite without warning, an arm swung out from his body and came at me like the boom on a boat. I had to duck down out of the way as it swept around the room. When it finally came to rest I saw how the finger at the end of it was pointing towards a glass cabinet on the other side of the room.

'Have a gander at my old John Weiss,' said Bannister.

So I made my way over to the cabinet and found behind the glass a slim case, about ten inches by five. In its open mouth lay a row of evilly-gleaming instruments.

'A trepanning kit, Your Grace,' said Bannister, coming alongside. 'A little out of date, but beautifully made, wouldn't you say?'

It certainly was. Like terrible jewellery; each piece very snug in its own velvet bed. The centrepiece resembling a small carpenter's drill – but not so modest – with a finely turned wooden handle at one end and all glinting metal at the other. Its own little army of apostles lined up on either side. But I was baffled by a tiny brush and a phial of oil which lay in their own little concavities.

'For lubrication,' Bannister explained.

I was so completely taken with this macabre machinery that I asked the Professor where one might purchase such a trepanation kit. But he was quite emphatic that such things were not commonly available to non-medical folk, so I said no more on the matter.

*

Bannister took me out to his dining club for luncheon, which was entirely unexpected and very kind indeed. I have had very little appetite lately, the food in the hotel being far too fancy, but when we were seated and served and Bannister launched into another incomprehensible monologue (something to do with carbon this time, I think) I rather found myself tucking in. We had a thick broth, grilled trout, spicy plum pudding and a bottle of sweet red wine. I was sleepily spooning the plum stones in the bottom of my bowl when some sort of rumpus went off at the table to my right.

There was the scraping of chair legs, the clatter of abandoned cutlery and the sound of conversations being hastily brought to a halt – in other words, that particular atmosphere which usually precedes some sort of fight. I was still trying to identify the protagonists (and praying the mêlée would not spread and engulf any innocent by-standers, such as myself) when Bannister suddenly sprang up from the table, sending his chair skittering off across the floor.

I had not the slightest idea how he had been drawn into it. Perhaps looks and glances had been exchanged. But in a couple of strides he was at the next table, had a fellow by the throat and was pushing him right back in his chair. The chap with Bannister's hands clamped on his windpipe was flat on his back in no time at all, whereupon Bannister jumped on top of him, sat on his chest and pinned his arms down with his long legs. Then his hand went hard down into the fellow's face. Screams now came from all parts of the room and one woman (who I took to be the fellow's wife) tugged vainly at Bannister's shoulder as he drove his fingers down into the fellow's throat.

When his hand came back up it had a piece of pork fat dangling from the fingers. It was very white and very wet. Bannister dropped it into a nearby saucer, then helped the unfortunate diner back to his feet.

'Thank you, sir. Thank you,' said the red-faced fellow. 'The damned thing got caught right under my tongue.'

But Bannister merely bowed a restrained little bow and returned to the table, while the rest of the room babbled admiringly.

'Some people simply refuse to chew their food,' he confided in me, wiping the grease from his fingers with his napkin.

The dining room slowly restored itself. The conversation

settled, the broken crockery was cleared away. The chap who had got the chop fat lodged in his gullet came by to shake my companion's hand and heap yet more praise on him.

When he was finally out of the way Bannister got to his feet.

'Well, onward and upward,' he announced. 'What says Your Grace?'

I said that 'onward and upward' sounded like good advice. So we collected our coats and hats at the cloakroom and went out into the already-darkening day.

*

That morning Bannister had suggested I look around his Special Collection, the implication being that this was something of an honour for a layman such as myself. By the time we emerged from the dining club, however, I would have been happy to go back to my hotel and spend the rest of the afternoon in bed. But, as I have already mentioned, William Bannister is very keen on remembering those details others might be inclined to forget. So, with his long arm around my shoulders, I found myself escorted back to the Anatomy Department and being led left and right and right and left and eventually down into the deepest depths of the place.

At the bottom of the steps stood a pair of doors with frosted windows which I thought very pretty indeed, and I might have stood there admiring their wintry sparkle a good while longer had Bannister not given me a smart shove towards them.

'You should find everything labelled,' he told me. 'Enjoy yourself,' and disappeared back up the steps.

It was not long before I was regretting having eaten such a substantial lunch or, come to that, having lunched at all. The vast white room was much too brightly lit and the bottles and jars and glass cases all gleamed like great chunks of ice. But as I made my way among them I recoiled not from the piercing light and its many reflections but from the overwhelming, all-pervading smell. The air was awash with formaldehyde – was warm and sticky with the stuff – so that, advancing down that first aisle of exhibits, I wondered if, by the time I came to leave the place, my own organs might not be as pickled as those on show.

That atmosphere of profound liquidity encouraged in me the notion that I made my way through some underwater world, for I found myself in the company of entities so wet and strange they would have looked more at home on an ocean bed. I could have read my *Gray's Anatomy* cover to cover a thousand times without preparing myself in the least. The lasting impression was of my having come upon an awful carnage, the result, perhaps, of a terrible explosion, which had scattered its victims into several hundred jars.

Handling the bones of an Ancient Brazilian may be fairly gruesome but coming face to face with his descendants' bottled brawn is something else again. Man had never seemed to me so mortal, had never seemed so sad. For as I slowly padded through that vast stinking room the voice which spoke to me most intelligently was a melancholy one – seemed to seep right through the thick glass jars.

Having never previously come across a man's vitals I was hardly likely to recognize them. Thus, here (the label assured me), suspended in alcohol, was a human heart, looking like nothing but a soft black stone. Here was a sectioned kidney, like a mushroom ready for the frying pan. All around me the innermost, most secret pieces of man were laid bare, hanging slack and horribly sodden in their prison-jars.

A Cumberland sausage of intestine.

A single eyeball dangling in fleshy mid-trajectory.

A human tongue, long enough to choke a man, coiled up like an eel.

And a brain – a man's brain, for goodness' sake! – with all

the contours of a bloated walnut. And not the ocean-blue I had always imagined but a dismal, pasty grey.

A curious construction, marked 'broncho-pulmonary', sat atop a pedestal in a fancy bell jar and which, after much puzzled label-reading, I finally understood as being an intricate representation of the interior of a lung. Again, I found my own picture of a body's mechanics well wide of the mark. The inside of my lung is apparently less like the branches of a leafless tree and more like a coral bouquet. Yet even this beautiful, bizarre lung-tiara, I thought, seemed to sparkle in a mournful way.

The whole collection evoked in me tremendous feeling. Certainly there was horror in those glass cases and some peculiar pulchritude to admire, but above all else I sensed that every organ was drenched in the same sad concentrate and that disappointment filled every last vessel.

I had wandered up and down those humid aisles for getting on half an hour and, rather surprisingly, my lunch had stayed where it was, when the following idea occurred to me . . .

> Is it not possible to take all these marinaded pieces and reintroduce them to one another? To recreate out of all these miserable, disparate parts one frail but functioning human being?
>
> But the answer was all too apparent.
>
> No, of course it is not possible. He has been unwhole for far too long. If he was put back together there would be no making sense of him. He would be an altogether too vinegary man.

By now, I had had enough of the place and was making my way towards the door, eager to fill my lungs with fresh air, when I came across an exhibit which struck such a deep chord in me that it stopped me in my tracks. Through the jar's inch-thick glass I saw what appeared to be a tiny but perfectly-formed child. The little fellow was all hunched-over. His bald head was bowed in meditation, his hands rested delicately on his knees. He seemed to float in an entirely different world to me, looked to be scowling with concentration. But from under his right knee I saw that there dangled an umbilicus, which hung uselessly like a disconnected pipe. And at that moment I realized that he had, in fact, never lived outside the confines of his mother's belly – was but a foetus of a child. He must have gone straight from the warmth of the womb to the awful chill of the jar, effectively living and dying without ever having breathed a mouthful of air.

How close he had come to being born or the circumstances of his death I could not tell. The label made no mention of these facts. Yet he had on his head a smattering of hair, had fingernails and neat little toes . . . all the detail of a born boy-child.

There was something familiar in his luminosity. Something in the magnification of the water and the glass. I looked in on him, hoping he might unfold himself and look me in the eye. But he did nothing but peer down into the solution which buoyed his poor body up.

*

As I was sitting here in my hotel room and recording the entry above I was reminded, no doubt by all the meaty imagery, of the one time I saw a rabbit being prepared for the pot.

I happened to call in on one of my gatekeepers and found him sharpening up a knife for the job. I remember the rabbit hanging forlornly in the corner from a hook on one of the kitchen's beams and my keeper going over and gently lifting it down and laying it on the table top. The prospect of a rabbit-skinning quite intrigued me, so I asked if he would mind me staying to see how it was done.

I reckon I must have thought back to that day a hundred different times in an attempt to get a hold on that transformation; trying to locate the precise moment when the rabbit ceases to be a creature and becomes nothing more than a piece of meat. Certainly, when one looks upon a dead rabbit one easily senses the difference between it and the rabbits which live and breathe. Its head hangs too heavily, its limbs are limp, it is too deeply asleep. Yet one somehow imagines the situation might be resolvable. As if the rabbit has just temporarily lost its quick. One feels that if one could only summon up in one's lungs some essential heat or spirit one might breathe some life back into it.

But to see the rabbit stripped of its fur and see its flesh bloodily gleam is to admit to some important threshold having been crossed and that only a genius with a needle and thread could return this animal to its previous form. I recall the fur being peeled back with care (even kindness), as if helping an aged relative off with her coat. The leg-joints were neatly bent and tucked in order to ease them out.

Only when the creature's head is detached from the body can one say with certainty that the process is complete. For when the cleaver strikes cleanly through the neck and its awful edge is sunk in the chopping block, then both parts of the bloody rabbit must know how significantly they have been rent. And when the head is gone we have no eyes, either conscious or unconscious, and it is there that we plumb for life.

When the belly is slit open and the innards are removed (although, to be perfectly honest, I cannot now recall at which point in the proceedings this took place) we are, without doubt, in the domain of the butcher, not the open field. And by the time the keeper had done with his twitching knife and gone off in search of herbs and onions to accompany the grey-red chunks into the pot, what I looked upon was not a rabbit but most definitely rabbit-meat (which, not surprisingly, I have never had much fancy for).

*

EDINBURGH, JANUARY 9TH

*

Last night, when I was all tucked-up in bed with the light out and just beginning to drift away, I caught a glimpse of the most distant, yet heartfelt memory. A recollection of some moment before my birth. There I was in my mother's belly; warm. My whole world very close to me. Yet there was something else – something important. Some other aspect which has slipped away. It is hard to find words to describe a time before words were available to me. But I have no doubt that what I momentarily caught hold of was a memory of the womb.

*

This morning I decided to stroll up to the Castle and break in a new pair of boots. Allowed Clement to come along, on the understanding that he walk several yards behind. I think the wind must have been behind us for we reached our destination in no time at all and finding I still had a little spirit to spare I left Clement at a chop house and carried on down the High Street to pick up some tobacco.

Bought a 'Visitor's Guide to the City' from an old woman on the corner of Bank Street and was pleased to find it contained a folded map – very simple, about two foot wide. The old lady, who wore a pair of spectacles with one lens missing, said it was by far the best street map of Edinburgh . . . of such quality that it had won an award.

'What sort of award?' I asked her.

'A map award,' she replied.

No doubt. Well, I asked if she knew a good tobacconist in the neighbourhood. A straightforward question, one would have thought, but one which provoked in her no end of personal discord and face-pulling before she finally reached some tentative agreement with herself. Having firmed up her directions she informed me how if I took the next-but-one passage off to the right and descended two long flights of steps I should come out right opposite one of the best tobacco shops in town.

Well, I thanked her, set off and, as directed, turned right at the second passage along the way. So confident was I of my imminently entering the tobacco shop and hearing the 'ding-a-ling' of the bell above my head that I had gone down, I think, three flights of steps and was climbing a fourth before I sensed that I might have gone awry.

Twenty yards further down the passageway I found myself at the wrong end of a cul-de-sac. A huge iron gate stood before me, bound by a rusty chain and lock. At this point I felt distinctly worried. No, why should I lie? Panic is what I felt. I saw at once how that old crone had led me – a stranger in town and about as green as the hills – into an easy trap and how, any minute now, some great lumbering nephew of hers would descend on me, club me on the noggin and rob me of every last penny in my purse.

So I filled my lungs in preparation for a desperate cry for help and my head prepared itself to be clubbed. I waited . . . then waited a minute longer. The lumbering youth must have forgotten our violent little tryst, so I set off back down the steps as fast as my old legs would go.

When I descended that first flight on returning I saw a

passageway off to the left which I must have gone straight past before. It looked long and dark and full of drips. Was it possible that the old woman had included an extra turn in her instructions and that I had not taken it in? Perhaps she had meant to mention it but had omitted it and the mistake was on her side? Either way, I decided to follow the passage for a minute or two and that if the tobacco shop had not given itself up by then, I would simply turn myself around and come straight back.

Well, I can only imagine that I took another left or right which went unaccounted when I tried to return. For within five minutes I was feeling as if I were the object of some practical joke, whereby a half-dozen stagehands constantly switched the set between my going and coming back. The passage walls, however, seemed quite solid and not like the set of a play at all. My bearings found no tally in their surroundings. In other words, I was completely lost.

Then I suddenly remembered my award-winning map and got it out and studied it very hard, as if the sheer intensity of my gaze might draw from it the information I required. But, of course, a map is absolutely useless unless one can say for certain whereabouts one is on it, and as there was not a single street sign on the walls around me I might as well have held up a blank sheet of paper and tried to set a course from that.

Well, I must have bounced around those passageways for getting on three-quarters of an hour, with that map flapping uselessly in one hand. My mind became the debating chamber for two fiercely dissenting voices . . . one reassuring me that I would be out of this awful stone maze the next minute, the other screaming that I would never get out alive.

All this time I did not come across a single other soul. It was bitterly cold and every door and window was firmly shut. If I had been wandering across a desert, I thought to myself, I would have about as much hope of finding a helping hand. Tenement buildings towered all around me and every once in a while I would come out into their yards. No doubt there were people within a few feet of me who knew this labyrinth like the back of their hand, but they were too busy warming them by their firesides to be bothered with an old man's distant halloos. The only signs of life were an occasional baby's cry or the distant bark of a dog, which echoed up and down the empty passageways. Given the choice, I think I would have elected to hear nothing but my own footsteps than those eerie, anxious sounds.

I trekked up cobbled valley and down cobbled dale. Turned myself about so many times I became dizzy and forgot which city I was in. I had marched myself deep into a state of exhausted fretfulness when I came out suddenly into broad daylight on a narrow footbridge which spanned a busy road below. Beneath my feet, on the floor of that city-canyon, the street was hectic with carriages and shopping-folk, all flowing merrily along. But my footbridge leapt straight across it, to disappear into a dark passageway on the other side.

As I peered hungrily down at all that humanity I noticed a row of three or four tiny shops. In the middle of them I saw one whose windows housed many mounds of freshly-rolled tobacco and many shelves of pipes. I saw the door of the shop open, heard the bell faintly ring and the proprietor, in a neat white apron, step out into the street. He looked left and right, as if he expected me, checked his watch, then turned to go back into his shop.

I shouted – at the top of my voice I shouted – so loud I felt sure I would set in motion tobacco-avalanches in his window display.

'Halloa! Below there!' I yelled through cupped hands.

But the tobacconist disappeared. As he closed the door I heard the bell briefly jingle again but it was soon gathered up and washed away by the wind and wheels and horses' hoofs.

I pushed myself back from the railing and there and then consigned myself to being for ever stuck up in the sky.

*

It would be as impossible for me now to explain how I managed to extract myself from that conundrum as it would be to explain how I became lost at the start. Certainly it was not due to any resourcefulness or calculation on my part and, though it is strange to hear myself say it, I can't help but feel that some piece of me is still trapped in those passageways . . . doomed to wander, exhausted, for evermore. The rest of me suddenly found itself pitched back onto the High Street, as if the malevolent force which had held me for its entertainment had at last grown tired and spat me out.

By now the very idea of tobacco repulsed me. So I brushed myself down and, in the poorest condition, set off to try and find old Clement. On my way I passed the spot where the old lady with one lens in her spectacles had stood with her visitor's guides. If she had still been there I might have had a good old shout at her, though I am not sure what I would have shouted, or if I would have had the energy to shout for long.

*

Edinburgh, January 10th

*

It must have been late afternoon when I came across the bleak little cemetery at Greyfriars'. The air particles which had held the daylight were being slowly vacated and made cold.

I strolled between the gravestones in their weathered gowns of green and brown and read the epitaphs of horse-dealers, pulpit orators and medical men. Took some comfort from the fact that even the most patronizing, puffed-up doctors do not escape the earth's deadly pull.

Sat on a bench and pulled my coat about me and watched the world slip through gradations of grey, a change so incremental in its nature that it was as if my own lungs were bringing it about. I remember pondering how an Edinburgh dusk might be different to an English one and chewing over corresponding matters of light and dark and, one way or another, reached such a zenith of enlightenment that I inadvertently drifted off.

I must have tumbled in the shallows of unconsciousness for quite a while, for when I came to things were altogether darker and chillier. My left leg, which was crossed over my right leg, was completely senseless and my fingers, which had formed a small cairn on my knee's hilltop, were similarly numb.

I carefully set about disentangling my frozen joints, thinking how this is becoming something of a habit with me, when I became conscious of the most heavenly music slowly pouring over me. A whole host of celestial voices were singing their Praises Be, as if welcoming me to the kingdom in the sky. The graveyard was utterly dark and dank but my mind was filling up with light. And though the air particles remained tight and empty, they had become enlivened and quivered amongst themselves.

It was some time before I gathered my wits and understood that the glorious sound which had stirred me emanated from the church behind my back. The choir was rehearsing the harmonies of 'Father Who Didst Fashion Me' and had not quite reached the end of the second verse when they were pulled up by their master's muffled voice and, after a short pause, made to recommence with the first line of that same verse.

I was stamping some life back into my dead leg and

rubbing some heat back into the palms of my hands when I saw just how marvellously the church was lit up, so that all the tableaux in the stained-glass windows radiated from the candlelight within. The saints, the angels and even the lambs – all brimmed with a heavenly glow. It was as if a great ship had stolen up behind me, with its cargo of hallelujas and kindly light. And no one else there to witness its arrival – just me and the grudging graves. I was struck by how a church's windows might be admired from outside as well as in, and I stopped my stamping to watch as the blues and purples were gently coaxed from the glass by the choir.

I was sitting up in the bath back at the hotel with Clement scrubbing my back before the significance of my experience in Greyfriars' cemetery truly came home to me. That here, if I could only put my finger on it, was a demonstration of the duality of man. We are not, as I had feared, simply a camera obscura – just a spectator of the light of the world. No. We are both the camera obscura and the lighthouse. We receive light and we send it out.

*

EDINBURGH, JANUARY 11TH

*

Called in again on Bannister. He did not answer his door. In fact, he had rather carelessly left the thing unlocked. I was in and out without anybody paying me much attention. Perhaps they think me some learned old gent.

Skipped down the stairs and was halfway back to the hotel before I realized I had cut my hand on the glass. Bandaged it with my handkerchief.

Clement wanted to know how I had come to hurt myself. Told him I had taken a fall. Packed up my bags without too much interference from him and we got to the station with hardly a minute to spare.

*

January 12th

*

Home again. The estate looks even colder and more wretched than before.

Unpacked and bathed and was back in my old routines within a couple of hours.

A month ago, I was quite convinced how my own body, or some element in it, was intent on bringing me down.

I see now how it is upstairs I am akilter – my mind which is askew.

*

January 20th

*

Out onto the balcony late last night. The wind was all around. Fished out my father's Dutch clog pipe from my pocket but found it broken in two. Must have sat on it. So I stood there in my slippers and leaned against the balustrade and let the breeze billow in my dressing gown and whistle in my ears.

A while later – perhaps an hour or so – a strange mist crept in from the lake. It rolled silently over the orderly lawns and seeped right through the hedges. I stood and watched it thicken up, watched it lap against the walls below. And quite soon the whole house was adrift in it and beginning to gently creak and sway. And we were advancing through a milky sea, with me in my slippers at the helm.

The clouds stole back at some point to reveal a sky alive with painful stars. And I became cold and tired and empty and my legs began to ache. I felt lost in the world and lonely and found no purchase in the mist below. So I took a reading from the heavens, set a course for the Cotswolds and retired to bed.

*

In the night I had a terrible vision.

> I saw a small ship with twenty men aboard, trawling off some Icelandic shore. The nets had been cast and the crew stood by to heave in the evening's catch. But the captain, who was up on the bridge and whose company I shared, saw that something was amiss. The compass was twitching in its glass and the vessel shifted towards starboard of its own accord.
>
> Orders were given to bring her back about but the young man wrestling with the wheel complained that his efforts all came to naught. He turned to the captain. 'It's the North Pole,' he cried. 'It is pulling us in.'
>
> Then I am no longer alongside the captain but floating high above the sea in the cold night air.
>
> I hear men wailing, calling out in the darkness. Some jump overboard into the freezing waves. And I see how it is the magnetism of the pole which has got a hold of the metal ship and begins to haul her inexorably in. And that when they reach the North Pole the compass will be spinning and the ship will be torn apart in the jaws of the ice.

*

This morning, peering at myself in the mirror, I noticed a mole on my left shoulder which I had never seen before and, turning, saw how it was just one of a considerable scattering, spread diagonally across my back. A great constellation of freckles, stretching from my shoulder right down to my waist.

Is it possible, I wonder, that there might be some correspondence between these moles and the stars I watch at night? There is something undeniably Orion-like about that cluster just beneath my shoulder blade.

The next time I am out on the balcony at night I shall compare them. I shall use a mirror.

*

January 24th

*

A grey and tedious day today. Nothing worth noting at all with the exception of a letter from Professor Bannister (threatening me with all manner of things, including policemen, which I chose to ignore) and an experiment I undertook in an idle moment, as I sat at table waiting for lunch to arrive.

Found my attention drawn towards a jug of water, about two foot in front of me. No doubt the same jug which has sat there every day for the last ten or twenty years. Today, however, I noticed how its little spout was turned up and away from me most contemptuously and how, when I moved my head to get a better view of it, the water in its belly threw back all sorts of refracted and untrustworthy light.

My first thought was to put something in it. Put something in the water and spoil its fun. I thought, 'If there is mashed potato on my plate when lunch arrives I shall drop a spoonful straight in.' But then I thought, 'No, not mashed potato. I shall harness the energy of my mind to send the blasted thing whistling across the table and crashing to the floor.'

I should mention that, for quite some time now, I have been wondering if it might not be possible for a man to cause objects to move by using the power of his mind. (I have some notes somewhere.) So I went straight ahead and concentrated my attention on that patronizing jug, glaring at it with undiluted fury and bringing to the boil such quantities of psychic energy that my ears were soon as warm as toast. I glared and I stared and grunted, but my efforts were all in vain. The damned jug did not budge a single inch, which was, of course, deeply humiliating. Outwitted by a common jug!

When my lunch finally arrived I told Mrs Pledger that I was sick of the sight of the water jug and asked it to be removed at once. I now wonder, however, if the experiment's failure might be down to not just my mental shortcomings but an unusually stubborn jug.

Lying in bed this evening, I eyed all the phials and bottles on my bedside table which contain all my preparations and powders and pills. How merrily they jangled against each other as a maid strolled past my door. I feel sure this has some bearing on the water jug business, though I cannot think just what.

*

January 28th

*

Most of it fades or falls away. We are more like Mr Snow than we care to think. But the odd memory, or sliver of it, perseveres. Nags away, like a stone in the shoe.

It is as if it has been stalking me since I first disturbed it in the Deer Park in the mist but even if I had known it was closing in on me I somehow doubt I would have been able to get out of its way. It had a fair old head of steam on it, had momentum on its side.

I happened to pick up my *Gray's Anatomy*, as I am in the habit of doing, and it fell open at the title page, where I clearly saw the name 'Carter', who is credited for all the illustrations in the book. I was not aware that the name had so profoundly registered in me – I must have picked that book up a dozen times before – and was half out of my chair to poke at the dying fire when I became suddenly aware of something moving powerfully in on me . . .

I froze. I listened hard. Something inside me stirred. As if a whole series of forgotten cogs had been set in motion; some deep-sunk machinery in my memory fired-up by the name in the book.

My free hand clung to the mantelpiece and I felt my presence in the room diminish. I heard a voice cry 'Carter' down all the years. Then,

I am a boy again, in the old family carriage, come to a halt on the beach with the mist creeping in.

My father has his head out of the window. The driver argues with another man, whom I cannot see. I do not understand what they are saying. All I hear are the voices to-and fro-ing towards a crescendo, before suddenly giving out.

A man with a long branch in his hand and a leather cap on his head passes the carriage window, heading back the way we came.

'Carter,' my father calls after him.

This Carter-man with his cap and his stick means nothing to me. I only know that I wish he would stay. I watch him marching off into the mist across the cold flat sand and when he has been all but swallowed up by the mist I see him turn and shout,

'This way. For the very last time.'

He waits a second, then turns and is gone.

I believe my mother is crying. Her tears start off some tears in me. After a minute she says, 'Not to worry. Not to worry.' But it is no good, for we are all of us worrying a very great deal.

Then my father pulls himself back into the carriage and gives me an unconvincing smile. He tells us how our driver is

certain he knows the way. And as if to back him up the brake is let out and we are moving again. We travel through the mist, which goes a little way towards relieving me. And I concentrate all my attention on the sand thrown up by the wheels, so as not to be frightened by my mother's tears and my father's unconvincing smile.

So successfully do I wrap myself up in my own small world that I have almost forgotten to be afraid. My father is talking and watching the sand with me and my mother has dried her eyes. But then the carriage suddenly comes to a dreadful halt and my precious sand stops flying for good.

My father has his head out in the mist again, which now carries on it the smell of the sea.

The driver is saying to my father, 'Sir, I think perhaps we should turn about.'

My hand has the poker in a fierce grip, as if I am about to do someone some terrible mischief. But whatever machinery previously stirred in me has all but seized-up again and I am left clinging to the mantelpiece, staring into the fire.

I prod and I poke at the embers, but they refuse to come back to life.

A Housemaid's Account

Three things always stick in my mind about him . . . You're quite sure it is all right for me to speak? . . . Well, the first is when I had only been at the house a month or two and was still finding my way about and I was right down in the basement and heading for the kitchens, I suppose, when I came across him in the shadows, sitting on a step.

He seemed to think my name was Rosie. There's no knowing where he got that idea from. But I had been warned by Mrs Pledger that he was confused enough to begin with and that in such an event it was probably best not to bother to put him right.

Well, he asked me where the trolleys had got to. I should explain that between the kitchens and the lifts up to the dining room is a fair old stretch, so there are tramlines set into the flags of the basement corridors and when the food is ready to go upstairs it is put inside the metal carts, then wheeled down the tracks. So I understood that these were the carts the old Duke was after, but seeing as how I did not know where they were kept I told him, in my politest voice, that I supposed that they were all locked up and I was about to carry on my way when he jumped up and grabbed me by my hand and insisted that I help him hunt them down.

Well, to be honest, I hoped we would not find them. I was very nervous about the whole affair and not half as pleased as he was when we came across one, tucked in a corner, just by the cupboards off the main corridor. Well, having found the cart I made my excuses and was all set to leave again but the old Duke ... beg your pardon, His Grace ... was having none of it and insisted I help him out.

Well, he ... Oh, I don't quite know how to put it ... but he made me ... made me ... push the cart up and down ... with him inside. He climbed inside the cart, where the plates and tureens would normally go, and had me push him up and down the corridors ... at speed.

There I've said it. Oh, dear ... You'll have to excuse me a second ... Oh, my goodness ... What a to-do.

The second thing ... now what was the second thing? Oh, yes. That they discovered His Grace ... and I should say here that I was not personally present at this one, but my good friend Molly was and she's no reason to lie ... but that they found him one morning in the dumb waiter which we use to bring the coal up from below. Just sitting there when they pulled it up, he was. All squashed up in the coal lift, with his face as black as you like.

Molly told me she was all set to scream – as indeed you would be – but he raised a finger to his lips so she never got the chance. He said that if she listened very hard she would hear the coal miners far below. Said you could hear them digging up the coal.

Well, she asked to be taken off coal duty after that one. Said she'd rather sweep the mausoleum every morning than risk another episode like that.

The third and final thing which stays with me, and the last thing I want to mention here, happened really not that long ago when I was coming in to work one morning, at the very crack of dawn. I was almost at the house and thinking to myself how the world was freshening up and was very much looking forward to spring when I saw a strange shape hanging from a tree. Very peculiar. I thought to myself, it looks just like a man. And of course it *was* a man. It was the

Duke himself, caught by his trousers. Just dangling from a tree.

I went to the bottom and shouted up to him. Asked if he required assistance of any sort. And he explained that he had been checking on the bud situation and that he appeared to have got his trousers snagged. I asked if he had been there very long and he said that he did not think so, but that whatever it was I intended doing I should hurry up because there was no knowing how long his trousers would hold out. It was a fair old drop.

So I went and called Clement, who came running. We had to fetch a ladder to get him down.

Yes, that last one will certainly stay with me. His Grace hanging from a tree.

[illegible] to the [illegible] and [illegible] [illegible] practical [illegible] of our [illegible] [illegible] [illegible] [illegible] [illegible] [illegible] [illegible] [illegible] [illegible]

[illegible]

[illegible] my [illegible].

The next [illegible] spent was [illegible] in the [illegible] [illegible] who [illegible] her head, just as cool as [illegible]. Then [illegible] and [illegible] above her [illegible] the [illegible] Arthur [illegible] back from the

From His Grace's Journal

February 3rd

*

I must be over-tired or in some way nervously exhausted. Something is certainly up with me, for I have recently been afflicted with what I can only describe as 'imaginings' – brief slippages of the mind. Spent the whole morning worrying about the memories of church spires I brought back from Edinburgh and how they have been scratching away at the inside of my skull. Then this afternoon had a very bad session with that head-picture Mellor gave me – the phrenology chart with Man's characteristics laid out in tableaux of tiny men.

I had it pinned on the wall above my shrine and stood there meditating on the various rooms within the head. I went slowly from one room to another and everything was right as rain, when I thought I saw one of the little chaps wriggling in his seat. Nothing much, just the straightening-out of the back a fellow does after he has been sitting for too long at a time. When I looked back at him he was perfectly still again, but now sat, I felt, a little more stiffly, as if he was holding his breath. I waited, did not take my eyes off him until, at last, he let out a tiny sigh.

The next thing I spotted was an old lady in the next compartment who scratched her head, just as cool as you like. Then a young girl in the room above her bent down to adjust the lace of her shoe. At this point I stepped back from the picture and saw how all the little figures had become minutely animated and how all now went about their chores. 'How marvellous,' I thought. 'Such harmony. Each inhabitant happy in his own four walls.'

But as I watched, the grim fellow in the room marked Acquisitiveness (a miser counting his piles of coin) leaned back in his chair and took a long look about him, until his gaze lit on Tunefulness' maiden, who gently strummed her guitar. The miser's gaze now turned distinctly lecherous. He sneaked a glance over each shoulder and got to his feet. Then, without a by-your-leave, he took up his walking stick and started to smash right through the separating wall and in no time was upon the maiden and looking her up and down in the most wicked way.

Meanwhile, the fox in nearby Secretiveness had started scratching at the wall, having sensed that on the other side Cautiousness' plump hen brooded over her clutch of eggs. The fox had soon scratched a hole for himself and squeezed right through; had got the bird by its throat and was shaking it this way and that.

And now Combativeness' burly pugilists heard Tunefulness screaming and broke their bout to listen for a moment or two and when they realized that the poor girl was in distress, began battering their bare fists towards her cries. And very soon they were through and upon the miser, one holding him down while the other struck him in the face, whereupon Benevolence's good Samaritan heard the miser moaning and abandoned the care of his patient to join the fisticuffs below.

Destructiveness' big cat caught a whiff of Alimentiveness' succulent joint of meat and started clawing its way through to it. Philoprogenitiveness' loving father, it seemed, had grown bored with his wife and child and began to look lustily across at Friendship's embracing girls.

Elsewhere, I saw Amativeness' cherub fix an arrow to his bow and train it on the fox with the hen in its mouth, while Conscientiousness doggedly held his scales in the air and looked impotently on.

The whole head was in a state of anarchy, walls were being torn down everywhere as the façade of civilization slipped aside to reveal Man's savage nature beneath.

*

February 15th

*

I have been working on a theory, quite unusual and primarily to do with bones.

First of all, I must say that not nearly enough is made of bones. I reckon they are all too frequently overlooked. When one considers how every creature which walks the earth leaves behind its own set of ribs and hips and tibia-fibias, one begins to grasp just how many bones there must be scattered about the place. The world, one might say, is nothing more than a vast burial ground on which we briefly picnic.

But my thoughts have been focused mainly on whalebones, which are, it goes without saying, the biggest in the world. How many whales are there, altogether? Millions, to be sure. The question, therefore, is: what happens to all those whalebones once their owners have passed away? They cannot all of them be picked clean by tiny scavengers and left to rot on the ocean bed. If that were the case there would by now be great piles of them poking out of the oceans. Shipping would have been brought to a halt.

No. The truth is that they are somehow organized – laid out in lines to form some sort of World Bone Network. Who is in charge of the enterprise? An international committee, presumably. No doubt the French are involved. As far as I can tell, this network consists of both longitudinal and latitudinal bone-lines, the majority of which are under the sea. On land this vast net is buried deep underground.

The purpose of this bone arrangement? I am not yet certain, but have narrowed down the options to . . .

(i) some sort of 'brace'. A way of cradling the Earth, to stop it splitting and coming apart from old age;
(ii) some powerful means of communication, via tremors, between governments;
(iii) bars of a prison. The world is but a cage.

I note all the above in order to prevent them drifting off into the ether, but also as a means of introducing another aspect of this whole business which has recently come to my attention . . .

At four o'clock this afternoon it occurred to me that Mrs Pledger is, in fact, a ship and that all the house's little gusts and zephyrs are what fill her skirts and blow her from room to room. It was only her breezing into my rooms this lunchtime with a bowl of minestrone in her hand which finally provoked in me this nautical connection. She was tacking her way around a sofa, plotting her course by way of Fowler's head on the mantelpiece to the north and the bureau to the east. As she approached I thought to myself, 'There must be a good deal of hidden rigging to keep her so navigable and trim.'

I watched with interest as she dropped anchor on the fireside rug and placed my soup on the table by my chair. As she bent down her bosomy cargo swung into view, all splendidly girdled and packed, and when she saw how I was spying her she gave me one of her frostier looks. Things were now falling very neatly into place, so I gave her a cheeky little wink. It was my way of saying, 'The game is up, Mrs Pledger!'

But she wasn't for coming clean. O, no. She became all tight-lipped and hoity-toity. I could see I was going to have to squeeze the truth right out of her.

'You're a sizeable lady, Mrs Pledger,' I told her, and waited to see how this little observation went down. She stared at me but not a word came out of her, so I continued. 'Be kind enough, Mrs Pledger, to tell me about the bones.'

She did her best to assume some incredulous air but it was quite plain I had caught her out. 'And which bones might they be, Your Grace?' she replied, reddening.

'Why, the whalebones that hold us all together,' I countered calmly, and leaning over toward her, added, 'And maybe the secret ones, Mrs Pledger, which keep you so shapely-looking.'

She was properly horror-stricken. I leaned back triumphantly in my chair.

I believe I might well be the first mortal man to understand the significance of the whalebones which are stitched in every woman's corset. For all I know, Mrs Pledger is, at this very moment, down in the kitchens sending out signals to the bone organizations. Perhaps *this* is why women are so peculiar. They are all in league with the whales.

Whatever lies at the bottom of this whole business – and I must say I believe there is still a great deal to dig up – it was clear from Mrs Pledger's reaction that I had struck a nerve. A whole lifetime of bone-secretion exposed!

I gave her another big wink then watched as she marched straight across the room. She stopped by a fruit bowl, picked up an orange; turned and threw it at me. It was headed right between my eyes. I ducked down too late, it bounced off the top of my head and landed smack in the middle of my soup.

We were both silent for a moment.

'Excellent shot, Mrs Pledger,' I announced.

She swept out of the room, leaving the whole place rocking in her wake.

Now, I have no problem having in my employ a woman who is up to her ears in bones. Mrs Pledger is a very fine woman – I have always said as much – and I sincerely hope that her paymasters do not punish her for being found out. After all, we are none of us entirely guiltless in that department; we all hide our bones away.

The orange bobbed in the remains of my minestrone.

'Fruit in my soup again,' I said.

*

February 19th

*

I have been poorly as long as I can remember. Upstairs as well as down. Long before this pain set off on its travels something nagged at me. Something has always nagged.

The problem, I am slowly beginning to understand, is that we are all prisoners of our own skin. Our bodies, with their incredible capacities, are also the gaols in which we are sentenced to languish. Our ribs are the bars of our tiny cells. We are entombed in flesh and blood.

Sooner or later our body's frailties begin to drag us down and we have no choice but to go. Illness, when it strikes, is a torture we are bound to suffer. We cannot be removed.

As often as not my own feelings are a mystery to me. Most days, the best I can hope for is to weather them, to endeavour not to get washed away. How wonderful it would be to let the mind roam freely, unencumbered by the fetters of skin and bone. To be able to come together and communicate with all the other souls.

I am, I now see, two very different people. The mind and

the bag of bones it heaves behind. The body, I suppose, is simply a vessel. The next man might regard it as a temple but, then, what a foul and decrepit ruin in which to worship.

What I long for is transcendence. To let the deepest part of me rise up and breathe the air. It is the awful separateness of life, foisted on me by flesh, which I have slowly come to detest.

All I want is to let a little light in. To let a little of me out into the world.

*

February 24th

*

The razor felt strange in my hand. Unfamiliar. The scissors too. So excited that my whole body itched. Something very odd about being beardless after so many bearded years. My neck now feels absolutely naked. As fleshy as a freshly-plucked goose.

The scissors took the bulk of it off in a couple of minutes – clumps of white hair, tumbling into the sink. Small bushy balls of the stuff resting on the porcelain, then flushed away with a twitch of the tap. Me left looking almost bruised, battered. But then, after the soap and the razor, a little less fierce. My neck has collapsed while it has been hidden from view. A baggy abundance of chalky skin hanging over a pair of straining guys.

So, all in all, I must say quite a surprise, which is more or less what I expected. The chin not the one I buried under the bristles all those years ago. The dimple disappeared. How curious to be reintroduced to oneself. To find one's most intimate relationship changed.

When I first started snipping away at the hair on my head

I had a fit of giggles. Simply couldn't help myself. Like trimming away at the clouds. Felt quite light-headed and as I lathered it up (a wonderful feeling) had further giggles to quell. Had to breathe slowly and get a grip on myself. Just my eyes staring back at me. Calmness. Calm.

My whole dome a-froth, with just the odd blossom of blood where I nicked myself. The razor's rasp very loud around the ears. Shaved away from them, so that if I slipped I would not lop them off. Left the old eyebrows well alone and, before I knew it, was rinsing away the soapy-suds.

I may have missed the odd little tuft or two, around the back of the head. I will need another mirror for that. But finally, there I am – a genuinely shocking sight. No longer laughing. A withered stump of a man. Thought I might suddenly start crying, like a baby.

Talcum-powdered the whole thing, so as to cover up the tiny scars and try to distract myself. Then, for a minute or two, sat in the bedroom and busied myself, pretending to read. Rose and returned to the mirror.

Much calmer now. Less giddy. Not worried like I was before. Stood there at the mantelpiece mirror, saying, 'Yes. The right thing to do.' And then, suddenly, I saw it. It leapt right out at me. To the right of my reflection sat Fowler's porcelain head with his usual inscrutable look and, what with my own head so white from the talcum, the two of us looked like kin. How strange. It would never have occurred to me. All I lacked were his labels and dividing lines.

Undid my gown and went over to the full-length mirror. Removed my trousers. What a white old man. Stared at me until I became a stranger. And in time I saw projected onto the flesh the *Ancient Chinese Healing* chart, with all its tributaries running up and down my arms and legs.

I imagined my belly, packed with Mrs Pledger's various herbs. Saw me stuffed full of them, like a turkey.

I saw the same organs the Oakley sisters had seen in me, the sleepy fish.

And in the middle of all this I saw the bone-tree, my very own skeleton-man.

With my white head perched on top, just like Fowler's, and those two eyes staring back at me from the void, I saw myself as some sort of living synthesis. An amalgamation of all the maps of man.

*

February 25th

*

I locked myself in my bedroom and walked around awhile. Unlocked the door, called out, 'Do not disturb,' then stood there while the words went galloping up and down the hall. I was already quite inebriated, having consumed a quarter of a bottle of brandy. Perhaps even staggered a little as I ushered me back into my room and locked the door behind. I had not yet crossed that threshold into flailing drunkenness, but was in no doubt that I was by now sufficiently anaesthetized.

Slumped down at my dressing table, where all the towels and instruments were laid out. The mirror which usually sits on the mantel I had placed flat on the table top. I tilted the middle of the dressing table's triptych of mirrors forward, at an angle of some forty-five degrees, and leaned my head between them both, which was a little like inserting one's head into a lion's open mouth. With a slight adjustment to the upper mirror the top of my head swung into view. The brandy bottle was close at hand in case I needed another swig.

I remember tapping the top of my skull with a finger before I started. The flesh was pliant and warm. Then I picked up the scalpel and made the first incision – about two inches in length – from back to front. I pressed down until I felt the blade scrape against bone. It made a grinding sound in my ears. Almost immediately blood welled up from the neat little line; a single black-red bead rolling forward and another one rolling back. I made a second incision, roughly the same length, which perfectly bisected the first, so that I now had a cross – a bleeding cross at that – on the crown of my head.

There was pain, certainly, but it was distant and somewhat blurred. I took a couple of gulps from the brandy bottle, and waited for the alcohol to find its way into my veins. Then I positioned myself between the mirrors again, reached up with both hands and carefully peeled back the four pointed flaps of skin. It was as if I was opening out an envelope, the flesh dragging a little as each fold reluctantly came away. There was pain, as I say, but it was secondary to a curious coolness and was dulled by my fascination. When I had done, the effect was quite fetching – like four petals on an exotic plant.

I mopped at my head with a towel (which went up white and came back very red) and succeeded in soaking up enough of the small pool of blood to reveal a startling flash of bone.

I fixed Bannister's trepan together. I had practised holding it several times. For all its finely-worked woods and metals and the plush upholstery of its case the implement is essentially little more than a corkscrew, the significant difference being the tiny-toothed circular bit which I now fitted to the end.

I had chosen one with a diameter of three-quarters of an inch, with a depth of about an inch and a half. I considered taking another swig of brandy but decided more alcohol might affect the steadiness of my hand. So, with the aid of my mirrors, I inserted the trepan in the very eye of that bloody blossom and slowly began to turn. The sound of the bit scraping out its circle made a terrible groaning sound – like a chair dragged across a bare floor – which resonated right through me, especially through my jaw and teeth.

One's skull, I discovered, is surprisingly hardy. More like teak than the shell of an egg. After three or four minutes both my arms were completely drained and I had to bring them down and rest them a while. When I paused that first time I removed the trepan and could clearly see the ring it had cut in my skull. I recommenced a few minutes later, having oiled the bit with the tiny brush, and found it fitted easily back into the groove.

The next time I rested I found I could actually leave the tool in my skull (or, rather, that it would not easily come out). So I sat there at the dressing table for a minute and took another swig of brandy, with that corkscrew poking out of my head. In all, I think I must have stopped and rested my arms about half a dozen times in this way, the whole operation lasting somewhere in the region of half an hour. Certainly, the deeper I drilled down into me, the harder each turn became. The operation also produced a rather acrid smell, which I did my best to ignore.

As time went by I became quite exhausted and began to wonder if I would ever finish the job. Once or twice a nauseous wave swept through me and I had to hold on to the dressing table until it passed. The trepan became very sticky with blood and I think I had paused to wipe my hands when I heard a tiny hissing sound.

I pushed on with the infernal winding – my head fairly throbbing now – until I felt the tool lurch a little to one side. I continued to carefully wind the apparatus – slowly now – and, by jiggling it a little, managed to extract the instrument from my head. In the end of the trepan I found a circular piece of bloody bone. I was through! I had uncorked myself! Had finally managed to break down that wall between myself and the outside world.

I sat back in the chair. A little dizziness, perhaps, but vision surprisingly steady. An assortment of wheezes and sucking sounds emanated from my head. I could feel tiny pockets of air creeping under my skull and at one point watched as a bloody bubble slowly inflated itself, right over the hole, before disappearing with a pop.

I can only describe the overall sensation as being somehow similar to the tide coming in.

Once I had restored some sort of equilibrium I raised a tentative hand to my head and very gently inserted a finger into the hole. It was quite deep and wet, like an inkwell. My finger went down until it eventually touched something moist and warm. Was that really my little box of tricks? Was that the terrible fruit?

Bandaged myself up, went into the bathroom and vomited several times. Dozed in an armchair for an hour or two. Woke and recorded this entry. Have applied a little ointment to the wound. Am about to pack myself off to bed.

*

February 26th

*

I hear voices. Beautiful voices. Voices all around. Last night, as I sat by the fire putting a fresh bandage on my head, I picked out the distant voice of a young woman reading a bedtime story to her child – a tale of a boy and a girl who get lost in a wood. The mother's voice was pure amber. It shone across the night. I saw her perched on the edge of her child's bed, wearing a dress of many pinks and blues. Pictured her perfectly in her cottage, all those miles away.

Sounds which had previously hid from my ears now shyly make themselves known. This morning I heard a young boy whistling as he strolled along a lane. The song danced among the hedgerows before winging its way to me.

I hear a maid down in the laundry, asking how much starch she should add to the water. Hear a young girl knocking on a neighbour's door and asking if her friend may come out to play.

But what came creeping in a little later and what most uplifts me are all the natural sounds. The heaving of the daffodil bulbs, unravelling beneath the thawing soil. The mighty heartbeat of every oak.

The seasons sweep about me. 'Prepare' is whispered down every root and vine. The great conspiracy of spring is almost on us. The buds have all been primed.

*

I must have fallen asleep in the flower beds. I remember my creeping out in the night. I believe I was listening for something. Perhaps I was being a sentry. My only recollection is my lying down on the cold, hard earth and looking up at the ocean of stars. The pruned stems of the roses pointed out the stars for me and were like branches of tiny trees. I remember imagining I was a very big fellow on the floor of a stark, empty wood.

When I came to the night had been swept from the sky and the stars had been moved along, but they had left their twinkling in a fine frost which had fastened itself to the bare roses and the fellow who lay below.

Getting to my feet took me several minutes. Bones extremely stiff. My trousers had a boardlike consistency but, once I had plucked myself from the roses, I felt altogether quite healthy and fit. Sneaked back up to my bedroom. Slept until almost four.

*

Mrs Pledger found some discarded bandages this morning and left a message asking what was up. I explained down the pipe that I had had a minor accident. She asked if I needed a doctor. I replied that I did not.

*

February 28th

*

I have in my hand a chalky coin. A small disk from my very own skull. I scrubbed and scrubbed away at it until it came up white.

Question— How many coins make up a man? How much is your average man worth?

This coin bought me my freedom. (There's a thought.) I just opened up my purse and took it out. In so doing I managed finally to heave back the door which opens on to the world. And now parts of the world come through to me which had previously been out of reach. In return, my thoughts go out into the world. It is a fair exchange.

I am doing so much wondering these days. Wondering full-time. This morning I wondered what I should do with my coin. Pickle it, perhaps? Or have it framed? Give it to someone as a gift, maybe? Who then? Clement? Mellor? A child? I decided the best thing would be to bury it. Put it deeply in the ground. There are Roman coins down there, I hear. I shall simply add one of my own.

The wound is healing up very well. Some pain, but it goes out of me and does not hang around, although I sometimes see its shadow. I have put some lint on the wound and a bandage, which goes round and round, under my jaw and over my head. It stops me talking (except through my teeth, like a bad dog) which is no great sacrifice. I now converse with the world in other ways and, I might add, with a good deal more success.

I have decided not to let my staff see me. I think they would be alarmed. Perhaps later, when things have settled down. Meanwhile, I have asked for my meals to be left outside my door. I wrote a note to Clement. One day, the whole world will send notes to one another. Our pockets will overflow with them.

Clement brought some stew, just now. I felt him approaching, one warm footfall over the other. Heard him thinking at the door. Eventually he came to a decision and crept away like a bear. I have not touched the stew.

*

MARCH 1ST

*

Dawn was but an inkling as I tiptoed from the house. My first time out in many days. I wore a woollen bonnet.

Is it milder? I think it is milder, although my wound still aches somewhat. If it is not yet milder, there is the prospect of mildness. Mildness is at hand.

Strange, but when I gauged myself at the edge of the Wilderness I found hardly a trace of fear. An ounce of apprehension, maybe, but nothing more. Nothing flighty.

Clambered through the creaking fence and eased myself into the foliage. Crept forward. Stealthily, just like a fox. Winter still insisted; an old darkness lingered among the bushes and the trees. The ground surrendered beneath my boots – like walking on an old damp mattress. But such richness all a-brimming. Such leafy promise everywhere.

Made my way deeper into the wood. Not a single bird sang. Took the trowel from my coat pocket, knelt and plunged it in. The soil was like black pudding. Very moist and many worms. Dug up a dozen trowelfuls, then brought out my handkerchief. Carefully unfolded the four corners and removed my bit of bone.

Placed it into the cold hole. I remember holding it there a while. I believe I may have said a few words. The occasion would have called for them. I replaced the earth over the bone-coin then gently patted it down.

Wandered for a while, touching fern and branch, then rested on a stone. Found a twig to scrape the soil from under my fingernails. Warmed a smudge of earth between finger and thumb.

'Are you alive?' I said.

As I rose, the stone seemed to shift under me. I looked down at the thing. With a little effort I managed to haul it over and found myself staring into what looked very much like a well. Had no matches with me but stared long enough into it to make out a raggedy flight of stone steps. So, not a well at all but some sort of shaft. And it slowly came upon me how it was the place where the old monks' tunnel emerged. The modest passage which is the great-great-ancestor to my own subterranean lanes.

Had I a lamp I might have taken a step or two down it but resolved instead to come at it from the other end. Returned to my rooms without being spotted. Cantered much of the way.

*

March 2nd

*

Left a note for Clement . . .

> Please remove all chains from entrance to monks' tunnel. Also, please note that, for the foreseeable future, I shall be com-

municating with all members of the staff via messages such as this.

Slipped it under the door into the corridor and within half an hour felt Clement heading this way. Heard him gently unfolding the note and in my mind's eye saw his face – at first puzzled, then slowly crumpling. After a minute a rough piece of paper appeared under my door with, *Is Your Grace ill?* scribbled on it in pencil.

'Not at all,' I whispered at the door.

Another note.

Then why does Your Grace hide away?

There was no satisfactory way of answering this last question, so I let the tight, round silence speak for itself and after a minute or two he left me alone.

I have my voices to be getting along with. I find that if I come within twenty yards of another mortal their thoughts tend to interfere with my own. Yesterday I heard a farmer in Derbyshire complaining about his dinner. 'This meat is too tough,' he said.

*

March 3rd

*

Blew down the tube around ten o'clock tonight and Clement came puffing up the stairs. I had posted a note requesting a lit lantern and, five minutes later, he deposited one outside my door, with a note of his own suggesting I wrap up warm. Took the stairwell through the door by my fireplace and went down, down, darkly down.

The chains to the monks' tunnel lay neatly coiled on the ground. I raised my lamp and headed in. The tunnel is a very long and narrow affair, apparently hacked right out of the earth. Its floor is littered with many mounds of crusted dirt where the roof has come away. Halfway along, where it dips a little, there is a huge patch of flowering mould, about fifteen foot long in total and the same colour as crême caramel. After a while I began to feel cold and tired, so to pass the time I imagined myself as a monk, tramping down that same tunnel several centuries before, in sandals with open toes. Composed a sort of madrigal. My lamp pumped out its meagre light and the darkness comprehendeth it not. It was as if I advanced in my own box of light, with darkness fore and aft. It slowly receded before me and came along behind.

Eventually my feet came down upon paving stones and I could tell by the change in temperature and the quality of the air that I was in the Wilderness. I came to the bottom of the old steps. The stone over the entrance was ajar, as I had left it, and a slice of moonlight shone through. I shouldered it open and the night air slid slowly in. Then, like a natural man, I crept out of the cold earth and into the mumbling wood.

*

March 4th

*

I eat just about next-to-nothing these days and sleep right through the afternoons. But each morning, before the aching dawn, I take my private stairwell down to the grotto and, with my lantern out before me, creep undergroundly out to the Wilderness. Down the earthy-reeking tunnel I go, with the spirits of the bony monks.

Have recently been giving some thought to clothing and begin to grasp how, for far too long, collar studs and cuff links have been keeping me locked-up. How, since infancy, I have been bound by belts and buttons, by too-tight jackets and over-starched shirts. Fairly got myself in a tangle with it. I became angry and stamped about the place. So now, on my nightly trips down the monks' tunnel, I pause at the bottom of the stone steps before emerging and remove every last constricting thread. Only the insects bear witness to this ceremonial casting-off. The earth finds nothing wrong with me.

In the Wilderness the lost moments give themselves up. The terrible grinding between Past and Future is quietened, calmed. There is something at work in the soil – something industrious – which fills up every last atom, emboldens the very bark on the trees. It gives the insects their tiny intensity, the birds the courage to call.

But all the little Lucifers are also out there, with their little forks and their eager grins. One of them told me how he fancied looking at my blood. But I find a modest garland of ivy keeps them at a distance. I knocked it up in no time and wear it with pride.

The last hour before daylight is the hour I love most. I go between the trees. My bare feet listen and Nature's ticking clock comes through to me. I hear the fixing of bayonets. I hear the buds contemplate their cannonade.

A Second Footman's Account

About this time I began to receive messages. Slipped under my door in the middle of the night and waiting for me when I got up.

The first one I got was on a Tuesday.

> The moon is, in fact, a hole in the sky. Consider.

or something along those lines. Well, I must say I considered it for quite a while, but it still meant nothing to me.

I didn't mention it to anybody at first. I was rather hoping it might be from one of the girls. A late 'Be my Valentine'. But the next night I got another one which said something like,

> What is that state of mind we call "consciousness"
> if not the constant emerging from a tunnel?

and then I knew it had to be His Grace.

I must have said something to one of the other lads on the Wednesday, most likely, who said he'd just received his first that very morning, written on a scrap of paper and slid under his door, just like mine. His had something to do with sarsaparilla. *Sarsaparilla – fact or fiction?* I think it was.

It turns out we were nearly all of us getting them. Maggie Taylor claims she opened her door and saw him scampering away.

He must have been using the secret passages he had put in for the tunnels. I should know because one of them goes right past my room and sometimes I would hear him sneaking about. That's a very peculiar feeling, I should say, to be lying in your bed late at night and hear someone creeping up and down between the walls.

From His Grace's Journal

March 5th

*

Out in the Wilderness late last night or very early this morning. The moonlight came down through the trees and dappled me but there was some mist to be waded through. I stopped to relieve myself against a bush. When I looked about to see where I might go stalking next, my eyes came to rest on an ivy-coated rock some twenty yards away which was picked out by the moon.

I approached, naked, garlanded, thinking, 'It is a very slim rock ... No, not a rock at all. Too square and upright for a rock.' And even then some instinct warned me. Some doomy inner-voice started up.

I tugged at the ivy but it bound the stone like string. Was reluctant to give its secret up. But I persisted and found that the stone beneath was smooth and flat with perfectly finished corners. This was no natural rock, crouched in the undergrowth. This was the headstone to a grave.

And horror quickly filled me up. I was weeping before the first word was revealed. Slid my fingernails under the moss and tore it back. There was twisting and snapping as I hacked it away. But I kept on tearing, desperately tearing until the headstone was bare. And I saw my own birth date chiselled in the stone.

I heard me say, 'I am a dead man.'
Read the words,

Our Beloved Son
Born
March 12 1828
Drowned
1832

and the sky presses right down onto me. And I am running for all I am worth.

I run through the mist just like a madman. Then I am out of the woods and into an open field. As I run I let out a miserable groan, but it will not fill my ears. I am an old man trying to outrun a memory, but my footsteps only drum it up. And now the memory is almost on me. Looming up. Slowly descending. No mercy. Merciless.

The carriage has been abandoned and we are hurrying across the misty sands. My father has a hold of one of my hands and is dragging me forward as fast as I can go. Over my shoulder I see my mother, with her skirts all gathered up as she runs along. She holds the hand of another boy, about the same size as me.

The memory carries me through the early morning mist and sweeps me towards the house.

'Faster than a galloping horse' comes to me. An old man's face, right up to mine, saying, 'Just you mind that tide, boy. It comes in faster than a galloping horse.' And I finally understand what we are running from – Mother, Father, myself and the other boy.

As we run across the sand we trip and stumble. But we pick ourselves back up to go on stumbling some more. And my child's mind is full of that galloping horse, which is now the tide's messenger and brings the whole sea charging in. I hear its terrible hoofs hammer behind me. I imagine its terrified eye.

We are all of us breathless and exhausted. I trip and tumble to the sand again. My father hauls me up, saying, 'Come on, boy. Come on. Another minute and we'll be there.'

The mist is clearing and in the distance I see tiny cottages, set back from the shore. I am back on my feet and running for the blessed cottages, knowing we are almost there. And then the water is suddenly upon us. We are running through it. It races under me and sweeps ahead of me and makes me dizzy to look down at it.

'Don't stop, boy,' my father shouts at me. But now the water is all around. It has climbed my legs and, in a second, is almost up to my waist. I hear a shout, and turn to see my mother disappear into the sea. When she comes back up she is all drenched and bedraggled and the small boy no longer holds on to her hand. She stands there in her wet dress, looking all around.

'Where's my boy?' she screams. 'Where's my boy?'

And I go down. I am under the water. Every sound in the world has been washed away. And I see the small boy floating close by. The floating boy with his back turned towards me and his child's hair shifting in the stream. He turns . . . slowly turns towards me. And when he finally faces me I see how his face is very much like my own. He is lost in thought. I reach out to touch him . . . to touch the floating boy . . . but the water grows cloudy and the tide rolls over us . . . and the floating boy is carried away.

*

The house is all in darkness. I grab a frock coat from the cloakroom and race straight up the stairs. But Mrs Pledger is on her way down in her slippers, with her lamp held out in front. She catches sight of me. Lets out a terrible scream.

'Your head, Your Grace!' she cries.

And then I am charging up and down the corridors and I

am bouncing from wall to wall. So late in the day yet I am still chasing, still searching for that one elusive thing. And I find myself at the door to the attic. Locked. I hammer at it with both hands. And now my hammering and Mrs Pledger's screaming have the landing filling up with staff. Their staring faces all lit with their candles and lamps. All wanting a little look-see at the mad, bald, beardless Duke.

They congregate at the bottom of the attic steps and watch me scratching, scratching at the door. Until at long last Clement – dear Clement – appears among the throng.

'The door's locked, Clement,' I call down to him. 'Where's the key, man? Where's the key?'

Mrs Pledger comes along beside him. Her eyes look straight at me but she speaks to Clement out of the side of her mouth. And I pay close attention to these sideways words.

'We have sent for Dr Cox,' they say.

And then I am filled up with all sorts of panicky feelings which make me rush at the faces, waving my arms about. And every last one of them is scattered, and the maids go shrieking down the corridors. I battle my way down to my bedroom door and the next minute I am back here in my hidey-hole, with the bolts all firmly locked.

I must have stood at the door a full five minutes, trying to catch my breath. And the noise in the house slowly subsided and there was less and less scurrying about, until at last I found myself wrapped in silence. All the beautiful voices had raised a finger to their lips.

I waited. O, I can be a patient man. I waited until one of the voices got around to whispering to me. And in time, deep inside, I felt some connection coming about. The planets slowly aligned themselves. I came over to the bureau and looked it up and down.

My fingers began working it over. Eager fingers, searching

out its little switches and nooks. But I was like the conch-boy who fails to produce a note. The thing just sat there, unmoved by my embrace. I covered every last inch, but it refused to let me in. And then my patience failed and I was in a frenzy again, kicking at it and howling and rocking the whole thing back and forth.

And as I rocked, the middle finger on my right hand found an unfamiliar purchase at the back. A square of wood which was loose and very well hidden away. I pressed it and deep inside the desk heard an old spring being triggered. A slim drawer popped out at me.

Two folded pieces of paper trembled in the tiny drawer. I reached in and picked them out. The first was a Christening Certificate. My name, in a barely legible hand. The name of another boy next to it. The word 'twins' somewhere.

The other was a Death Certificate, for the same boy, filed four years after the first. In a column on the far right of the paper I read, *Drowned, Grange-over-Sands*.

And then there is silence. A terrible silence. A cavernous pity with no way of filling it.

When I have finished setting down this entry I shall take the staircase to the tunnels. I shall go out into the Wilderness and wait to hear what is to be done.

Mr Walker's Account

Mostly I would use the bag-net or the gate-net or a simple trap or snare. Some nights I might take along a dog or ferret but very rarely would I take my father's old fowling gun. Too much noise and, of course, being caught with it would only make a bad situation worse. But it had been a moonlit night and I had a lucky feeling so I took the wretched thing along.

Well, I was about to head home and was moving up the hill from the lake, with the gun primed across my arm. I came up alongside the Wilderness, where I've had some success before, and decided I would have a look around.

I was in quite deep when I heard something stirring. Like a panting or a groaning sound. So I slowed right down and crouched there, very still, to see where the noise were coming from. Then, quite close by, there was the sound of grinding stone – an awful rumble, it was – no more than thirty feet away. Well, I did not dare move a muscle.

And I saw how he came up out of the ground. Crawling. A fleshy creature. Never seen anything like it before in my life. He came out on all fours and slowly turned himself about. Went over to a nearby stone, as if he might bask upon it. And by now I was sick with fear.

I was so afeard I must have shifted. A twig snapped under my boot. And the creature swung round to see what went on there. He looked all around him from the stone where he squatted and I saw how his eyes settled themselves on me.

On my life, I thought he were some sort of monster-man. I thought he were after doing me harm. And in a second I had brought the gun up and let it go. God have mercy on me, but that's what I did. And he flew up and back, twisting every way. And he fell back into the ferns.

When I was sure he was not moving I went up to him and turned him over with my foot – like he were nothing but a dog – and straight away I saw how it were a man that I had shot. An ordinary man, but bald and naked, with a great hole in his chest where I had shot him, lying there among the leaves.

AUTHOR'S NOTE

*

Astute readers will have noticed that I used as my point of departure for this novel the life of the fifth Duke of Portland, William John Cavendish-Bentinck-Scott. They will also recognize just how swiftly and significantly the lives of the real and invented dukes diverge and the downright liberties which have been taken.

I am deeply indebted to the following people who, one way or another, helped me convert a handful of ideas into some sort of book . . .

Kevin Hendley, who first brought the story of the real duke to my attention and gave me his own guided tour of the estate; his parents, Tom and Win Hendley, who made me very welcome in their home while I was researching the project and his sister Diane for ferrying me about the place.

The Worksop Trader, Iris Exton, Caroline J. Bell, Doreen Smith, Jack Edson, Brenda Penney and Margaret Carter.

David J. Bradbury, a local historian and author of several publications on Welbeck Abbey.

The local studies departments at Worksop Library and Mansfield Library (where George Sanderson's map is on display); Miss E. Allen, The Hunterian Museum, London; Richard Sabin and Ben

Spencer, The Natural History Museum; Professor M. H. Kaufman, Department of Anatomy, the University of Edinburgh and The Wellcome Institute.

The University of Nottingham Library for their kind permission in allowing me to reproduce the recipe for 'rheumatics' (ref: Pw K 2739) and the advertisement for 'Essence of beef' (ref: Pw K 786).

Joe Mellen, Tony and Mary Laing, Wendy Jilley, Ian Jackson and Adam Campbell for help with some of the more arcane details.

Rose Tremain for much-appreciated encouragement.

And, as always, my friend and mentor Peter Kiddle who got me chasing after the green man fifteen years ago.

Most of all, special thanks to Cath Laing for providing me with the time and space to indulge myself in the writing of this book.